SUDDENLY THE night was split by an ungodly scream of sheer, animal terror. Then just as quickly all went still, and the lawman could feel a vagrant breeze cooling the sweat on his forehead. Wondering if Bajeca had met his match, Stoudenmire scrambled up the hill, trying to make as little noise as possible. Within moments he topped the rise and plowed down the other side, cocking both hammers on the shotgun as he skidded through the dusty soil. Moving cautiously now, he eased through another stand of juniper and tangled underbrush, gliding silently from tree to tree. Abruptly he broke out into a small clearing and froze dead in his tracks.

Beside a crackling little fire sat Bajeca, calmly wiping his knife clean on Kale's shirt. Glancing up, he grinned like a playful wolf and lifted Kale's severed head from the ground.

"A gift for *el patrón*. One *gringo pistolero* who will kill no more."

DON'T MISS THESE OTHER
CLASSIC WESTERN ADVENTURES FROM

MATT BRAUN

Dodge City
Dakota
A Distant Land
Windward West
Crossfire
Highbinders
The Warlords
The Spoilers
Hickok and Cody
The Overlords
Tombstone
Rio Grande
Brannocks
The Gamblers
Rio Hondo
Savage Land
Noble Outlaw
Cimarron Jordan
Lords of the Land
One Last Town
Texas Empire
Jury of Six

AVAILABLE FROM ST. MARTIN'S PAPERBACKS

EL PASO

MATT BRAUN

St. Martin's Paperbacks

EL PASO

ISBN: 978-1-250-01351-4
EAN: 1250013518

Printed in the United States of America

Previously published in 1973
Signet edition / March 1989
St. Martin's Paperbacks edition / July 1999

St. Martin's Paperbacks are published by St. Martin's Press, 175 Fifth Avenue, New York, NY 10010.

P1

For
Barry Winston
who stuck through all the wars
and
Elizabeth and Paul Shumski
whose support was ever valued

AUTHOR'S NOTE

El Paso is essentially the story of one man, Dallas Stoudenmire. Lawman, gunfighter, mankiller, he was all these and more. Yet unlike the cotton-candy heroes of western folklore, Stoudenmire was imperfect, flawed; a man who lived by his own code in a land where it was often difficult to separate evil from good.

Born to German parents who had immigrated to the Lone Star State, Stoudenmire was named after George Mifflin Dallas, a Texan who served briefly as vice-president of the United States. After four bloody years fighting for the Confederacy, Stoudenmire returned home a trained killer; cold, impersonal, something of a loner. Over the next decade he became a lawman of formidable persuasion, killing an unrecorded number of badmen with the precision and stoic disinterest that was to remain his trademark. Along the way, he served variously as a Texas Ranger, deputy sheriff, and city marshal, evincing little concern for titles so long as he had a star pinned on his chest.

When the call came to tame El Paso, Stoudenmire was ready. Everything past, from the killing ground of the Civil War through the deadly years as a Ranger, had been but a preliminary to this main event. Like some intricate jigsaw puzzle of destiny, the toughest bordertown on the frontier and the lone-wolf lawman were brought together in a clash that reshaped western legend.

Although the events depicted in *El Paso* are based on documented records, certain liberties have been taken with time, place, and various names. The fact remains, however, that what is written here was essentially what occurred along the banks of the Rio Grande during that desperate summer of 1881.

Dallas Stoudenmire left his mark on El Paso, as well as on the era of the gunfighter. Yet, in passing, it must be noted that he bore small resemblance to the mythical lawmen of folklore. He was simply a man doing the job for which he had been trained, perhaps colder and more deadly than most, but fairly typical of his breed. Resourceful, honest to a fault, brave beyond the measure of other men; a mankiller who coincidentally happened to wear a star.

Matthew Braun

CHAPTER ONE

1.

LIEUTENANT JOHN Tays found himself at a slight tactical disadvantage. He was leading a force of eighteen Texas Rangers, and his orders were to safeguard the journey of three American businessmen. But at the moment, he was standing eyeball to eyeball with close to a thousand Mexican insurgents, and whoever blinked first would very likely wind up cold meat. Somewhat like a man who has a bear by the tail, Lieutenant Tays had developed a sudden liking for far away places.

That morning, as false dawn had given way to first light, the besieged Americans saw that all hope of escape was gone. Under cover of darkness the villagers of San Elizario had encircled with hastily dug rifle pits the adobe hut in which the Americans were trapped, and the sun's brilliant streamers glinted off a solid ring of blued steel. Rangers and civilians alike gazed at the fortifications in dull apathy. After seven days of intermittent fighting, any hope that the army would lift the siege had long since faded. Time had run out, and to a man they knew full well that the Mexicans would exact a grim price for the misery inflicted on them in the last few months.

Waiting for the final attack, Charles Howard could only reflect on the vicious bitch called fate. Earlier that year he had formed a combine with various El Paso businessmen for the sole purpose of cornering the Rio Grande salt trade. East of town, across a hundred miles of barren desert, lay a small chain of salt lakes. Though only recently arrived in Texas, Howard was a man of considerable ambition; an opportunist not above an unsavory deal if enough money were involved. And he was quick to grasp that whoever held a monopoly on the salt lakes could name his own price for that precious commodity.

Though Howard bore a remarkable resemblance to a well-fed hog, he was an affable, persuasive talker. Political skulduggery was a game he understood well, and within a short time, his combine had been allowed to file a claim on the distant lakes. While such grants were normally restricted on public service lands, the burgeoning salt cartel had in effect been given a license to steal. With legal possession of the lakes, they could collect a fee on every *fanega* of salt hauled away, and there were none to prevent them from raising the price to whatever the traffic would bear.

But Howard and his cronies had miscalculated the temper of the people. Throughout the memory of many generations, natives from both sides of the Rio Grande had driven their oxcarts to the dry lakes, braving a fortnight in the waterless desert so that their families might have salt. Moreover, they also bartered salt in the interior regions of Chihuahua, and the gummy cakes they gouged from the earth represented the primary money crop of every village along the border. The El Paso combine posed a threat not only to the natives' own humble needs, but more significantly to the meager livelihood they had been able to glean from the salt trade itself. Reaction was swift and violent.

Under the leadership of Don Luis Cardis, the insurgents had captured Charles Howard at San Elizario, the village closest to the salt lakes. There they forced him to relinquish all claim to the disputed lands, presumably squelching his salt racket in the bud. Then, in exchange for his life, they extracted his promise never to return and sent him packing down the road. Though Howard was built along the lines of a whale, he was hardly a jovial fat man accustomed to turning the other cheek. Ten days later, he caught Don Luis alone in El Paso and gave him an overdose of buckshot, leaving the Mexicans leaderless, if not wholly defanged.

Public officials immediately set the telegraph wires humming, urging the governor to request assistance from troops stationed at nearby Ft. Bliss. Of the fifteen thousand souls along the upper Rio Grande, roughly a thousand were *norteamericanos*. Should a race war erupt, they would be doomed by the sheer weight of numbers. More distressing still, El Paso was isolated by an arid waste of some five hundred miles from the nearest American settlement. With visions of the entire community being wiped out overnight, local politicians demanded forceful action from the government in Austin.

Characteristically, the governor disdained the use of federal troops and sent instead a company of Texas Rangers, commanded by Lieutenant John Tays. Never wanting for a glib argument, Howard somehow convinced Lieutenant Tays that the Mexicans were in open revolt. *After all, fewer than five decades had passed since Texans defeated Santa Anna at San Jacinto. Only a fool would doubt that the greasers remained loyal to Mexico!* Accompanied by the Rangers, Howard and his cohorts had returned to San Elizario, determined to recover what was theirs by right of connivance and political clout.

But natives along both sides of the border were also marching on the sleepy village. Chico Barela had emerged as their new leader, and his call to arms drew upwards of a thousand fighting men even as Howard prepared to reclaim the salt lakes. No sooner had the businessmen arrived in San Elizario than they found themselves confronted by an ugly mob. The cry went up for blood, retribution for the murder of Don Luis Cardis, and the Rangers were barely able to hold them off. Retreating to an adobe hut on the south side of the plaza, the hated *gringos* quickly found themselves under siege by the frenzied Mexicans.

The next week proved a hellish nightmare for the Americans. They ate horse meat, rationed their water, and waited anxiously for federal troops that never came. Instead of attacking directly, the Mexicans pinned them down with sniper fire night and day, certain they couldn't hold out longer than the dwindling water supply in their canteens. Then, as the seventh morning dawned, the natives waited in their newly dug rifle pits, ready for an all-out charge should the *gringos* prove unreasonable.

Shortly after sunrise Chico Barela called for a parley under a white flag. Lieutenant Tays stepped from the adobe, and the Mexican leader's conditions were heard clearly by everyone in the hut. The Rangers would be allowed to depart in peace, but Howard and his partners, John McBride and John Atkinson, would remain as hostages in the village. The *gringos* had one hour to consider the offer, and if they refused, then their company would be killed to the last man. With that, the Mexican flashed an arrogant grin and strode back to the rifle pits.

Turning, Tays moved through the door of the hut, only to be greeted by a deadly silence. None of the Rangers could bring themselves to look at the three businessmen. While they were sworn to uphold the law, they had families to think about, not to mention their own skins. *And besides, hadn't the greaser promised that the three men would simply be held as hostages? Like as not, they'd be released just as soon as things calmed down. Probably no more'n a day or two at the most.*

Charles Howard was many things, but above all else he was a man who believed in hedging his bet. Even if the Rangers agreed to fight, which seemed highly unlikely, he would surely be killed. That was a foregone conclusion. No, the wiser move was to surrender. Although he wouldn't trust a greaser's word any further than he could spit, it made sense to get the Rangers clear and hope they could return in time with a cavalry troop. Briskly confident, he outlined the plan to Lieutenant Tays and saw the strain wash out of the Rangers' faces. McBride and Atkinson weren't too happy with his decision, but then they didn't have a hell of a lot of a choice. Come to think of it, none of them did.

Thirty minutes later Tays and his Rangers pounded out of the village, spurring their horses for El Paso. Behind they left Howard and his partners the featured attraction amidst a howling mob. Some years would pass before even the strongest of them could erase the scene from his memory.

Chico Barela was no less pragmatic than Charles Howard. He remained a leader only so long as he served the will of his people, and right now, his ragtag army was calling for blood. *Gringo* blood! With the Rangers hardly out of sight, the hostages' arms were bound behind them, and they were marched across the plaza to an adobe wall beside the ancient mission. While McBride and Atkinson seemed numb with shock, Charles Howard allowed his captors nothing more than a tight smile. He had gambled and lost. And where he was headed, he had best enjoy the fresh air while he could.

Without benefit of prayer or even a blindfold, the prisoners were shoved against the wall as a firing squad was hurriedly formed. Lacking a sword, Barela borrowed a *machete* and raised it overhead. When it fell, the roar of gunfire thundered across the plaza, instantly followed by the maddened shout of the onlookers. Atkinson and McBride dropped lifelessly in the dust, but Howard had been gutshot, and he staggered forward, knees buckling.

"¡Más arriba, cabrones!" he moaned through clenched teeth. "Higher, you stinking goats!"

"¡Acábenlos!" roared the delighted mob. "Finish him!"

Chico Barela marched solemnly to the wounded man. Deliberating a moment, he gauged the blow, then swung the *machete*. Charles Howard's head toppled to the ground, ending his brief moment as salt baron of the Rio Grande. Spurting bright fountains of blood, his body simply collapsed, and the crowd went mad with a spasm of sheer joy.

"¡Hecho!" cried Chico Barela. "It is done! Don Cardis is avenged. The salt lakes belong again to the people!"

2.

SHORTLY AFTER suppertime, the men began drifting into the compound. Spread along the banks of the Rio Grande just west of town, Hart's Mill was an imposing structure. The river had been channeled and damned so that it flowed through a high stone arch erected on one side of the millhouse. Locally, it was said that the sluggish river was a mile wide and a foot deep; too thin to plow and too thick to drink. But as it tumbled from the towering arch, sufficient force was generated to turn a huge creaking waterwheel. Seth Hart had copied it directly from those he remembered as a boy in New England, and along the upper Rio Grande, his was the only gristmill. Somewhat like its owner, the mill seemed formidable, unrelenting as it ground inexorably on; one of a kind in a land where industry and determination often fell victim to the drowsy pace of the natives.

Near the mill stood Seth Hart's home. Overlooking the river, it was built of foot-thick adobe and surrounded by tall shade trees. And it was here that various El Paso businessmen who shared Hart's political persuasion met once a week for a bruising, heads-up poker game. The house rules were table stakes, check and raise, and a good stiff jolt of rotgut for those left sucking hind tit. As in his business and political endeavors, Seth Hart played poker to win.

After being greeted by their host, the men took their usual seats and settled down for a long, spirited night. They were old friends, each having come to El Paso when it was still a stopover to somewhere else, and there were few secrets among them. They loved whiskey and cards, shared a long standing dream to make El Paso the hub of power in west Texas, and considered themselves ethical businessmen as well as adept politicians. They saw no contradiction in this latter belief, for they readily agreed that a man of substance must play many roles. While there were no saints among them, neither were there any scoundrels, and on this bedrock, their friendship had taken root and grown.

With drinks served and small talk out of the way, the men sat back to await the first deal. But Seth Hart absently riffled the cards, as if pursuing some elusive thought that resisted words. His thatch of white hair spilled over his head like an unkept mane, and the soft, cider glow of the lamp gave his face the flat sheen of weathered rawhide. Were these men his sons, or had this been a land of clans, he would have ruled as patriarch, the venerable elder to whom all others looked for guidance. Although neither condition existed, Hart was still a man of considerable influence, and his four friends seldom made a move without seeking the miller's counsel. Curiosity whetted, they waited in deepening silence as he sifted the chaff from what it was he had to say.

Hart cleared his throat and spat a wad of phlegm at a cuspidor beside the chair. When he spoke his voice was gravelly, as if he had spent too many years swallowing the dust from his own gristmill. "Boys, before we get sidetracked on poker, I'd like to get your ideas on this hornet's nest Charlie Howard stirred up. We're looking down a long, hard road, and if somebody doesn't calm the Mexicans pretty quick it's liable to be a bloody one." He paused, mulling the thought further. "One thing's for certain. Just as sure as we're sitting here, Ed Banning and his bunch aren't going to do a damn thing except keep right on lining their pockets."

"Maybe the greasers'll ventilate Banning the same way they did ol' Charlie." Doc Cummings, owner of the local mercantile emporium, chuckled softly at his own wit. "After all, Charlie was a spoon-fed piker compared to the Banning boys."

Horace Adair reared back in his chair. Noted for his hair-trigger temper, the Irishman was general manager of a mine north of town. "Jesus Christ, Doc! You made your point and missed it, all in the same breath. Granted Ed Banning would skin a flea for its hide and tallow, but he only steals from poor folks indirectly. Political corruption and cattle rustling rarely matter one way or the other to *peones*. Come to think of it, they might even admire him."

Curiously, Horace Adair was closer to the truth than he realized. There were many in El Paso who openly admired the Banning brothers, and their ranks weren't limited to saloonkeepers, madams, and cardsharps. Ed and Sam Banning had hit town in the spring of '79, shortly after word leaked out that three railroads were laying track toward the border. At the time, El Paso was little more than a crossroads. The trail from Santa Fe to Mexico City ran directly through the center of town, while the stage route connecting San Antonio with the Pacific Coast meandered off in the opposite direction. And El Paso's chief claim to fame lay in the fact that the Butterworth stage stopped there twice a day.

But with the arrival of Southern Pacific's first train only last month, the little border town had undergone some startling changes. Trains were daily disgorging a horde of mercenaries who smelled loose money on the freshening wind. For those with a strong stomach, there were fortunes to be made, and whores, tinhorn gamblers, thimbleriggers, and gunslicks had descended on El Paso like swarming locusts. Hardly to anyone's surprise, the Banning brothers were running strong at the head of the pack, welcoming outlaw and harlot alike with open arms. With liberal doses of bribery, intimidation, and outright murder, they had taken over city hall and virtually dominated the city council. Although it saddened early settlers like Seth Hart and his friends, there was no denying that in only two short years Ed Banning had become the power to be reckoned with in El Paso.

"Horace, as usual, your logic is devastating." Doc Cummings cast a mischievous smile around the table, amused by the Irishman's pugnacious manner. "But I'll tell you one thing. Ed Banning's day is coming. He's got his finger in everything else, and he'll probably get around to trying to steal the salt lakes just like Charlie Howard did. Maybe if we wait long enough, the greasers'll settle his hash for us."

Before Adair could frame a reply, Seth Hart broke in sharply. "Doc, you and Horace are both missing the point. Howard trying to grab the salt lakes only aggravated a sore that's been festering for years. And mark my words, the Bannings' rustling operation across the river will one day force the *patrones* to lead their people against us. So far they've sat back and watched, but if their ranches keep getting raided, they'll organize those *peones*, and God help us then."

The men silently glanced at one another, weighing Hart's words. Nate Hobart, proprietor of the Alhambra Hotel, sucked nervously at his drink and tried to think of something profound to add. But his natural reticence won out, and he merely waited for the shaggy-haired miller to resume.

When the stillness thickened without anyone venturing a solution, Hart tossed out another firecracker. "Boys, what I've been leading up to is simply stated. El Paso is just facing too goddamned many problems all at one time. Ed Banning is stealing the town blind, and when you get right down to cases, his political shenanigans are one of the big causes of our Mexican problems. Appears to me that, if we solve one, we'll have gone a long way toward solving the other. What I'm suggesting is that we put Banning to the skids and send him packing."

"Well, we could always have George Campbell run him out of town," Cummings observed dryly. The comment was greeted with grunts and snorts by the other men, for it was common knowledge that City Marshal Campbell was one of Banning's political flunkeys.

"Shit fire," Adair remarked acidly. "George Campbell couldn't catch his ass if he was tied hand and foot in a tow sack."

"By God, what we need is a *town tamer!*" John Simmons, owner of the livery stable and feed store, suddenly came alive. His eyes glittered with comprehension, as if the answer had been revealed to him alone. "Someone like Wild Bill Hickok, or Bear River Tom Smith. A real head-cracker!"

"There's only one problem with that, Johnny. They're both dead." Horace Adair's sardonic comment brought chuckles from the other men, and a withering look from Simmons.

Doc Cummings abruptly came up on the edge of his chair. "Maybe so. But by Jesus Christ, I know one that's not dead! He's a deputy sheriff up in Colorado County, and, gents, he's the meanest sonovabitch that ever got up and walked on his hind legs. Name's Dallas Stoudenmire, and lemme tell you, he eats knotheads like Ed Banning for breakfast."

"Is that a fact?" Adair inquired innocently, glancing about the table. "And how is it you know so much about a Dutchy gunslinger?"

"Horace, he just happens to be German. Or at least his

folks were. And for your information, he's gonna marry my sister later this month."

"Doc, we're not playing for chalkies, you know." Seth Hart gave him a searching look. "This is serious business. You sure you want to get your brother-in-law hooked up in a deal like this?"

"Hell, Seth, I can't see how it'd hurt to ask," Cummings replied. "He's full grown, and I reckon he knows how to say no. Besides, he's been a lawman of one kind or another since the end of the war, and even if he don't want the job, he could sure as hell give us some powerful advice. Offhand, I'd say it's as good a place to start as any."

Hart pondered this for a moment, then nodded. "All right, send him a wire. But don't let the cat out of the bag. Just say you'd like to see him on a matter of some importance."

"And what will we accomplish, even if he's as tough as Doc says?" Adair's bulldog jowls set in an obstinate scowl. "You don't seriously think the city council will fire Campbell and hire a new marshal?"

Hart smiled patiently. "Horace, let's take 'em as we come to 'em. Don't forget that Doc and me both have a vote on that same council. And if we want to play dirty pool, we might just figure a way to ram it through."

The miller ran callused hands through his white mane, then picked up the deck of cards. The discussion had ended. "Boys, let's get down to some serious poker playin'. The name of the game is stud. Ante five dollars and take your licks like real white men."

3.

DALLAS STOUDENMIRE wasn't what folks would call a handsome man, but he looked like he had been built to last. Rangy and lean, he was hewed somewhat on the order of an oak door, standing six feet four and weighing in at a gristled two hundred twenty. Few men knew his full strength, and those who had tested it rarely came back for seconds. His very presence was enough to halt most troublemakers in their tracks, and his fearsome impact wasn't lessened by the craggy features, the jut of a heavy brow, and a shock of hair like burnished wheat. His face looked as though it had been hurriedly chiseled from a hunk of granite, and above the hollow cheeks his eyes touched lightly on all about him. As if it concealed some shallowly buried danger, his gaze seemed pale and depthless in its constant movement, like mountain water beneath freshly frozen ice. All in all, he was a solitary sort, a man best left to himself. And most people took him just as they found him. At a distance, in short doses.

When Stoudenmire stepped from the train at the Southern Pacific depot, he felt the stares of those crowding the platform. While he was used to it, the gaping looks never ceased to nettle him, like farmers gawking at some oddity in a tent show. He knew he was different from most men, colder, quicker to strike, drained of remorse once it was done. But it didn't bother him; he accepted it for what it was, wasting little thought on the compassion and gentleness that preachers rated so highly. Time lays scars on a man, bloody welts tracing a path from where he stands back to where he started. In the overall scheme of things, there were some men who needed killing, and it stood to reason that there had to be a few who were hardened to wield the instrument of destruction. Why he had been tapped for the job, or how it had come about, seemed unimportant, lost in the haze of long-ago, far-away things. Somehow it had started, leading him step by step from a wild young hellion to a man with a star on his chest. He was good at it, perhaps the best. And for now, being best at what he did was all that mattered.

Ignoring the stares, Stoudenmire turned his broad back on the train station and strode off down Main Street. Though he knew little of El Paso, he had heard that it was nestled in the Tularosa Basin and was thus unprepared for the pervasive sense of being encircled by mountains. The *Conquistadores* had named it El Paso del Norte, for it formed a natural pass to the north over the mountains that now joined Texas, New Mexico, and Mexico. The bare, craggy slopes of the Franklin Mountains dropped off from a high rim to the north, and the town itself lay in the shadow of Comanche Peak. To the east lay the arid plains he had crossed by train, broken only by the flat desert mesas, jutting unevenly from the parched earth. Beyond the tablelands, he could see the Hueco Mountains, with the sheer cliffs of El Capitán thrusting skyward as if to escape the desolation and heat.

Turning, he studied the land to the southwest, across the river. In the distance, he saw the Sierra Madre range, forming a backdrop for El Paso's twin sister on the opposite border, Paso del Norte. Even though the towns appeared similar in every respect, he had heard on the train that Paso del Norte was strictly for Mexicans, a place where a *gringo* wandered at his own risk. The thought brought his mind back to the reason for being here, and he crossed the plaza in search of Doc Cummings. The cryptic telegram in his coat pocket said little, and perhaps that was what made him curious enough to travel six hundred miles. Most times the things men left unsaid were what counted in a pinch, and knowing Doc, he had no doubt there was considerable yet to tell.

Later that night, Stoudenmire and Cummings met with Seth Hart and his poker cronies. Although the five businessmen were the only ones who knew the purpose behind the lawman's visit, Stoudenmire's presence in El Paso was hardly a secret. Earlier in the evening, Cummings had taken him on a tour of the town's gamier dives, and there was considerable talk in the red-light district about the solemn-faced jasper with the frosty eyes. But the brief walk through the southside had served its purpose. Within an hour's time the lawman had counted close to thirty saloons, an equal number of dancehalls, and a rash of whorehouses unlike anything he had ever seen. Moreover, he had observed two saloon brawls, a knifing, and a somewhat amateurish gunfight, all within the space of two blocks. Yet not once had he seen a man wearing a badge. Any lingering doubt in Stoudenmire's mind had fast been dispelled. El Paso was in desperate need of a responsible peace officer.

Once introductions were out of the way and the men seated in Hart's study, the miller briefed Stoudenmire on the extent of the problem they faced. Without need of exaggeration, he detailed events leading to the salt war, the general hostility that existed between whites and Mexicans, and the stranglehold the Bannings had secured on the political apparatus of the town. While he spoke, Seth Hart had been sizing Stoudenmire up, and he liked what he saw. But there was more to a man than what met the eye, and that's what they had to find out before the evening was finished.

"Frankly, Mr. Stoudenmire," Hart concluded, "if I were in your boots, I wouldn't touch this job with a ten-foot pole. Course, you're a lawman, and I'm not, so I suppose you know what you're gettin' into." Then he paused, letting the silence mount as he appraised the other man. "Well, no sense beatin' around the bush. What about it? Do you think you're man enough to cut the mustard?"

Stoudenmire's eyes narrowed at the outright challenge, and the room went still as the men waited to see how he would answer. "Mr. Hart, it sort of looks to me like you've got the saddle on backwards. I didn't come here begging a job. You sent for me, near as I recollect. Whether or not I can pull your bacon out of the fire is something you'll have to decide for yourself. My record as a peace officer isn't hard to track down, and if I'm any judge, you've already put out feelers in the right direction."

Doc Cummings couldn't restrain himself from butting in. "Dallas, don't be so infernal high and mighty. He's only tryin' to get your opinion of our predicament. Christ, I've already told them how you fought for the Confederacy and served as a Ranger before you took the deputy job. They know you can clean up El Paso. They're just tryin' to get you to say it."

The lawman just nodded, smiling tightly. "Well, I'll tell you, Doc. I'm not right sure I want the job. Leastways not until we come to an understanding about a few things."

"If you want my two cents worth," Horace Adair snorted, "I'm not convinced he can handle it. Running the Bannings out of town is gonna be like tryin' to pour hot butter in a wildcat's ear. All this bullshit about him being a gunslinger might impress the folks back home, but goddamnit, this is the border. If he starts playing the big, tough *hombre* on the southside, those boys are just liable to whittle him down to size."

Stoudenmire's flinty gaze swung around, and he looked at Adair as if he were something hairy that had just crawled out of the gravy. "Mister, I never had much use for little men with loud mouths. Now if you pop off once more, I'll be forced to forget you're Doc's friend. Savvy?"

"Hold it!" Hart's gruff command came just as the Irishman's jowls swelled with rage. "Horace, sometimes I'd swear you don't have sense enough to carry guts to a bear. Granted Mr. Stoudenmire might be young in years, but it seems you aren't able to see beyond that. There are other ways of measuring time, you know. Offhand, I'd say that anyone who has killed six men upholding the law doesn't need a wet nurse, even on the border." The startled looks from his friends brought a benign smile to the miller's face. "Why the surprise? You boys know I don't bet without peeking at the hole card. Like Mr. Stoudenmire surmised, I've already gone to the trouble of having him checked out."

Horace Adair glued a sheepish smile on his face and got busy sipping his whiskey. The big sonovabitch was for real after all! Silently, he wondered what went on inside a man's head who killed so easily, and for pay at that. The cold-eyed bastard probably pissed ice water and slept on nails.

"Well goddamn," Cummings crowed. "Are we gonna sit around on our thumbs or do we offer the man a job? How about it, Dallas? Want to try cutting El Paso down to size?"

"Trying won't get it. Not by half," Hart interjected. "He'll have to bet the limit and back every play to the hilt. Otherwise, he'll be cold meat inside of a week. But before we go too far with that, I'd like to hear more about those conditions Mr. Stoudenmire wants us to meet."

The lawman glanced around the room, studying each man in turn before responding. "Gentlemen, with the exception of Doc, I don't know any more about you than I do Adam's goat. You say you want your town cleaned up, and until you prove different, I'll take you at your word. But if I'm going to kick over a shithouse, it'll have to be done my way. That means no interference, no deals, and no special treatment for friends. Whoever gets in the way gets hurt. If you can't swallow that, then let's just shake hands, and I'll see about catching the next train out."

The men stared at Stoudenmire as if hypnotized, certain he meant every word he said. Whoever got in his way wouldn't just get hurt. They would get killed. And in his own way, the lawman was warning them that it could happen. Still, they didn't have a hell of a lot of choice. It was either suffer along under the Bannings or take a chance on a killer who just happened to wear a star. The one bled you dry with political corruption, and the other might just chase the whole damn town up a tree. But you paid your money and you took your chances. The odds came out the same no matter how the nut was cracked.

"Boys, it looks like we've got ourselves a new marshal." Seth Hart's tone left no doubt that the decision had been made. "Now we'd better get down to figuring strategy. I've got an idea the city council is gonna wet down their legs when we spring Dallas on them."

Stoudenmire leaned back in his chair and lit a cigar. As the men began talking, he sipped at his drink for the first time. Good whiskey. Damned good, in fact. And he had to admit that he was impressed with the company, too. Still, he'd seen sure-fire winners turn to busted flushes more than once. Better to bank on himself and forget about handouts. Storekeepers were generally soft in the guts anyway. Besides, when the shooting started, a man did well to forget he had friends.

4.

EL PASO's city hall fronted Oregon Street on the west side of the plaza. Once a month, Mayor Isaac Porter convened the city council in an upstairs meeting hall. There they met to consider the bagful of problems generated by the town's mushrooming growth.

Since the mayor, as well as two of the councilmen, Simeon Ogleby and Pud Brown, danced to whatever tune the Banning brothers happened to favor, the monthly meetings were generally cut-and-dried affairs. Occasionally, the irascible Doc Cummings would liven up what he called "The puppet show," but more often than not, the meetings made for a dull, frequently wasted, evening. The sole ambition of Mayor Porter and his two henchmen centered on milking the town dry with corrupt schemes, and even Seth Hart in his tenacious, probing way had been unable to get the goods on them to date.

The June council meeting promised to be little different from those in the past. After reviewing progress on current projects, which included a public waterworks contract awarded to Pud Brown's brother, the mayor opened the floor to new business. Hart and Cummings sat back to watch the show. While the council's shenanigans sometimes curdled their stomachs, there was a perverse fascination about the rogues' devious methods; as if a primer in civic malfeasance was being acted out right before their very eyes. Still, tonight might prove more interesting than anyone suspected, for Seth Hart planned to drop a bomb right in the mayor's lap. Just as soon as the four-flushers finished ramming through their latest swindle.

Isaac Porter was a beefy little man, whose spongy face was deeply pocked from a childhood bout with smallpox. Careful grooming did little to improve his chunky figure, and he had the disconcerting habit of peering at a man like some wise, inquisitive bird. The role of charlatan suited him perfectly, and as he faced the council, none doubted that he had few peers in the art of slick manipulation.

"Gentlemen, before the night's over I have every intention of breaking the faro bank at the Monte Carlo, so what do you say we get down to brass tacks? The floor's open, first come, first served."

Simeon Ogleby's hand shot skyward, and the mayor recognized him with a benevolent nod. "Mr. Mayor, I'd like to propose that the council entertain a motion to build a bridge over the Rio Grande. It's a public disgrace for a town of this size not to have a fine, substantial bridge joinin' us with our neighbors across the river. Besides that, now that the railroad has reached us, we should provide some civilized way of importing and exporting goods with Mexico. Trade is the backbone of commerce, and if this town's gonna grow, we've got to start thinkin' *progress.*"

Hart and Cummings exchanged glances, never ceasing to be amazed by the sheer audacity of these rascals. Though he knew it was futile, Doc couldn't resist a bit of heckling. "Simeon, what the hell are you gonna do with a bridge? You could wade that goddamn mudhole without gettin' your toes wet."

"Commerce, Doc. Commerce. The backbone of trade." Ogleby floundered, trying to remember if he had his terms in the right order. "And vice versa, of course."

Isaac Porter gave him a devastating look and jumped into the breach. "Gentlemen, I personally find great merit in this proposal. Why, just think of it! El Paso would be the only town on the border with a bridge connecting it to Mexico. The possibilities for international trade are enormous. I might even say, unlimited. As a matter of fact, the idea has such merit that I suggest we broaden the discussion to consideration of selecting a contractor to build this fine bridge."

"Hell, why not give it to Pud's brother?" Doc cackled. "He knows all about working in water."

Pud Brown shot a nervous glance at the mayor and smiled apologetically, like he expected someone to kick him in the ass. Porter studiously ignored Doc's wisecrack and went right on with the meeting. To no one's surprise, a building outfit resting in Ed Banning's hip pocket was selected, and an allocation of twenty-five thousand dollars earmarked for construction. The motion was quickly brought to vote and passed three to two. Hart and Cummings voting *nay* had somewhat the same effect as spitting into the wind.

As the mayor and his two cronies were congratulating themselves on their slippery footwork, Seth Hart decided it was time to rock the boat. But it would have to be done skillfully, in a roundabout manner. For if the Bannings ever tumbled to his real purpose, then no amount of pressure, deftly applied or otherwise, could force them to oust George Campbell.

"Mr. Mayor, I would like to bring a matter of some importance to the council's attention. Just now you made the point that our town is growing by leaps and bounds. And I agree wholeheartedly. Our first bank has just opened, we've got two newspapers, and before the summer's out, another railroad will reach us. All in all, I'd say we're about to become the biggest thing that ever hit West Texas. But if we're ever going to equal the likes of Austin or San Antonio, we've got to bring about some changes. To use your term, Isaac, we've got to get down to the brass tacks of civilizing a town that thinks it's still a frontier outpost."

Hart had their attention, though it was obvious they were waiting for the ax to fall. Looking around the table, he let the suspense build for only a moment, then pushed on. "We're faced with two problems that aren't about to solve themselves. First, there's the Mexicans. The army proved they're unwilling to take a hand in civilian matters when they let Charlie Howard get sliced to ribbons. And Austin isn't gonna keep sending a detachment of Rangers everytime we yell wolf. Which means we must solve it ourselves. As long as there's a threat of violence, El Paso won't be anything more than a jerkwater whistle-stop.

"Now the second problem is just as bad, from a standpoint of the town growing and attracting more business enterprises. Any night of the week you wanna go down to the southside, you can see at least one gunfight and probably stumble across two or three cadavers without even trying. And every last one of you knows it's true. Brawls, shootings, knife fights. The kind of violence people expect from a cowtown, but certainly not a progressive community. And to my way of thinking, gentlemen, the blame falls on our shoulders, not on the townspeople. Calling a spade a spade, I'm talking about the man we appointed to protect the citizens of El Paso. George Campbell is worthless as tits on a boar hog. He not only isn't man enough for the job, he doesn't even try. I can guarantee you he's sacked up in some whorehouse swilling whiskey at this very moment. And with my own eyes, I've seen him make a beeline in the opposite direction whenever trouble starts."

Mayor Porter chuckled softly, then broke in before Hart could catch his breath. "Now, Seth, it's not all that bad. George isn't the best peace officer, I grant you. But he's certainly not the worst. Good Lord, this town's still got growing pains, and you can't expect any man to civilize it overnight."

"Well, by God, somebody better," Cummings snorted. "Otherwise, we're gonna have greasers crawlin' over us like flies on a manure pile. That is, if the rowdies don't kill everybody in town first."

The mayor and his cohorts suddenly began squirming in their chairs. Huddled together at the end of the table, they peered blankly at Hart and Cummings, like a trio of owls caught in a chicken coop. Apparently, the businessmen were in dead earnest, and the Banning underlings had no desire to create a row over such an insignificant post as city marshal. Their crooked little empire was running under full sail, and anyone who made waves would have to answer to Ed Banning personally.

Porter blinked first, unwilling to start a fight without Banning's approval. Then in his oily, politician's voice, he began probing for a weak spot. "Now Doc, don't get yourself in a swivet. We're all reasonable men here. And I'm sure Seth will agree that we can come up with some way to get George Campbell back on the straight and narrow. Think about it calmly for a moment and then tell me where you think the marshal has gone astray."

Cummings regarded him with a brash, amused insolence. "Isaac, you're slick. Real slick. Remind me of a tomcat I heard about once. Seems like he got the hots for a little skunk pussy and started humpin' a female polecat. Well, sir, after a couple of whacks, he had to call it quits. Hadn't had all he wanted, you understand, just all he could stomach. What I'm gettin' around to saying, Isaac, is that unless you put a damper on the southside and the greasers, the voters of this town might start figuring they've had all of you they can stand."

"Doc's right, Mayor." Seth Hart grabbed the lead before Porter could gather his wits. "The marshal was appointed because you supported him, and everyone knows it, and as any fool can see, George Campbell wilted when the going got rough. He's your responsibility, Isaac, and if you don't do something about it, the decent people of El Paso are going to start having second thoughts about their mayor."

Porter glared at him across the table, trying desperately to muster some reasonable argument. But Hart's words had the ring of truth, and everyone in the room knew it. Ogleby and Brown simply held their breath, like something rancid had been smeared on their upper lips. Yet the silence deepened, and their faces went taut as they waited on the mayor to offer a snappy rebuttal.

Watching them, Doc Cummings couldn't resist the temptation. "Blessed are those who have nothing to say and cannot be persuaded to say it."

The sarcasm brought Porter out of his funk. He shot Cummings a stinging glance, then looked back at Hart. "Exactly what is it you're suggesting, Seth?"

"Not much, really. Just that Campbell be replaced with a man who can make El Paso a safe place to live."

"And I suppose you've got his replacement all picked out?"

"You might say that. We've been talking to a fellow named Stoudenmire. Got a fine record as a peace officer in East Texas. We think he's got the backbone the job calls for."

"And if I refuse to consider a change?"

"Why, Isaac, I suppose I'd be forced to call in the newspapers and tell 'em the mayor got skittish when we started talking about cleaning up El Paso. You know, elections are only a year or so away, and lots of people are just achin' to stir up a reform movement."

Porter mulled it over for a moment, desperately aware of the need to talk with Ed Banning. "Tell you what. We'll take it under advisement and come to a decision at next month's meeting."

"Sorry, Mayor, but that won't cut it." Hart's eyes hardened, and his jaw set in a stubborn cast. "I'll agree to twenty-four hours, which means we meet again tomorrow night. Otherwise I sic the newshounds on you."

Isaac Porter merely nodded, his face flushed with indignation and worry. Rising, he stalked from the room, trailed closely by Brown and Ogleby. Breaking the bank at the Monte Carlo was now the furthest thought from his mind. It had been a rough night, and right at the moment, he needed a good, stiff drink.

Observing their hasty departure, Cummings heard the warm, moist chuckle of a fat man laughing and turned to find Seth Hart thoroughly amused by the new order of things.

"Doc, just offhand, I'd say we've got 'em on the run. Goddamn me if they didn't look like three little shoats that just come out of the cuttin' pen."

The two men shook hands heartily and strode from the meeting hall with new zest to their step. Things were looking up, and if the Bannings weren't careful, they might just wind up snookered in their own game.

5.

SOME TWO hours after the council meeting, Isaac Porter wandered into the Coliseum Saloon. His step was slightly unsteady, and his eyes had taken on a glassy sheen, but otherwise, there was no outward sign that he was carrying a load. Since leaving city hall, he had belted down the better part of a quart, and at the moment he was feeling no pain. Still, he was in command of himself, and his confidence had risen sharply as he moved from saloon to saloon along San Antonio Street. Tipping his hat to the bartender, greeting his constituents with an expansive smile, the mayor eased through the boisterous crowd and headed for the Coliseum's back room.

Like most watering holes in town, the Coliseum had a

long mahogany bar with a smattering of nude paintings and French mirrors hung on the walls. But the similarity ended there, for the Coliseum was owned by the Banning brothers, and it was hardly an accident that their establishment was the showplace of El Paso. On one side of the large hall, there was a row of gaming tables, offering faro, chuck-a-luck, roulette, and other pleasant devices for separating the sucker from his poke. Toward the rear of the room, angled across one entire corner, was a small stage where dancing girls, Irish tenors, and stuttering comedians took turns competing with the roar of the crowd. Taken at a glance, it was quite a place, and for most men, owning the Coliseum would have represented the end of the rainbow. But Ed Banning had never considered himself molded from common clay; what was enough for the average pilgrim was merely a sampler for El Paso's political kingpin.

After threading his way through the packed house, Mayor Porter halted before a door at the rear, adjusted his coat, and knocked lightly. From inside came a muffled command, barely audible over the hubbub from the saloon. Sucking up his paunch, Porter twisted the doorknob and entered Ed Banning's office.

The first thing he saw was Sam Banning. The younger of the Banning brothers had a way of drawing attention, even in a crowd. For a big man, he was uncommonly handsome, and the fact that his nose had been broken on occasion somehow lent character to his broad, rough-hewn features. But after fashioning his face, the gods in their perverse way had played a cruel joke on Sam. His wide, heavily muscled shoulders gave way to long dangling arms, and his hands looked as if they could crush coconuts if the need arose. Still, the crowning touch was that Sam had grown to manhood almost as thick through the head as he was through the shoulders. All in all, the young Mr. Banning seemed only one step removed from walking on his knuckles.

Porter nodded to Sam, then turned to his brother who was seated behind a massive, ornately carved desk. "Ed, how's tricks? Looked like you're making money hand over fist out there.'' The mayor jerked his head back toward the door, and his hat tilted askew, cocked rakishly over one eyebrow.

Ed Banning regarded the dumpy politician with a speculative gaze. Isaac Porter had achieved minor fame as a boozer in earlier days, and Banning had a sneaking hunch he was on the firewater again. ''Mayor, what brings you down to this neck of the woods? Thought you had a council meeting tonight.''

''Oh, we did, we did,'' Porter assured him. ''Passed that bridge deal one, two, three, and awarded the contract to our sterling partner in illusion, Ab Roberts.''

El Paso's political boss just nodded, observing him closely, certain now that Porter's euphoric mood was about nine parts alcohol. Banning's frowning eyes slanted upward, two cold, ashen sockets in a long, bony face. Unlike Sam, he was a spare man, with a chalky, pallid look, almost as if he had been sickly as a child. Somewhat withdrawn by nature, he was an astringent sort, who usually spoke through clenched teeth, as if his jaws had been broken and wired shut. But the most disturbing thing about him was his eyes, menacing yet somehow lifeless, tinted a strange, dispassionate shade of gray, curiously suggestive of a cold winter cloud in a dead sky.

With the exception of his brother, Ed Banning had little use for other men; cynical of their motives, sharply aware of the imperfections that flawed their character. Remote, purposely holding himself aloof from the crowd, he played on other men's frailties and, with reasoned audacity, brought them to their knees in the crunch. Now, irritated by Porter's weakness for the bottle, he decided to whittle his political front-man down a notch or two.

''Isaac, you're soused. And the only thing lower in my book than a drunk is a reformed drunk. Now, suppose you pull up your pants and tell me what happened at the council meeting to set you off.''

The mayor's bonhomie wilted under the biting sarcasm, and his motley features dissolved beneath a mask of outright alarm. ''Ed, it wasn't my fault, honest to Christ it wasn't. That bastard Seth Hart has got it in his head that we need a new marshal. And he's threatened to blow the lid off unless we appoint some John Law he's scrounged up. I swear to you, Ed, I didn't have a thing to do with it. Absolutely nothing."

"All right, Isaac, keep your dauber up. There's a difference between having your tit in a wringer and losing all the marbles. Now just start at the beginning and tell me exactly what happened."

"Goddamn, Ed, you ain't gonna get nothin' out of him that makes sense." Sam's eyes flashed like coals of black ice as he gestured comtemptuously toward Porter. His normal disposition was something akin to a boar grizzly with its paw in a rusty bear trap, and right now he regarded the stubby little politician with a hungry glare. "Lemme take old swizzle-guts out and dump him in a horse trough. That'll bring him up talkin' a blue streak."

"Sam, try not to be so rash. Isaac's not that bad off. Are you, Isaac?" Ed Banning paused and Porter nodded dumbly, darting a nervous glance in Sam's direction. "See, what did I tell you, Sam? Isaac's got it all sorted out, and he's going to pony up just like he had balls. Now you go right ahead, Mayor, we're all ears."

Fumbling the words, Porter tried to flush the whiskey fumes from his spinning brain. Haltingly at first, he started to relate the gist of what had happened at the council meeting. Warming to his subject, the old warrior then launched into a vitriolic, damning tirade against Seth Hart and Doc Cummings. Gaining confidence as his grasp for the trenchant phrase returned, the mayor swept into the home stretch with a dire warning that all was lost unless the two businessmen were somehow thwarted in their underhanded conspiracy.

When he finished, standing spent and slightly breathless, the brothers simply stared at him with disgust. Ed Banning finally shook his head with a patronizing smile. "Isaac, if anybody ever takes the trouble to kick all the bullshit out of you, they could bury you in a matchbox."

Sam's hoarse grunt cut him off. "Forget him, Ed. We got to worry about them smart-aleck sonsabitches uptown. I say get 'em in a dark alley and split their heads with a bungstarter. Teach 'em they can't get away with muckin' up the water. Let everybody in this whole goddamn fleabag know who's callin' the shots in El Paso."

"You know, Sam, sometimes I think our old man's oats must've been thinned out when he get around to you. Killin' Hart and Cummings wouldn't do anything but get the reformers out on the street pounding their drums." When the younger Banning gave him a baleful frown, Ed chuckled lightly. "Now don't get all bent out of shape. Lemme have a minute to think this out."

Unlike his brother, who operated solely on raw instinct, Ed Banning was coldly phlegmatic when crossed; a calculating, passionless instrument even with his back to the wall. Leaning back in the chair, his eyes clouded over and fixed on the ceiling, as if the answer lay hidden in the broad crossbeam. Slowly, piece by piece, he took the puzzle apart and put it back together again, examining each possibility with precise care before discarding it. Then, as he stood back and looked at the situation as a whole, the jumbled parts abruptly fell into place, no longer obscured or muddied but suddenly clear and shiny bright.

With the solution now in hand, his eyes focused again, and he found Sam watching him intently. "Brother, it occurs to me that dogs don't lie down just one way. And I think this is one of those times when we're gonna let Mr. Seth Hart go away figurin' he's bluffed us out."

When Sam's forehead wrinkled in protest, Ed held up his hand. "Let me finish. We're gonna let them have this hayseed as marshal. Stoudenmire, is that his name? Well they can have him, and welcome to him. It's no sweat off our balls. So long as we control the courts and city hall it doesn't make a good goddamn who wears that tin star. Without the mayor or the judges to back him up, Stoudenmire is gonna be flounderin' around like a hamstrung calf. And the dandy part of it is that we have absolutely nothing to lose, whichever way the dice fall. If he does get the greasers calmed down and clamps a lid on the southside, then we'll take credit for appointing the man who cleaned up El Paso. Lookin' at it the other way, if he falls on his ass or gets himself killed, then we'll dump the blame right back on Hart's doorstep. Like I said, there's no way for us to lose. It's like playing with a stacked deck."

"By God, Ed, you've done it again!" Isaac Porter grinned broadly, nodding his head with a great show of awe. "I'll just walk into that meeting tomorrow night and tell Hart to bring on his horses."

"You do that, Mayor. Only make damn sure Hart and Cummings believe that their threats worked. Otherwise, they might shy off and start kicking over more rocks."

Later, after Porter had wandered back into the saloon, the Bannings broke out a bottle of their own. Downing a shot, Sam smacked his lips, like a dog sniffing horse apples. Then he started, as if the whiskey had jarred his dim wits, and peered quizzically at his brother.

"Say, Ed, I just thought of somethin'. What the hell kind of excuse are we gonna give George Campbell?"

"Don't worry about it, I'll think of something. Course, we could send him on a raid across the river. Maybe somebody'd put a hole through him and let a little of that rotgut leak out." Lazing back in the chair, he sipped the whiskey, savoring its pleasant bite as his eyes drifted off. "Sam, if you're ever gonna amount to anything in this game, you've got to get one thing through your head. Men are the cheapest commodity on God's green earth. You buy 'em like pig's knuckles. By the pound or by the keg. And even then, you've got to figure you've been robbed. No matter what you paid."

Sam Banning's thick brow wrinkled, and he dimly wondered what the hell his brother was talking about. Then he decided it wasn't worth the effort, and went back to the more inviting certainty of the bottle.

CHAPTER TWO

1.

"DOC! DOC!" Kate Stoudenmire rushed forward and threw herself into the storekeeper's arms. She hadn't seen her brother in almost a year, and she sorely missed the eldest of the Cummings brood.

"Lordy, Kate girl, just look at you." After a mighty hug Doc held her at arm's length, mumbling appreciatively as he made a slow appraisal. "Yessir, gal, you are purely somethin'. Can't rightly call you my baby sister anymore. All growed up and married. Say, speakin' of husbands, where's Dallas?"

Glancing around, they saw Stoudenmire threading his way through the crowd gathered about the train station. Behind him came two Mexican youngsters who had all they could do to handle Kate's assortment of luggage. Trailing at his heels was the biggest dog Doc Cummings had ever laid eyes on.

As the two men shook hands, Doc saw the dog give him a long, speculative stare. He was easily the most ferocious-looking beast Doc could recall having stumbled across, including a couple of brief encounters with grizzlies. Built along the lines of a mastiff, he had a deep bull-chest, an enormous furrowed head, and a jawful of teeth that looked like he'd traded them off a shark. And like his master's, the dog's eyes were cold, somehow menacing, constantly shifting as he noted the movement of all about him with a wary scowl. In the background, Doc overheard the little Mexicans talking about *el lobo hambre*. The hungry wolf! Somehow it fitted the dog perfectly, and he idly wondered what the hell Stoudenmire fed the brute.

"Dallas, it's good to see you," Cummings said, tearing his thoughts away from the dog. "How's it feel to be an old married man? And what have you done to Kate? Man, she looks like someone just handed her the keys to the goody factory."

Stoudenmire's face cracked in a rare grin. Kate was his one weakness, the only soft spot in some thirty years of steeling himself to toe the mark in an uncompromising land. "Doc, near as I can see, I haven't done a thing for Kate. She's just a natural looker, that's all. Trouble is, you've been sittin' out here remembering your baby sister, and all the time she was studying to be a real eyeful."

Kate was a stunner, no question about it, and a man needed only one look to work up a fit of envy toward the lawman. Standing about even with Stoudenmire's shoulder, she was what people back home called dainty. But unlike many delicate women, she hadn't been shorted when the sweetmeats were handed out. Her oval face was framed by hair black as obsidian, and her eyes shot sparks of fiery green, like some ancient feline goddess. She had a devastatingly winsome smile and a bewitching manner that was both seductive and impish in the same breath. Yet Kate somehow created the illusion of being one of those fragile, gentle things that would vanish in a wisp of smoke unless handled gingerly. And beneath these more obvious features was a sense of refinement and gentility that left even raw-boned Texans gulping for pretty words and mushy phrases.

Although one man's eye for beauty might easily leave another man doubting his judgment, there were few who wouldn't agree that Dallas Stoudenmire had snared a rare prize indeed when he got himself spliced to this toothsome young piece.

Cummings slapped Stoudenmire on the shoulder and crowed with laughter. "Maybe I remember her in pigtails, like you say. But I bet I wouldn't be wide of the mark thinkin' you got more than you bargained for too." Rolling his eyes, he chortled and nudged the lawman in the ribs, glancing slyly at Kate. "You're lookin' sort of peaked, son. Not lettin' Katie girl work you overtime, are you?"

"Honestly! Men are so crude." Kate blushed up to her hairline, eyes flashing with mock indignation. "You two act like you're in a stable discussing some high-stepping brood mare. Well you'd better take care, mark my words. I know enough about the both of you that, if I ever started talking, this whole town would roll over on its back."

"God save us, she'd do it too!" Grabbing his sister around the waist, Cummings struck off toward a horse and buggy hitched near the end of the depot. "C'mon, Dallas. Let's take your bride on a tour of the town before she ups and spills the beans." Over his shoulder he darted a quick glance at the dog. "That grizzly bear of yours can ride in the caboose. What's his name, anyway?"

"Tige. And you'd better take care what you call him." The dog's ears perked up at the sound of his name, and Stoudenmire knuckled his wrinkled brow. "He's sort of proud of being a dog, and he don't take kindly to most folks."

"Man or beast?" Cummings called back in jest.

"Both." The lawman chuckled softly, and Tige licked his hand, sensing in some distant way that his master had had the last word.

Shortly, luggage and dog had been loaded on the buggy, and they headed uptown. Chattering like a magpie, Doc Cummings enlightened them on the points of interest, allowing small room for questions. San Jacinto Plaza, renamed for the battleground where Texas had won its independence. The Notice Tree, an ancient shadetree on which proclamations and death warrants had been tacked in times past. The State National Bank, first of its breed on the upper Rio Grande. And its partner in commerce, the Parker House Hotel, even then rising from the dust in a whirlwind of mortice and wood.

Pausing at the native market, the storekeeper explained that the countryside abounded with Mexican *granjeros*, small farmers who spent their lives coaxing raisins, grapes, and various fruits from the hostile soil. Centuries ago, hard on the heels of the *Conquistadores*, Franciscan monks had planted vineyards across the basin, and Paso wine, along with a fiery *aguardiente*, were now relished throughout the

Southwest and Mexico. While the natives were far from prosperous, they seldom experienced the famines of old, and with the coming of the railroad, their produce could be marketed on an even vaster scale.

Kate was all eyes as the buggy trundled through El Paso. Her life had been spent in the backwoods village of Columbus, and she had always dreamed of living in a city. While a bit disappointed with the monotonous adobe buildings, she was enthralled with the bright costumes and gentle gaiety of the people. There were few Mexicans in East Texas, and by contrast, the border town seemed very colorful and exciting, almost quaint. Maybe it wasn't Austin or San Antonio, but it wasn't the sticks either. Besides, she was seeing it all for the first time with the man who had rescued her from a shabby life in the backwaters of nowhere.

Dallas Stoudenmire was her savior, sometimes gruff, often inscrutable, but a man of intense passion and hidden warmth. He had snatched her from the jaws of marrying some farmer with one cow and a boil on his rump. Had that happened, she would have ended up like her mother, old and worn before her time, having another baby everytime someone shook a pair of overalls at her. Now she was somebody, the wife of a man selected for an important civic post, a celebrity after a fashion. And while he had never suspected, she would have gladly kissed her husband's feet on their wedding day.

Thinking about it, she made a tiny gurgling sound deep in her throat, half wonder, half pure joy. With the excitement of the moment, it was a heady mixture, and her head spun with the sheer exhilaration of just being alive. Then the moment of reverie passed, and Doc's voice once again intruded on that highly personal little world of her private thoughts.

"Yessir, we're a community that's going places. Agriculture, ranching, mines up north in the mountains. And the railroad just puts frosting on the cake. Everything a town needs to thrive and grow, make something of itself. Wouldn't be surprised but what El Paso becomes a real force in this state's economy before we're through."

"Doc, I think the word you're hunting for is boomtown," Stoudenmire noted soberly. "But from what I've seen so far the biggest business in El Paso is vice. Leastways most of the *dinero* spent in this town finds its way back to the southside in one fashion or another. Course, I could be all wet. I'm sort of Johnny-come-lately around here, so I reckon I'll have to wait till I see the full show."

"No, you're right as rain, Dallas. Hit it dead center, as a matter of fact." The storekeeper's face twisted with disgust, and he spat over the side of the buggy. "Sometimes I get wrapped up in what this town *could be*, and I lose sight of what we've got to overcome to get there. Ed Banning and his gang are the nerviest bunch of cutthroats along the border, and they've got to be sent packin' before El Paso will ever amount to anything. That's why we hired you. And being plain-spoken about it, most of the townspeople don't care whether you run 'em out or kill 'em. Just so they're gotten rid of."

"We'll see, Doc," the lawman said. "I don't believe in callin' my hand till all of the cards have showed."

"Perfectly understandable. Anyway, you're the marshal as of tomorrow morning, and you can run it however you see fit." Doc's face suddenly brightened, and he leaned across to swat Stoudenmire on the knee. "Damnation, I clean forgot. Seth Hart pulled a few strings back East while you were gone. Might say he called some political debts. Anyway, he got a pipeline into James Garfield and had you appointed a deputy US marshal. What with wearin' two stars, I'd say you oughta be able to cover just about any play the Bannings make. Course, you might do best to keep that under your hat. Seth figures it's an ace in the hole you shouldn't play till your back's against the wall."

Stoudenmire just nodded, reserving comment one way or the other. "Likely it'll come in handy, but tell Hart I don't want any more favors. I took this job with the understandin' I wouldn't be beholden to anyone. I meant just that, Doc."

"Pull in your horns, boy. Nobody's tryin' to get you obligated. Seth just wants what's best for the town, and he figured you could use all the muscle we could muster."

"Doc, I've got no more use for a politician than a hog does a sidesaddle. Just keep your cronies clear of me and let me do my job. If gettin' the Bannings' ashes hauled is what they're really after, I reckon they won't have long to wait."

Doc Cummings hunched forward and gave the horses a good swat with the reins. Damned if his brother-in-law wasn't as contrary as an old mule about certain things. Stubborn as a Dutchman, people always said, and by God, these Germans sure fitted the ticket.

Seated between them, Kate had remained silent throughout the discussion. Dallas had told her little of what lay behind his appointment, and for the first time she became aware of the task he had undertaken. Deputy sheriff of a settled county was one thing, but marshal of an untamed border town was more than she had bargained for. As they drew up before the house Doc had rented for them, Kate decided that something would have to be done about finding her husband a safer line of work.

2.

THE DIM light of a quarter-moon cast a faint glow over Paso del Norte. Along the main street, soft music drifted from a scattering of *cantinas*, and in a large building to the west, the lively tunes of a *fandango* floated across the plaza. Horses lined the hitchrails, standing hip-shot in the warm, sleepy night, yet the street was nearly deserted. The festivities had only just begun, and those not attending the dance had settled in for a night at their favorite saloon.

But the sleepy tranquillity of the village was abruptly shattered by coarse laughter and drunken shouts that were unmistakably American. The doors of a *cantina* burst open and four men stumbled into the street, steadying each other as they lurched to a halt. They reeked of *tequila*, and as they wobbled about, their eyes searched the night for some devilment worthy of their rowdy mood.

"For Chrissakes, boys," roared one with a thatch of red

hair, "I still say we oughta slip on down to that *fandango* and find us some little chili peppers."

"That's the ticket!" another agreed drunkenly. "I'm a man that needs to get his log sapped, and them Mex gals purely know how to jitterate your juices. Whooeee! They is somethin', ain't they, Red?"

Before Red could answer the oldest member of the crew cut him off. "Listen you goddamn nitwits, you go down to that dance and you're gonna end up shootin' marbles with your balls. Them greaser bastards don't like whites messin' with their women."

With a wild screech a runty, bowlegged little man reeled away from them, violently flapping his arms to keep from falling. "Yellow sonsabitches! Yer nothin' but a bunch of gutless shitkickers. Gonna let them greasers run it over you? Bullshit! There ain't a man alive that can make me back up."

With that, he stumbled backwards and sat heavily in the dusty street. The other men regarded him solemnly for a moment, dimly attempting to sift out the gist of his angry tirade.

"Goddammit, boys, he's right," Red growled. "Them greaser pricks ain't gonna brace us. Long as we stick together and keep our guns handy, they'd let us hump their mammy right in the middle of that dancehall."

The horny one perked up at that, and the older man merely mumbled sourly to himself. The decision made, they ambled forward and clumsily lifted their sidekick from the dirt. Just then, an obscure figure materialized from the darkness and silently glided past them, hugging the shadows near the adobe buildings.

Glancing up, Red batted his eyes and squinted hard, not sure he was seeing right. "Boys, if these old peepers ain't playin' tricks on me, that there is a livin', breathin' chili pepper."

The men's heads swung around, and for a moment they stared drunkenly into the shadows. Then their eyes came uncrossed, and without a word, they moved toward the dim figure. Fanning out, they formed a half-circle, bringing their ghostly quarry to bay against a wall.

"*¿Quien es?*" a small, quivering voice implored. "What is it you want, *señores?* I was only on my way to the *baile*. I meant no harm."

Trapped between them stood a young girl, hardly more than a child. Her eyes went wide with terror, glistening in the soft moonlight as she cowered against the building. She pressed herself flatter against the cool adobe, paralyzed with fear, whimpering as the men advanced on her. Then they leapt forward like a pack of wolves on a bleating calf, dragging her to the earth in a silent rush. Beneath her simple cotton dress they could feel the ripe young breasts, the warm thighs, the gentle swell of her girlish hips. Suddenly their tongues went thick, and the brassy taste of lust flooded their mouths. Red clamped his hand over her face, and they wordlessly lifted her. Gripped with shock, the girl stiffened under their hands like some frozen little bird with a broken wing. Moving swiftly, they ducked through the alley and faded into the darkness.

Less than a quarter-hour later the men reappeared from the alleyway, brushing dirt from their clothes. The edge had been blunted on their drunken mood, and their words came in terse, surly grunts.

"Shit, boys, I've had better poontang'n that screwin' a knothole. Come to think of it, Mother Thumb and her four daughters has got that gal beat."

"Goddamn right! That little bitch just laid there like a board. I'll bet she didn't wiggle her ass once the whole time I was humpin'."

"Quit pissin' and moanin', will ya? It was free, and that's likely the first time you ain't paid for it since you quit jerkin' your pud."

"Listen, you little turdknocker, I've had about enough of your lip for one night. Keep it up and you're gonna get . . ."

The four men came to a halt as they emerged onto the street, falling silent as they blundered into the path of several horsemen. Riding past were seven *vaqueros* mounted on their best cow ponies, clearly dressed for the *fandango*. The Mexicans eyed the men haughtily, their gaze wavering between curiosity and outright contempt. Then, just as they drew even with the Americans, the girl stepped from the darkness at the *gringos*' backs. Blood streamed down her legs, staining her torn skirt the color of burnt ochre; the bodice of her dress had been ripped apart, revealing the delicate bud of her childish breasts. Her eyes seemed wide as saucers in the pale light, and beneath them lay the dull gaze of one who has just walked barefoot through the coals of hell.

The *vaqueros* reined their horses viciously, wheeling toward the Americans. Startled, the four men turned to see what had attracted the Mexicans and found themselves face to face with their own handiwork. The specter advancing toward them froze the Americans in their tracks, like the sightless dead come to exact some nameless vengeance. Suddenly the feisty little man with the bowlegs snarled and spun about, clawing at his six-gun as he turned. But before he could clear leather, the *vaqueros* cut loose with a ragged volley, and pockets of dust spurted from his shirtfront. As he slammed backwards, his legs folded beneath him, and he dropped to the earth with a dusty thud. His partners briefly considered making a run for the darkness, then discarded the thought. They had no more chance than a flea on a wet hog; any sudden movement would leave them as dead as the sawed-off runt lying at their feet. Slowly they raised their hands, halfway expecting to get it in the back even as they did so.

Within the hour, the villagers of Paso del Norte had gathered before the local *calabozo*. Inside the jail, Pedro Vazquez, their *alcalde*, was attempting to piece together the story. As mayor, it was his responsiblity to determine the charges and hold these men for the *rurales*. Quite by chance, his nephew, Ramón Vazquez, was the leader of the *vaqueros* who had captured the Americans.

Listening to Ramón recount what had happened, the *alcalde* sensed that the temper of the crowd was better suited to a quick hanging. But these were his people, and they would never go against his wishes. Quite clearly, the *norteamericanos* were guilty, and they would be executed without doubt. But all according to law. So long as he was *jefe* of Paso del Norte, there would be none of the senseless violence that went on across the river.

As his nephew finished speaking, Pedro Vazquez heard a sullen muttering erupt from the crowd and turned to see people easing away from the door. Then a man and a woman appeared in the doorway, shielding the girl between them. With great dignity, they moved across the room and stopped before the *alcalde*, looking neither right nor left. The girl simply stared at the floor, unable to look at anyone.

"*Mi niña*, I would spare you this if it were within my power." Pedro Vazquez lifted her chin and kissed her gently on the cheek. "But we must know who did this terrible thing. So you must be brave and force yourself to look upon these men. If they are the ones, then it is your duty to make this known. Have no fear. Just look and tell what you see."

The girl slowly turned her head and stared for a heartbeat at the three men, now securely locked in cells at the end of the room. Huge tears welled up in her eyes, rolling down over her cheeks, and she nodded. Just once, almost shyly. Then her gaze went dull, and a merciful darkness swept over her eyes.

When the girl had been led away by her parents, the *alcalde* turned back to the prisoners, speaking in broken English. "You have been identified as the men who did this horrible thing. Were it up to me, I would hand you over to the people. Instead, you will be tried by law and executed before a firing squad."

"Listen, you tub of guts," Red shouted, "we didn't do nothin' to that bitch that ain't been done before. She's a whore. You understand, a *puta?* Just come right out and offered it to us."

Ramón Vazquez advanced on the cell, his face twisted with rage. "*Gringo bastardo*. Only filth like you would do that to a young girl. She was an *inocente*, a virgin!"

Red swallowed hard, but he didn't back off. "You're not spookin' us, greaser. We're Americans and we know our rights. Besides, we work for Ed Banning, the big *hombre* across the river. If you do anything to us, he'll burn this goddamn pigsty down around your ears."

"*Tien cuidado, bárbaro!*" The *alcalde*'s warning sounded with all the finality of a death knell. "Take care, barbarian! Do not offend your God. You will have need of him where you are going."

"*Sí*, my uncle advises you well," Ramón Vazquez added. "Look to your God for *absolución*. You will find none from Señor Banning. Scorpions like him eat their young when the road grows hard."

The prisoners' faces took on a wooden look. They understood, even halfway believed it. But they didn't like what they heard. The horny one slammed up against the bars and shook his fist in Ramón's face. "You greaser sonovabitch! Your day's comin'. You just wait. We'll get out of here, and when we do, I'm gonna cut your nuts off and feed 'em to the pigs."

The *alcalde* turned and walked to the door, pausing before the jailer. "*Alguacil*, if these *gringo* dogs so much as rattle the bars on their cages, you are to shoot them without hesitation."

Pedro Vazquez stepped into the night, followed closely by Ramón and his *vaqueros*. The jailer closed and barred the door, then pulled an ancient Colt from its holster. Cocking it, he eased himself onto a stool and regarded the Americans like a fat snake.

Right about then, Red got to wishing he had a stump between his legs. Damned if it wouldn't make life a hell of a lot simpler.

3.

STOUDENMIRE CROSSED the plaza with Tige hard on his heels. The morning sun was barely two hours old, but already the broad square was a beehive of activity. Everyone in El Paso got an early start, for as midday approached, the heat became oppressive, downright unbearable for some. While greenhorns were known to laugh at the town's casual pace, they quickly learned that the afternoon siesta was a touch of genius born of sheer necessity. Those who didn't heed the message like as not ended up with sunstroke.

Walking north across the plaza, Stoudenmire reflected on the unsettling bit of news Doc Cummings had passed along only moments before. When he had stopped in at Doc's store, the tale of last night's trouble in Paso del Norte was already making the rounds. Bad news travels fast, and the young girl's rape along with the killing that followed had spread alarm among the townspeople. Something like this could trigger a shooting war with the greasers, and most everyone agreed that El Paso was sitting on a powder keg with a short fuse. The new marshal was of a similar opinion, for it was well known that the Mexicans thought highly of their women. And deflowering a virgin was damn near the last straw for anybody! Whichever side of the river they happened to call home. Thinking about it, Stoudenmire decided he hadn't come to town any too soon.

But at the moment, he had a more immediate problem. Namely George Campbell and his deputy, Bill Johnson. Against his better judgment, Stoudenmire had agreed to keep them on as deputies. Somehow he was skeptical of any man who meekly accepted demotion from marshal to deputy, and it occurred to him that George Campbell would likely try to undermine his efforts at policing the town. Seth Hart had termed it good politics, but it had left a bad taste in Stoudenmire's mouth from the very start. Still he had agreed, and like it or not, he would have to go through the motions.

Entering the office, he found Campbell seated behind the desk and Johnson stretched out on a rickety bunk. One glance was all he needed to catalog this pair. Throughout the war and almost ten years as a peace officer, he had dealt with their breed more often than he cared to remember. Shiftless, slovenly men without roots; warped in mind and filthy by choice; willing to cut their own mother's throat for a decent meal or a shot of cheap whiskey.

The men returned his look with casual indifference, neither stirring from their indolent pose. Plainly they had every intention of giving him a hard way to go, right from the start. Their attitude made it clear that taming El Paso was his ball of wax, and they were merely paid observers. They figured to lay up on their backsides and wait for him to get his nose bloodied. Chuckling to himself, Stoudenmire recalled he'd played this same game before, and he had picked up a few dodges that even these sharpies hadn't seen.

"Off your ass and on your feet, gents. The reins just changed hands, and we're gonna operate a little different around here from now on. In case you hadn't heard, my name's Stoudenmire, and that's my desk you're sittin' behind."

This last remark was aimed at Campbell, who blinked like a horny toad that had just stepped on a rattler's tail. He was a thin, stringy sort of fellow, who looked as if he had been stretched out to dry and left in the sun too long. As he unfolded from the chair and came to his feet, his beady eyes glinted with outright hatred. "Sure thing, Dallas. You just set right down and take over the ship. And if it gets a mite leaky, why Bill and me'll be real proud to give you a hand bailin'. Won't we, Billy boy?"

Johnson mumbled something under his breath and heaved himself off the bunk with considerable effort. From the look of his eyes, he might bleed to death at any moment, and anyone who doubted he was a confirmed rummy just couldn't read sign. Twenty years of beans and sowbelly and green rotgut were starting to show at his beltline, and from all appearances, he couldn't have fought his way out of a rotten gunnysack.

Stoudenmire merely glanced at him, then leveled a flinty gaze on the former marshal. "Campbell, let's get something straight from the outset. When you speak to me, it's Mister Stoudenmire, or Marshal. I'm sorta particular that way, and you'd do well not to make me tell you twice."

"Well, yessir. Marshal, sir. You play the fiddle and we'll do the dancin'. And Billy, let's not forget to salute when *Mister Stoudenmire* starts barkin' orders.

"Gents, I've got a feeling that ridin' double with you two is gonna be more than I could stomach." His pale eyes settled briefly on the rummy, then shifted back to Campbell. "There's two things I never had much use for.

Tin-horns with a flannel-mouth, and a swizzelguts that can't wean himself off the juice.''

Campbell's face blanched, and his Adam's apple bobbed like a fishcork. ''Lemme tell you somethin', *Marshal.* We been around a long time before this town ever heard of you, and we're gonna be around a long time after you're gone. There's more'n one way to skin a cat, you know. And I got an idea somebody's gonna nail your hide to the wall before you even get started real good.''

''Is that a threat, sonny?'' Stoudenmire deliberately goaded the man, enjoying himself immensely now that it was out in the open. ''Or are you just makin' promises you can't keep?''

''Mister, you're walkin' on eggshells, and you don't even know it. If I was you, I'd take to avoidin' dark alleys and lonely places.''

''Campbell, you just tied a can to your own tail.'' Stoudenmire's glare raked the other man. ''You and Johnson pick up your gear and clear out. You can collect your wages at city hall.''

Campbell took a step forward, his fists clenched. ''Listen, you overgrown sack of shit, you can't fire me. I don't take orders from anybody. . . .''

A pistol suddenly appeared in Stoudenmire's hand, and he laid it upside Campbell's jaw like a sledgehammer. Fiery sparks erupted inside the skinny man's brain, and the whole left side of his head went numb. Without a sound he crumpled to the floor as if his backbone had been snatched clean.

Across the room, Johnson's hand edged slowly toward his gun, almost as though he wanted someone to stop him before he worked up the guts to make a try for it. Snarling, Tige padded forward with hackles raised, baring his fangs. Johnson froze, eyes bright with fear, as if he had been turned to stone. One wrong move and he knew the ferocious-looking bastard would start at his boot tops and eat him alive.

Once he saw that Tige had Johnson cornered, Stoudenmire hefted Campbell, lugged him to the door, and tossed him into the street. Returning, he grabbed Johnson by the collar, waltzed him across the floor and planted his boot straight up the rummy's tailbone. Johnson shot through the door as though propelled from a cannon and came to a shaky halt beside his fallen partner.

Massaging the seat of his pants, he tried to suck up the nerve to stand and fight. "Marshal, you're a real stem-winder. But you ain't as big as you think. Things are gonna get plenty sticky around here, and it might just be I'll take a hand in it personal."

Leaning against the doorjamb, Stoudenmire smiled sardonically. "Johnson, find yourself another trough to swill at. You mess around with me and you'll get hurt."

Unable to stand up under the lawman's cold stare, Johnson turned and helped Campbell to his feet. Bleeding freely from a wide gash in his head, Campbell moaned something that didn't make much sense and slumped against his cohort. Supporting him, Johnson started off at a slow walk across the plaza. Every few steps, he turned to peek back over his shoulder, like a jowly old rooster twisting his neck to hunt for lice.

Stepping back inside, Stoudenmire took a seat behind the desk and waited for the explosion. Twenty minutes later it came. Mayor Isaac Porter stormed through the door in a faunching rage. Before the lawman could open his mouth, Porter launched into a frothing tirade that would have turned a faith healer green as pickle juice.

"By all that's holy, Mr. Stoudenmire, you are a very temperamental sort of man. You can't just go around whipping the bejesus out of your own deputies and dumping them into the street. Something like that creates a bad example for the rest of the town. Sets law and order back on its ear. Gives it a black eye, if you see what I mean. This is a civilized town, Mr. Stoudenmire, and we can't have the law fighting among themselves. It just won't do. By glory, it won't do at all!"

Porter's overbearing manner left the marshal thoroughly unimpressed. "Mayor, you might as well save your breath. What's done is done, and that's the end of it."

"Not by a damnsight it's not, Marshal. When you appeared before the city council to discuss this job, we took you to be a reasonable man. It was agreed that Campbell and Johnson would be retained as your deputies, and I'm just afraid we'll have to hold you to it." Porter's voice had risen sharply as he spoke, but he suddenly lost wind as he noticed Tige eyeing him with a strange look. "And if you don't mind, please call your dog off. I don't care for the way he's staring at me."

Stoudenmire rubbed behind the dog's ears, smiling faintly. "You can relax, Mayor. Politicians are a little rancid for his tastes. But that's neither here nor there. I've given your stooges the gate, and that's how it stands. If you or the city council try to interfere, then you can start hunting for a new marshal. Now, I haven't got all day to stand around listening to you preach, so fish or cut bait."

Porter was on the verge of blowing his cork when he thought better of it. Banning had ordered him to let the German have his head. And by God, that's just what he'd do. *He'd let the arrogant sonovabitch hang himself!* "All right, Marshal. Don't do anything rash. There's no need to get riled up over such an insignificant matter. We hired you, and we'll back you to the hilt. Even if we don't fully agree. But I feel duty bound to warn you that this isn't a town that can be policed by one man alone."

Stoudenmire grinned cockily. "Don't get yourself in a lather over that, Mr. Mayor. Just happens there's a fellow on his way here that I've already signed on as deputy. Name's Jim Gillette. He's not much to look at, but he's tougher'n most. Found that out when we rode together in the Rangers."

Mayor Isaac Porter just nodded and plastered an assy smile across his face. Someone had just been feinted into position and given a first class screwing. And he had the very distinct feeling that it was Mother Porter's youngest son. The slow one.

4.

RAMÓN VAZQUEZ had awakened earlier than usual that morning. There was a taste of ashes in his mouth, and it occurred to him that what lay suppurating in a man's mind often surfaced in his gorge. Dressing slowly, his thoughts returned again to last night, and he silently offered a prayer that it had been his bullet that killed the *gringo cerdo.* Since squeezing the trigger that once, he had cursed himself a thousand times for not continuing to fire until all the filthy beasts were dead. *Muerte!* That is what they each deserved, quickly and simply, without the mercy one shows even a dumb animal.

But then, a man could not easily escape the lessons of his youth. And a Vazquez would never lower himself to act in the manner of the barbarians across the river. Especially one who had risen to the position of *caporal* over the largest ranch in the district. After all, Don Miguel Salazar expected him to set the example! *El patrón* would hardly bestow his blessings on a foreman who taught *vaqueros* to shoot men down in cold blood.

Somehow the thought filled him with disgust. Mercy and aristocratic conduct were for the *hidalgos*, the ruling class. Perhaps compassion was a luxury the common people, the *peones*, could no longer afford. The time for civilized behavior was when one faced an honorable enemy, not when the *gringo* jackals were snapping at the heels of the poor and the defenseless. While he had been revolted by the brutal executions of the *norteamericano* businessmen at San Elizario, it came to Ramón that there was much to be said for dealing harshly with such scavengers. *¡Madre de Dios!* What he wouldn't give to be an Apache for a short time. There was a form of moral conduct the *gringo bárbaros* could understand. And never forget!

Leaving the bedroom, Ramón walked toward the center of the house. Though this was the *casa* of his uncle, he thought of it as his own, for he had grown to manhood within these walls. And it was good to have spent such a night in the place of his youth. Somehow he seemed stronger for having slept in his old bed again. Moments later, he entered the dining room to find Pedro Vazquez already seated at the head of the table.

"*Buenos días, mi tio,*" he greeted the older man. "*¿Como está usted?*"

"*Bueno*, Ramón." The *alcalde* paused just long enough to note the hollow cast to his nephew's eyes. "*¿Y tu?*"

Ramón merely shrugged, sliding listlessly into a chair. After pouring a cup of hot chocolate, he idly stirred it with a spoon, clearly absorbed with his own worrisome thoughts.

"*A quien madruga, Dios le ayuda,*" Pedro Vazquez observed. "God favors those who rise with the dawn. Are the circles beneath your eyes from early prayer, *mi hijo?*"

Ramón shook his head, then gestured heavenward. "Does He also favor those who cannot sleep for want of destroying their enemies?"

"My son, God overlooks much, but he would be displeased to see your hatred so quickly aroused." The older man examined the dregs in his cup thoughtfully, as if seeking some further enlightenment. "Ramón, no rational man could deny that the situation worsens between the *yanquis* and our people. I, too, spent a restless night considering this very thing. But if those to whom the people look for guidance were to sanction violence, then the Rio Grande would run red with blood. *¡La jugo de muerte!* The juice of death."

"*¡Bueno!*" Ramón's dark gaze crackled with sudden ferocity. "So long as it is *gringo* blood, then I would gladly cut the first throat. We have lived too long under the oppression of this filth. It must end. *¡Pronto!*"

The *alcalde* flinched, his face gone tight with shock. "And is spilling blood the only way it can be ended? Are we not reasonable men who can employ persuasion with our enemies? Have we learned nothing from the suffering of our *antepasados* under the Spaniards?"

"You talk in riddles, *mi tio*. The yoke of oppression was lifted from our people only after Juarez led them to war. It would seem that the way of our ancestors contradicts your cry for reason."

"So you would have our people take up the sword and march on El Paso. Slaughter the *norteamericanos* as if they were hogs in a charnel house. Is this what you are telling me, Ramón?"

The younger man flushed and looked away, shamed by

his uncle's heated rebuff. "You twist my words, *padrino*. I meant only that we should defend ourselves and have no mercy on these jackals when they swim the river to violate our lands and our women. How could anyone who values his manhood do less? Can you look inside yourself and state with certainty that the *gringos* would ever be swayed by reason? Even if they were, what would be gained besides a moment in time? We have seen them break faith again and again with the *indios* of the north. Are we *ingeui niños* to believe that they will treat Mexicans with greater honor than they have shown the red men?"

The *alcalde* nodded, more in understanding than agreement, as though weighing the younger man's words before he spoke. "Since your mother and father died and you came to live with me, I have tried to raise you as a son. *¡Mi hijo!* And now I will repeat a blasphemy to you that a man would dare whisper to none but his own flesh. I have lived long and seen much of the evil men practice among themselves, most of it so terrible it is best forgotten. As *jefe* of this village, I have learned that brotherhood is merely a word employed by priests, for if God smiles on a man, then he must afterward hold himself beware of his neighbors.

"But wisdom such as this often makes a man *cinico*, and we are confronted by problems, Ramón, that will never yield before cynicism alone. Certainly we can open our eyes to the *gringos*' treachery, but to fight them is to do battle with the wind. There is no end to it. A man must ultimately tire, and when he does, he will be blown away, as chaff from wheat. Somehow we must seek out men of reason among the *yanquis* and deal with them not so much from trust as from necessity. Until then, we must not provoke our people to foolhardy acts. Among the old ones it is well known that even the bravest *toro* can thrash himself to death in a spider web."

Ramón heeded the wisdom of his uncle's counsel, but it did nothing to lessen his hatred of *gringos*. Nor did it have much effect on his fear that even then the *norteamericanos* were planning reprisals against their village. Although it was true that the cloud of rage no longer blinded his thinking, he still saw the situation for what it was.

Last night's tragedy was but a quirt to the hostility that existed between the two races. Perhaps the last in a dreary chronicle of injustice and duplicity that would soon drive his people beyond the point of reason. Regardless of his uncle's belief that decades of humiliation could be resolved with pretty words and unstinting faith.

Long before his time, it had started with the Treaty of Guadelupe Hidalgo. That infamous document, which had allowed a river to split a city in half, leaving thousands of their people to suffer under the rule of arrogant *tejanos*. While it had never touched him personally, he had seen with his own eyes the degradation of those who lived north of the Rio Grande. It was not a sight easily forgotten.

Yet that was only the beginning. Wherever a man turned, he seemed to find *gringos* blocking his path, scheming and clawing to satisfy their monstrous greed. There was the constant rustling of cattle from Mexican *ranchos*, an indignity that *patrones* and *vaqueros* alike had suffered for much too long. The *yanqui* mining interests were burrowing like moles throughout Chihuahua, sapping the strength and the spirit of *peones* enslaved in those dungeon pits. Even the salt war had been the *norte-americanos*' fault, for it was they who sought to rob the poor by withholding the very substance of life itself.

Now they had committed the unforgivable indecency. Despoiled a young girl of her virtue. And he had no doubt that those across the river were at that very moment planning to rescue the three barbarians held prisoner in Paso del Norte.

The *alcalde* had waited patiently while his nephew sorted out his thoughts. When Ramón finally looked around, he smiled and clasped the younger man's arm. "It occurs to me that you are a good man, *mi hijo*. Never had I heard you speak out against the *gringos* with such anger until the ordeal of this young girl. Compassion for the weak is a commendable thing, particularly in a man. But never should it be allowed to cloud your judgment. The people look up to you, and in time, you could become their *jefe*. Yet I would caution you that there is more to being a leader than making impassioned speeches and provoking men to spill blood. A fool often regrets his words, but a wise man seldom regrets his silence. You would do well to think on this in days to come."

Ramón stared at the old man for a long time, wondering if wisdom and reason could, after all, bring about justice for their people. Troubled beyond measure, he had allowed himself to be persuaded that nothing should be done to incite violence. And for the moment, he would respect his uncle's wishes. But persuaded or not, he fully intended that the *cabrones* in jail would never again cross the Rio Grande. Except as dead men.

5.

JIM GILLETTE arrived on the afternoon train. While he was glad to get his feet on solid earth once more, he didn't waste any time gawking at the sights. Like the man, his gear was honed to essentials, and he came straightaway to the office. When he stepped through the door, he carried a warbag, a mule-eared sawed-off shotgun, and a Colt .44 cinched high on his hip.

Stoudenmire came around the desk, and the two men shook hands. Though they hadn't seen each other in over a year, they had kept in touch, and there was little need for small talk. They liked each other, respected one another's skills as a peace officer, and felt confident enough in their friendship that there was no need to prime it with meaningless words.

With greetings out of the way, they had gotten down to business. Gillette hitched a chair over beside the desk, and Stoudenmire proceeded to brief him on what they faced. In a detached, unemotional voice, he related each incident in the long chain of bloodlettings leading to the present tensions between Mexicans and Yankees. Then he covered the Banning Brothers in similar detail, stressing their political stranglehold on the town and their dominance of the vice district. Much as an afterthought, he next outlined the support they could expect from Seth Hart and the council of businessmen, noting wryly that it was something on the order of a fresh water spring in an alkali desert: just when you needed it most, it would more than likely go bone dry.

Gillette toyed with his mustache and asked few questions, occasionally snorting like an old plow horse when a particularly juicy item was ticked off. In one form or another, he had seen this pathetic little drama repeated almost endlessly across the frontier. After twenty years, he had become a jaded warrior in a land where every dusty, ramshackle crossroads had both an arena and its own version of the Christians and the lions. Only the names and faces changed. And sometimes the death list.

Observing his calm, unruffled manner, Stoudenmire was again reminded that the former Ranger wasn't much to look at, coming or going. Gillette was whipcord lean, gaunt as a skinned lizard, and his washboard ribs gave the impression he hadn't had a decent meal since he quit the farm. Beneath a mop of shaggy hair, his narrow face was set in a woebegone, saturnine mold, as though he toted the troubles of the world on his bony shoulders. While he wasn't a jolly man, occasionally he would grin like a horse eating briars, and at the oddest times. Like at a funeral or when he was headed into a gunfight. His watery eyes were uncommonly tranquil, like a pool of maize pudding, and to all outward appearances he seemed mild as a sucking dove. But a man's looks could be curiously deceptive. Stoudenmire had seen this long drink of water in action. When push came to shove, he was fast as a snake, and what he could do with that old Colt .44 made greased lightning look like molasses at twenty below.

The rest of the afternoon had been spent in war council, with the two men discussing how best to approach the double-barreled dilemma confronting El Paso. Stoudenmire's disposition improved markedly just knowing Gillette was on hand to back his play. Having the gloomy-faced deputy around was much like pulling on an old pair of boots, comfortable and somehow reassuring. Along toward sundown, they had mapped out their opening strategy, leaving plenty of room for fancy footwork in the clinches. Once they started booting asses, there was small likelihood of predicting which way the worm would turn, and neither man tried to fool himself on that score. Looking ahead, they were agreed that, after a certain point, they would just have to play the cards as dealt.

Stoudenmire invited Gillette home for supper and positively glowed under the old lawdog's praise of Kate and her cooking. Afterward, they strolled downtown and began a systematic tour of the southside dives. Much to the marshal's amusement, Gillette's doleful features took on a spark of liveliness as they inspected row after row of whorehouses, saloons, and gambling dives. Never had he seen so much vice crammed into so little space, and he noted that, heathen for heathen, the sporting crowd of El Paso more than likely topped Dodge City in its heyday. Then the pensive look returned to his face, and the deputy observed that it was a shame to put the skids under such a testament to man's moral blight. After all, it was the nature of the beast to wallow in fornication and sin, and who were they to upset the Good Lord's grand design. Stoudenmire just chuckled, never quite sure whether the old fox was pulling his leg or actually making some profound comment on the shaky state of men's affairs.

Later in the evening, they swung back toward the plaza and decided to have a look at the Coliseum Saloon. So far, they hadn't seen anything they couldn't handle, and the only unknown factor remaining was the Banning brothers themselves.

"Just might as well let 'em know we're in town," Stoudenmire remarked. "Sooner we put a bad taste in their mouth, the quicker we'll get 'em to come out in the open."

"Dallas, you're a natural wonder. Back 'em into a corner, twist their tail, and make 'em howl! Yessir, there's more'n one way to make a dog shit peach seeds. Present company excepted, of course."

Gillette glanced down at Tige, who was trotting along at Stoudenmire's side. The dog returned the stare with a kindly light in his eyes, and even gave his tail a patronizing wag. The new deputy was one of the few men Tige tolerated as an equal, and Gillette considered it an honor that he had been accepted into the dog's select circle of friends.

Together, the three of them marched through the swinging doors of the Coliseum and halted to give the place the once-over. Other than the fact that the room was jammed to the rafters, there wasn't anything noteworthy going on, and after a few moments they took up positions at the end of the bar. But even in the mad swirl of roughly dressed men and spangled saloon girls, their arrival hadn't gone unnoticed. As they bellied up to the bar, an undercurrent swept through the crowd, and within moments everyone in the room knew that the town's new marshal had paid an unofficial visit on El Paso's political kingpin.

Before Stoudenmire and Gillette appeared out of the night, conversation at the bar had centered around the three men being held in Paso del Norte. Sam Banning had been right in the thick of the discussion, occasionally prodding the crowd on with a bitter comment about the uppity greasers. Talk had slackened momentarily with the arrival of the lawmen, but hard whiskey makes for loose tongues, and before long the angry shouts began anew.

"Boys, you can say whatever you damn well please," barked a chunky man built along the lines of a beer keg. "But I'm here to tell you that there ain't a man-jack among us that's safe once them Mexicans get the idea they can jail a white man."

"Goddamn right!" growled a beefy miner with hands like ore crushers. "We oughta go over there and wipe out the whole fuckin' village. Just like the Indians." He slammed his fist on the bar, and bottles rattled its entire length. "Nits and lice, by Christ!"

Sam Banning's bullish roar drowned out the crowd's response. "Now wait a minute, boys. You're going off half-cocked. There's no need to start a war. The way to teach them greasers a lesson is to show 'em we won't stand still for white men being arrested. Ride over there a couple of hundred strong and just flat-ass free them three men. Show them *cholo* bastards who's boss around here, and by God I'm layin' money our troubles are ended."

"Sam, you're all wet," the big miner shot back. "There's only one thing them sonsabitches understand, and its name is Judge Colt. What we gotta do is make a lead mine out of a few of them greasers. That'll take the kinks out of their tails once and for all."

While the men were arguing, Ed Banning had eased through the crowd and now stood beside his brother. Word had reached the backroom that Stoudenmire was on the premises, and the boss decided to have a look for himself. What he saw left him thoroughly unimpressed, and it occurred to him that the crowd would enjoy a little sport at the marshal's expense. *Might as well put the big bastard in his place right from the start!*

"Marshal Stoudenmire, we'd like to hear your opinion about all this." The crowd went silent, sensing that Banning was out to gig the new lawdog. "We know you haven't had time to get your feet on the ground just yet, but we'd be interested in hearing how you'd go about freeing those poor boys."

Everyone at the bar turned to look at Stoudenmire. Although they had heard of him, few had seen him before tonight, and they were openly curious as to where the new marshal stood. Stories were already circulating that the city council had been blackjacked into hiring the German, but as yet no one had figured out to what purpose.

Stoudenmire's flinty gaze rested on Banning for a moment, then swung around the crowd. "Gents, if you want some good advice, you'll stay on this side of the river. Mexicans are about as fair as anyone else unless they're curried the wrong way. If those three fellows really did gang up on a young girl, then I reckon they deserve whatever they get."

A murmur of resentment swept through the crowd, ending with hoarse muttering from those nearest the lawman. Then the one built like a beer keg spoke out. "Shit, I always heard that rapin' a Mexican gal was no more a crime than humpin' a nanny goat."

The men laughed good naturedly, turning back to the marshal for his reaction. But the miner with the fearsome hands wouldn't let it drop. "You know, I've heard of nigger-lovers. But I'm a sonovabitch if I ever heard of a greaser-lover. Marshal, you're wearin' a badge on the wrong side of the river. Why, over there, I'll bet your shit wouldn't even stink."

In one stride, Stoudenmire was on him, pistol barrel flashing in the dull glint of the overhead lamps. The Colt landed with a mushy thud, and the miner's eyes rolled back in his head like glazed stones, flat and unseeing. With a great sigh, he simply collapsed and sank to the floor.

Stoudenmire spun on the crowd, his eyes cold as chilled glass, every fiber of his body prickly and tensed. This was the part he enjoyed, the moment that made all the drudgery and routine bearable. Meeting the bullyboys and hard-cases head-on, cracking their skulls with the old buffalo trick, or forcing their hand until they did something even more foolish. Like going for their guns.

"Anybody else got something on his mind?"

The crowd remained curiously still, stunned by the speed with which Stoudenmire had floored the ruffian. They were also distinctly aware that Gillette was covering the marshal's back, which meant that whoever got brave would be caught in a cross fire. To make matters worse, Tige had materialized beside his master, showing a row of teeth like a shark. Between the guns and being chewed on by a snarling brute, the men just held their breath and waited it out.

Then the blood pounding against his temples eased off and Stoudenmire relaxed. "Gents, in case someone forgot to mention it, the Bannings are playing you for fools. The men being held over in El Paso del Norte are on their payroll. They were just setting you up to do the dirty work for them. If I were you, I'd think it over before I risked my neck to pull someone else's fat out of the fire."

Casually reholstering his gun, Stoudenmire turned his gaze on Ed Banning and waited. But the political boss wasn't about to face another man at his own game, especially with the deck stacked against the house. Smiling tightly, he just nodded. This was only the opening gambit, and until the odds suited him better, he wasn't going to be pushed into anything hasty.

After a moment Stoudenmire turned and walked leisurely from the saloon, trailed by Gillette and Tige. As the batwing doors swung shut, the crowd let out a huge sigh, and everyone started talking at once.

El Paso had a new marshal, and he gave every indication of being man enough to handle the job. But anyone who had seen the look of evil stamped on Ed Banning's face would have laid odds that Dallas Stoudenmire was a walking dead-man.

CHAPTER THREE

1.

SAM BANNING kept a loose rein on the high stepping bays, letting them pick their own way over the rutted, twisting trail that led eastward from El Paso. Beside him, Ed sat lost in contemplation, stewing on the way Stoudenmire had jackassed him the night before. The political boss was a man easily affronted, and he wasn't about to overlook outright contempt from anybody. Especially a two-bit lawman set on making a name for himself. Stoudenmire had called the tune last night, but there were ways of bringing the big German to earth.

Their buggy raised a rooster-tail of dust as they traversed the desolate country east and north of the Rio Grande. It was an arid, hostile land, filled with sand, rattlesnakes, and thorny chaparral. Yet it wasn't a barren land, not if a man knew where to look. There were vast, hidden stretches of buffalo and grama grasses, generally sharing the soil with yuccas that sprouted stalks of brilliant, white blossoms. Scattered waterholes seldom went dry even in late summer, and spring rains usually brought the countryside alive with Tahoka daisies, buttercups, and fiery paintbrush. Stands of lacy mesquite and barbed cat's-claw fought for the earth's moisture, but somehow the sparse grasslands survived, mocking the fallow plains that dominated the cardinal points of the compass. And curiously enough, that remote, seemingly ravaged land provided a bountiful life for great herds of longhorn cows.

But while the arid flatlands offered bounty of sort for the mossyhorns, they held forth even greater lure for the

Banning brothers and their night riders. Within such desolate country was to be found the isolation and secrecy so highly prized by those who prey on other men's possessions. Especially the four-footed variety.

Shortly after arriving in El Paso two years earlier, Ed Banning had undertaken a search for ranchlands far removed from the settlements along the Rio Grande. After crisscrossing the countryside for nearly a month, he finally found exactly what he had in mind: a rundown spread so far back in the wastelands that a man needed a map to find it. The next step had been to hire a crew and flush out the half-wild longhorns inhabiting the brush and thorn patches dotting the land. Once he had a going concern, Banning began greasing the right palms, and before long his outfit was awarded the beef contract at Fort Bliss. With a legitimate front firmly established, he then branched out, regularly ordering his crew into Chihuahua and Sonora to raid the wealthy Mexican *ranchos*. The rustled cattle were herded back to the ranch, given a brief introduction to a running iron, then either sold to the army or trailed to Fort Worth. With the coming of the railroad, the operation was simplified even further, and the gratifying part was that hardly anyone cared how or under what circumstances the cattle came to be north of the Rio Grande.

The ranch itself was little more than a wilderness outpost, consisting of two adobe buildings, a cookshack, and a log corral west of the compound. Northeast of the ranch, the terrain lifted gradually to a chain of stunted mesas, and in the distance hung the towering peak of Cerro Alto. Beneath the sheer cliffs of this great mountain, the adobe structures looked small and insignificant, dwarfed by the immensity of rock and sky that dominated the landscape for twenty miles in every direction. All things considered, it made for a foreboding, uninviting scene. The kind that people normally went out of their way to avoid.

When the Bannings pulled up before the main house, Tom Kale stepped through the doorway and ambled toward the buggy. Kale had worked for Banning from the beginning, ramrodding the ranch, organizing and leading forays into Mexico; in general, contributing greatly to the devious schemes of his boss. He was a leathery man, tightlipped and unsmiling, as if the merciless sun had long ago melted both the suet and the humor from his lean frame. Weathered by a lifetime in the saddle, his features looked as though whittled from some dark, resisting wood, and his nose jutted from between sharp cheekbones like a jagged outcropping of rock. There was no sign of warmth in his long, dour face, just as flaked stone seems all the more cold for its lack of expression.

Those who best knew Tom Kale seldom let their guard down whenever he was near. For like the land itself, the Banning foreman was a brutal, often murderously savage man who derived some queer satisfaction in watching both man and beast suffer at his hand.

After alighting from the buggy, Ed Banning led the way toward the house without uttering so much as a word. Kale knew a thundercloud building when he saw it, and rightly suspected that a storm was about to break. Once inside, out of sight of the bunkhouse, Banning turned on him like a sore-tailed bear in fly season.

"Kale, you've got my ass between a rock and a hard spot, and something has to change or else you're gonna be looking for a new meal ticket. I've told you till I was blue in the face that our men aren't to be allowed in Paso del Norte. Yet you just go your own way and let 'em do as they damn please."

Kale opened his mouth to speak but Banning cut him off with a dismissive gesture. "Now don't give me any of that horseshit about having to play nursemaid. You're paid to ramrod this outfit, and that includes seeing to it that they follow orders. Well, by Christ, crossing the line and raping a Mexican girl right in the middle of the village isn't my idea of sticking to business."

In a cold, metallic voice, Banning related the gist of what had happened in Paso del Norte the night before last. Sparing no detail, he then recounted Stoudenmire's visit to the Coliseum and the duel of wits that had subsequently ensued. When he came to the part about the marshal's outright challenge, Banning's face blanched. As he remembered how he had been ridiculed before the townspeople, his voice went shaky with rage, and for a moment, Kale thought he was going to come unglued. But Banning quickly got hold of himself and resumed in the flat, menacing tone he normally employed.

"I blame you for this whole goddamned mess, Kale. If you'd been minding the store none of it would've happened. And just in case you've got any doubts, *you're* the one that's gonna get it straightened out. We've got too much at stake to let things get out of hand now."

Tom Kale got busy rolling a cigarette and made a stab at changing the subject. "Boss, I've never let you down yet, even if them knuckleheads did sneak across the river. But the thing that's got me bumfoolzled is this new marshal. What the hell's he doin' in El Paso anyway? Some of the boys say they heard of him when he was a Ranger, and the way they tell it, he's just about as good with a gun as he makes out. You reckon we've done bit off more than we can chew?"

"That big crock of shit?" Sam blurted angrily. "Listen, when Ed gives the word, I'm gonna tie a knot in his tail so hard he'll never sit down. Near as I can tell, the only thing he's good at is makin' fools out of other people."

Ed glanced sourly at his brother. "You don't need to keep harping on it. But you're right about one thing. We've got to act fast to save face in town. Stoudenmire has rigged it so that everyone is waitin' to see if we're gonna let those boys go up against the wall. If we leave 'em to a greaser firing squad, we're gonna be the laughingstock of West Texas."

Kale peered at him owlishly through a haze of smoke. "You mean you want us to raid that Mex jail?"

"Kale, if you had dynamite for brains, you couldn't blow yourself off a jonny pot." Banning shook his head sadly, as if reprimanding a backward child. "Now pay attention, just like you had good sense. Tonight I want you to raid one of the big *ranchos* south of Paso del Norte. Make it worthwhile in terms of cattle, but the important thing is to shoot up the *hacienda* and the Mex crew. That'll scare the bejesus out of every greaser in the district, and tomorrow night they'll all be home with their doors barred."

"Then we raid the jail!" Kale laughed, slapping his thigh.

"No, you goddamn nitwit! You're not to go anywhere near that jail. I wouldn't trust your boys to piss on a dead dog. What I'm gonna do is send a buggy over there about an hour after suppertime. Three of my girls will be decked out like housewives, and they'll say those boys are their husbands. Only they're gonna have guns under their dresses, and when they leave, those boys won't be so helpless anymore. Later, they can make a break and swim the river. If nobody shits and steps in it, I figure we can get 'em free and make an ass out of Stoudenmire all in one stroke."

"Boss, that's slick," Kale snorted, shaking his head with admiration. "We'll have them boys back over here before anybody even tumbles to 'em being gone."

Banning's eyes leveled down on the foreman, fixing him with a malevolent glare. "And once you get 'em back here, I want you to march them over to the bunkhouse and shoot 'em right in the doorway. It's time you and the rest of these bastards learned that when I give an order I expect it to be followed. Savvy?"

Tom Kale wasn't easily frightened, yet he swallowed nervously under Banning's harsh scrutiny. Killing was his stock in trade, and adding three more to the list was all in a day's work. But the death sentence he had just heard pronounced indirectly included him. Should he foul Banning's nest again, his life wouldn't be worth a plug nickel. Kale's mouth suddenly turned dry as a gourd, and his guts went stone cold. Working for this ruthless scutter was like being harnessed shoulder to shoulder with Lucifer himself, and he had the very distinct feeling that he was running dead last in a two-horse race.

2.

DOC CUMMINGS could smell the aromas while he was still a good stone's throw from the house. No doubt about it, Kate had acquired their mother's knack for southern cooking, the kind that stuck to a man's ribs and left him wishing he could have eaten more. He could tell from the smell alone, and it set his mouth to watering. Reflecting back over the carefree days of their childhood, Doc was suddenly warmed inside by the thought of having Kate so near. She had always been his favorite of the Cummings' brood, and he was immensely pleased that he had been able to finagle a way for her to live in El Paso. Suddenly it occurred to Doc that things were really looking up.

As a widower, he had become used to the heartburn served up in the local greasy spoon, but with Kate in town, it stood to reason he'd get a decent meal occasionally anyway. Perhaps being invited to supper tonight was only the beginning. Maybe if he played his cards right, it would become a regular thing. Whistling a catchy little tune, he entered the Stoudenmire home, beaming like a chessy cat as Kate came to greet him.

When she led him into the living room, Doc's mouth popped open in astonishment. "Great jumpin' jehossafat! Katie what have you done to this place? Why it looks like a palace. A goldang palace!"

Kate flushed, and her eyes took on a little girl sparkle. Considering that she'd had little to work with, she was justly proud of the transformation. That first evening in El Paso she had stood looking at the austere interior of this adobe monstrosity, wondering how in the world she could ever make it appear anything more than a mud hut. But in only three days she had wrought a minor miracle, decorating it with all the frills and foofaraw so dear to a woman's heart.

Each window was now festooned with gay curtains, done in bright, cheery colors that distracted the eye from the stark adobe walls. The spartan furniture did little to liven the room, but somewhere, Kate had found an ornate Persian rug, that covered nearly the entire floor. Like a peacock amongst a flock of brown hens, the rug somehow lent beauty to the dull ugliness of the room itself. Pictures of solemn ancestors and pastoral landscapes had been hung judiciously along the walls, and everywhere there was evidence of Kate's remarkable cleverness with crochet and needlepoint. From the native market she had bought great batches of wild flowers and small boxed plants, which even now were beginning to sprout tiny blossoms. But the *pièce de résistance* had been reserved for the mantel over the fireplace. There in somber dignity hung a strangely lifelike portrait of Kate and Dallas on their wedding day. Framed in gilded wood with a delicate carved design, the portrait dominated the room, evoking a degree of elegance that was curiously foreign to the wattled adobe.

While the Stoudenmire home was located on Magoffin Avenue in the better district of El Paso, there were few houses that could match its comfortable atmosphere and simple grace. Kate had ample reason to be proud, and as she luxuriated in Doc's praise, it somehow seemed right that her brother was the first outsider to observe the results of her handiwork.

The meal she served was no less impressive than the house itself, particularly to a widower who had grown accustomed to the chili pepper and raw spices of local cafes. Spread across the table in lavish array was fried chicken, mashed potatoes, cream gravy, blackeyed peas, snap beans, cornbread, and a huge pitcher of buttermilk. For a crowning touch, she served a steamy peach cobbler with great gobs of fresh whipped cream.

Doc Cummings unbuckled his belt and set to with the gusto of a starved mongrel trailing a gut wagon. Between mouthfuls he raved incessantly about the food, the house, his sister's beauty, and his own great fortune in them having chosen El Paso as their home. Watching him, Stoudenmire was reminded of a gluttonous bear fresh from a winter's hibernation. And it came to him that with little or no prompting Doc could easily become a steady boarder.

After a particularly effusive compliment on the house, Doc helped himself to another load of potatoes and gravy. "Dallas, you oughta be mighty proud of this gal. It's not every woman that could turn an outsize *jacal* hut into a dazzler like you've got here."

Stoudenmire pretended to consider it a moment, watching Kate out of the corner of his eye. "I expect you're right, Doc. Course, this place might be too fancy for some folks' tastes. Not everybody can get used to being just another ornament in his own house."

"Oh, what gratitude!" Kate's eyes flashed with feminine outrage. "Dallas Stoudenmire, sometimes you drive me to distraction. After I work my fingers to the bone, you have the unmitigated gall to say it's too frilly. Honestly!"

She knew he liked the house from the little things he had said, but it exasperated her no end that he was so close-mouthed with compliments. Still, she should be getting used to it by now. This great bear of a man she had married was no talker, to put it mildly. What he left unsaid about home, job, and his own thoughts would fill volumes. She sometimes had the feeling it was like extracting teeth to get him loosened up for even a pleasant little chat.

Stoudenmire grinned slyly at her obvious indignation. "Doc, I hate to carry tales on your sister, but she's laying it on a little thick. The fact of the matter is, she enjoyed sprucin' this place up so much that I couldn't get her to quit till it was plumb finished. Put me in mind of a speckled pup with a fresh bowl of cream."

"Yeah, her mama was like that." Doc paused with a drumstick in midair, and a mellow look came into his eyes. "Turn her loose cleanin' a house or whippin' up a big meal, and she acted like the Good Lord had just passed out a dipperful of heaven on earth."

"You two should just hear yourselves," Kate exclaimed. "Honest to gracious! It's like you were talking about a doll that just happens to speak passable English. Doc, if mama were alive she'd jerk your britches down and paddle your rump with that drumstick. I swear she would."

The two men couldn't help but laugh, and after a moment, Kate gave in, smiling good-naturedly. But Doc wasn't about to risk spoiling his chances as a steady guest, and he very shrewdly changed the subject.

"Dallas, there's talk around town that Banning is planning something that'll bring both sides of the river up short. Nothin' you can hang your hat on, but the word is out that he means to show everyone just who's runnin' El Paso. You heard anything?"

"Not much. People are still a little leary about where I stand in this deal." Stoudenmire stirred his coffee thoughtfully for a moment. "There's one thing you can bank on, though. Banning will have to act soon. He can't afford for folks to get the idea he's going soft. Which is what'll happen if he lets the Mexicans get away with killin' his men. Just offhand, I'd judge he's giving it some serious thought."

Doc came up for a breather after his second helping of peach cobbler. "Well it's for damn certain he's been too quiet. Especially after you faced him down in the Coliseum the other night. To my way of thinkin', that's a sure sign something big is brewing. But when and where it'll happen is up for grabs. Most of his boys develop lockjaw when anything really salty is hatching."

Stoudenmire's mouth lifted in a tight, sardonic smile. "Just between you and me, we're real lucky he opened his mouth in front of that crowd. I'd been wonderin' how we could stop a mob from crossing the river, and he set it up easy as pie by tryin' to show off. The way things worked out it's a matter of *his* honor at stake. Unless the wind changes, none of the townspeople are gonna get involved, no matter what he does. Now if we can just keep it that way, then maybe folks'll think twice about taking pot shots at one another across the river."

"Oh, I've got no doubt it headed off an open war between us and the greasers. But I'm not so sure I agree with your bracin' Banning the first crack out of the box. Seems to me you might've led up to it slowly. This way he knows you're after his hide even before you've started."

"Doc, there's no easy way to rid yourself of lice. Banning has to be crowded so hard he'll get mad enough to act, and sooner or later he's gonna make the *big* mistake. Think back to when you were a kid, and you'll remember that, once the hounds start snapping at a coon's heels, he doesn't have time to make plans. He has to move fast and hope he doesn't stub his toe along the way. That's why there's more dumb hounds than there are smart coons."

"Maybe you're right." The dubious look on Doc's face belied his words. "I just hope you haven't stirred up a hornets' nest before you're ready to burn 'em out. Now, for example. What've you got in mind if Banning sics his gang on your tail? You know, it's just possible he's got plans to run you out of town. Did you ever think of that?"

"Doc, if I'd let you, I suspect you'd talk the molars right out of my jawbone." Stoudenmire pulled a huge pocket watch from his vest, noting the time as he pushed his chair back. "But I've got evening rounds to make, and Gillette's gonna be champin' at the bit if I keep him waiting. Now you just have another piece of cobbler and don't get yourself in a lather about me and Banning. When he stumbles, I'll be there to dust him off, and it'll likely be all over before you even hear the shoutin'."

The lawman gave Kate a peck on the cheek, then walked from the dining room with Tige at his heels. After a moment, the front door closed with a gentle thud, and the house went still. Brother and sister sat staring at each other, both troubled by the same doubts yet tempted to leave their thoughts unsaid.

3.

THROUGHOUT THE meal Kate had listened silently to the casual exchange between Dallas and Doc, learning more in a few minutes than her husband had told her in three days. Now she felt herself being swamped by an outpouring of fear and downright bafflement about the grim, unyielding man she had married. Suddenly she couldn't hold it in any longer.

"Doc, I'm so worried I don't know what to do. Dallas treats this whole thing so lightly. He won't even talk to me about it. Whenever I bring it up, he just pats my head like I was a child and goes back into his shell. But the way you talk, he's got half the men in El Paso out gunning for him."

Doc made a good try at grinning and clucked sympathetically. "Katie, don't let your imagination run away with you. All of that was mostly talk, nothin' else. Listen, you've got one hellava man there, and he cut his teeth on hardcases like Ed Banning."

"That's something else that bothers me." Kate's words came awkwardly, and she found it difficult to look at him. Somehow her thoughts seemed too terrible to share with anyone, even her brother. "Dallas changes when he starts talking about the law. Almost as though killing another man was some kind of game. It's frightening to say, Doc, but he's like a cat playing with a mouse. Only he's not playing. He's deadly serious, and it's as if he just can't wait for those men to start fighting back." She shook her head numbly. "I just can't understand the change in him. When we're here alone, he's so warm and gentle. Then he puts that badge on, and he becomes someone else, a stranger almost. And that part of him scares me, Doc."

Doc Cummings just looked at her, searching desperately for something to say. But what could a man say to a sister who had blindly married a gunfighter? She hadn't the slightest notion that her husband was a trained killer, the kind that hunts men much as a great cat instinctively hunts animals of prey. How could any woman understand that the man who shared her bed was a specialist at a very dirty game? Dallas Stoudenmire was a professional mankiller, and anyone with a lick of sense never doubted it for a moment.

Doc glanced at her out of the corner of his eye. "Sis, what do you know about Dallas?"

"That's a strange question to ask." Kate gave him a mildly puzzled look, not quite sure what he meant. "I know that his folks, came over from Germany and he was born outside Mineral Wells. He's thirty-three, doesn't drink much, and behaves himself around women. I know lots about him, Doc. Enough that I wanted him to be my husband."

"Sure. But those are things girls're just naturally interested in. What I'm drivin' at is, do you know anything about his life before you met him? What he was doing for thirty years before he turned up in Columbus."

"Well, of course, I do," Kate said indignantly. "I'm

not some schoolgirl ninny with stars in her eyes. He was city marshal at Nacogdoches, and before that he was a Texas Ranger, and before that he fought for the Confederacy. Just for your information, he'd never been married before, either."

Doc poured himself another cup of coffee, trying to keep his tone casual. "Didn't that strike you as a little odd? Him being that old and never married, I mean."

Kate shook her head, more puzzled than ever. "Why would it strike me as odd? Lots of men wait till they've sown their wild oats before they settle down. They don't all jump the broomstick with the first thing that comes along in skirts."

"Dallas never seemed to me like a man that'd sowed any wild oats." Doc hesitated, mulling it over, and his next words were those of a man thinking out loud. "Unless I miss my guess, there wasn't much to tell on that score."

"That's ridiculous, Doc. Why should he tell me things like that, anyway?" Kate was growing exasperated with her brother's prying manner. "If you're hinting that Dallas isn't . . . oh, damn, you make me so mad sometimes I could just scream. If you're trying to say that Dallas isn't like other men, then you'd better drink your coffee and go on home."

"Katie, I don't mean it like you think, but in a way, that's what I've been drivin' at. He's not like other men." He faltered for a moment, wracking his brain for a way to open her eyes about the man she had married. "Did he ever tell you that his folks were killed by the Comanche when he was just a kid?"

She stared at him blankly, hardly able to credit her own ears. "Indians?"

"You remember when I came home to visit last year?" Kate bobbed her head, and he went on. "Well I decided to find out about this fella my little sister was stuck on. So I took Dallas out and got him drunk. Leastways as drunk as Dallas can get. Loosened up might be more like it. Just enough so's he would talk some."

"But, Doc, I don't understand. What have his folks getting killed got to do with anything?"

"I'm comin' to that. Just give me time. You see the Civil War was going rough for the South about then, so he ups and enlists. Course, he lied about his age, but the Confederates needed men, and since he was bigger than most already full-growed, they didn't ask any questions. He ended up fightin' with General Joe Johnston. Matter of fact, he was still at it when Lee called it quits at Appomattox."

Kate nodded impatiently, somewhat irritated by his roundabout manner. "I know all that. He told me about being in the army."

"Sure, but I'll bet he didn't tell you what it was like." When she failed to answer, he smiled dryly. "Thought so."

There was a pause while Doc collected his thoughts, searching for some way to break it to her gently. "Well now, keep in mind he was only fifteen when he started in at this business of war. Maybe you never thought about it, but that's sort of an early age to get baptized in the ways of killin' men. Fact is, he wasn't but seventeen when the war ended. Those two years had a mighty big effect on him, Katie. Had to. Couldn't have been no other way. There he was, just a kid, watching men being slaughtered like cattle, seeing 'em maimed and going mad with fear. Still, them things was only part of it. More'n likely just a small part. What I'm gettin' around to sayin' is, they took an overgrown kid and taught him to kill, showed him how easy it was. Just pull the trigger and a man falls down. More'n that, though, they taught him there wasn't nothin' wrong with killin'. Not so long as a man's in the right. Don't you see, they wiped away that old bugaboo about 'Thou shalt not kill.' A green kid marched off to war, but an old man came marchin' back. Something had been burned clean out of his soul. Call it feelin', or pity, or whatever you want. Killin' came natural to him now, and he didn't have no more conscience about it than if he was swattin' flies."

Kate stared at him in sheer horror, her eyes wide and glistening wetly. When she spoke her voice was tremulous, shrill. "Doc, are you trying to tell me that the man I married isn't human? That he's some kind of mad-dog killer. If you are, I won't listen to another word. That's sick, to talk like that, and you're no friend of Dallas's to say such wicked things."

Doc winced, stung by her fiery accusation. "Kate, I was your brother before I was his friend. Maybe it's not pretty, and like as not I'm being rash tellin' you all this, but if you don't come to understand the man, your life's gonna be pure hell."

"Understand him? Don't try to play God, Doc. I understand him very well. He's a gentle man underneath all that bluster, and I know it in ways that nobody else could know."

"Is that why he keeps that man-eatin' dog with him all the time? 'Cause he's so gentle." The little merchant's face saddened, and he cursed himself for having ever broached the subject of Stoudenmire's character. "Sis, I'm not tryin' to run Dallas down. I like him, even admire him in a way. Guess I always have. But if I didn't understand him, I'd find him mighty hard to like. Maybe you oughta give that some thought where lovin' him's concerned."

"You're the one I don't understand." Kate appeared bemused, uncertain of her feelings just at that moment. "You tell me all these dreadful things, and in the same breath, you try to convince me that it's for my own good. How, Doc? How is knowing all this going to make my life with Dallas any better?"

"Because there's more to being a man's wife than sleepin' with him. More'n likely, you've already found that out." He studied her for a second, watching the hurt and fear kindle in her eyes, yet he was determined now to see it through. "Kate, this man's whole life is tied up in some funny kind of way with doing what he thinks is right. Upholding the law, destroying the lawless. Sorta like the great god Jehovah visitin' wrath and damnation on the sinners. After the war, he drifted around for a while, then joined the Rangers. First he fought the Indians up north with Jones's company, and considerin' how his folks was killed, I suspect he took few prisoners. Later, he served with McNelly down on the border, and that wasn't no picnic either. Don't you see what I'm gettin' at, Sis? Ever since he was a kid, somebody's been trainin' him to kill and givin' him a license to make it legal. They taught him that killin' is all right so long as it's the sinner that gets killed. That's how he was raised up and that's how he believes."

Then Cummings hesitated, groping for some justification that would absolve the man his sister had married. "Whatever your man is Kate, he's what the people of Texas made him. What they needed, what the times called for. That's all I'm tryin' to say."

Kate regarded him vacantly, her face drained of emotion. "You're saying he kills other men because he has to, because no one ever showed him another way. You don't condemn him, but at the same time, you don't approve. He's the lesser of two evils. A good badman hired to hunt down the common, garden-variety badmen. That's very charitable of you, Doc. Almost Christian."

"Damn, I wish I'd never opened my big mouth." He rubbed his face with both hands, like a man that has sore eyes and a long way yet to go. "Kate, regardless of what you thought I said, I don't believe there's a bad bone in Dallas Stoudenmire's body. Matter of fact, he's about the most decent man I ever met. Otherwise, I'd have raised holy hell before I let you marry him. I'd trust him with my life sooner'n anybody I know, and you damn sure don't put that kind of faith in a man that's not straight. That's what I meant a while ago about him being my friend whatever he is. What he isn't has got nothin' to do with it."

Kate didn't say anything for a few seconds, almost as if she had dismissed the subject from her mind. Then she glanced up with renewed curiosity. "Did Dallas tell you all this the night you got him drunk? Or are you just guessing?"

"Tell you the truth, Seth Hart had him checked out through the governor's office. Most of it came out there. The rest I put together from little things Dallas said. Damn little, I'll admit. He's not the most talkative man I ever met."

"No, he's not that." Kate smiled wanly and sighed. "But deep down he's as good a man as any woman could ask for. And somehow, I'm going to get him out of El Paso and make him forget this horrible life. I don't know how, but I will.''

Later, walking back to his room over the store, Doc Cummings had the feeling that he had only made matters worse. He had meant it the right way, for it was plain to see that Kate couldn't go on much longer with the way things were. But then, as parsons were so fond of reminding folks, the road to hell was paved with good intentions. Chalk one up to damn fools and good deeds. Lately they seemed to be a matched pair.

4.

THEY CAME like ghostly shadows in the night. The moons' golden streamers lighted the compound with a dusky glow, just bright enough for a man to catch his rifle sights when the time was right. Kale placed each man in position, carefully selecting an open field of fire, and by midnight they had the *hacienda* surrounded.

The night riders had split into two parties after Tom Kale personally scouted the layout. The smaller group was to raid the northernmost herd of cattle just as soon as firing broke out in the compound. Leaving nothing to chance, Kale had selected to lead the assault on the *hacienda*. The sole purpose of this raid was to punish the greasers in their own backyard; scare them so badly that they would be posting sentries for a month to come. The cattle herd was strictly a secondary target, and like any guerrilla leader worth his salt, Kale had chosen to direct the main attack himself.

The *hacienda* of Don Miguel Salazar lay some twenty kilometers southwest of Paso del Norte. The aristocratic *hidalgo* had inherited a Spanish land grant from his father and ruled a small kingdom stretching to the headwaters of the Rio Santa Maria, nearly a hundred kilometers further south. Located on a tree-sheltered plain alongside a sleepy brook, the *cuadrilla* consisted of the master's *casa* and various outbuildings, which included bunkhouses, *jacal* huts, stables, and storage sheds. The compound was enclosed on three sides by a low adobe wall with the brook forming the remaining boundary. Don Miguel's large, sprawling home overlooked the stream just south of the main gate and commanded a view of the entire *rancho* headquarters.

Kale had posted half his men on the far side of the brook behind trees and the remainder in a grove of giant *maguey* near the opposite side of the compound. Once the shooting started, the Mexicans would be caught in a deadly cross fire, with virtually no chance of mounting a counterattack. While greatly outnumbered, the Banning night riders had the element of surprise working in their favor, and their tactical advantage promised to make it a costly night for Don Salazar's *vaqueros*.

Shortly after midnight, three of Kale's men slithered into the compound and set fire to a large stable near the west wall. Within moments the building was engulfed in flames, and squeals from the terror-stricken horses could be heard a mile away. *Vaqueros* poured from the buildings in their nightclothes, forgetting guns, boots, and all else in their rush to save *el patrón*'s prized breeding stock. Among the first to reach the blazing stable was Ramón Vazquez, who had served as Don Salazar's *caporal* for close to five years. Shouting commands above the raging inferno, Ramón quickly organized a bucket brigade, then led a handpicked crew through the flames to rescue the panicked horses.

Waiting patiently, like a tawny panther watching a game trail, Kale bided his time as the crowd thickened around the stables. Soon every man on the place was frantically engaged in dousing the fire, and the leaping flames silhouetted their every movement within the confines of the *cuadrilla*. Observing the rushing figures closely, Kale selected the one who seemed to be giving all the orders. Carefully aligning his sights on the man's chest, Kale squeezed the trigger and felt the Winchester buck against his shoulder.

Ramón Vazquez would always think back on the night of the fire as a moment of *buena fortuna* for him personally. Had he been standing still he would have been a dead man, *muy muerto*. But at the split second the rifle cracked, he stooped to retrieve a fallen bucket, and the slug ripped through the fleshy part of his arm. Spun around, he dropped to the earth, knowing even as he fell that his people had been skillfully lured into a trap.

Suddenly the night came alive with the yellowish flash of gunfire, and lead hissed across the compound like a swarm of angry wasps. *Vaqueros* fell right and left, clutching their wounds, and those left unscathed after the first volley ran for cover. Rolling beneath a *carreta*, Ramón peered cautiously around the wooden wheel, trying to ignore the dull throb in his left arm. One glance was enough to confirm his suspicions. Their attackers had them neatly scissored in a cross fire, and unless something was done fast, every man in the *cuadrilla* would be snuffed out like defenseless insects.

"*¡Dispersad, hombres!*" Ramón shouted over the roar of flames and rifle-fire. "Scatter! Run for the buildings! Get your guns and form along the walls. *¡Pronto, hombres! ¡Pronto!*"

The *vaqueros* came off the ground as if electrified by his hoarse command. Scuttling crablike across the open compound, they dodged and weaved in headlong flight toward the adobe structures. The gunfire increased in tempo as they ran, upending an even half dozen before they reached the sanctuary of the buildings. Moments later, they boiled from their *cabañas* like frenzied ants, clutching rifles and bandoliers as they darted toward the walls. Five more of their number jackknifed into the dust as they ran the gauntlet of lead for the second time, but more than forty *vaqueros* made it safely. Within the beat of a heart, their rifles leveled over the walls, and the night was split with a thunderous fusillade as they returned the raiders' fire with a vengeance.

Three miles to the northeast another deadly engagement was being played out with equally savage results. Ten raiders had infiltrated the cattle herd, moving stealthily through the pale darkness as they waited for the signal. When the ragged sound of shooting drifted in from the *hacienda*, they opened fire on the night guards, presumably killing every man in the first volley. But among the *vaqueros* was an *anciano* of great resourcefulness and daring. The slug meant for him had pulverized his pommel instead, and he very cunningly tumbled from the saddle, squirming off into the brush with the noiseless wrigglings of a chubby snake. From there, he watched silently as the bushwhackers mounted their horses and set about trailing the restless herd in a northerly direction.

But this ancient one wasn't a man who accepted such insult lightly. In his prime, he had been *macho hombre*, and it went against the grain to cower in the brush like a steer with an empty bag. Removing his rowled spurs, he waited until the herd had been lined out and started north. Just as he suspected, one of the *gringo ladrones* fell back to ride drag on the skittish longhorns. With that, the *anciano* exploded from his hiding place, displaying the agility of one half his age as he collared the raider in a bounding leap. Cartwheeling over the horse, they struck the ground, and he scrambled erect as if shot from coiled springs. Balanced catlike on the balls of his feet, the ancient one's heart thudded with the excitement of an old *guerrero* who has forgotten nothing about the deadly games men play. Jerking a battered cap and ball Remington, he clouted the raider upside the head, grunting with satisfaction as the man settled limply into the dust.

¡Caramba! The old fox had lost none of his juices after all. And he, Hector Lizardi, the *vaquero* they had thought to retire to the goat herd, would personally present *el patrón* with this *gringo abominación. ¡Madre de Dios!* It had been a good night indeed for old men.

While Hector Lizardi was gloating over his prisoner, Tom Kale decided it was time to break off the fighting and make a run for the border. Withdrawing his men in small bunches, he managed to keep the *vaqueros* pinned down until everyone was mounted. Moments later the raiders thundered northward, intent on putting distance between themselves and the Salazar *rancho*. Circling back to assign a rear guard, Kale was astounded to find that he hadn't lost a single man in a firefight that had raged for nearly a half-hour. If the cattle raid had come off anywhere near as well, he'd really have something to crow about to the Bannings!

But if Tom Kale was exultant, Ramón Vazquez was seared clean through by a fury unlike any he had ever known. The Salazar *hacienda* was devastated, a burned-out ruin where only an hour before there had been a magnificent ranch. With no one to halt its advance, the stable fire had spread rapidly to other buildings, and the entire *cuadrilla* now lay in smoky rubble. With the exception of Don Miguel's *casa* and a single bunkhouse, every building in the compound had been leveled to the ground.

Still, buildings could be erected again; their loss was but a thing of the moment. Men were something else entirely, and short of *Jesucristo* himself, there was no one with the knack of pumping life back into the dead. With a quick count, Ramón made it eleven dead and twenty-six wounded, some mortally. There would be much wailing in the *vaqueros'* quarters before another dawn, and the thought of his people being shot down like dogs brought a sickening taste to Ramón's mouth. Someone would pay dearly for this slaughter, eye for eye, just as it has been in the old days when they fought Comanches instead of *gringos*.

After seeing to his men, Ramón sought out Don Miguel, who was wandering through the rubble in a numbed daze. *El patrón* had little to say, staring blankly at the carnage and death about them. Ramón tersely explained what must be done, then left him gazing sorrowfully upon a brood mare that had not survived the fire. Ordering horses brought in from the nearby *remuda*, he called on every *vaquero* who could ride to take the saddle. Less than a quarter-hour after the shooting had ceased, the *caporal* led a force of nineteen men toward the Rio Grande.

With fresh horses under them, the *vaqueros* set a blistering pace, and some ten kilometers from the border, they overtook the *gringo* column. Kale and his raiders had joined the tail end of the rustled herd only minutes before and were hanging back in event the greasers gave pursuit.

Upon sighting the Mexicans, Kale ordered the longhorns stampeded toward the river and formed his men to fight a delaying action until the herd was safely aground on Texas soil.

Over the next hour, a running battle raged across the countryside. The villagers of Paso del Norte heard the gunfire and promptly bolted their doors. Those engaged in the fighting seemed to be doing a good job of it, which meant that only the *estúpido* would venture forth to satisfy their curiosity. Wise men minded their own business, behind locked doors, leaving other men to attend to such affairs as they saw fit.

But the villagers' relutance by no means extended to Ramón's *vaqueros*. Repeatedly they charged the *gringos*, only to have their attack blunted by the accurate fire of the Texans' rifles. Kale kept his men fanned out in a compact crescent behind the rushing herd, never once allowing them to bunch together. After losing several men in futile charges, the Mexicans splintered off, every man for himself in a ghostly, moonlit duel. But Kale directed the raiders' fire with telling deadliness, and as the last of the herd was driven into the river, the *vaqueros* called it quits.

Drawing to a halt on a rise overlooking the Rio Grande, Ramón and his men watched helplessly as the raiders swam the lazy current. On the other side was Texas, and over there a *vaquero* had one foot in the grave when he stepped from the water. Better to wait, to make plans, Ramón counseled. There was always another day, and the *gringos* had departed owing a debt that would be collected manyfold in time to come.

Reining his horse about on the opposite bank, Tom Kale observed the distant Mexicans with a throaty chuckle. By God, this was a good night's work well done! He had lost only two men, and as near as he could count, they had put at least a dozen of those greaser bastards under for keeps. That's the kind of fighting any man could be proud of!

Thinking on it, he decided he might just hit the Bannings up for a raise.

5.

THE SUN had barely topped the horizon when Don Miguel and Ramón came out to survey the damage from last night's raid. While the *hacienda* itself had suffered only minor damage, the outbuildings were nothing but charred ruins, and a sense of loss hung over the compound like a shroud. Upward of two hundred steers had also been lost in the raid, but among Don Miguel's people, there was a greater sorrow that left no room for smoldering homes or scrubby longhorns.

After the abortive chase to the Rio Grande, there were now fourteen dead *vaqueros*, and the mournful cries of their women was enough to make a strong man lose his breakfast. When Ramón saw the bodies laid out, his guts shriveled into a hard knot, strengthening his resolve that retribution must be swift in coming. There were some things upon which no price could be set, except in blood.

Later in the morning, after the dead and the wounded had been attended to, the captured *norteamericano* was brought forward. Hector Lizardi had become an overnight hero among his people, once again *macho hombre*, proudly leading the barbarian around for everyone to see. The prisoner was a large, fleshy man, towering over his shrunken captor, but a deft tug on the rawhide *reata* around his neck quickly brought him to heel.

When the raider was hauled before Ramón, the *caporal*'s rage centered wholly on him, just as a hawk selects a single dove in flight. This lone man was the one visible symbol of the unspeakable filth that had devastated their homes and murdered their *compañeros*. What he had to say would make interesting listening, and the *vaqueros* gathered closer, eagerly awaiting Ramón's choice of persuasion.

The raider was jerked and shoved across the *cuadrilla* grounds and roughly bound to a tree near the brook. The questioning began, but the prisoner proved a stubborn witness. First, he professed no understanding of Spanish, then when Ramón switched to broken English he simply refused to speak, sulling up like a paunchy old mule. The night rider had no illusions about what was coming; he had lived on the border long enough to know that his fate was sealed. It was only a matter of what device would be used and how long it would take. Determined to go under like a man, he clamped his jaws shut and gave every indication of never opening them again. These greaser pricks could do whatever they wanted, but he'd show them the kind of grit a real *hombre* had.

Ramón studied the problem for a moment, then stepped off a few paces and drew his pistol. Aiming with utmost care, he squeezed off a shot, and the man's right ear disappeared in a frothy, pink spray. The prisoner banged his head against the tree as he jerked backwards and a steady stream of blood trickled down his neck. Ramón waited, giving him an opportunity to speak, but the Texan merely gritted his teeth and returned the stare defiantly. The *caporal* raised his pistol again, and when it exploded, the man's left ear disintegrated in a shower of bloody tissue. The raider groaned, yet so slightly that only those standing nearby heard it, and spat a wad of phlegm at Ramón's feet.

Ramón glanced at Don Miguel, who was standing off to one side, and smiled tightly. This *gringo* promised to be a tough one; but the day was long, and they had plenty of time. Perhaps he had greater fear of a slow death than a quick one, and in that, they could accommodate him easily. The *caporal* ordered the prisoner's shirt removed, then looked slowly around the circle of hard, brown faces. For what he had in mind, there was one above all others who deserved the honor, and he selected Hector Lizardi.

"*Abuelo*, it comes to me that your knife needs practice. This vermin is yours to whittle on, old one. But take care you do not kill him. The *bárbaro* has much to say before we allow him to die."

The old man's eyes went moist with pride. "*Sí jefe*. I will treat him gently, as if he were merely a child whose manners must be corrected."

Walking forward, Hector Lizardi stopped before the prisoner. With great ceremony, he slipped a long, wicked looking stiletto from its scabbard. Testing its edge with his thumb, he squinted up at the raider, flashing a mouthful of scraggly, brown teeth. "*Amigo*, you are about to witness a miracle. With one swift stroke of the blade, I will reveal how it is possible for you to change from man to *manso*, the tame bull. Have you ever seen a man gelded, my friend? It is an ugly thing, and sad. Very sad. No longer will his pole grow stout, and the women find him a source of much amusement."

Suddenly the narrow blade flicked out and down, slashing the man's belt and pants so that they fell over against his hips. A thin ribbon of blood appeared from his belly-button to his groin, seeping down over the short, curly hairs that showed above the crotch of his trousers. The raider's buttocks slammed up against the tree as his manhood flinched from the knife. Then he sucked up his nerve and closed his eyes, waiting for the final cut.

But men are unlike cattle, as Hector Lizardi well knew. They die quickly from loss of blood or simply from shock when their *pequeñas rocas* are cut from the sack. Better merely to carve on the *gringo* dog and break his spirit little by little. Suiting action to thought, the old man hefted the stiletto like a surgical instrument and began tracing a pattern of precise slits across the man's belly. When that failed to draw any response, he neatly severed each nipple, watching the exquisite agony on the raider's face as the blade razored through his tender flesh. Still the *ladrón* refused to speak.

Losing patience, the ancient one grasped the Texan's lower lip between thumb and forefinger and gauged an arc from corner to corner with the tip of the stiletto. But as the blade pierced the man's fleshy jowls, Ramón halted Hector Lizardi with a sharp command.

"Enough, grandfather! I see now that this *piojo* is more stubborn than we suspected. Either that, or he is more of a man than his fat belly would lead you to believe. Still there are ways to loosen any man's tongue. Eh, old one? Perhaps we should let him share a moment with the crawling death." Turning to his men, Ramón searched their faces. "What do you say, *caballeros?* Shall we introduce our silent friend to *el culebra?*"

The men roared their approval, flashing curious glances at the prisoner as they nudged one another in the ribs. While the raider hadn't the faintest idea of what was coming next, it seemed fairly clear that it would be worse than what he had already undergone. Bathed in a slime of his own sweat and gore, he sagged against the ropes, thankful for even this brief respite. Galvanized by Ramón's brisk orders, the *vaqueros* set about collecting empty grain sacks and took off in all directions across the parched countryside.

Don Miguel spoke briefly with his *caporal*, nodding occasionally at the prisoner, then walked off toward the *hacienda* What was about to happen wouldn't be pretty to watch, and there were some things that even *el patrón* preferred not to witness. While he saw the necessity, it nonetheless left him revolted. As he knew full well, Ramón and his *vaqueros* had not fought the Apaches and Comanches without learning something about the limits of a man's courage. And the Texan was about to be tested in a way that Don Miguel considered harsh even for a *gringo*.

Shortly the prisoner was marched to a small, open-sided *ramada* and stripped naked. Four ropes were thrown over the rafters and secured to his hands and ankles. Then, before he had time to gather his wits, the man was hoisted aloft in a spread-eagle position. *Vaqueros* strode forward clutching sacks and dumped the contents on the earthen floor of the *ramada.*

The morning stillness instantly came alive with an ungodly buzzing sound, and a dozen furious rattlesnakes coiled to strike. Leaping back, the *vaqueros* grabbed long poles and surrounded the shed, forcing the snakes to remain inside. Being poked and shoved with the sticks infuriated the rattlers even more, and their angry warning swelled to a deafening pitch.

Ramón stepped as close to the shed as he dared and peered up at the helpless raider. "*Gringo*, you can halt this game whenever you feel the urge to speak. From this moment on, whether you live or die is a matter of your own choosing."

Moving back, Ramón barked an order, and the Texan was slowly lowered from the rafters toward the floor. After a moment, the snakes became aware of the new threat and switched their attention from the *vaqueros* to this strange enemy who hovered overhead like a taloned hawk. The raider jerked violently, arching his buttocks high in the air, trying desperately to push himself back up the ropes. But his struggles were in vain, for the lines inexorably lowered him into the viper pit below. As he neared the floor, the snakes poised to strike, and the enraged whir of their rattles came like the call of death itself. Dripping sweat, his eyes bulged out of their sockets, shot through with crazed terror.

Suddenly the man gasped as he spotted one especially large rattler eyeing his dangling manhood. Every fiber in his body strained backwards with inhuman will, for it now became clear that whatever part of him reached the snakes first was exactly what they would strike. Already he could feel the slithering filth gnawing on it, gouging and chomping as they pumped their venom deep within his precious rod. Death came to every man, and once cold, it mattered little how he had gone under. But not like that. *Holy Mother of God, not like that!*

The *vaqueros* watched in frozen awe, wondering if the *yanqui* would hold his tongue until it was too late. Some of his breed were *muy valiente*, brave beyond the measure of other men, and perhaps this fat-gutted barbarian was one. Whatever he was, he would shortly be dog meat unless he opened his mouth soon.

Then, with little more than a yard separating him from the rattlers, the Texan broke. Screaming hysterically, his face etched with mortal fear, he swore to tell all if they would only save him. Ramón ordered him hoisted aloft, but refused to untie him just yet. Drained of the last ounce of courage, the raider hung limply from the ropes, swaying overhead like a gutted steer. Every muscle in his body quivered uncontrollably, his eyes twitched with spastic madness; like a man already dead, his bowels flushed in final release.

The questioning began again. This time Ramon was confident that they would come to an understanding, for they were both reasonable men, and as such, there should be no secrets between them. But should he prove stubborn with certain answers, of course, they would not hesitate to lower him again among those who waited below. *¿Comprendes, amigo? ¡Bueno!*

6.

SHORTLY AFTER noon that day, a carriage crossed the Rio Grande and drove straight to the Paso del Norte jail. There three girls alighted, their faces wan and solemn, dressed demurely as befitted housewives. Their driver escorted them into the *calabozo*, and as they entered the door, the portly jailer came forward to meet them. Four *gringos*, three of them women, was hardly an everyday occurrence in his flea-bitten lockup, and he instinctively grew wary.

"Buenos días, Mariscal," the driver greeted him in passable Spanish. "These *señoras* are the wives of the prisoners now in your custody. They humbly request permission to speak with their men for a few moments. Since it is well known that their husbands are slated for *rapida ejecución* the ladies feel honor-bound to look upon them once more."

The jailer sucked up his stomach and sauntered around for a better look at the ladies. Seldom had he been called marshal, and the title had a heady effect on him in the drowsy heat. Still one could never be too careful where *gringos* were concerned. They were a devious race, given to great cunning and duplicity in their dealings with his people. Yet the man looked harmless enough, and the women certainly presented no threat. After all, he, José Flores, was a man of some experience in such matters, not to mention his remarkable facility for sizing up a person in one glance. Besides, he was a family man himself, and it was only right that *hombres* who had an appointment with the firing squad should be granted one last visit with their loved ones. Such a thing would do much for a man on his way to hell.

"*¡Hecho!*" His eyes warmed, and he smiled benevolently. "Consider it done, *señor.* But the ladies will be allowed only ten minutes, and under the circumstances, I fear they will be afforded no privacy."

"*Gracious, Mariscal.* You are very kind." Looking around at the women, the driver related the gist of the conversation, then turned back to the jailer. "The *señoras* thank you and indicate that ten minutes will be more than enough. After the beastly thing these men have done, the ladies wish only to fulfill their wifely duty, and nothing more."

Tipping his hat to the women, the driver turned and walked out the door. José Flores smiled solicitously and ushered the ladies toward the rear of the jail. This was a sad thing, and he felt very *simpático* about these poor, betrayed women. Still, they were exceptionally pretty in that pale, *gringo* way, and doubtless they would have little trouble finding better husbands once this dirty business was finished. He would light a candle and pray to the Virgin that their bereavement not be too incapacitating.

Red and his two cellmates had watched this little charade with mounting interest. They weren't too sure about the play, but there wasn't a doubt in the world that Banning had hatched this scheme personally. The girls were regulars in the Coliseum Saloon, and they wouldn't be here unless the big boss had a hand in this deal. While the prisoners' grasp of greaser talk was limited, they had caught enough of the conversation to understand that the women were posing as their wives. Considering that each of the girls would hump a drunk Indian if the price was right, the three men had all they could do to keep from laughing. Watching the tubby jailer herd them along like lily-pure doves was more than a man could rightly stand with a straight face.

When the girls stopped before the cell, the three Texans crowded against the bars. José Flores thoughtfully backed off a few paces, not wishing to intrude on their tender, yet somehow pitiful, moment. Out of the corner of his eye he saw the men clasp their wives' hands, and the soft mur-

murings he took to be words of endearment brought a sorrowful frown to his face. *¡Madre mio!* It was indeed a cruel thing that these men had brought such disgrace to their women. The sooner they faced the firing squad the better for everyone concerned!

Suddenly the girls' escort appeared in the doorway and again stepped inside. Instantly alert, the jailer walked toward the front of the room, keeping his hand near the ancient Colt resting on his hip. But the driver seemed peaceful enough, wishing only to inquire if it would be possible to get a cup of coffee. José Flores apologized profusely, for the coffee pot had grown cold since morning. More to the point, he was disgusted with himself at having suspected the man simply because he was a *gringo*. Chattering like an amiable bear, he walked the driver back to the door, and they parted with a warm handshake.

While José Flores was salving his conscience, things in the back of the jail were moving at a furious pace. In a flash the girls hiked their skirts, pulled guns from their underclothes, and passed them to the prisoners. With the jailer's attention thoroughly diverted, it was a simple matter for Red and his partners to stash the guns beneath their mattresses. When the *alguacil* returned, he found everything as serene as a high mass, marred only by an occasional sniffle from one of the women. Again he was struck by the rightness of allowing these doomed men one last glimpse of their wives. Somewhere a man's good deeds were being recorded for that final day of judgment, and his actions here this afternoon would not go unnoticed.

When the girls were ready to leave, he escorted them to the carriage and stood watching as it pulled away. Dabbing at their eyes with delicate hankies, they waved goodbye, and José Flores felt a lump the size of a gourd form in his throat. *¡Madre de Dios!* Such gentle creatures to be married to those filthy *cabrones* back inside.

The day passed uneventfully, and after giving the prisoners their supper, the jailer stepped outside to sit on the front step. Each evening when darkness fell, a freshening breeze drifted in off the river, and it was good to be rid of the heat for another day. The night seemed alive with fireflies and the chirp of crickets, and for the first time in longer than he could remember, José Flores felt at peace with himself. This was a thankless job, one seldom appreciated by the people, but it had its moments. Gazing up at the sky, he watched the moon play hide and seek with the clouds and reflected once again on the skinny beauty of *yanqui* women. *¡Sí!* Today had been one of those moments.

Back in their cell, Red and his cronies stared up at the same moon through a barred window. Yet their thoughts had little to do with cool breezes and pretty women. They would have much preferred a dark night for a jailbreak, but beggars couldn't be choosers. The greasers could easily take it into their heads to march them before a firing squad at any time, and escape might be tonight or never.

They had spent the afternoon planning just how it would be done, and with the village quieted down, there was no reason to wait longer. On signal, two of the men started scuffling, cursing one another in loud, fluent terms. Jerked from his reverie by the commotion, José Flores hurried into the cell block, ordering them to cease fighting. But the tables suddenly turned, and before he suspected what was happening, the jailer found himself staring down the bores of three Colts.

"All right, you greasy tub o' guts," Red snarled. "We'd just as soon kill you as not, so don't fart around or I'll put a slug right through your gizzard. Now get them keys and be damn quick about it."

The jailer wordlessly crossed the room and took a ring of keys from a wall peg. But as he turned back, his offside was hidden for a moment, and his hand stealthily crept toward the gun on his hip. *¡Jesucristo!* If he let these animals escape, the villagers would more than likely decorate a tree with his plump neck. Three to one were bad odds, even for a *pistolero* like himself, but he had to try.

"Hold it!" Red's sharp growl brought him up short. "Listen you fat prick, you're about a hair away from going under. Savvy, greaseball? Now heist your hands and trot over here with them keys."

José Flores did as he was told. Even the most fearless *guerrero* knew there was a fine line between bravery and foolishness, and the big, black holes centered on his belly-button seemed very persuasive indeed. Besides, he had seven children, who would take it very unkindly if their father suddenly left them orphaned. Unlocking the cell door, he stepped aside to let the Texans out.

Without warning Red whacked him over the head with the heavy Colt. The jailer's knees buckled, but the *gringo* thumped him twice more before he hit the floor, striking savagely as one would club a fattened steer. José Flores made no sound as a widening pool of blood puddled up around his head. Had Red not feared risking a shot, he would have been a dead man instead of one with a cracked skull.

Easing through the front door of the jail, the Texans stuck to the shadows and began a cautious approach to the river. The streets were deserted, and Paso del Norte seemed quiet as a graveyard. But they took no chances. Moving silently from building to building in the tawny moonlight, they passed through the village without arousing a single dog. Though this struck Red as curious, he chalked it off to an overdue change in luck and plowed on toward the border.

Minutes later, they reached the river, and the sight of it made them bolder. Freedom lay on the other side. A land where there were no lice, ravenous fleas, or firing squads. The thought alone made them dizzy with relief. Sliding down the bank in a shower of dust, they plunged into the water and went splashing across the Rio Grande like frisky yearlings.

But even as they ran, Ramón Vazquez and fifteen *vaqueros* emerged from the treeline bordering Paso del Norte. Armed with rifles; they watched impassively as the Texans neared the opposite shore, awaiting their *caporal*'s order. When it came, the night was rendered with a hollow roar, and the three renegades pitched forward on the riverbank, dead even as they hit American soil. The *vaqueros* continued firing until their rifles were empty, shredding the lifeless bodies with a hail of lead. Only when the hammers clicked on empty chambers did they lower their weapons and fade back into the trees.

The debt had been repaid in part. Not fully by any means, and after the savagery of last night, perhaps never. But now there would be no doubt as to the fate of those who violated Mexican women or ravaged the land of their fathers.

CHAPTER FOUR

1.

EL PASO was alive with talk of last night's brutal slaying of the three Americans. Frank Hollingsworth, the local butcher, happened to be on his way home and had actually witnessed the slaughter, which was the term already being applied to the killings. The townspeople were in a shaky mood, appalled by the savagery of the incident. Though the dead men were generally considered nothing more than common rapists, border scum really, they were human. When the riddled bodies had been carted up to the funeral parlor, word quickly spread that they were as full of holes as a leaky sieve. Such an end was better suited to animals, for whatever else they had been, the men were Texans. The way things were shaping up, no man was safe outside the sanctuary of his own home. Maybe not even in it.

Although the people were unnerved by the Mexicans' savagery, there was also an undercurrent of ill feeling directed toward the Bannings. They had clearly masterminded the escape attempt, and it had been their ranch hands who had stirred up the Mexicans. Though no one could fault them for trying to save their own men, it now became clear that the life of every *anglo* along the river had been placed in jeopardy. The Mexicans meant to fight if pushed, and stirring up a hornets' nest to save three men was hardly the act of a civic benefactor. What had been whispered in the past was now being bandied about openly. Ed Banning was a conniving bloodsucker, and so long as he ended up with all the marbles, he didn't give a tinker's damn for the fate of the town itself.

Tom Kale rode into town late that morning, eager to report the success of his raid. Touching up the brands on the rustled longhorns was taking longer than planned, and he had finally decided it was best to ride on in and let the Bannings know what was happening. Besides, he was a little concerned that Red and his two partners hadn't shown up at the ranch. Assuming the jailbreak came off without a hitch, he had fully expected them to come loping into the home base sometime last night.

Upon entering the office in the Coliseum he found the Bannings sour-tempered and curiously untalkative. The grim scowl on their faces was clear enough to read, and to an old scout like Kale, the sign said to walk lightly.

"Mornin', boss," Kale's voice was neither chipper nor solemn, just sort of neuter in tone. "How's tricks, Sam?"

"Not worth a shit." The burly man's features twisted in a bilious grimace, like he was having gas pains and couldn't break wind. "In case you hadn't heard, somebody just kicked the crapper door off the hinges."

"Yeah? Well maybe I've got a little news that'll cheer you up some." The ramrod wasn't sure what Sam's cryptic observation meant, but where the Bannings were concerned he had found it best not to prod them with questions. "Night before last we whipped the livin' piss out of them greasers and got away with near two hundred beeves. The boys are finishing up the brandin' right now. Sorta puts a new light on things, don't it?"

Ed Banning came erect in his chair. "Kale, you're a day late and a dollar short. Last night your asshole buddies got themselves pumped full of lead. What Sam's trying to tell you is that the greasers let 'em get to this side of the river before they gunned them down. Evidently they got wind of the break somehow and had a whole goddamn regiment lined up along the south bank."

"Sorta like a turkey shoot," Sam growled. "Only your boys didn't have near as good a chance of walkin' away."

"Well I'll be dipped in shit," Kale said, clearly thunderstruck by the news.

"We're all gonna be double-dipped if we don't get things back on an even keel pretty damn quick." The gang leader's waspish comments sizzled with anger. "Instead of busting those three nitwits out of jail and making a fool of Stoudenmire, we've made jackasses out of ourselves twice running. Once more and folks around here are liable to start thinkin' we've gone soft in the head."

"That's for damn sure." Kale shook his head ruefully, still slack-jawed with the turn of events. "Us losin' five men in two days might give the wrong people some big ideas."

"Five men?" Ed Banning snapped. "What the hell are you talkin' about? I only count three."

"Oh, I lost two in the raid the other night. Taylor and Pickens. Guess I forgot to mention it."

"Just clean slipped your mind, did it? Like you'd lost a couple of steers out in the brush somewhere. Kale, honest to Christ, sometimes I think your wits are about as sharp as a dull butcher knife."

"Boss, I ain't no dummy, but you plumb lost me." The foreman glanced at Sam for some clue and got only a dour look in return. "We've lost men on raids before. Plenty of times. Where's the difference this go-round?"

"You thickheaded ox. If you had sense enough to pour piss out of a boot, you wouldn't have to ask." Banning's eyes narrowed with scorn, and it was all he could do to hold his rage in check. "The greasers got hold of one of your men and made him talk. That oughta be plain enough even for you. Otherwise how would they've known about the jailbreak and had a whole goddamn army waitin' with Winchesters?"

"Well hell, Mr. Banning, I ain't no mind reader. We shot it out with the greasers the better part of the night, and I just sorta figured them boys went under when I wasn't lookin'."

"That's the trouble with you, Kale. You figure too much. That kind of thing has been known to ruin a man's health."

Banning's surly threat brought the ramrod up short, and he wisely concluded that it was best not to try defending his actions further. Sam was just looking for an excuse to beat the whey out of somebody, and if the elder brother blinked in his direction, he might easily come out on the short end of the stick. Not that he was afraid of Sam one way or the other. It was just that if he had a choice, he'd rather fight a cross-eyed gorilla.

When Kale held his silence, the gang leader cooled down somewhat, sinking back into his chair. "If you'd let me know in time, we could have changed the plan, instead of making asses out of ourselves. But there's no use cryin' over spilt milk. What we've got to think about is that the greasers are holdin' either Taylor or Pickens over there somewhere. And sure as Christ made green apples, he's talking his head off, whichever one it is. If the greasers got cute and handed him over to the Texas Rangers, we'll be hung by our balls on a short string."

Banning's gaze shifted to the ceiling, and his eyes went cloudy, somehow out of focus. Sifting the known from the unknown, and holding it to the light of what urgently needed doing, he slowly came to the only reasonable solution. "Kale, whoever they've got, they're probably holding him at the same hacienda you raided. I want you to make sure he never sets foot off that place except in a box. If you foul this up, you'd better keep right on going."

Kale just nodded, needing no explanation. Once more and he would be playing on borrowed time. That was the message, and he had every certainty that, if he stumbled again, it would be a long fall.

Sam's brutish grunt snapped his thoughts back to the present. "Well I'm damned if I see why we ought to bother about somebody the greasers've got. There's only one man we've got to thank for this whole mess, and it's that shit heel marshal. I say get rid of him. Once he's out of the way, them bleedin' hearts uptown won't have anybody to hide behind."

"That's the ticket!" Kale agreed brightly, trying to regain lost ground in his deadly race against ill wind and piss-poor luck. "Hell's bells, I'd be willin' to do the job just to see the bastard's face when he got chopped down."

"You two make a pair," Ed Banning observed testily. "Damned if I ever saw anything to beat it. If Stoudenmire turned up dead, everybody in town would know who did it, and there's a limit even in El Paso. That's all the reformers would need. Give 'em a martyr and they'll start poundin' drums all the way back to the statehouse. Now both of you pay attention, 'cause I'm only gonna say this once. Until I give the word, we'll just lay low and keep our eyes open. One way or another, we'll get Stoudenmire, but nobody makes a move till I say the time is ripe."

When neither man seemed inclined to argue the matter, Banning waved his hand dismissively. "Why don't you two trot out and get yourselves a drink. I've got some things to think out."

Sam bobbed his head dumbly and turned toward the door. Kale followed him out, amused by the fickle tides that momentarily put him to rowing with the boss's brother. Over drinks at the bar, they agreed that Ed was a very deep man, hard to understand. But other than this shallow observation, they were unwilling to speculate further about the man they both served so meekly. Some things were just better left unsaid.

2.

SHORTLY BEFORE noon, Stoudenmire was crossing the plaza when he met Mayor Porter headed in the opposite direction. Although the two men were on speaking terms, neither was laboring under any illusions about where the other stood. Stoudenmire served but one mistress, the law, while Porter had cast his lot with corruption and personal gain in the form of the Banning machine. Like two battle-scarred old dogs eyeing the same bone, they feinted this it way and that, sparring verbally whenever they met, each seeking some advantage before the fight was joined. Though the marshal respected Porter's skill as a manipulator of men and things, he found the mayor an insufferable bore, not to mention the fact that he was something of a windbag in the bargain. Porter was simply scared witless of the marshal, for after twenty years on a lawless frontier, he had grown accustomed to a certain tolerance where men's misdeeds were concerned. Clearly Stoudenmire couldn't be classed as a tolerant lawman, and it was a bit unsettling to meet a man who had some Jehovah-like concept of himself as the dispenser of justice.

Stoudenmire nodded to the mayor and started to pass on by. But Porter had other ideas. "Marshal, I wonder if you have a moment? As a matter of fact, if you're not too busy, I'd like to buy you a drink."

"Thanks just the same, Mr. Mayor, but I rarely drink before noon." The sarcasm was thinly veiled, just the way Stoudenmire meant it. "Besides, my wife is expecting me home for dinner."

"Well land's sakes, man, she'll keep it hot for you." Porter's tone seemed almost desperate, and he clutched at the marshal's arm with a feeble, birdlike grasp. "This is important. Official business in a manner of speaking, and I'd think that takes precedent over a paltry noon meal."

Stoudenmire sensed some curious change in the politician. Nothing he could put his finger on, but a noticeable crack in the wall nonetheless. "Since you put it that way, Mayor, I'll take you up on the offer. But no drinks, just talk. Suppose we try your office instead of a saloon."

"No. Not city hall," Porter said a bit too quickly. "Let's go to your office. There'll be less . . . ah . . . interruption that way."

Without a word, the marshal turned and began retracing his steps across the plaza. Whatever was on the portly little man's mind, it would prove a hell of a lot more interesting than Kate's incessant whining about the risks he took. Come to think of it, there were times a man could get a gutful without ever touching food.

Trotting along at his side, the mayor would have given considerable for a drink right at that moment. Isaac Porter was a troubled man, more than he cared to admit. He sensed that the townspeople were growing more and more disgruntled with the state of affairs that existed along the border. They had been brought to the brink of outright warfare with the Mexicans more times than anyone cared to remember; there was no longer a soul among them who questioned how far the Mexicans were willing to go to exact retribution. The fact that the Texans were vastly outnumbered sobered them even more, and it was hardly surprising that few men expected to come out of it alive if the bloodletting ever started.

More significantly still, word was spreading that the Bannings, along with their political and business cronies, were at the root of the trouble. Though this was only partially true, Porter could see that any further problems could easily bring about the downfall of the political machine he had helped to establish. Should that happen there was every likelihood that some of his more unsavory deals with the Bannings would come to light, and he had no wish to end up as an ornament on a telegraph pole. Which was just where this game might lead if something wasn't done fast. The Bannings weren't about to look out for anyone but themselves, even if the whole town was leveled to the ground; so that left it up to him. But it would be touch and go if Ed Banning ever got wind of what he had in mind.

When they reached the office, Stoudenmire sent Gillette to see about his own dinner, and they had the place to themselves. Porter took a chair across from the desk and gave the room a quick once over, like he expected a barrel of whiskey to roll out from under the corner bunk. The marshal just sat and waited, an old hand at the game of "out of the skillet and into the fire."

Porter had a distinct aversion to silence, as if a moment uncluttered by words was an opportunity lost forever, and he soon broke under the lawman's stony gaze. "Marshal, instead of beating around the bush, I'll come straight to the point. El Paso is faced with a crisis. Perhaps the one that could break the camel's back, in a manner of speaking. The killing of those three scoundrels last night has unsettled the people more than any other single incident I can recall. Even the salt war didn't frighten them like this. It's just too close to home."

"Mayor, before you start stretchin' for a second wind, why don't you get down to the point. It's beginning to look like a long day on an empty belly."

"To be sure, Marshal Stoudenmire. To be sure. But let me first impress on you the need for urgency. The Mexican populace on both sides of the river is only one step away from being up in arms. It would take nothing more than some insignificant mishap to put them at our throats.''

''Like raping another little girl?'' Stoudenmire remarked stiffly.

Overlooking the sarcasm, Porter pulled out a large handkerchief and mopped his face. ''Perhaps. Who knows what governs a Mexican's actions. The thing I'm leading up to is this. I believe the citizens of El Paso to be in greater mortal danger at this moment than ever before. The Mexicans lack only a leader to bring them storming across the river by the thousands. While we could put up a stiff fight with the help of the army, I harbor no illusions about the outcome. And unless we move quickly, that day may arrive sooner than anyone suspects.''

''I'll have to hand it to you. You're just a sack full of surprises.'' Stoudenmire scrutinized the politician's face for a long moment before resuming. ''Let's get our cards out on the table. You could talk till you were blue in the face, and I still wouldn't believe you're worried about the townspeople. Now suppose you quit making speeches and tell me what all this is about.''

''My boy, there are times in a man's life when he must set aside the lessons of the past and deal with the moment on its own merits. Perhaps your cynicism is well founded, but is it so hard to believe that even a politician can want what's best for his community?''

''Maybe. Maybe not. Most times when a politician gets to worrying about the lowly citizen, it's brought about by some threat of his own political survival. If that's what you're sayin', then I reckon I could swallow it.''

''Marshal, I won't deny that a certain concern for my own skin prompted me to arrange this discussion.'' Porter swabbed his face again with the handkerchief, shrewdly appraising his adversary. ''Just between us, I would even admit that those who view me as being corrupt are not without cause of a sort. But even if those things are true, a man can still have a genuine feeling for the people.''

Stoudenmire snorted contemptuously and gave the older man a flat, uncompromising stare. ''Whatever it is you want, why don't you just spit it out? All this hemming and hawing won't change things between you and me one iota.''

''Very well. To be perfectly frank about it, I was hoping you would have a talk with the *alcalde* of Paso del Norte. Word is spreading that you have done your best to head off trouble, and I have a feeling the Mexicans would listen to you. They already know what you've done to calm folks over here, and a request from you to hold their own people in check would carry a lot of weight. More than anyone else in this town, you have a strong chance of preventing further bloodshed.''

The mayor paused, meeting Stoudenmire's gaze squarely for the first time. ''Whatever your opinion of me, I hope you'll believe that I'm sincere in wanting to halt this violence.''

''Sure, I believe you. Your kind always gets squeamish when they see blood.'' The lawman gave him a look that would have raised frost on a brass cannon. ''I'll see the headman across the river, but don't think its got anything to do with you. If it was up to me, I'd feed you and your cronies to the Mexicans like dog meat.''

After a moment of strained silence, the mayor rose and walked out the door. There was nothing more to say. Stoudenmire would see the Mexicans well enough, but afterwards, he would be right back dogging the Bannings' tracks. And if some of the Banning underlings happened to get caught in the crunch, it wouldn't bother the marshal in the slightest. Thinking back to those cold eyes, it came over the dumpy little politician that Stoudenmire would probably even enjoy it.

Isaac Porter suddenly needed a drink in the worst way. The furies seemed to be gathering, and he had fought enough battles for one day.

3.

LATER THAT afternoon Stoudenmire crossed the Rio Grande and inquired directions to the *alcalde's* home. The somnolent village was like a hundred others he had seen along the border while serving with the Rangers, and it occurred to him that time had little effect on the casual pace of these people. Naked, taffy-skinned children rolled in the dirt right alongside mangy dogs, runty pigs, and a motley assortment of bleating goats. Women in sleazy, faded dresses tended the dirt-floored adobes while their men rested in the shade, ever confident that *mañana* would bring about a sharp reversal in their fortunes. They asked little of life, expected less, and somehow struggled along on the lean times that were part and parcel of border living.

Watching them as he rode along the dusty street, Stoudenmire was reminded again that at heart the Mexicans were warm, peace-loving people. They wished only to bask in the mellow sun, to be left alone. Still, even the most gentle creature on earth would turn and fight when driven to the wall. Thinking about it, he recalled that Mexicans weren't exactly disciplined fighters, but they were mean as a barrelful of snakes when it got right down to cut or be cut.

Dismounting before an unusually large adobe, he walked to the door and knocked. Even before the sound of his knuckles faded, the door swung back, revealing an elderly man who somehow appeared taller than he actually was.

"*Buenos días, señor,*" Pedro Vazquez greeted him. "How may I serve you?"

"*Buenos días, Alcalde.*" The lawman flashed that rare smile, which made it seem all the warmer. "I am Dallas Stoudenmire, marshal of El Paso. Pardon this unannounced intrusion, but I come hoping we might speak of matters mutually important to our people."

"Come in out of the heat, Marshal. I am honored that you would call on me and always welcome an exchange of ideas with our *americano* neighbors."

The *alcalde* led him back to a cool, high-ceilinged study and courteously offered refreshments. While they sipped hot chocolate, Vazquez held the conversation to idle small-talk, obviously trying to put the lawman at ease. After an appropriate round of pleasantries, centering on the weather and the merits of Paso wine, the older man sat back in his chair and folded his hands. With formalities out of the way, the serious business could now begin.

"My friend, I have long wanted to talk with a leader from your side of the river." Chuckling, Pedro Vazquez tapped his chest with a deprecating gesture. "But I am an old man given to excesses in speech. Suppose I first listen to what you have to say, for I am sure your errand is of no small consequence."

"*Gracias, Alcalde*. Your concern is not misplaced, I assure you." Then, without mincing words, Stoudenmire came straight to the point. "I am here seeking some way to bring about peace between our people. Failing that, I would hope to arrange a truce of some sort so that tempers on both sides of the Rio Grande might have time to cool."

The Mexican's brow furrowed in thought as he studied his guest. "This is no small thing you seek. Your countrymen are not noted for their peaceful ways, and unfortunately my people long ago lost faith in the honorable intentions of any *yanqui*."

Stoudenmire's mouth tightened at the blunt words, but there was no denying the truth behind them. "*Jefe*, your words are harsh, but not without justification. Like most men, Americans come in all shapes and sizes, some good, some bad. Yet it is a curious thing that the bad ones are always more visible; that they somehow seem to lead the good without a struggle, much like a tame bull with a ring in his nose. Still, if those same people are shown a way, they would much prefer to live in peace. Perhaps I reach too high, but should we be content with anything less than our people living as neighbors once more?"

"We also have our bad ones, the *bandidos* in the hills But strangely they prefer to prey on their own kind." The *alcalde* puzzled on this for a moment, wondering why the bandits never dared cross into Texas. It was a thought that would bear examination. "How would you propose to bring about this truce? It is an ambitious undertaking."

"Ambitious perhaps, but not impossible." The lawman searched Vazquez's face for any sign of guile, then decided to go whole hog. "The men responsible for our troubles are mostly Americans. This I admit freely. Already I have taken steps to calm the good ones among my people. Now, I will reveal for your ears alone, that I have taken the trail of the bad ones and hope to have them in jail soon. They are called Banning, and once I bring them to earth, many of our problems will be resolved."

"Yes, I have heard that name. Are these men responsible for the terrible raid of two nights past?" When Stoudenmire nodded, the Mexican came up on the edge of his chair. "This is a good thing you do, Marshal. *Bichos*, vermin like these men, should be stamped out wherever found."

Vazquez had watched his visitor closely, purposely letting him do the talking. Now he was convinced that this large, soft-spoken *gringo* before him was an honorable man. Within the last week, he had heard tales from his people across the river about Stoudenmire's efforts to avert open hostilities, and there appeared every reason to credit them as true. Suddenly a thing he had once said flashed through his mind. *There are times in a man's life when he must blindly trust other men, even* yanquis. Perhaps this was the place to start.

"Marshal, I wonder if you would care to join me in a humble supper? I wish to send for my nephew so that you might speak with him. What he has to say will prove most interesting, you can be sure."

Stoudenmire readily agreed, not quite sure what the *alcalde* had in mind but willing to gamble a few hours to find out. The supper they shared was far from humble, consisting of choice beef, various native dishes, and an unusually fine wine. After working his way through a second helping of everything, it occurred to the lawman that Mexican politicians must eat as high off the hog as their American counterparts. Still, the old man was chock full of amusing stories, and over brandy and cigars it came to Stoudenmire that he wasn't being entertained so lavishly without some purpose in mind. Whatever the game was, the stakes seemed right, and as long as he had taken a seat, he decided to enjoy himself. Listening to the *alcalde* launch into another whopper, he came to the conclusion that the old Mexican might just be a match for Doc Cummings. The two of them in the same room would probably be more than a man could take in one night.

Toward dusk, Ramón Vazquez arrived on a lathered horse and went into a whispered conference with his uncle. He, too, had heard stories concerning this *gringo* lawman and felt there was no harm in discussion. Walking forward, he shook Stoudenmire's hand with a firm grip.

"Our people across the river say you are *simpático* to the Mexican cause. We find this a very strange trait in a *yanqui*, especially one who serves the will of the *ladrones* who rule El Paso."

Stoudenmire was amused yet a little nettled by this shallow test. "You are a foolish young man to judge people so casually. Were I working for the *gringo* thieves, I wouldn't have missed." Jerking his chin, he indicated the arm that Ramón favored with every movement.

"*¿Quien sabe?*" Ramón shrugged, gigged on his own shaft and unable to wriggle free. "Who knows, perhaps there is such a thing as an honest *yanqui*?"

"Perhaps." Stoudenmire's mouth curled in a tight, dry smile. "But if you meet one, I wish you would point him out to me."

The young *caporal* laughed outright, turning to his uncle. "This hombre bears watching. It comes to me that the man hasn't been born who could order him against his will."

"In your own way, *mi hijo*, you have come to the right conclusion." The *alcalde* had been sitting back watching the exchange with much zest. "Now that you have taken his measure, I suggest you tell him of the matter we agreed upon."

Ramón glanced back at Stoudenmire, less suspicious now, but still not wholly trusting of any *gringo*. "Even if you betray us, I see no harm that can come of it. We are holding one of the raiders prisoner, and he has been persuaded to talk. Other than the details of the jailbreak last night, he has also revealed that one calling himself Ed Banning is the head of these *piojos*. We are still thinking on ways to make use of the one whose tongue has been loosened."

The lawman paced to the window and stood staring out into the night. Here was a chance to put a rope around Banning's neck, and it had been handed to him on a silver platter. Mexican silver at that. But if he was to pull it off, it would take the help of this young firebrand, and that might require some powerful convincing.

Facing the two Mexicans, he thanked them for their trust and asked that they consider what he had to say without judging it too quickly. Then in a terse, businesslike manner, he outlined his plan.

Ramón must accompany him to the Banning's ranch and identify the stolen cattle. As a US marshal, he would then arrest the Bannings and arrange their extradition to Mexico on charges of rustling and murder. With the testimony of the captive raider, they were certain to be convicted. Once they had had their moment before the firing squad, peace would again come to the border. There were many dangers involved, and the plan could easily fail. But as leaders of their two peoples they were obligated to try.

The *alcalde* thought on it for only a moment, then drew Ramón into another guarded conference. There was much risk to the plan, just as the *yanqui* lawman admitted. But then peace was rarely purchased cheaply. Somewhere in the midst of all this violence and bloodshed, men had to begin trusting one another. If the men to whom the people looked for leadership were unwilling to try then where would it ever begin? They must place themselves in the hands of this quiet *tejano* and pray to the Virgin that their faith had not been misplaced. How could a *jefe* do less and still look his people in the eye?

The old man and his nephew swung around to find Stoudenmire watching them closely. Ramón Vazquez stepped forward and extended his hand. He would appear at the marshal's office in the morning.

4.

EL PASO was just coming to life when Ramón crossed the river accompanied by two *vaqueros*. Townspeople blinked the sleep from their eyes and gaped in astonishment. Considering the temper of the moment, it was most unusual, if not downright alarming, for armed Mexicans to boldly ford the Rio Grande. Word raced ahead of them along the street, and by the time they reached Stoudenmire's office, a small crowd had gathered on the plaza. Speculation was rife as to their purpose, for it was indeed baffling to see greasers calling on a Texas lawman. That was one for the book, no doubt about it!

Then someone recalled seeing the marshal cross to Paso del Norte just yesterday. Suddenly this strange turn of events took on even more significance. Yet to what purpose? The reason for the Mexicans' presence still eluded them despite a rash of conjecture, and the onlookers were more bewildere than ever.

But if the townspeople were mystified, Ed Banning struggled under no such drawback. One of his men had spotted the brand on the *vaqueros*' horses, the Salazar Bar Lazy S. Hotfotting it over to the saloon, he blurted out that it was the same brand they had doctored on the rustled steers. The ones grazing contentedly on the Banning ranch right at that moment. Only the new brand was still fresh, and any fool would take it for exactly what it was. The Bar Lazy S doctored with a running iron.

Banning was a man who believed in hedging his bet, especially in a game where the stakes included his own neck. After pondering the matter briefly, he sent a rider to warn Kale. Under no circumstances were the Mexicans to reach the ranch alive. Stoudenmire wasn't to be touched, but if the greasers came anywhere near Banning range, they were to be gunned down on the spot. Perhaps they were in town for another reason entirely, stranger things had happened. Still, there was nothing to lose by playing it safe.

When Ramón dismounted before the jail, Stoudenmire stepped outside. "I see you have drawn a crowd, *amigo*. Come inside where we may talk freely."

"*Glacias*, Marshal," the *caporal* replied. "I would be the first to admit that such a pack of *gringos* makes my back itch in a most peculiar way."

The *vaqueros* left their horses ground-reined and followed Stoudenmire through the door. Gillette came forward with a glum smile, and after introductions had been attended to, they got down to the business at hand. Motioning Ramón to a chair, the marshal took his seat behind the desk.

"I am pleased to see that you had no second thoughts about out little venture. Many men would place a greater *precio* on their lives."

"*De nada.*" Ramón waved aside the compliment. "It is nothing, I assure you. There are many things a man can live with, but fear makes a jealous companion."

As he spoke, the Mexican glanced uneasily at Tige. The big dog hadn't moved from Stoudenmire's side, and Ramón found it difficult to ignore his cold stare. "This one could teach us both the meaning of courage, I suspect. With such a dog even the darkness holds no secrets for a man. *¿El lobo bajo, eh?*"

"The little wolf?" Stoudenmire gave Tige a rough pat. "Yes, I suppose he would accept that well enough. Yet he was named for the one *vaqueros* have learned to respect above all others. *El tigre.*"

"*Sí*, and rightly so. Never have I seen a dog whose manner so closely resembles that of the spotted death. But enough of such things. We have more important matters to discuss. How are we to proceed with our own hunt?"

The lawman tilted back in his chair, hands locked behind his head. "The Banning *rancho* lies something over twenty kilometers to the northeast. We will ride there and conduct a quiet search for your cattle. If we can avoid being seen, so much the better. If not, then we may be forced to fight. Either way, we will stay until we find what we seek."

"*¡Está bueno!*" Ramón flashed a pearly grin. "I like your view of things, *amigo*. We go, we look, and if anyone objects, we fight. *¡Madre de Dios!* You should have been born a *vaquero*."

"Perhaps it is good I wasn't." Stoudenmire smiled lightly. "One *charro* of your boldness seems to be all Chihuahua can afford at the moment. Now, let us come to the crucial part of what we do. Suppose you draw for me the brand used by Don Salazar. Then we will attempt to determine how these *ladrones* might have altered it."

Ramón took the pencil and paper Stoudenmire indicated and slowly began sketching the Bar Lazy S. Gillette and the two *vaqueros* moved in closer until the five men were huddled around the desk. Once the drawing was completed, they began experimenting with various ways it could be changed. But they had more ideas than pencils, and before long, a lively debate was raging as to exactly what they should look for once on Banning land.

Some twenty minutes later, Stoudenmire and Ramón rode east from El Paso, trailed by the two *vaqueros*. Gillette had argued to be taken along, but the marshal ordered him to remain behind. Someone had to police the town, and it would never do for both of them to be gone at the same time. Tige didn't care much for the arrangement either, and as the four men rode off, it occurred to the long-faced deputy that they had been left to hold a fort that hardly rated defending.

After traveling eastward on the main road for some miles, the horsemen swung north on a narrow, rutted trail. There wasn't much to see in this desolate land, and Stoudenmire used the time to get better acquainted with the young *caporal*. The lawman found him a very likeable sort, maybe a shade too formal for a Texan's tastes, but the kind of man a fellow wouldn't mind having at his side when push came to shove. Like many Mexicans, he was a little short-fused, and there was no doubt that he was headstrong. Too much so. The way an unbroken stud has a mind all its own. A pound of daring in the same keg with fiery temper made for an explosive mix, one that could get everyone around it blown sky high if sparks ever flew the wrong way. Still he was an engaging cuss when he wanted to be, without a devious bone in his body, and it was a damn cinch he didn't fear anything this side of perdition itself. That kind were few and far between, and a man was lucky if he crossed trails with two or three in an entire lifetime. Yet Stoudenmire wasn't the sort who committed himself quickly where people were concerned. Ramón had the stuff to make a good friend, no two ways about it. Something on the order of Jim Gillette, only a feisty pepper-ball instead of plodding foxiness. But there was plenty of time, and thinking about it, he decided to reserve judgment until they had been back to back a couple of times.

Something over an hour after taking the winding trail, the riders approached a small chain of sandhills, bordered by an outcropping of huge boulders and mesquite trees. While there were no fences or boundary markers, the men knew they were nearing Banning land, and they became alert for any sign of cattle. As the road entered a draw, flanked on either side by higher ground, Stoudenmire felt his hackles come up.

Something was out of kilter, but he couldn't quite put a name to it.

Before he could react, both sides of the draw came alive with a sharp crack of Winchesters. The lawman rammed his spurs home, but his horse needed little urging. The chestnut hit a gallop in three strides, and Stoudenmire hunched low over the saddle. Out of the corner of his eye, he saw two of the Mexican horses falter and go down, then he was out of the draw and running clear.

Glancing back, he caught a quick glimpse of Ramón and another *vaquero* returning the fire from behind their downed horses. The other Mexican was spraddled beside the road, obviously dead. But even as he turned his horse to assist the trapped men, the hills and rocks erupted with flame, slamming Ramón and the *vaquero* to the earth.

Wheeling the chestnut, he cursed himself for a fool and rode north, circling the sandhills. The blood pounded against his temples, and his teeth gritted so hard his jaw-bone hurt. *Why them and not me*? Did some ungodly specter ride with him that neither he nor his horse had been hit? By what miracle had he come through that hail of lead without so much as a scratch?

Then it came clear. *They hadn't meant to shoot him!* They were after the three Mexicans, and as sure as Christ was spiked to a cross, that stolen cattle herd would be off Banning range before nightfall. For that matter, the bastards might already be trailing the longhorns toward some more remote spot. But with the thought came a vivid kaleidoscope of the murderous fire he had just ridden through, and he knew that every gun on the Banning payroll must have been hidden in that draw.

Suddenly it dawned on him why he had been allowed to live. The Mexicans would blame him for Ramón's death! When violence flared anew, he would be caught squarely in the middle, and he could almost hear the angry chant of the townspeople when they denounced him as a meddling fool.

The chestnut grunted as he raked savagely with his spurs and cut cross-country toward El Paso. The least he could do was get a wagon and return the dead men to their native land.

Then he'd see about settling the Bannings' hash. After today they were past due. Way past due.

5.

SHORTLY AFTER midnight Stoudenmire walked through the doors of the Coliseum with Tige at his heels. Word of the ambush had swept through town like wildfire, and a hush fell over the crowd as he crossed the room. The head barkeep exchanged nervous glances with a pug-nosed bouncer, but neither of them stirred from their tracks. Something about the look on the marshal's face made a man think twice, and it took more nerve than they had between them to try blocking his path. Without bothering to knock, Stoudenmire entered Banning's office and slammed the door behind him.

Ed and Sam Banning were startled by the lawman's sudden appearance, yet they returned his cold stare evenly. Stoudenmire's features were ashen, somehow wooden looking, as though he had just cut the cards with death itself. His hooded eyes gave off a flat sheen, like stained glass in strong sunlight, and every fiber in his body seemed taut as shrunken rawhide.

Ed Banning had seen the killing urge in men's eyes before, but he wasn't particularly intimidated by Stoudenmire's flinty gaze. He had faced many mankillers in his day, and he was still around to tell the tale. Fear was what got a man laid out on a cold slab, while caution was what separated the quick from the dead. The lawman had plainly come looking for trouble, primed to kill—the way a bear thinned by winter noses fresh scent. The gang leader never doubted for a moment that one miscue on his part would trigger a gunfight. But this deal shaped up as a cold deck, and he hadn't the slightest intention of being provoked into a showdown. Stoudenmire's death at their hands would serve no useful purpose, and Banning had already decided to remain calm in the event he forced the issue.

"Evenin', Marshal. Have a seat and rest your feet." Banning's amiable manner was decidedly strained. "Sam, get Marshal Stoudenmire a drink of the good stuff."

When Sam started out of his chair, Tige gathered himself, growling low in his throat. The burly ruffian eyed the dog, then glanced up at the lawman. "Call your hound off or I'll twist a knot in his tail."

"Sonny, you lip off to me and I'm gonna stunt your growth." Stoudenmire's tone was flat, deadly, clearly inviting him to pick up the dare. "Crawl back in your cage or get stomped. Your choice."

"Back off, Sam!" Banning's sharp command froze the younger brother in his chair. "Just keep your mouth shut and let me do the talking. Now, Marshal, let's get down to brass tacks. Since you're not here on a sociable visit, suppose you just state your business."

"Banning, your string has run out in El Paso. From here on it's devil take the hindmost." The words whipped across the room like pearls of stinging frost. "If you're still around when your number's called, I'll come looking."

The Bannings simply watched him, neither man moving so much as a hair. Stoudenmire remained motionless just inside the door, yet he somehow seemed calmer, even stoic now that he had kicked the lid off. But his unruffled manner was merely the cool shell that settles over an old hand as he steels himself for a fight. His hand hung loose, poised at his side, awaiting some flicker of movement that would send it streaking toward the Colt on his hip. He was ready to kill, and they both knew it.

''Marshal, that's a real pretty speech, but it won't hold water.'' Banning was very careful with his hands, but his voice was steady and firm. ''You're gonna find yourself choppin' tall cotton if you try to run us out of town. And I don't think you've got what it takes to shoot us down in cold blood.''

''Banning, you've been drawing aces so long you forgot what it's like to wind up on the short end.'' Stoudenmire saw they weren't going to fight, but he wasn't ready to call it quits. ''Tonight I posted a wanted circular on the Notice Tree. It's got Tom Kale's name on it, and the charge is murder. I'm tempted to save the state the cost of a trial when I run him down. On the other hand, I might just bring him into court and let him put a noose around your neck. Sorta makes your milk curdle, don't it?''

For a moment Ed Banning was too dumbstruck to reply. The Notice Tree in the center of the plaza hadn't been used since Texas won independence. Only in extreme cases was a man's name tacked to the ancient trunk, for it meant he was wanted dead or alive. And few were ever brought in except across the back of a horse.

''Stoudenmire, it appears to me your luck is runnin' a mite thin. I assume you're talkin' about those Mexicans getting killed north of town this morning. But it's gonna be kinda hard to hang a man without witnesses. Course, you're such a smart fellow you might figure out some way to bring them greasers back to life.''

The lawman's mouth twisted in a grim smile. ''I already have. Leastways one of them is healthy enough to identify your ramrod as one of the bushwhackers. Besides, I was there myself, and I'm not likely to forget Kale's face. Offhand, I'd say my testimony, along with the Mexican's, would just about make him a cinch bet for the scaffold.''

This latter statement was sheer bluff. Stoudenmire hadn't seen anything but smoke and gunflashes that morning, and even that had been from the back of a galloping horse. Still there was no one to dispute his claim, and it might just force Kale to come looking for him.

The marshal glanced over at Sam, then back to the older brother. "Banning, I always believe in giving a man an even break. I'll spot you gents a headstart, and we can settle this whole deal right now. Otherwise, I'll crowd you so hard you'll kiss my ass and bark like a fox before we're through."

Ed Banning was tempted, but only for a moment. While one of them might get the lawman, he was damn near certain that the big bastard's first slug would catch him about brisket high. And he hadn't the slightest intention of becoming the late political boss of El Paso.

"Sorry to disappoint you, Marshal, but we'll sit this hand out. And if you're bankin' on that tin star to see you through, you're gonna find out it's nothin' but a damn fine target. When you walk out that door, you'd better keep right on going."

"Banning you can cut your wolves loose anytime you want. Makes no difference to me. I'll still get you."

Stoudenmire turned and walked from the room. When the door slammed shut, the Banning brothers breathed an immense sigh of relief. They had come close, perhaps closer than they had ever been in their lives. For the last few minutes, Old Scratch had been leaning over their shoulders, and his breath had a hot, fetid smell. Like a bouquet of dead snapdragons.

Crossing the plaza moments later, Stoudenmire cursed the Bannings for a pair of gutless fourflushers. While they wouldn't hesitate to shoot a man in the back, they didn't have the stomach for a face to face showdown, even with two to one odds. The thought touched a raw nerve and his mind drifted back to that afternoon when he had returned to the draw with a wagon.

Already the vultures had gathered, circling ever nearer as the sun warmed their supper. The Mexicans called them *buitres*, and the name fitted like a glove. Filthy scavengers who spent their lives squabbling over rotted carrion in a land that seemed as dead as the flesh they ate. Watching them glide overhead, he had thought that it really didn't matter much one way or the other. When you are dead, a box or a buzzard amounts to about the same thing. Maybe one is a little slower, but no less final.

When he pulled up in the draw, the Mexicans lay just as they had fallen. Walking among them, he again cursed the dirty bastards who had gunned them down so mercilessly. But when he rolled Ramón over, his pulse quickened, and cold beads of sweat popped out on his forehead. Astonishing as it seemed, the young *caporal* still had a spark of life in him. Not much, but a hell of a lot more than Stoudenmire ever expected to find in a man carrying at least four slugs.

Plugging up the holes as best he could, the lawman loaded Ramón in the wagon and raced for El Paso. A doctor worked over him until late evening, pronouncing it an act of the Almighty that the greaser had survived. Somehow none of the slugs had struck a vital organ, and while his days as a *vaquero* were finished, the sawbones gave him a fifty-fifty chance of pulling through.

Leaving Gillette to guard Ramón, the marshal had then returned to the jailhouse to think out his next move. With his blood running cold, the decision wasn't long in coming. *Force the Bannings up against the wall. Make them fight or run.* But the Bannings seemed disinclined to jump in either direction. They refused to fight, and they showed no signs of making a run for it. Like the *buitres,* they were going to wait and watch, and whatever they had up their sleeves would more than likely come on a dark street when a man least expected it.

Passing the Notice Tree as he headed back to check on Ramón, the lawman had a feeling that El Paso was about to live up to its reputation as the toughest town along the border.

CHAPTER FIVE

1.

EL PASO hadn't exactly returned to normal, but in the two weeks since the bushwhacking, a guarded calm had settled over the town. Like a man holding a stick of dynamite with a sputtering fuse, the townspeople waited for an explosion that seemed dreadfully slow in coming.

Though an inquest into the killings was to be held, it had been delayed until tempers on both sides of the river cooled down. Ed Banning had pulled strings to force an immediate hearing, but when Stoudenmire threatened to expose it as a political fix, the coroner hastily backed off. The local gadflies chalked this up as another point for the marshal and sat back to await results.

Mayor Porter trotted out one lame excuse after another for the postponement, but the real issue behind this political infighting was hardly a secret. Stoudenmire was determined there would be no inquest until his key witness was able to testify. As the sole survivior among the ambushed Mexicans, Ramón Vazquez had much to tell, and the gambling fraternity was laying odds that his testimony would send half the Banning gang scurrying for their holes.

After a week of guarding the *caporal* around the clock, Stoudenmire had secretly moved him to Paso del Norte, figuring he was considerably safer among his own people. Ramón's recovery had been little short of remarkable, considering his wounds; yet he was mending slowly, and the marshal had to curb his impatience as best he could. Until an inquest was held, the wanted circular on Tom Kale was strictly unofficial, and he desperately needed the Mexican's testimony in open court to nail it down tight.

Then, as the uneasy standoff entered its third week, the turning point came. Just before leaving the office for his noon meal, the marshal received word from Pedro Vazquez that Ramón was much improved and anxious to testify. Stoudenmire immediately paid a call on the coroner, who seemed delighted that the troublesome affair was at last coming to a head. When Stoudenmire suggested that the fewer the spectators the better, the nervous little official agreed wholeheartedly and set the inquest for the middle of the week. That way people would have to choose between curiosity and their livelihood, which would hold down the size of the crowd some at any rate. Whether it was enough to maintain order remained to be seen.

Arriving home for dinner, Stoudenmire seemed in a zestful mood for the first time in longer than Kate could remember. As she was serving the table, he playfully swatted her on the rump, something he hadn't done since the day of the ambush.

"Better watch it, missy." Patting her hips again, he gave her figure an appraising look. "Feels like you're putting on a little beef in the wrong places."

Kate shot him an indignant glance and moved around the table to her seat. "How would you know? The last couple of weeks I began to think you had lost interest in things like that."

"Lost interest? Hell, I've just been restin' up." Smearing butter over a slice of bread, he grinned mischievously. "You pretty near wore me down to a nubbin' there for a while. Course, I'm not complaining, mind you. It's just that I thought I'd married a tabby cat, and it turns out I got myself a lady catamount."

"Oh, that's not fair. You're the one that always starts it." Kate's face turned beet red as she toyed with the food on her plate. "Besides, you said yourself that there's nothing wrong with a woman wanting to please her husband."

Stoudenmire chuckled deep in his throat. "And herself, too. Don't forget, it takes two to ring the bell."

Kate had never seen him so talkative. And playful, like a naughty little boy with some prank in mind. Coming out of a clear blue like this, it left her a bit flustered. "My, but aren't you chattery today. Did the city council give you a raise or something?"

"Better than that." The lawman paused in the midst of spearing another pork chop. "Ramón Vazquez is ready to talk, and we're gonna hold the inquest day after tomorrow. Christmas comes early this year."

She watched his sure hands carve the pork chop, her own food now forgotten. "That means you'll finally get the evidence you've been waiting for."

"Not just evidence, Katie. There's more to it than that. Once Vazquez says his piece, it'll force the Bannings' hand and they'll have to fish or cut bait."

"What you really mean is that they'll have to fight or run. And either way, you'll go after them."

"Sure. What do you think I've been after since we came here? Tom Kale is their foreman, and once he's indicted, it'll smoke the Bannings out in the open. That's what I've really been waiting for. Evidence is all right, I reckon, but the only way to nail the Bannings and make sure they stay nailed is to crowd 'em into a corner."

Stoudenmire's eagerness for this encounter was readily apparent, for he clearly saw it as the most expedient means of putting the Bannings on ice. Seldom was he so enthused about anything, and it was as though the prospect of a good fight had rekindled his sense of humor. But Kate found it difficult, if not outright impossible, to share his mood. They had been married less than two months, and she was discovering that the law is a demanding mistress. Stoudenmire seemed like a man possessed, as if his every waking thought was devoted to the downfall of the Bannings. That left room for little else—wives included—and more than ever, she had begun to question the wisdom of marrying a peace officer.

With some reluctance, she had admitted to herself that she was jealous of his dedication to the law. This wasn't married life as she had envisioned it, especially since the gaiety of their courtship had been replaced with his grim compulsion to tame El Paso. Still, even that would have been bearable if she weren't so frightened. This stranger who shared her bed was plainly more concerned about some piddling inquest than he was with the shaky state of their marriage. But while she resented that fiercely, she felt numbed by the thought that the hearing would place him one step closer to a showdown with the Bannings. Some inner premonition told her that he hadn't a prayer of living through the fight that was sure to follow.

After all, what effect could one man have on a town like this? He was backed only by Gillette and that ungodly dog, while the Bannings had a small army at their beck and call. It wasn't just foolish, it was downright thoughtless! When it was over, he would be conveniently dead, and she'd be left to do all the suffering alone. Just thinking about it made her blood boil, and it came over her that she must have been mad to marry a selfish little boy who liked dangerous games better than he did a warm bed.

"Dallas, we're going to have this out here and now. You have no right to go out and get yourself killed. It's just not fair. Even if you don't care for your own sake, you should be thinking about me."

Stoudenmire just smiled and shook his head, thoroughly amused by her petulant little tantrum. The thought of getting killed had never entered his mind. The likelihood was so farfetched that it was almost laughable. "Kate, you're gettin' goosebumps where it's not called for. Whenever I start something, I generally manage to finish it."

"Dallas Stoudenmire, don't you dare take that tone with me! I won't be treated like a simpering little schoolgirl, not by you or anyone else. And while we're at it, you might as well know that I didn't get married just to become a grass widow before I've even gotten used to sleeping with a man."

"C'mon, Kate. You're acting like a spoiled brat, yet you want me to treat you like a woman. You know a man can't turn his back on a job and walk off. Not and live with himself."

"You would if you loved me! Don't you understand, Dallas? I want a live husband, not a dead hero. If you loved me, you'd take me away from here this very day, before something terrible happens."

Stoudenmire rubbed his forehead with growing exasperation. "That's what I'm trying to tell you. Nothing's gonna happen. Not to me leastways. Why can't you get that through your head?"

Huge tears welled up in Kate's eyes, and she hid her face in her hands. "Oh, Dallas, please take me away from this horrible town. Please. I just don't know how much more I can stand."

Stoudenmire came around the table and took her in his arms, tenderly consoling her. But the more he talked the harder she cried, and it seemed like a losing proposition. Then a curious thing happened. Irritating as her nagging had become, something about Kate's utter defenselessness aroused him, making his breath come short and fast. Switching tactics, he began to kiss the soft hair at the nape of her neck and, after a moment, started fondling her breasts. At first she lay rigid and unyielding in his arms; then she slowly began to respond, and a hungry little moan escaped her lips.

"Oh, God, it's been so long. I thought I'd just shrivel up and die waiting for you to touch me again."

Stoudenmire kissed her gently, rubbing his hands lightly along her thigh. "I know. I'm a damn fool to get so wrapped up in a job. But everything'll be all right now. You'll see. There's nothin' at the office that can't wait, and we've got all afternoon to ring those bells any way you want."

Lifting her in his arms, he felt Kate nuzzle softly against his shoulder. Women were strange creatures, so easy to neglect and so damned miserable to live with when they weren't being bedded properly. Maybe an afternoon of diddling every now and then was just what she needed. Certainly it would keep her spirits shored up, and that alone would make it worthwhile. Come to think of it, a matinee here and there wouldn't do him any harm either.

But even as he carried her toward the bedroom, he knew

it wouldn't change things for him. The job still had to be done.

2.

ED BANNING sipped at the whiskey, only vaguely aware that the henna-haired whore had snuggled closer to his lean body. She had been working on him for nearly an hour without noticeable results, and it seemed apparent she would have to go some to earn her keep tonight. Yet the gang boss made no sign that he wanted her to stop, and the girl never once slackened her efforts. She had seen what happened to other whores who couldn't get it up for Banning, and her instinct for survival was too finely honed to take chances like that. But as her fingers teasingly probed his body, she wished mightily that his rod could become as hard as his face. Around the house, the girls had coined a saying for men like this. *Stone face—soft tool.* And with the exception of a wooden Indian, she couldn't think of anyone who had a better claim to the title than this unresponsive turd sharing her bed at the moment.

Boss Banning was a man with a wide assortment of problems, most of which remained obscured behind an aloof, somewhat haughty manner. The outward, more obvious troubles had to do with the threat to his control of the town. He was a lifelong believer in the process of corruption and deeply suspicious of those who advocated the straight and narrow. From his warped perspective, men were greedy, selfish, lacking in either scruples or anything even remotely akin to brotherhood. While he hadn't invented the rules, he was a master of the game and found it well suited to his ruthless nature. Corruption and fear were the tools of his trade, employed mercilessly in his drive to dominate those around him. The strong ruled the weak, just as it should be; the only part of the earth inherited by the meek was the six feet that marked their passing. And until Dallas Stoudenmire came to town, the essential weakness of other men had served him well.

But on this particular night, Banning's thoughts were

focused on a problem that had little to do with politics and forthright lawmen. While he would be the last to admit it, the gang leader was a man of flawed character. The obsession with power that governed his life was merely a manifestation of some inner compulsion; the need to be accepted as a man of substance and stature. His origins were of the dirt poor, beans and sowbelly variety, and within him smoldered the effects of having been born on the wrong side of the blanket. Every facet of his life was tainted by the lowly circumstances of his birth, and from it sprung a bitter resentment of both the haves and the have-nots. He despised the masses for their docile fatalism and hated the wealthy few with the passions of a man reared amidst constant want. The gritty flintstone of his life had chipped and flaked with each blow, leaving a man of choleric malice in the aftermath. As if human warmth had been seared from his being, he was a man devoid of compassion, even for himself. The only emotions he had ever known were a hard fist and a stiff prick. So it was that his life had become a mockery of what other men held sacred, one in which there was neither feeling nor mercy. In Ed Banning's world, force of will alone prevailed, and strength was rarely tempered with selfless motives.

Yet something had gone awry in his relentless pursuit of prominence. The most visible symbol of all he coveted was denied him, and without it he remained but a pale reflection of the man he had set out to become.

Never in his life had he lain with a decent woman.

Well-bred girls wanted nothing to do with a man whose very existence was a blasphemy in itself, and since boyhood, his overtures had been met with the casual disdain reserved for those beneath contempt. Instead of the mansion and genteel wife he had envisioned, he constantly deluded himself in the belief that saloon girls could actually be seduced. When even that became too bothersome, he simply returned to the whorehouses. Strangely, he felt some kinship with these soiled ladies of the night, for his own origins were only one step above the kingdom of whores. And although he detested himself for wallowing in such filth, it was almost as if he had come home each time he returned.

But it was far from a satisfying experience. Amidst frowzy women and stale whiskey, he attempted to elude the furies of his personal hell, only to find that a man can never really outdistance the stench of his own soul. That fickle bitch called fate had allowed him to play with crooked dice well enough but loaded them in her own sly way so that he turned up craps with every roll.

There, sipping whiskey and watching a whore sweat over his intractable body, was where Tom Kale found him. When the knock sounded at the door, the redhead hastily covered them both with a sheet, as if modesty dictated that only her partner of the moment be allowed to gaze upon the merchandise.

"Come on in," Banning called. "We're not bashful."

The door opened, and Kale stepped into the room, peering owlishly through the cider glow of the table lamp. "Howdy, boss. Didn't mean to catch you with your pants down, but I've got to see you *pronto.*"

Banning untangled himself from the girl and gave her what passed for a smile. "Sugartit, why don't you run down and get us another bottle. Give me ten minutes, and then we'll pick up where we left off."

The whore scrambled from the bed and into a robe, then headed for the door. She was happy for the respite, no matter how brief. Maybe with a little rest the cold bastard would get some lead back in his pecker. Otherwise, she was in for one long, asshole of a night.

When the door closed behind her, Banning's words came like a slap in the face. "You pinheaded sonovabitch! I oughta have you skinned alive. You've got a lot of nerve showin' up here after you let one of them greasers get out alive."

"Boss, you're treein' the wrong squirrel." Kale moved toward the bed, trying his best to look innocent. "Honest to Christ, them greasers looked deader'n old horse turds. There wasn't no reason to think otherwise, and we was in a hurry to get on back to start trailin' that herd outa there."

"I've told you before, you're not paid to think. You're

paid to . . ." Banning bit off the words with a sharp click of his teeth. "What the hell are you doing in town? I thought I sent word for you to lay low."

"Sure, I know. But I got somethin' I figured you wanted to hear."

"Well isn't that dandy? Stoudenmire's got you posted, and you come lollygaggin' into town like school had just let out. You fuckin' dingbat, what if he caught you up here whispering in my ear? You figure to talk us both out of jail?"

"Boss, if you'll quit rawhidin' me, I'll say my piece and get on back to the ranch." The foreman sucked up what backbone he had left and met Banning's stare head-on. "Hell, I wouldn't have come in if it wasn't important."

The gang leader snorted derisively and polished off his drink. "All right, Kale. I'm listening. But you'd better make it damned good."

"It's better'n that." Kale leaned over the brass frame at the foot of the bed, grinning like a skunk in a cabbage patch. "I just had me a little sashay across the river, and I found out where them greasers are holdin' the boy we lost in that raid. They got him locked in a shed close by the *hacienda,* and they feed him once a day, just like he was some kind o' pet dog. I was sorta thinkin' me and the boys would scoot in there some night and bring him back to the fold. That'd really teach them Mex bastards a lesson."

"Your thinkin' is gonna get you killed yet." Banning jabbed his finger in Kale's face, and the ramrod backed away from the bed. "I don't want the sonovabitch rescued. I want him dead! He broke once and he'll break again, even if we get him out. They're planning to spring him on us at the inquest, just as sure as you're standin' there. And if they do, we're gonna be up shit creek without a paddle. Understand, Kale? We'll be swingin' on the wrong side of a long rope."

Kale shook his head with a bewildered frown. "Boss, you're gonna have to run that one by again. How can they lynch us for rustlin' Mexican cattle?"

Banning sighed heavily, staring at the foreman with disgust. "The law calls it corroboration. They've got that greaser you missed, and they've got one of our own men. If those two get up in court and tell the same story, then the fact that we rustled those steers will tie us to the killings. In case it slipped your mind, in Texas they hang people for murder. Even if it was greasers."

Kale nodded dumbly, thoroughly convinced they were in mortal danger. The gang leader poured a shot of whiskey and knocked it down in one gulp. Only then did he look back at the bemused ramrod.

"I don't care how you do it, but I want you to make sure neither of 'em gets to that inquest on his feet. If you miss this time, don't bother coming back. That's my last warning, and you're a dead man if you don't deliver the bacon this trip out."

Kale didn't even bother to argue the point. Banning held the case ace, and only a fool bet into a sure-fire lock. The ramrod simply nodded and walked from the room.

Banning watched him out the door, then settled back against the pillows. No damn wonder he couldn't get up a boner lately, what with Stoudenmire breathing down his neck and numbskulls like Kale stepping in shit everytime they turned around. Thinking about it reminded him of the redhead, and he began listening for her footstep. Maybe the little bitch had thought up a new trick while she was gone. If she knew what was good for her, she had better come up with something. His pole needed greasing, and this goddamn waiting around for her to get it hard was enough to set a man's teeth on edge.

3.

THE DAY of the inquest was overcast and unusually muggy, a bad sign according to those who believed in such things. Tension among the townspeople was thicker than ever, and as the final hour approached, a crowd began to gather on the plaza. Stoudenmire's hopes of holding the hearing without a bunch of hotheads jamming the streets were fast dwindling. The people of El Paso had as much at stake as the Mexicans, maybe more if violence erupted, and they fully intended to be in on the showdown.

When it became known that a time for the inquest had finally been set, word circulated through town that an army of Mexicans planned to attend the hearing. Like most rumors, nobody knew if this one was true or not, but it was enough to make grown men lay awake at night. The town began to bristle with armed men, carrying not just pistols but a regular arsenal of rifles and scatterguns that hadn't seen use since the last Indian scare. The stage was set for a bloody war, one the Americans couldn't hope to win, and Stoudenmire suddenly awoke to the fact that he desperately needed help.

Bracing Mayor Porter two nights past, he had demanded official action of some sort. The army had already shown its reluctance to interfere in civilian matters; and on the face of it, that left only the Texas Rangers. Porter had no choice but to approve the marshal's request and promptly fired off a wire to Austin appealing for reinforcements. Once again, the aging politico found himself unable to guarantee the safety of his own town. Perhaps Ed Banning would raise hell about calling in state police, but under the circumstances, their options seemed severely limited.

After a flurry of telegraph messages between Porter and the capital, the governor had finally authorized his request. But there was considerable resentment in Austin about the whole affair, and Porter was given to understand that he had better straighten the mess out once and for all, and be damned quick about it. Otherwise, the governor would declare martial law and dump the entire nest of worms right in the army's lap.

The Ranger company had arrived late last night on the evening train. This time they were commanded by no less a veteran than Capt. Frank McCormak, and it was clear that there would be no repetition of the salt war fiasco. Though McCormak and a goodly number of his men were old friends, Stoudenmire found them strangely distant. Their attitude inferred that he, like everyone else in El Paso, had his own bone to pick. With so many factions in contention, the Rangers simply couldn't afford to take sides, and McCormak made it clear that, unless violence broke out, his company would remain in the background.

When Stoudenmire attempted to brief him on the Bannings and the political struggle underlying the conflict with the Mexicans, Capt. McCormak had cut him off short. The Rangers were interested in safeguarding the citizens of El Paso, and nothing more. The political bickering among the town leaders was none of their concern, and Stoudenmire would just have to skin that cat the best way he could. The marshal had turned on his heel and walked off, thoroughly baffled by McCormak's contemptuous manner. So far as he was concerned, the Rangers would be about as much use as a busted paddle, and he had the very distinct feeling that it was going to be all upstream from here on out.

The hour for the inquest was drawing near, and as the crowd on the plaza continued to swell in number, Stoudenmire found himself growing more apprehensive by the moment. This deal had about it everything necessary for the worst massacre since the Alamo, yet there wasn't a damn thing he could do to head it off. Worrying about Kate, and Ramón, and how to nail the Bannings had been enough for any man, not to mention the subtle pressure from Seth Hart and his crowd. But wondering if the Rangers were going to sit on their thumbs until it was too late had hatched a quandary that left him surly and foul-tempered. If the bastards weren't anything more than official observers then they should have stayed in east Texas, where the battles had already been fought. Still, their presence alone might put the damper on a few hotheads, and right now, he would take all the help he could get. Folks always talked about not looking a gift horse in the mouth, and in this instance it seemed to fit.

Abruptly, his sullen mood was broken when yells went up outside that the Mexicans were coming. Stepping to the door, Stoudenmire watched with some amazement as Ramón drove up in a buggy, surrounded by nearly fifty mounted *vaqueros*. The Mexicans presented quite a formidable appearance with their wide brimmed, floppy hats, bandoliers crossed over their chests, and rifles resting on the pommel of each saddle. They plainly meant business, and if anybody was fool enough to try crossing them, there would be a whole batch of new widows in El Paso tonight.

Walking toward the buggy, Stoudenmire gestured at the *caporal's* escort. "*¿Que pasa, Ramón?*" Such a show of force is indeed surprising. I thought we had agreed to keep this affair peaceful."

Ramón was dressed in the traditional short black jacket with large silver coins for buttons, and his pants had a faint silver pattern woven down each side. Despite a slight pallor to his features, he appeared as fiery as ever, and it seemed hard to believe that he was still recuperating from the murderous wounds of a fortnight past. He looked like a young *caballero* on his way to a fiesta, though on closer examination, there was something older and infinitely sadder about his eyes.

Leaning forward, his voice dropped to a near whisper. "*Hombre,* much has happened this day. None of it good. The *gringo* prisoner was to be brought from Don Miguel's *hacienda* to Paso del Norte early this morning. I regret to say that he and his guards were ambushed by *yanquis pistoleros*. He was killed with the first shot, and it goes without saying that he has been silenced forever concerning who is behind the *conspiración* among your people."

"Dirty bastards." Stoudenmire's eyes narrowed, and he unconsciously glanced in the direction of the Coliseum Saloon.

"*Sí.* That is the least of what they are." Ramón's mouth was set in a tight, thin line. "Without the *gringo*, I fear our cause is hopeless, but I am still willing to testify. As for these *vaqueros*, I had no choice. Don Salazar refused to allow me across the river without a large escort. You would do well to caution your people, for after this morning, these men would gladly spill *gringo* blood."

The lawman was silent for a time, gazing thoughtfully at the armed horsemen. "*Un momento, amigo*. Let me have a word with the Ranger leader."

Turning, he walked toward the Rangers, who were standing in a small knot beside the jail. Capt. McCormak saw him approaching and stepped forward a few paces.

Stoudenmire gave it to him straight, without any frills.

"Frank, those *vaqueros* are spoiling for a fight. We can go into the reasons later, if you're interested. Right now, we've got to keep 'em apart from the local hotheads, or we're gonna have more dead bodies around here than you've seen since Shiloh."

McCormak studied the Mexicans for a moment, then looked back at the lawman. "I reckon we can help you that much. I'll put it down in my report as a preventive measure."

Stoudenmire's mouth twisted in a sardonic grin. "You're a real sport, Frank. The next time you see the governor, be sure and tell him I said to kiss my ass."

Wheeling about, he returned to the buggy and helped Ramón to dismount. The Mexican hobbled a bit from his wounds, but he was game as ever, and Stoudenmire led him toward the coroner's office on the north side of the plaza. McCormak quickly brought the Rangers forward and formed a line separating the *vaqueros* from the townspeople. In a loud, contentious voice, he announced that no one would be allowed inside the hearing room except officials and witnesses. A sullen groan went up from the crowd, but nobody made a move in the direction taken by Stoudenmire and the *caporal*. The Rangers alone would have been enough, but with fifty armed greasers right behind them, it was a little more than anyone cared to tackle on an empty stomach.

Jim Gillette fell in on the other side of Ramón, and as the three men neared the coroner's office, Gus Krempkau, the court interpreter, stepped outside. After being introduced to the witness, Krempkau briefly outlined the inquest procedure, then turned and started back toward the hearing room.

Suddenly a volley of gunfire erupted from the opposite side of the plaza and a storm of lead swept over the four men. Spurts of dust mushroomed off the back of Ramón's jacket, and he staggered on a few steps as if nothing had happened. Then his knees buckled, and he slowly toppled over, dead before he hit the ground. Directly in front of him a few paces, Krempkau clutched his gut, his eyes gone wide and horribly white with shock. The force of the slug had slammed him up against the building, and he very gingerly slid down the wall. But even before he touched the boardwalk, his head lolled over at a crazy angle and he slumped forward in a pool of blood.

With the outbreak of gunfire, the townspeople scattered like fat quail, running for the nearest cover as fast as their legs would pump. Capt. McCormak and his Rangers fanned out in an arc before the *vaqueros*, covering them with cocked Winchesters. While they were outnumbered, the Rangers had the drop on the Mexicans, and for the moment no one seemed inclined to push the matter further.

Stoudenmire and Gillette had instinctively dropped to the ground when Ramón was hit, jerking their sixguns in the same movement. But within a split second, they came up firing, racing across the plaza in a dodging, bobbing run. The bushwhackers had split and run by the time the lawmen reached the opposite corner, presenting them with something of a problem. Then Stoudenmire caught sight of Tom Kale and George Campbell hurrying down a side street and took off at a dead lope. Turning the corner at the end of the block, they saw Kale already mounted and spurring south out of town. Campbell's horse had suddenly gone skittish, rearing and backing away as the former marshal fought to catch a stirrup.

Gillette opened fire on the fleeing Kale, emptying his pistol in a staccato roar. Just then Campbell abandoned his horse and turned to fight, triggering three shots at the lawmen. Stoudenmire's arm came level, and his Colt spouted flame. Deliberately, with precise care, he stitched a pattern of bright red dots across Campbell's shirt front. At each shot, Campbell's body jerked uncontrollably, and he lurched backwards, sinking lower and lower until the last slug pounded him into the dust.

A blue haze of gunsmoke hung in the still air as the lawmen began shucking empties and reloading. Without a word, they came together and turned to stare toward the river. In the distance they saw Tom Kale flogging his horse through the shallow ford, headed southeast into Chihuahua.

4.

STOUDENMIRE AND Gillette returned to the plaza only to find themselves confronted with an even graver situation. Townspeople were scurrying about the stores and buildings fronting the square, preparing to defend El Paso. Everyone fully expected the *vaqueros* to begin shooting at any moment, and not a man among them doubted that the Mexicans in Paso del Norte would come running after hearing gunfire. Barricades of trade goods and furniture were being erected on the boardwalk outside a number of stores, and already the plaza seemed encircled by an ominous ring of gun barrels.

The marshal took only a moment to gauge the situation, then turned to his deputy. "Jim, hotfoot it around the plaza and tell those nitwits to get inside and stay there. The man that fires the first shot will answer to me personally. You tell 'em he won't like the way I ask questions, either."

Gillette moved off at a brisk trot, and Stoudenmire headed across the square toward McCormak and his Rangers. But before he had gone ten paces, he heard his name called and turned to find the town leaders bearing down on him like a phalanx of scalded owls. Mayor Porter headed the delegation and close on his heels was the full city council, including Seth Hart and Doc Cummings.

"Marshal Stoudenmire, this madness has gone far enough!" Porter's tone was one of outraged indignation. "You're the one that brought these Mexicans into our town, and I demand that you resolve this dreadful affair immediately. I warn you, sir, we won't stand by and watch our people slaughtered like so many sheep."

Stoudenmire advanced on the jowly politician with a swiftness that rocked him back on his heels. "Porter you're nothing but a conniving old blowhard, and I've had about all of you I'm gonna take. Lip off to me once more, and I'll break your back. That's a promise."

Porter swallowed hard, wilting under the lawman's brutal glare. When Stoudenmire saw that the mayor had run out of juice, he wheeled around and started off. But Seth Hart's gruff rumble again brought him up short.

"Marshal, that won't cut it. We're the elected leaders of this town, and we have a right to know what you're planning. After all, we're not talking about jailing a bunch of rowdy drunks. Man, this whole town could be put to the torch!"

Stoudenmire spun on him, freezing the miller in his tracks with a flinty look. "Mister, you've sorta forgot who's callin' the shots around here. When I took the job, we had the understanding you'd stay off my back. The only conditions were that I run Banning out of town and get the Mexicans cooled off. Maybe it's not as neat and pretty as you'd like it, but that's what I'm doing. Now if you'll just button up your pants and quit dribblin' nonsense, I'll get on about my business."

Doc Cummings stepped forward, grasping the lawman's arm as he turned to leave. "Dallas, don't go off half-cocked like that. These men are only trying to help. They're concerned about the town and trying to figure out what our next move should be. Just slack off and listen to their ideas for a minute. That won't hurt anything."

The marshal shrugged his hand off, scowling at the other men as if they were worrisome gnats. "Doc, I don't have time to listen to a bunch of politicians blather about if maybe and how come. While they're talking, this whole goddamn deal could blow up in our faces. I know what needs to be done, and as soon as things get quieted down around here, I'll do it. In the meantime, I've got no use for a lot of preachin' from these bullshit artists."

When a crestfallen look came over Cumming's face, Stoudenmire clasped the older man's shoulder. "Listen, Doc, I appreciate what you're trying to do. But if you really want to help, you can go over to the house and keep Kate company. I left Tige with her, and that ought to be enough in case of trouble. But it'd sure take a load off my mind if I knew you were with her."

Cummings just nodded, clearly hurt that he was being elbowed aside like some doddering old man. But Stoudenmire didn't have time to spare his feelings. Out of the corner of his eye, the lawman saw that things were coming to a head between the Mexicans and the Rangers. Without another word, he took off across the plaza at a fast dog-trot.

Though the Rangers still had the upper hand, it was something akin to having a tiger by the tail. Outnumbered as they were, the peace officers wouldn't have a chance if the Mexicans ever went for their guns, and that was exactly what had brought the kettle to boil. As he approached, Stoudenmire heard McCormak arguing with a *vaquero* who appeared to be the spokesman for the Mexicans. When the Marshal came to a halt at the Ranger's elbow, McCormak turned away from the *vaquero* with a troubled frown.

"Dallas, we've got ourselves a real pisscutter. I offered to let these greasers ride out if they'd just lay their guns down, but it's no dice. This bird says they'd as soon die fighting right here as get shot in the back before they reached the river."

Stoudenmire looked from McCormak to the Mexican and back again. "Can't say as I blame him much. In case you hadn't noticed, this town's pretty damn close to being a shootin' gallery."

McCormak glanced around the plaza, and his eyes squinched up like an old coon. "Maybe so. But we better do somethin' *pronto* or these boys are gonna get tired of palaverin' and start doing some shootin' of their own."

"Tell you the truth, Frank, I don't know what's holdin 'em back. If it was me, I'd have shot my way out of here ten minutes ago." The lawman's gaze again wandered over to the Mexican, who was staring at them with a hostile frown. "Tell you what. Let me have a crack at him. Maybe we talk the same language."

McCormak just shrugged and stepped aside. Stoudenmire turned to face the *vaquero,* gripped by an awareness that what was said in the next few seconds might easily leave El Paso's streets littered with dead. This was the crunch old timers liked to talk about, and it was a damned uneasy spot to be standing in, no matter how big a man's boots were.

"*Está día triste, amigo.* Very sad. We share a great

burden in the death of your *caporal*, and no one mourns his passing more than I."

"Don't call me friend, *gringo.*" The Mexican spat the words with an angry hiss. "You have a peculiar way of remaining alive while your friends are being killed."

"Perhaps. But your leader believed me to be *simpático* to your cause, and he was not a man easily fooled." Stoudenmire felt his mouth go dry as he prepared to turn the corner. "Still that is neither here nor there in this thing of the guns. The *tejanos soldados* want only to see you safely across the river, and they will guarantee your lives with their own."

"*¡Válgame Dios!* You must think me *loco.*" The *vaquero* gestured toward the coroner's office, where the bodies of Ramón Vazquez and Gus Krempkau lay as they had fallen. "There is the truth of what comes to those who trust *gringos*. We keep our guns! Let us say no more about it. Anyone who tries to take them from us will pay dearly."

The lawman knew a dead end when he saw it and, on the spur of the moment, decided it was whole hog or none. "Let us compromise then, *señor*. You may keep your guns, but the *tejanos* will accompany you to the river. That way we can watch each other. If you are truly the *teniente* of Ramón Vazquez, then you will see the wisdom in what I propose."

The other *vaqueros* had been listening closely to this exchange, and they now edged forward, awaiting some reaction from their new leader. But before the Mexican could answer, Frank McCormak stepped between the two men.

"Stoudenmire, you just hold your horses. Before I take them greasers anywhere, they're gonna give up those guns. There ain't no two ways about it."

"Whatever you say, Frank. It's your tea party." The lawman moved back a pace and waved McCormak toward the Mexicans. "Just walk right in there and collect their rifles. There's only fifty of 'em, and I seem to remember you always did like long odds."

The debate ended right there. Capt. Frank McCormak decided to temporarily join forces with the *vaqueros* and get them the hell out of El Paso. It had been a trying kind of day, and his only regret was that he couldn't leave with them. Chasing bank robbers and horse thieves back on the Pecos was beginning to look like real soft duty.

While Ramón's body was being loaded in the buggy, Stoudenmire pledged to the *vaqueros* that his killer would not go unpunished. They didn't say much, and he let the matter drop there. But he knew the promise would get talked about across the border, and it might just hold the Mexicans in check until Kale could be caught.

When the *vaqueros* were mounted, Stoudenmire and McCormak led the procession across the plaza. Gillette fell in at the rear and the Rangers rode shotgun on either flank. Once out of the center of town, everyone began breathing easier. The real danger was past, and the Rangers were no less relieved than the Mexicans. Moments later, they reached the river without incident, and the *vaqueros* spurred their horses through the shallow stream. Watching them cross to Paso del Norte, Stoudenmire reflected back over the morning and decided it had been a sorry mess for everyone involved. Especially Ramón Vazquez.

Back on the plaza, the townspeople slowly emerged from the buildings under a sky that was curiously chilling to the bones. They still clutched their guns, like little boys playing at being soldiers, and when they spoke, there was a trace of false bravado to their words. The greasers were gone for the moment, well enough, but few believed the trouble would end there. The murder of the Mexican *caporal* was certain to bring reprisals. Maybe not tomorrow, or the day after, or even the day after that. But it would come.

5.

STOUDENMIRE STEPPED from the courthouse, crossed South Oregon, and headed back toward his office. He had just sworn out a federal warrant for Tom Kale. The next step was to hunt the backshooter down and capture him. Or kill him. That was up to Kale. So far as the lawman was concerned, it made little difference which way it went.

If the bastard resisted, Stoudenmire meant to kill him, with no wasted motion. With or without Kale, he would still get the Bannings. Even if he had to call them out in public where they had no choice but to fight or get laughed out of town. Justice could be served in many ways, and when a man started out killing snakes, he couldn't be too squeamish about his methods.

But as he strode along streets that now seemed hauntingly quiet, it came to the marshal that he was letting his temper get the upper hand. Though Kale deserved no more mercy than a rabid dog, there were factors that overshadowed killing him out of sheer revenge. Alive and kicking, he represented a greater threat to the Bannings. On a witness stand in court, the ramrod could put a rope around Ed Banning's neck without batting an eye. It was entirely possible he even had a few juicy tidbits to relate about the political shenanigans going on in town, which was another can of worms that badly needed opening. And nothing would warm the heart quite so much as watching the Bannings accompany Kale to the gallows. That was for damn sure!

Reflecting on it, Stoudenmire decided there was much to be said for the majesty of the law. Without it, the world would be a dog-eat-dog slaughterpen, with the little guy coming out on the short end of the stick everytime. Not that it wasn't much the same even with the law, but at least the fainthearts had some chance so long as there were courts and men willing to pin on a star. There was even something wholesome about an old fashioned neck-stretching every now and then. Strange as it sounded, folks went away feeling just a little more civilized after seeing a renegade take the long drop. Just knowing that the covenant of an eye for an eye even existed was somehow reassuring, and when a hired killer like Kale tried walking on air, it made a man think twice about flaunting the rights of others. Naturally, if the men who gave the orders, like the Bannings and Isaac Porter, got strung up in the bargain, it made the law seem all the more invincible. Godlike somehow, as if nobody was immune from the rope.

Still, awesome as the formalities of the law might be,

there was much to be said for a good, clean bullet just below the brisket. It was neat, saved the state a lot of money and, in the long run, served justice near about as well as a hangman. Folks respected a bullet, too, maybe even more than the rope. And when a fellow started chalking up things like personal satisfaction, there just wasn't anything so deep-down gratifying as putting a slug through some badassed jasper that hadn't gotten the message. Especially a sneaky shitheel like Tom Kale.

Yessir, the law was a good thing. Made people mind their manners and probably converted more heathens into straight-arrow Christians than any Bible-thumper ever thought about. But with snakes like Kale and the Bannings, there was a swifter, more certain law. Which meant that the man wearing the star sort of had to play it by ear. Depending on how the cards fell, some might get hung and some might get shot. Like any sporting proposition, you pays your money and you takes your chances.

Chuckling to himself, Stoudenmire entered the office, noting in the back of his mind that the Rangers had just trooped into a cafe for dinner. The fact that three men had been killed this morning didn't seem to bother their appetites in the slightest. The thought jarred some dim memory of the war, and the lawman remembered how he had always been ravenous as a gaunt wolf after a day on the killing ground. Odd maybe, but nothing startling. Lots of things made men hungry, and if killing happened to whet a man's appetite, that didn't make him some kind of freak. Just different.

Gillette looked up from pouring himself a cup of coffee, his expression just the least bit puzzled. "I sorta figured you'd gone home for dinner. Anything wrong?"

"Nothing that can't be cured I reckon." Stoudenmire eased down in a chair and propped his boots on top the desk. "I'll head home directly. Thought I'd check in with you first."

"Well you needn't have bothered." The deputy took a cautious sip from the steaming mug, then cracked a sly grin. "After you left, I took a little jaunt around town, and it's quiet as a church full of bats. Maybe too much so. But

I'll tell you one thing. It's a damn cinch nobody's gonna be visitin' Paso del Norte for a spell."

"If I was you, I wouldn't lay any money on that." Stoudenmire leaned farther back in the chair, locking his hands behind his head. "The way things stand now, I'll be on the other side of the river before nightfall."

"Jesus Christ!" Gillette's startled look was one of sheer bafflement. "What in the raw name of common sense would cause you to do a thing like that?"

"Well, for one thing, I want to have a talk with the *alcalde* over there. See which way he figures his people are gonna jump. For another, I've got it in mind to bring Tom Kale in. Tracking a white man in Mexico won't be hard after what happened here this morning."

Gillette squinted, lifting one eyebrow scornfully. "Dallas, I'm gonna flat-out tell you something. You're out of bounds crossin' the river. Even a US marshal don't have no jurisdiction over the border, and them Rurales are gonna howl like you'd just stuck a hot poker straight up their ass."

The marshall didn't appear too impressed with the argument. "I reckon Ramón's *patrón* will keep the Rurales off my back when he finds out who I'm after."

"In a pig's ass!" Gillette snorted. "Sometimes talkin' to you is like feedin' oats to a dead mule. Even if you run Kale down, the greasers'll likely declare first claim. And to get him back here you're gonna have to fight your way across half of Chihuahua."

"Maybe. Maybe not. But I'm going after him whichever way it works out." Stoudenmire lowered his feet to the floor and began rummaging through the desk drawers. "Ramón got killed because he trusted a *yanqui,* and people over there aren't gonna have any faith in our word until Kale's been measured for a box."

"Pardner, I'm tellin' you for your own good, you'd better chew on this deal for a while. Chances are Mama Stoudenmire's firstborn ain't too popular over there right now. If you keep pushin' your luck, we're liable to have to gather you up with a rake."

The lawman grinned in that cryptic way, like he was

thinking of some secret, highly personal joke. ''Stranger things have happened. But there's one thing you can't argue. If we're gonna head off a bloodbath along the Rio Grande, then we've got to show that the authorities over here won't condone the killing of Mexicans.'' Locating a box of shells in a drawer, he paused and began filling the empties in his shellbelt. ''Besides, Pedro Vazquez went out on a limb to help me nail the Bannings and lost his nephew in the bargain. I owe the old man, and I mean to pay up.''

''Oh, you'll pay all right. Don't fret that.'' The deputy stared into his coffee mug, as though something profound might be revealed in the dregs. ''Trouble is, I've got a feelin' you won't care much for the interest they're gonna ask.''

Stoudenmire came around the desk and selected a rifle, then a sawed-off shotgun from the rack on the wall. ''Listen, we could sit here jawbonin' till hell freezes over, and it wouldn't change a thing. Unless someone goes after Kale, we might as well shit in one hand and wish in the other. 'Cause he's not coming back this way. Not as long as he's able to talk and get the Bannings fitted out for a rope.''

Gillette shook his head slowly, searching the marshal's face for some sign that still eluded him. ''Dallas, there's times you act like some kid that's green an' limber an' full of sap. Every now and then I get to watchin' you, and it plumb baffles me where the hell you got off to when the good Lord was handin' out nerves.''

''Don't get your bowels in an uproar, Jim. I'll be back before you can say scat. Come to think of it, instead of worrying about me, you oughta light a candle for Mr. Kale.''

''Well, you're full growed for a fact, and I reckon your mammy taught you what teeth was for when she weaned you. Just make sure you get first bite.''

The two men shook hands, and Stoudenmire walked from the jail. Turning the corner, he headed toward Magoffin Avenue and home, dreading the scene he would face there. After the shootings this morning, the fireworks were sure to go off the minute he walked in the door. But when

Kate found out he was riding into Chihuahua alone, she would likely pitch the granddaddy of all screaming fits. Already, he could hear her pleading with him not to go, snuffling and sobbing, harping on those lame-brain premonitions of hers.

Women were damned hard to savvy. When they got married, they prayed to the Almighty that they had gotten themselves harnessed to a real man. Then little by little, they tried to cut his balls off.

CHAPTER SIX

1.

SHORTLY BEFORE sundown, Stoudenmire crossed the Rio Grande. The Winchester was snugged down in a scabbard beneath his leg, and the shotgun hung from a rawhide thong over the saddle horn. His chestnut gelding was as frisky as a colt after two weeks on oats and hay, and behind him trailed a packhorse loaded with grub. Like any hunter of dangerous game, the marshal had come prepared.

Running Kale to earth wouldn't be done overnight. The outlaw had a good lead, more than Stoudenmire cared to admit, and had doubtless swung southwest toward the Sierra Madres after circling Paso del Norte. Once in the mountains, he could lose himself for a lifetime, for few there cared if a man was being hunted. Since the time of the Spaniards, the Sierra Madres had been a haven for *bandidos* and *insurrectos* alike; so long as a man tended to his own knitting, there was no safer hideout within a thousand miles in any direction.

Though the lawman had few qualms about the outcome of the hunt, he would have felt even more confident with Tige along. The big dog was like an extra right arm, an infallible sixth sense that never faltered. Without him, it was as if Stoudenmire had left part of himself behind, and it wasn't a good feeling. But where he was headed wasn't a fit place for a dog, or a man either when it came down to cases. Before reaching the mountains, he had to cross vast stretches of desolate wasteland, and just worrying about himself and the horses was going to be chore enough. Besides, Kate needed some sort of protection around the house, and next to a double load of buckshot, Tige had few equals at scaring off uninvited guests.

Right now though, he had other things to worry about. Riding along Paso del Norte's dusty main street, Stoudenmire could feel the villagers' hostility all about him, almost as if their malevolence were alive and breathing deeply of his loathsome scent. Though they refused to look at him directly, he sensed their dark eyes boring holes through his back. It was somewhat the same feeling a stray dog has when he wanders into strange territory, not hunting trouble but pretty damn certain the neighborhood pack is going to give him a good chewing just on general principle. When he reined to a halt before the *alcalde*'s home, the lawman felt a mixture of surprise and relief. That no one had taken a shot at him wasn't just remarkable, it was downright astonishing. As he dismounted, it occurred to Stoudenmire that it might be a sign. A good sign, for a change!

Pedro Vazquez admitted him with the haggard look of a man who has lost that which he treasures most. The *alcalde* was a widower, and after Ramón's parents had died in an epidemic, he had taken the boy to raise. Through the years, they had become like father and son, and Pedro couldn't have been more grief stricken if Ramón had been of his own flesh. But misery was the companion of all men in Mexico, with the exception perhaps of the land-wealthy *hidalgos*. Those who survived learned to bear the pain of life with grace, for within this stoic fatalism lay their only measure of defense against the hardships each must endure. Pedro Vazquez had learned the lesson well over his threescore years, and as he led Stoudenmire inside, his face was a stony mask. Yet beneath this outer serenity, he was a crushed man; it showed in his eyes, vast pools of exquisite sorrow.

Ramón was laid out in the parlor, his face frozen in waxlike tranquillity. The coffin was a simple affair, as unpretentious and as lacking in vanity as the man himself had been. But as Stoudenmire stood over the casket, looking down on the dead man's pallid composure, it struck him that Ramón in death wasn't anything like the fiery young *vaquero* he had grown to admire. Maybe death was the great leveler after all, just like the wise men said. Perhaps when a man went under, he left the bad things behind, all the heartaches and inequities that seemed to dog a fellow's tracks while he was alive and kicking. How else could you account for that petrified smile on Ramón's face? If ever a man crossed over with reason to hate a goodly share of those left behind, it was this young Mexican. And the peaceful calm spread over his features right now was a far cry from the rage he must have felt in those last moments. It was damned strange, more than a man could rightly come to grips with. Like something out of a jumbled-up dream that didn't make much sense but seemed real as hell all the same.

Still, whichever way the dice fell, Ramón was long past caring. The warm climate made it unwise to keep the dead above ground longer than overnight, and by morning he would have a fight of another kind on his hands. Earth to earth and dust to dust, the preachers always said. But the fellow being turned into worm meat might see it a damned sight different. Especially since he was planted six feet deep and couldn't outrun the slimy little bastards.

Villagers filed past the coffin in a steady stream, and a priest was mumbling and waving his hands around like a rainmaker in a dutch oven. Watching them, the lawman wondered who they pitied the most, Ramón or themselves. The young *caporal* would soon be buried and forgotten, but they'd still be trudging along in the same old sea of shit. Before he had time to think that one through, Pedro Vazquez took his arm and guided him toward the study.

After seating Stoudenmire, the *alcalde* went to stand before the open window. Gazing out into the dusky nightfall, he seemed worn and beaten, a tired old man who had outlived everything that mattered. His shoulders slumped, giving him a stooped appearance, as if the burden was simply too much to carry farther. The lawman regarded him silently, sharing his remorse to a small degree, yet somehow complimented that the *jefe* would allow him to see beneath the passive mask. Then the older man's bent figure straightened, and Stoudenmire realized that it had been only a momentary lapse. When Pedro Vazquez turned, he was himself again.

"I have often thought that the good die before their time," Vazquez said, taking a seat across from the Texan. "After today I am convinced of it."

"In my country we have a saying, *Alcalde*. Only cream and bastards rise to the top. So it is with death. Sometimes evil flourishes on the bones of those who least deserve to go under."

"There is much truth to that. Yet I wonder if it is *mala suerte* or did God intend it that way? Perhaps the good ones have merely lost the instinct for survival in this harsh land."

"Perhaps. But that is a question best left to those wiser than myself." Stoudenmire thumped his head with a deprecating gesture. "I am a practical man, *sin astuto*, and for me the direct path is the most agreeable. When I see a snake, I kill it, and in time there will be no snakes where I walk."

Pedro Vazquez gave him an appraising look. "Senor, it comes to me that there is more than one kind of cunning. I believe you are attempting to tell me something that resists words."

The lawman nodded, returning the old man's quizzical gaze with a solemn frown. "*Jefe*, so long as I remain above ground. I will blame myself for Ramón's death. Had I been wiser, he would not be lying in the next room at this moment. But while I live, those who killed him will sleep in fear. Tonight I begin the search for the one who actually held the gun."

The *alcalde*'s eyes brightened and he came up on the edge of his chair. "*¡Madre de Dios!* It is what I had hoped to hear you say. After this morning, I am convinced that revenge is a good thing. When we heard the *gringo asesino* was riding south, I prayed it would be you who took his trail." Then the old man leaned forward, giving Stoudenmire a fatherly tap on the knee. "But on this other thing, you do yourself an injustice, my friend. Ramón was a man, and he conducted himself as a leader should. What he did was done for our people, and your influence played only a small part. Do not reproach yourself. He died fighting for our cause, and few men go to their grave with such honor."

Before the marshal could answer, a knock sounded at the door, and Don Miguel Salazar stepped into the room. Striding forward he embraced Pedro Vazquez, mumbling condolences in a choked voice. Watching them, Stoudenmire decided it would be a tossup as to which one had loved Ramón the most. Then they separated, and the *alcalde* began talking so fast the lawman could catch only a word here and there. But he heard his name mentioned a couple of times, and when Don Miguel glanced in his direction, it became apparent that their discussion centered on him. After a final exchange, *el patrón* smiled and came forward, offering his hand.

"I have heard much of the *yanqui* whose words are untainted, and I am honored to meet you. Pedro tells me you are going after Ramón's killer, and for this gesture you will be doubly honored among our people."

"*Gracias*. But it is not a gesture, señor. It is a debt owed to a brave man."

"*Sí*. He was that above all else. A man of courage." The *hidalgo's* eyes glistened and he swallowed hurriedly. "But you chose a bad night to ride south, my friend. Chihuahua is no place for an *americano* to be caught alone. Not tonight, perhaps never."

Stoudenmire's expression remained firm. "That is a chance I will have to risk. To delay longer would mean losing the man's trail entirely."

"Yes, I see your point." Don Miguel grew thoughtful for a moment, then suddenly clapped his hands together. "*¡Caramba!* Perhaps there is a way after all. Señor Stoudenmire, tonight you will be a guest at my *hacienda*. Since it is south of here, it is in the direction you travel. Tomorrow I will provide you with the one thing that insures success on any hunt. Regardless of the quarry."

Stoudenmire didn't have the least idea what he was talking about, but there was no reason to refuse. He had to spend the night somewhere, and so long as it was headed south, one spot was as good as another. The two Mexicans chatted a few minutes longer, then *el patrón* indicated it was time they be on their way.

Pedro Vazquez walked them to the door and took the lawman's big paw between his hands. "Ramón will rest easy knowing that you ride in his place. *Vaya con Dios, mi hijo.*"

Only after he had mounted and pulled the chestnut abreast of Don Miguel's stallion did the *alcalde*'s words register on Stoudenmire. Wasn't that something! That old bugger calling him son. He'd been dubbed lots of things for taking a man's trail, but usually it was closer to sonovabitch. Maybe things were looking up after all.

2.

ALTHOUGH JIM Gillette hadn't let on to Stoudenmire, he was just a little put out with the lawman's brash scheme. Maybe the marshal's plan to sweet-talk the *alcalde* would work. And maybe it wouldn't. It seemed just as likely that the stubborn German would get himself killed poking around Paso del Norte, and that would really tear things. One thing was sure, the greasers wouldn't be real fond of the man who had gotten Ramón Vazquez killed. Expecially when he was the same one that had gotten those *vaqueros* perforated in an ambush only a couple of weeks back. Where Mexicans were concerned there was a time to be tough and a time to be smart. Some men never lived long enough to learn which was which. But right now, everybody on the other side of that river had a mean hair up his ass, and it would have been a dilly of a time to lay back and play it smart.

Still, there was more at stake here than Stoudenmire's neck. There was a whole damn town sitting on a short fuse, not to mention a deputy that couldn't hardly work up a good spit. Though he had no qualms about handling roughnecks or diving into a gunfight, this deal was just a bit over his head. The only consolation in the whole sorry mess was that the Rangers were still in town, and if the greasers came storming across the river, he would damn sure dump it square in their laps. But what the hell would he do if they suddenly decided to move on?

While he was ruminating on that unpleasant dilemma, Doc Cummings walked through the door. The storekeeper was just on his way to supper, but he had stopped in on the off chance he could finagle an invitation to one of Kate's meals.

"Evenin', Deputy." He gave the office a quick once over. "Dallas already gone home?"

"Last time I heard, he was headed for points south." Gillette's tone was dry, slightly caustic. "First stop bein' Paso del Norte."

"Paso del Norte!" Cummings parroted incredulously. "What in the name of Christ is he doing over there?"

"Funny. That's the same thing I asked him." The old lawdog grinned like his teeth hurt. "Said he was gonna pour a little honey over their *jefe*, and then he figured to beat the bushes for Tom Kale."

"Well kiss my ass! Doesn't he know a man could get killed that way?"

"Your guess is about as good as mine, I reckon. Dallas is double wolf on guts and savvy, but sometimes I get to wonderin' if he hasn't got more of one than he does the other."

Cummings batted his eyes nervously, thoroughly perplexed by the whole affair. "Damn, I grant you Kale has to be caught, but trailin' him across the border is overdoing it. Dallas oughta know better'n anyone else that he's got no jurisdiction over there."

"He knows, right enough. Just didn't pay it no mind." The deputy spat a black stream of tobacco juice in the general direction of a spittoon. "Thing about Dallas is, he don't like folks fartin' around in his business. Once they do, he'll chase 'em clean to hell and back. I got an idea Tom Kale is gonna learn that the hard way."

"Well, everyone wants to see Kale's neck stretched. But tryin' to take him in Mexico is nothin' but damn foolishness. Right now those greasers figure any white man is fair game." The storekeeper dropped into a chair, staring morosely at the wall. "Besides, it's the Bannings we oughta be worryin' about. Kale's just hired help."

"I don't know as I'd get all bent out of shape worryin' about Dallas. Tanglin' with him is sorta like kickin' a porcupine. You generally come away wishin' you hadn't." Gillette grew silent for a moment, puzzling over something that had only just now occurred to him. "Course, maybe I was a little too quick to fault Dallas. Appears to me he figured the Bannings could wait. 'Bout the only thing that's gonna put a damper on them Mexicans is to get the fellow that actually done the killin'. Lookin' at it that way, I reckon Kale sorta comes up with a ring in his nose."

Cummings was becoming testier by the moment. "Well I don't know as I'd buy that. We're facing a bad situation here, and Dallas has no business off chasin' around Chihuahua. Brother-in-law or not, he was hired to protect this community, and his place is in El Paso. All I've got to say is that his plan better work, or we'll all be out on our ear."

"Mr. Cummings, where I come from, folks used to say hindsight ain't no better'n hind tit. Dallas did what he thought was best, and I reckon we'll just have to wait and see how it pans out. Come to think of it, we haven't got a helluva lot of choice. Once he gets his mind made up, he's mighty hard to swing around."

"Damned if that's not the truth. I never met a man so all fired set in his ways. Now you take this Banning thing, for instance. We tried to keep him from crowding them so fast. But no, he had to shove 'em up against the wall. Bang! Bang! Bang! And now look where it's got us."

The deputy eyed him quizzically, wondering if the man knew the first thing about bringing law to a border town. And making it stick. "Just offhand, I'd say that Dallas has got 'em suckin' wind. Every move they've made has turned sour, and if he brings Kale in, their goose is cooked. Course, Dallas would just as soon shoot 'em as send 'em to jail. Can't say as I blame him much."

"Well let me tell you something, deputy. He might not get the chance to do either one." The storekeeper hunched forward, lowering his voice to a conspiratorial whisper. "Seth Hart says he has it on good authority that they're gonna try to kill Dallas just as soon as this Mexican scare eases off. Now, what d'ya think of that?''

Gillette had been a lawman too long to get in a dither over small town rumors. ''Seems to me they're going about it bassackwards. Why not just have the city council fire him? Solves the whole problem.''

''Not accordin' to Seth Hart, it don't. If they fired him, it'd turn into a political bombshell, and come election time, their boys might just get eased out of city hall. Besides, Dallas is still a US marshal, and gettin' him off the city payroll wouldn't mean a hill of beans.''

''Yeah, I can see that. But damned if it don't seem like killin' him would stir up an even bigger political rhubarb. I mean, it ain't like nobody'd have to be told who did it.''

Cummings tapped the desk with his finger, grinning like a bloated old cat that had just swallowed the last canary. ''There's where you're missin' the boat. People just naturally give a fellow the benefit of the doubt. Even a no-account bastard like Ed Banning. They're too goddamn lazy to get all worked up over something that can't be proved. Especially if there's a chance it might get them shot, too.''

The deputy pursed his lips, mulling it over for a moment. ''From what you say, it's a matter of who eats who first. That being the case, if I was Dallas, I'd get Banning before he got me. There's all kinds o' ways to egg a feller into a gunfight, you know.''

The storekeeper's head jerked around and his eyes widened. ''You're talkin' about forcin' a man to fight just so you can use the law to kill. That's a little cold-blooded, isn't it?''

''Why not? You think the sonovabitch is gonna be mannered about it when he has Dallas backshot in some alley?''

''No, I don't suppose he would. But that doesn't excuse using the law to suit your own ends. I've got a strong hunch the respectable people in this town wouldn't condone that kind of thing. Not for a minute.''

''Shit fire and save the grease!'' Gillette's rubbery mouth twisted in an amused grin. ''Man, you've got a lot to learn about the law. It's not what's written down in books. It's what men like Stoudenmire can enforce at the end of a gun. Anytime you don't believe it, you just try pullin' the props out from under the man holdin' that gun. That's the day you'll quit havin' law. *Muy pronto.*"

"Well, that's neither here nor there, is it?" Cummings was on the verge of losing an argument, and he decided to pull in his horns. "All I know is that Dallas acts too hastily sometimes, and one of these days, it's going to be his downfall. Assuming he makes it back from Chihuahua in one piece, tell him I said he'd better watch his step around the Bannings."

"I'll do that very thing." The deputy smiled wryly. "Dallas'll be right proud to know you're lookin' after his welfare."

Cummings saw nothing to be gained by arguing further with the contentious old lawdog. Bidding the deputy good night, he walked from the office and headed uptown. Maybe Dallas Stoudenmire didn't know enough to stay at home where he belonged, but that was no reason to let good food go to waste.

Quickening his pace, the storekeeper hurried toward Magoffin Avenue, savoring the smell of Kate's cooking as if he were already seated at the table.

3.

STOUDENMIRE AWOKE shortly before sunrise and dressed hurriedly. Through the window, he noted that the dawn sky was metallic, colorless clear to the horizon; to the west he could make out the rugged humps of the Sierra Madres. There was no wind, no sign of rain clouds, nothing to cover a horse's tracks through the parched lands this side of the mountains. A good day for a manhunt.

Moments later, he was striding down the long corridor leading to the center of the house. The lawman had seen many fine homes in his time, but Don Miguel's *casa* was in a class by itself. Though they had arrived late in the night, he could tell that a stranger would do well to have a map if he started roaming these halls alone. The passageways, corridors, and wings would be damned confusing if a man wasn't familiar with the layout. Maybe when things calmed down a little, he would come back with Kate and let the old man give them a guided tour. But right now wasn't the time, not with Kale making dust somewhere ahead.

Stoudenmire's gut rumbled, and his thoughts turned to food. Hopefully he could find the kitchen and get something hot in his belly before riding out. While he would have liked to wait around for a chat with Don Miguel, he just couldn't spare the time. Whatever *el patron* had in mind to help him with the hunt would just have to wait for another day. Every minute lost merely widened a gap that was already pushing twenty-four hours, and that was too big a lead to give any man on the run. Still he was curious about the old *hidalgo's* cryptic offer of last night. *Something that insures success on any hunt.* Damned strange when a man stopped to think about it.

Heading in the general direction of where a kitchen ought to be, he walked through a wide doorway and came to an abrupt halt. Don Miguel was seated at the head of a table big enough for a platoon, calmly working his way through a bowl of fruit. The lawman hadn't figured him to be stirring around at this hour. It was something of a shock to find a *grandee* bright-eyed and bushy-tailed so early in the day.

"What troubles you, my young friend?" The Mexican indicated a chair beside his own. "You appear startled. Is it so remarkable that an *anciano* like myself still rises with first light?"

"*De ninguna manera, Patrón.*" Stoudenmire seated himself as servants began carrying in platters of food. "Not at all. It is only that I fear your sleep has been disturbed on my account."

"Old men sleep lightly. Particularly when all they hold dear is being destroyed about them. *¡Bastante!* Enough of my troubles. I have ordered the *tejano* breakfast for you, pork and eggs. I hope it meets with your satisfaction."

"*Gracias, Don Miguel.*" The lawman dug in hungrily,

bothered not at all that his plate was swimming in grease. "It was kind of you to be concerned with so small a thing."

"No, not kind. *Egoista.*" The *hadalgo* smiled benignly. "But selfishness to a purpose. I want your stomach content and your mind strong for the ride ahead. Even Pedro Vazquez's desire for vengence pales beside my own."

"That was clear last night, *Patrón.* Only a blind man could have failed to observe your sorrow. I suspect Ramón was as much your son as he was that of the *alcalde's.*"

Don Miguel's eyes clouded over, the bowl of fruit now forgotten. "*Sí. Mi hijo.* He was that and more. When the Comanche killed my wife and children some years ago, I became a man without a soul. Then Ramón came to the *hacienda* as a simple *vaquero.* What a man, even as a boy! He was what I hoped my son would be. And soon that is what he became. *Mi hijo segundo.*"

The old man fell silent, staring at his plate as if some vision from the past had been brought to life on its glossy surface. The moments ticked by in utter stillness, and tiny smile played at the corners of his mouth. Finally, the mist of what once had been faded from his eyes, and he glanced back at the lawman, blinking sheepishly.

"*Usted dispense, amigo.* Excuse me for looking back to more pleasant times. Today it seems I have nothing to look forward to but the quick death of the one you seek. Now! Tell me how you would go about trapping this *bárbaro.*"

Stoudenmire pushed his plate away and sat back. "I believe he will attempt to reach the Sierra Madres. Chihuahua to the south has many villages, and it seems unlikely he would ride in that direction. The mountains would appear a safer refuge, and if I am right, I will cross his trail somewhere to the southwest. The man must have food, and wherever he stops he will be remembered."

"Your reasoning is sound. It is obvious you have had much experience with *piojos* of this sort." Don Miguel hesitated, searching for a tactful way to phrase his next question. "But what if he reaches the mountains, my friend? The *bandidos* rule the Sierra Madres like kings. Not even the Rurales dare to travel there. Should this man ever join the *bandoleros*, he would be safe for as long as he cared to remain in Mexico."

"This is true, Don Miguel. Somehow I must overtake him before he crosses the flatlands this side of the mountains. Speaking of that, I fear I must take leave of your hospitality. The one named Kale is many hours ahead of me, and I must find a way to narrow his lead."

"Now you touch on the heart of the matter. This is precisely why I asked you to be my guest. Come, we are expected outside."

The *hidalgo* pushed back his chair and headed for the door at a fast clip. Stoudenmire tagged along in his wake, still thoroughly puzzled by the old man's air of mystery. When they emerged on the front porch of the *casa* a cluster of *vaqueros* waited at the bottom of the steps. As *el patrón* came to a halt, the men doffed their sombreros, darting hidden glances at the *americano*. The marshal returned their looks with growing curiosity, and in that moment, his eye was drawn toward a man at the rear. Looking closer, Stoudenmire suddenly realized that the man wasn't Mexican. He was a *mestizo*. A half-breed Indian.

Don Miguel motioned with his hand, and the breed edged through the crowd, slowly mounting the steps. When he came to a stop before the old man, the Indian bowed his head, not humbly but proudly as a warrior would honor a king. Watching him, Stoudenmire was struck by the sheer force of the man's physical presence. Unlike the plains Indians he had known, this *mestizo* was remarkably tall, with broad shoulders, a deep bull-chest, and bulging, sinewy legs that looked like gnarled saplings. His hair hung loosely over his shoulders, black as the darkest ebony, and his sharp, angular features brought to mind images of a fierce, predatory hawk. Strapped around his waist was a knife distantly related to a machete, and his clothing consisted solely of breechclout and moccasins.

But the thing that men remembered most about this *mestizo* were his eyes. They were black and piercing, in the way fire sears whatever it touches, and among the *vaqueros* it was said that this strange one could see through other men's souls. The lawman wouldn't soon forget those eyes either. When the Indian looked at him, Stoudenmire could think only of Tige. The same inhuman brilliance, somehow bristling with hunger; the eyes of a beast that had been weaned on raw meat and warm blood.

Like Tige, the *mestizo* also served but one master, in this case Don Miguel Salazar. Observing the Indian's manner before *el patrón*, it occurred to Stoudenmire that any one who messed with the old man was the same as dead. It was a handy item to keep in mind. While the Texan had never been bested in a fight, he sensed instinctively that tangling with this half-breed could get a man killed. Stone-cold—and sliced to ribbons in the bargain.

Don Miguel waited until they had finished their inspection of one another before he spoke. "Señor Stoudenmire, this is the man who will guide you in your hunt. His name is Bajeca. If you were familiar with his tribe, you would know he is a Yaqui. A race of *guerreros*, descendents of the Incas. Unfortunately, Porfirio Diaz declared war on them some years ago, and the Yaqui nation is now scattered across all of Mexico. When Bajeca came to us, he was near death. But we nursed him back to health, and he has remained with us ever since."

Turning, *el patrón* smiled benevolently, and a spark of warmth flickered and died in the *mestizo*'s eyes. Glancing back at Stoudenmire, the old man waved his hand toward the distant countryside. "We only see him occasionally. He lives out there among the wild things. No one knows where, or cares to know I would imagine. But when we need him, he somehow comes to us, and never have we needed him more. Bejeca can track *el tigre* through running water, and if ever a man lived who can find the *gringo pistolero* in that wilderness, you are gazing upon him at this moment."

"Bejeca," Stoudenmire spoke the name with simple dignity, extending his hand. "I am honored to have a *yaqui guerrero* at my side. Together we will bring this pale-eyed *comadreja* to bay."

The *mestizo* pumped his hand once, then dropped it, staring through him as other men would look past a shadow. "Among the people of *el patrón*, it is said that you are *macho hombre*. When a man sets out on the *jornado del muerto* that is a good thing to be."

"The man we pursue will determine if it becomes a journey of death. If he resists, then he must die. But there are reasons for wanting him taken alive."

The Indian shrugged, inscrutable behind a stony expression. "How had you thought to conduct this hunt?"

The lawman gestured toward the Sierra Madres. "Unlike *el zorro*, this man is not cunning. He will run toward the mountains without bothering to cover his tracks. Somewhere to the southwest we will find his sign."

Bajeca studied him for a moment, watching everything and nothing in the same look. "It comes to me that this *cabrón* you seek was wise to run. If he fears you as greatly as you believe, then we will find his tracks at the village of Los Papalotes. That is the fartherest from the Rio Grande a horse could run without resting."

With that, he turned to Don Miguel, bowed his head slightly, then walked down the steps. The old man looked around at Stoudenmire and smiled. "Bajeca is not a tactful man, but he will never fail you. Give him a free rein, and he will lead you to the *gringo* dog."

Out of the corner of his eye, Stoudenmire noted that the *mestizo* was already mounted and had led his own horses forward. Nodding to Don Miguel, he moved down the steps and climbed aboard the chestnut. Without a word, Bajeca wheeled his scruffy mustang and rode south from the compound.

El patrón clearly wanted Kale brought back in a basket. Stoudenmire had no doubts on that score. And unless he missed his guess, the breed had been ordered to do the dirty work. The only thing that had him puzzled was what the old *hidalgo* had in mind for a certain *tejano* lawman.

4.

THE MEETING had been called to decide their next move. By now it was common knowledge that the lawman was off hunting Kale, and if he were captured, then the fat was in the fire. Ed Banning laid it out in cold, precise terms. Kale could send them all to jail, probably even get them hung, despite the fact that every judge in town was on their payroll. Should the ramrod be returned to El Paso, their chances were slim indeed, for there was every likelihood they would never live to stand trial. Lynch mobs couldn't be bribed or scared off, and once Kale started squealing, the townspeople might just decide to take matters into their own hands.

Isaac Porter was only about half-stewed, but far enough along to be amused by this little charade. Ed Banning had his mind made up before this meeting was ever called, and to say that they were here to decide a plan of action was like the Almighty asking Moses what should be inscribed on the rocks. It was downright laughable, assuming a man could keep his sense of humor while he was being insulted. They didn't want his advice today anymore than they had in the past. They only wanted to make sure his hands were as dirty as their own. That way they could always toss him to the wolves if and when a mob came pounding on the door. It was the oldest trick in the book. Divert the pack's attention with a juicy bone, and then run like hell.

But on the face of it, there was damn little Isaac Porter could do to protect himself. Though he bitterly resented the Bannings' imperious manner, there was no way he could avoid being used by them. They made the decisions, and it was up to him to perform the political skullduggery. They were always in the background, screened by the simple expedient of staying out of sight. Though everyone knew who pulled the strings, it was the mayor standing stage center who actually danced the jig. And that made him a very vulnerable fellow. People had a way of remembering what they saw rather than what they heard, which meant he was a prime candidate for a lynching bee if things ever came unwound.

Yet if it weren't for the Bannings he would still be scratching out an existence in one grubby scheme or another. They had made him mayor, and like it or not, he was bound to them by a cord that could take a half hitch around his windpipe if he weren't careful. Once a part of their organization, a man did well to toe the mark, even if he didn't care much for their methods. Where the brothers Banning were concerned, loyalty was wisely cultivated. Regardless of how disgusting it might be to play the toady for outright hooligans. Otherwise, a fellow ran the risk of claiming his reward in the hereafter somewhat prematurely.

Whenever he was with them, he felt like a man juggling vials of nitro. Sam was the most dangerous simply because he was the least predictable. He was nothing more than a common thug with a brain the size of a dried prune, someone to be avoided whenever possible. Even Ed had his darker side, though he could be reasoned with if a man had a sound argument. But that made him no less dangerous. Those who crossed him never lived to regret it, no matter how fast they could talk. Generally they just disappeared, buried out in the desert probably, and the message wasn't lost on whoever remained.

Still, a man had to protect himself in the clinches. Even if it meant jabbing Ed in the eye when he wasn't looking. The way things were shaping up, someone was being ticketed for a lengthy stay at Huntsville, maybe even a noose. And it damn sure wasn't going to be Isaac Porter. Listening to Ed rehash their predicament, he decided that a wise man would start hedging his bet. After all, there was no harm done if he put out feelers in the other camp. Not if he played it close to the vest and kept his mouth buttoned when he was drinking.

"Kale is gonna have to be rubbed out." Banning's words came as no surprise to the mayor. This was what the gang boss had been leading up to for the last ten minutes. "If Stoudenmire brings him in, we've got no choice. Maybe he won't talk, but that's a risk we can't afford to take. Better men than him have cracked when they came face to face with a hangman's knot."

"Very true, Ed. Very true indeed." Porter nodded sagely, wondering all the while if Banning's last comment hadn't also been meant for his benefit. "The expedient thing is to silence him. Otherwise, our own necks go on the block."

Banning shot him a curious look. "Isaac, you must be getting smarter in your old age. What happened to all that holier-than-thou bullshit about never resorting to violence?"

The mayor made a game effort at grinning wickedly. "An extreme disease requires an extreme cure. Sometimes a man must forfeit his life so that those about him can carry on the good fight."

"Jesus Christ," Sam growled. "What kinda crock is that? We're gonna kill him 'cause he's got a big mouth. Why don't you just say it straight out?"

"Sam, don't let him get under your skin." Ed cocked an eye in Porter's direction. "When our friend here starts soakin' up the juice, he just naturally can't resist two-dollar words. Isn't that right, Mayor?"

"Ed, you do me a grave injustice. Nothing could be farther from the truth. Why, I'm sober as a judge and twice as circumspect."

"Porky, lemme tell you somethin'. When my brother says you're drunk, you're drunk." Sam jabbed at the pudgy little politician like his finger was a battering ram. "And if you're not careful, I'm gonna give you a fat lip to go along with your fat head."

"All right, that's enough horsin' around. We've got more important things to talk about." Ed's crisp tone stopped both men cold. "That's better. Now whether Stoudenmire brings Kale in dead or we kill him only solves part of the problem. The biggest thing hangin' over our heads is the German himself, and as long as he's kickin', we're not safe. Believe it or not, I've come around to Sam's way of thinkin'. Stoudenmire has got to go. Until he's laid out, we're up to our necks in a bucket of shit."

"Hotdamn! Now you're talkin' my kind of game." Sam swelled up his chest and crowed loud enough to raise the sun. "I'll break that sorry bastard's head in so many pieces he'll look like a junebug in a meat grinder."

Ed glanced around at Porter, again eyeing him in an odd way. "What about you, Mayor? How's your stick float now?"

Porter appeared shaken, though he tried desperately to

hide it. The murder of Ramón Vazquez and Gus Krempkau had aroused the townspeople unlike anything in the past. They knew the gang was responsible, and if an innocent bystander like Krempkau could be gunned down, then nobody was safe. What was even more unsettling, they believed the town to be on the verge of a war with the Mexicans simply because the Bannings were out to protect their own hides. Graft and corruption could be tolerated in reasonable doses, but people drew the line when their lives and property were endangered. Just as sure as he was sitting here, the mayor knew that, if Stoudenmire were killed in the wake of yesterday's murders, it might well be the final straw.

"Ed, I'm not sure but what that wouldn't be a mistake. Killing Kale is one thing. Nobody's going to shed any tears over scum like him. But killing Stoudenmire might just be more than the people will stand for."

"Then I reckon that's something we'll have to worry about when it happens. Stoudenmire is more dangerous to us alive than dead, even if it splits this town right down the middle. I'm gonna tell you something, Porter. I think that bastard is crazy as a loon. He means to shovel dirt in our face even if he goes under doing it. When you're up against somebody that likes killin' that much, you'd better get him before he damn well gets you."

Isaac Porter didn't say anything. From where he sat, there was nothing left to say. Banning had clearly made up his mind, and if he talked till doomsday, it wouldn't change things by a hair. They were going to kill Kale, then Stoudenmire; and afterward, the whole goddamn town would come crashing down around their ears. And when it did, anyone standing close by was going to be sucked under with them. If he wasn't sure before, he was now. The time to make a deal with the opposition was before the worm turned. Which meant that he would have to move fast, before these lunatics had a chance to start taking pot shots at the marshal.

Later, reflecting back over the discussion, Ed Banning came to the conclusion that his political frontman was getting weak-kneed. The signs were all there, and if he was right, it could be serious. Damn serious if the old reprobate started talking to the wrong people. Kale was bad enough, but if Porter ever started blabbing, then the Bannings might as well eat shit and bark at the moon. That's about all that would be left.

After puzzling over it for a while, he ordered Sam to have the mayor watched around the clock. It wouldn't hurt anything, and it might just be the shrewdest move he'd made yet.

5.

STOUDENMIRE AND Bajeca pulled into Los Papalotes as the red ball of fire in the sky came directly overhead. They were covered with grit and sweat, and a growing uncertainty. Along the road south they had stopped at a dozen or more native huts, only to be told the same story each time.

The *gringo* they sought had not passed this way. On that the natives were emphatic, for it was a much discussed event when a lone *yanqui* dared to travel so far from the border. Had the man they described ridden past, someone would know, which meant that everyone would have known.

Still the lawman hadn't abandoned hope so easily. This was a much-traveled road, and a man riding fast might have gone unnoticed. On the other hand, perhaps Kale was foxier than he thought. If he had laid up somewhere yesterday and ridden through the night, then there was little likelihood that anyone would have spotted him. Had Stoudenmire been on the run that's what he would have done. And at the moment, he was damn hopeful that Kale had figured it the same way. Otherwise they could spend a month crisscrossing the countryside before they picked up the trail.

Stoudenmire waited outside while Bajeca entered Los Papalotes' one general store. Maybe if the *mestizo* was alone, he could get more information. Mexicans down this way certainly made no effort to hide their dislike of white men, and it could be that his presence was putting a quietus on the whole deal. Through the open door he could see the storekeeper nodding and flapping his arms around like a windmill whenever he answered a question. The man's eyes were wide as saucers, and even from a distance it was obvious that he was frightened out of his wits by the fierce-looking breed. After a final volley of excited chatter, the storekeeper jerked a soiled rag and began mopping his face. Without so much as a thank-you, the Indian spun on his heel and walked from the store.

Something about his stride alerted Stoudenmire that they had struck paydirt. The *yaqui* swung into the saddle before looking at the lawman, but his eyes smoldered with a peculiar glint.

"The fat *cochino* inside says he was awakened at dawn by a *gringo* not unlike the one we seek. This man purchased food and an *olla* for water, then departed hastily."

"That is good news, Bajeca." Stoudenmire had the feeling his companion wasn't too keen on sharing all he had learned. "And which direction did this man take upon departing?"

The *mestizo* seemed impatient to be off, but he gestured down the road. "This pig of a merchant says he rode south along the road. Yet he made the *consulta* about a trail across the dry lands."

"Then he is headed toward the mountains as we suspected. Is there such a trail?"

"Only in a man's head and his nose. Even a *gringo* can cross the *arido tierra*, but not without much difficulty."

"*¿Quantos los Sierra Madres?*" The lawman pointed toward the distant mountains. "How far across the bad lands?"

Bajeca shrugged, seemingly bored with the incessant questions. "*Quien sabe. Todo día.* Perhaps a day. Perhaps more. Much depends on the man and the horse he rides."

"And what of the horse our friend rides? Did the *mercante* relate the condition of his mount?"

"*Sí.* The fat one says that the *caballo del gringo* had been ridden hard and would most certainly collapse unless treated gently." The *mestizo* cast Stoudenmire a scornful look. "While we talk, the *yanqui* filth moves farther from our reach. *¡Andale!* Let us ride before he eludes us forever."

Bajeca jerked his mustang around and kicked him in the ribs. The lawman was only a few strides behind, and they trotted southward in the noonday sun. Thinking back over what they had learned, Stoudenmire estimated that Kale was probably five hours ahead of them. Six at the outside. More to the point, he was riding a jaded horse, and it was a cinch he couldn't push the animal over the wastelands this side of the mountains. Most likely he figured no one was on his trail at this point and wouldn't risk killing his horse. Maybe he would even hole up somewhere during the heat of the day. If they could somehow cut his sign, there was every likelihood they could close the gap by nightfall. The other side of the coin wasn't pleasant to consider. By morning Kale would be in the mountains, and tracking him there was a foolhardy proposition any way a man sliced it.

Once they were out of sight of the store, Bajeca left the road and began casting in ever widening circles over the broken ground to the west. Kale wouldn't have headed for the mountains until he was sure no one could see him, and this was as good a spot to start as any. Within a quarter-hour the *mestizo* found sign and signaled Stoudenmire. The lawman had only to look at the tracks, and he knew they were on the right trail at last. Yesterday, after Kale had spurred out of El Paso, he had inspected the hoofprints carefully. Two caulks had been built up more than usual on the inside of a back shoe, and it left a distinctive imprint. This track matched it perfectly. The road south had been too heavily traveled to make out one hoofprint from another, but there was no doubt in his mind now. He nodded to Bajeca, and they struck out at a steady lope headed due west.

The earth was sandy in most places, with clumps of stunted mesquite and yucca scattered over the countryside, all of which made tracking fairly simple. There wasn't a tree worthy of the name for miles around, and in the distance they could see the Sierra Madres range climbing skyward from the desert floor. The terrain grew more hostile as the afternoon wore on, and the sun hammered down with a ferocity that was unlike any heat Stoudenmire had ever known. Bajeca took it all in stride, seemingly oblivious to anything save the tracks stretching westward before them. But the lawman felt as though every ounce of sweat in his body had been drained off, leaving him as dry and parched as a weathered slab of rawhide.

Surprisingly, there was no sign that Kale had any intention of halting to rest his mount. The tracks showed that the horse was nearly spent, dragging his hooves through the clutching grip of the sand. Occasionally the rider had dismounted, walking a ways to give the animal a breather, but it was all too clear that Kale meant to cross this desolate wilderness before the day was out. The two hunters held to a grueling pace, taxing the endurance of their own mounts to the limit. They were gaining, and each time the trail showed signs of freshening their spirits climbed. But they couldn't slacken the pace or allow time for even a brief rest. Kale was still running scared, and if he was to be caught, it might just be now or never.

Through the afternoon they trudged on, following tracks that deviated only to skirt stands of giant saguaro, prickly pear, and Spanish bayonet. Rattlesnakes, tiny desert rodents, and a startling variety of lizards were the only life they saw stirring, and along toward sundown it became apparent that there was small likelihood of overtaking the hunted man. As dusk settled over the vast emptinesss surrounding them, the two men decided to call it quits for the night. There was no sense in going on and running the risk of losing Kale's tracks in the dark. Better to wait for first light and put on a final burst of speed in the hope they could close the gap before he reached the sanctuary of the mountains.

They halted to make camp in the foothills bordering the Sierra Madres. Here the land was a jagged upheaval of deep canyons, arroyos, and treacherous barrancas, all the more reason not to chance traveling at night. Although water was to be found only during the spring rains, their *ollas* were still half-full, and they could at least afford the luxury of quenching their thirst. What remained would go for their horses, to prepare them for the sprint that would come with false dawn.

Stoudenmire had just begun loosening the straps on the pack horse when he heard Bajeca grunt in that odd way Indians use when they run up on something unexpected. Turning, he saw the *mestizo* staring off toward a distant hill at a somewhat higher elevation. Though dusk had fallen there was still a murky half-light in the sky, and he could just make out a stand of gnarled juniper trees on the hillside. There wasn't anything strange in that, and for a moment he thought the breed must be having a bit of fun at his expense. Indians had a peculiar sense of humor, and they weren't above a practical joke on occasion. Then he took a closer look and saw a slight movement among the trees. Rubbing his eyes, he peered into the gloomy twilight, and any doubts fast went by the boards. A wispy tendril of smoke floated skyward through the stand of junipers.

Tom Kale had just played out his string!

Clearly he was on the back slope of the hill and had built a small fire in the belief that there wasn't anything but coyotes and gila monsters within miles of his camp. It wouldn't be easy crossing this nightmarish terrain in the dark, but with any luck at all they would have him trussed up like a yearling steer before the stars came out.

Moving up to stand beside Bajeca, the lawman nodded toward the hill. "It appears the pale-eyed *diablo* has been brought to bay."

The *mestizo*'s eyes remained fastened on the smoke. "An animal being hunted is allowed no mistakes. This one was cursed by a *bruja* even before he started."

"Perhaps it is so." Stoudenmire paused, watching the Indian closely. "Bear in mind, he is to be taken alive unless there is no other way."

Bajeca's stoic features gave no hint of what he was thinking. Without a word he strode to his horse and pulled an ancient Henry repeater from behind the saddle. Stoudenmire thought of saying something else, but gave it up as a waste of breath. Walking to the chestnut, he jerked the scattergun and quickly checked the loads. After a few moments discussion, the two men separated and melted into the darkness. Bajeca would circle in from the south, and the lawman would approach from the north. Once in position, they would sneak up and try to jump the man as he slept.

Working his way through a series of arroyos and rock studded hogbacks, Stoudenmire spent the next hour in a cautious advance. After skinning both knees and a set of knuckles, he was worming his way up the hillside when the dull boom of a pistol shattered the inky stillness. No mistaking it, the shot had come from a Colt and not a Henry repeater. Whatever was happening on the other side of that slope, Kale had gotten in the first lick.

Suddenly the night was split by an ungodly scream of sheer, animal terror. Then just as quickly all went still, and the lawman could feel a vagrant breeze cooling the sweat on his forehead. Wondering if Bajeca had met his match, Stoudenmire scrambled up the hill, trying to make as little noise as possible. Within moments he topped the rise and plowed down the other side, cocking both hammers on the shotgun as he skidded through the dusty soil. Moving cautiously now, he eased through another stand of juniper and tangled underbrush, gliding silently from tree to tree. Abruptly he broke out into a small clearing and froze dead in his tracks.

Beside a crackling little fire sat Bajeca, calmly wiping his knife clean on Kale's shirt. Glancing up, he grinned like a playful wolf and lifted Kale's severed head from the ground.

"A gift for *el patrón*. One *gringo pistolero* who will kill no more."

CHAPTER SEVEN

1.

STOUDENMIRE RODE into Paso del Norte just before noon two days later. Since there was no need to push themselves or their horses further, the lawman had set a leisurely pace on the trip back from the mountains. The chase was over, and the bloody sack hanging from Bajeca's saddle horn made it unnecessary to reach El Paso with any haste. Tom Kale's death had turned the clock back almost to where he had started, for without the ramrod's testimony, there wasn't much to be gained by dragging the Bannings into court. The marshal had thought about it plenty in the last couple of days, roundly cursing the way fate sometimes bollixed up a man's best shot. It was a bitter pill to swallow, but there just weren't any witnesses left. First the rustler captured in the raid on Don Miguel's *hacienda*, then Ramón, and now Kale. People who had the goods on the Bannings somehow seemed to wind up stone cold and six feet under. It was a sorry goddamn mess, no two ways about it.

When Stoudenmire and the *mestizo* had ridden into the *rancho* the evening before, Don Miguel insisted he spend the night. They had much to celebrate, *el patrón* announced, and he promptly ordered a royal *banquete* in honor of the successful hunt. After presenting his gory trophy, Bajeca had quietly disappeared. Clearly he preferred the solitude of the wilderness to a Mexican shindig, and Stoudenmire couldn't fault him there. The lawman wasn't in a particularly festive mood himself, what with being fresh out of witnesses. But he had little choice in the matter since everyone on the place took to addressing him as *compadre*.

Damned if a man could figure these people out. Only a few days ago, the *alcalde* started calling him son, and now he had been appointed sidekick to a whole crew of Mex cowhands. That was heady stuff, and he could see how the *hidalgos* had made a good thing for themselves by playing on the herd instinct of their people.

Kale's head was mounted on a pole in the courtyard and anyone who could still fog a mirror filed past to have a look, women and kids included. The *vaqueros* swarmed around Stoudenmire throughout the entire night, pumping his hand till it was sore. He was *macho hombre*, the man who had avenged the murder of their young *caporal*, and from this night forward, his name would be honored among the people of Don Miguel. Somehow Stoudenmire took it all in stride, and even managed to loosen up a bit after a few shots of tequila. But Kale's swollen eyes staring down on the festivities played hell with a man's appetite, no matter how much firewater he downed. The lawman ignored the food and stuck to drinking, all the while wishing there were some way to wind that head up and let it speak its piece in a courtroom.

Thinking back on it as he reined to a stop before the *alcalde*'s house, Stoudenmire seemed to recall having held a conversation with the head sometime during the night. But it was all a little muddled, and he couldn't remember exactly what Kale had said. If anything. That tequila was wicked stuff, probably the very drink people had in mind when they started talking about popskull. Anytime it made a stray head start popping its jaws, there was damn sure more to it than a fellow might suspect. But what the hell, he was among friends. And near as he could recollect, they had listened to the conversation like a flock of stewed owls anyway.

Pedro Vazquez threw open the door at his knock and embraced him with a great show of affection. The *alcalde* had already heard about the outcome of the manhunt, as had everyone in Paso del Norte. Ramón's killer had been tracked down and executed, which was the kind of justice people understood best; and so far as the old man was concerned, Stoudenmire wasn't far shy from walking on water.

Vazquez ordered a lavish meal in his honor, then made him sit down and relate every detail of the chase. When the lawman came to the part about finding Bajeca with Kale's severed head, the *alcalde*'s eyes glistened brightly, and for a minute Stoudenmire thought he was going to jump up and shout *¡Ole!* But the aging politico merely nodded with vast approval and listened attentively as the Texan concluded with the highlights of Don Salazar's impromptu fiesta. When he finished, Vazquez chuckled happily and slapped his knee.

"*¡Madre mio!* I would have given much to see that *monfeta*'s head on a pole." Then he darted a sheepish glance at the lawman. "Do not be offended by our barbaric ways, *amigo*. We Mexicans are a peaceful race, but even the *santos* might become bloodthirsty if their loved ones were being slaughtered like mad dogs."

"My only regret, *jefe*, is that the head belonged to Kale instead of the man named Banning. But that is a problem I will face tomorrow. Tell me now of what happens between our people during my absence."

"Absolutely nothing, my friend." The old man scratched his head as if studying an unusually complicated riddle. "Trade has come to a standstill, but other than that there have been no *incidentes*. Not even one. It surpasses all understanding."

Stoudenmire found it equally bewildering, even unsettling in some curious way. "That is more than I had hoped for. I expected the pursuit of Ramón's killer to calm the more reasonable among our people, but there are many hotheads on both sides of the river. Perhaps the *salvajes* among us tire of fighting after all."

"Perhaps. Yet it is known that a stillness always moves ahead of the storm. Pardon an old man's *cinismo*, but I fear that even a slight rupture would once again set the people at one another's throats."

"*Sí*, there is truth in that. Though the one who must

enforce the law sometimes finds himself wishing it were not so."

"You are a young man, and it is only natural that you would wish away the bad. I have lived much too long for such things. Occasionally I can deceive myself into believing that the human race is human after all, but only for a moment. Late at night when I face my God and myself, I must admit that brotherhood is a false dream echoed by false prophets.

"You paint a bleak picture, *anciano.*" Stoudenmire tapped the star pinned on his shirt. "Perhaps if men like myself kill enough of the evil ones, there will one day be peace over this land."

The *alcalde* chortled skeptically. "You had best start with the women, my friend. Only when there are none left to bear sons will we eliminate the greed that drives men to kill. The Spaniards took this land from the *indios*. The *juaristas* took it from the *españols*. And now the *gringos* would take it from my people. There is no end. Only change."

"You are no doubt correct, *jefe*. Still there are many who would prefer to live in peace. Otherwise, they would not hire men like me to rid the world of lice. Perhaps the day will yet come when the good ones can set their *diferencias* aside and live in harmony."

"Only a foolish man would cease to pray for such things. To abandon all hope is to renounce *Jesucristo* in the same breath." Pedro Vazquez's deadened eyes belied his words, and it occurred to the lawman that Ramon's death had turned the old man into a devout cynic.

"I am not a religious man, but in my own way I help *Padrenuestro* along." Stoudenmire rose and settled his gunbelt in place. "Now I must leave you. There are those across the river who grow anxious for my return."

Vazquez came erect and shook his hand warmly. "What will you do now, *mi hijo?* All who could have helped you have been silenced forever."

The lawman grinned. "I will do what it is that I do best, *jefe*. Kill a few more of the evil ones."

"*Excelente!* There is always room in the graveyards for

those who prey on the weak. *Buena fortuna*, my young friend. Walk lightly and *vaya con Dios*." The *alcalde's* eyes twinkled and a sardonic smile spread over his brown features. "*Y el diablo* if need be."

Ten minutes later Stoudenmire nudged the gelding into the water and forded the Rio Grande. For no particular reason it passed through his mind that Pedro Vazquez, was a man who had lost his grip on his own soul. The old Mexican no longer believed in anything, least of all himself. Losing faith in God was one thing, that happened to lots of men who still somehow managed to toe the mark. But when a man lost faith in himself, he was treading on a real hellish piece of quicksand.

The marshal's hand lightly brushed over the holstered Colt, finding curious reassurance in the cold metal. There were some things a man never lost faith in, no matter how troublesome times became.

2.

PEOPLE ALONG San Antonio Street stopped to stare as the lawman rode past. Behind him Stoudenmire could hear their excited chattering, and as he neared the plaza, a small crowd had formed in his wake. They appeared neither pleased nor distressed by his return; their attention centered solely on the fate of Tom Kale. Everyone knew the marshal would come back, and seeing him in the flesh only piqued their curiosity all the more. What they really wanted to know were the particulars of his widely discussed manhunt in Old Mexico.

Presumably Stoudenmire had caught up with Kale; that much was taken for granted. But the wanted man wasn't strapped across the marshal's packhorse, and that raised questions of an even more intriguing nature. Had he killed the Banning ramrod and buried him across the border? Or had Kale somehow outwitted him, maybe even outshot him, and reached the interior safely? Both possibilities had an appeal all their own, and the crowd batted them back and forth as if Stoudenmire weren't anywhere within spitting distance.

The lawman wasn't especially interested one way or the other, and he simply ignored them, reining the chestnut catty-cornered across the plaza. He was so tired he felt like he had been run through an ore crusher; over two hundred miles in less than three days was enough to wear any man's tailbone down to the nubbin. Yet physical weariness was only part of the dull ache that rode with him. Tom Kale's death had been a bitter disappointment and returning without a witness against the Bannings only rubbed salt in an already festered sore. Maybe if it had been he who killed Kale, it wouldn't have galled so much. But he felt like he had just been along for the ride, and the scenery damn sure wasn't anything to write home about.

The crowd was still hard on his heels, and their curiosity had been whetted to the point that one man finally worked up the gumption to address Stoudenmire directly. "Marshal, if it ain't too much trouble, we'd be obliged to know what happened over there."

"Mr. Kale won't be coming back." Stoudenmire didn't bother looking at them. Instead, he kicked the chestnut into a trot and left the crowd gawking at his broad back.

But his cryptic answer was clear enough, if somewhat short on details. *Tom Kale had gone under!* How or where wasn't all that important, not at the moment. The thing that mattered was that Stoudenmire had returned, and the wanted man was dog meat. The news swept through El Paso like wildfire, cresting from building to building as if fanned by a hot wind. *Dallas Stoudenmire had pickled the fastest gun in town, and the Bannings were next!*

The marshal didn't give a good goddamn what they thought. By tonight it would be all over town how Kale had actually died, and that would really give them something to talk about. Maybe it would even put the fear of God in some of Banning's cutthroats and set them to making tracks for parts unknown. As for the Bannings themselves, they might just drop around to shake his hand. Kale's death had damn sure gotten them off the hook, and unless he missed his guess, the Coliseum would start serving drinks on the house in about ten minutes. Cursing under his breath, Stoudenmire dismounted in front of the jail and looked up to see Gillette hurrying across the plaza.

The lanky deputy ambled to a halt and eyed him critically. "Well I see you made it back. But damned if you don't look like somebody rolled you over a cliff in a gunnysack."

Stoudenmire tied the horses to a hitch rack and smiled tightly. "Jim, that's pretty much how I feel. Either I'm not used to sittin' a saddle three days straight, or else my rump's gone soft with city living."

"Probably a little bit of both." Gillette craned his long neck around and gave the packhorse a quick once over. "See you didn't bring Kale back after all. Don't tell me now, lemme guess. The Rurales have got him, and they've done thrown away the key."

"Matter of fact, I didn't see a Rurale the whole time I was gone." The lawman grunted as Gillette's wiseass grin evaporated. "C'mon, let's get in out of the heat, and I'll tell you all about a sneaky half-breed I've been keepin' company with."

Once inside, Stoudenmire got himself a cup of coffee, then settled down behind the desk. Skipping minor details, he briefly sketched out what had happened across the river, winding it up with a step by step account of the manhunt's grisly finish. Gillette appeared speechless for a moment, and the lawman chuckled to himself. Anything that could silence this old turkey-gobbler must be hair-raising enough for the best of them.

"Jeeesus Christ!" The deputy looked like a man with a harelip trying to quote scripture. "That's the goddamnedest thing I ever heard tell of. Them bastards sorta play for keeps, don't they?"

"Yeah, I reckon you could say that. They sure as hell snuffed out our last witness against the Bannings, and that's about as permanent as you can get. Looks to me like we're right back where we started."

"Noooo. Not just exactly, that is." Gillette rubbed the back of his neck, and his forehead wrinkled in a frown. "Way I hear it, the Bannings are about half-froze to lift your scalp. So it's just likely you might've smoked 'em out in the open after all."

Stoudenmire's mouth cracked in a tight smile, and the weariness seemed to drain out of his face. "Well now, that's a horse of another color, sure enough. Did you happen to hear when they would make a try, or how they'd go about it?"

"Nope. Just heard that Ed Banning's been kickin' up dust like a pony going off in four directions. Don't take much savvy to figure out how they'll try it, though. Their kind always comes at a man from behind."

"I expect you're right. But it doesn't make much difference one way or the other. Just so long as we can force 'em to show their hand, I won't be too particular. Where'd you run across a juicy tidbit like that, anyway?"

"Well it starts to get a little dicey right about there." Gillette absently twirled the ends of his mustache and cocked one eye. "Doc Cummings got it from Seth Hart who got it from somewheres else. Accordin' to Doc it came straight from the horse's mouth, or pretty damn close thereabouts."

The lawman grimaced and shook his head skeptically. "Hell, I thought you'd got it from one of those unimpeachable sources the newspapers are always carryin' on about. Listening to Doc talk is like pourin' shit through a tin horn. No matter how it comes out, there's not a clear note in the bunch."

"Maybe. But I've been hearin' the same story all over town. The word's around that Banning's not just bowed up anymore. You got him plumb spooked and from where he sits, it's you or them. Folks allow that he don't mean to leave any loose ends this time, either."

"Jim, it sounds to me like someone just made an educated guess and started themselves a fair-sized rumor. Hart and Cummings can speculate all they want, but that's not gonna get the Bannings off their duff and into the street."

The old lawdog splattered the spittoon with a brown wad and licked his mustache. "When it comes to hardheaded, you could spot a jackass a city block and win going away."

Stoudenmire blew steam off his coffee and mulled it over for a minute. "I'm not sayin' it won't happen. Where there's smoke, there's always fire. Even if it's only a little one. I just don't happen to think the Bannings are rattled enough to start doing their own dirty work. Not yet, at any rate. If they try anything, it'll come from one of those knuckleheads on their payroll."

"Damnation, that's all I've been tryin' to say! Somebody's gonna be layin' to kill you. What the hell difference does it make who it is?"

"None, I suppose. Except that the only way we're gonna get the Bannings is to rawhide 'em into a gunfight." The marshal considered that at some length before he looked back at Gillette. "What about Hart and his crowd? How are they taking all this?"

The deputy's mouth split in a big, horsey grin. "Well, I'll tell you. 'Pears to me they don't know whether to shit or go blind. First they got a case of the hives 'cause you lit out after Kale. Then they started bendin' my ear about Banning plannin' to catch you in a dark alley. Sometimes I get to wonderin' if they've still got to have a light when they get tucked in every night."

Before Stoudenmire could frame an answer, Kate burst through the door and ran around the desk. With a tiny cry of delight she threw herself into his arms and began smearing his face with wet, sticky kisses. Gillette guffawed behind his hand, watching the lawman turn beet red with embarrassment as he tried to fend Kate off.

"Slow down, girl. I've only been gone three days."

Ignoring him completely, she smoothed back his hair and settled more securely into his lap. "Oh, it's so good to have you back. It seems like you've been gone forever, and I promise I'll never be cross again. I was over in Doc's store, and when I heard you were back, I said to myself, the very first thing I'm going to say is that I'm sorry. Well, I'm sorry. So don't you dare act grumpy." Clutching him around the neck, she gave him a big kiss square on the mouth.

Stoudenmire lifted her easily and set her feet on the floor. Rising, he gave Gillette a helpless look. "Jim, how about taking care of my horses. I can see we're not gonna get much work done around here today."

With an arm around Kate's waist, he headed for the door, and she snuggled hungrily against his chest. Just as they disappeared through the door, he turned and called over his shoulder. "Mind the store, deputy. I just decided to take the night off."

3.

AFTER CHECKING in with Gillette next morning, Stoudenmire strolled over to the mayor's office. Overnight a scheme had occurred to him that could easily drive another nail into the Bannings' coffin. Whether it worked out or not, he had nothing to lose except a little conversation. Talk was cheap enough, and he might just wind up with a songbird who knew where all the skeletons were buried.

After Kate finally fell asleep in his arms, he had lain awake far into the night sorting through the alternatives that remained. There were many ways to make a gang run for cover. The quickest was to force their boss into a gunfight, but Ed Banning showed a decided reluctance to accept the challenge. Some men preferred to hire others to do their killing for them, and the weasel-faced saloon owner was plainly of that stripe. Whatever it was that would make him stand and fight hadn't come clear as yet, so the lawman set that tactic aside until he could get a better handle on what made Banning tick.

Another method was to whittle away at the lesser gang members, undermining confidence in the boss as his flunkeys were fed to the meat grinder one by one. This was the tack he had followed from the start, yet he had to admit that the score seemed a bit lopsided. Campbell and Kale had gone under to be sure, but at a cost of Ramón, a court official, and two *vaqueros*. Somehow it seemed like a damned poor trade, even though Banning had lost four men in the rhubarb over the young Mexican girl. Besides, taking a bit here and there was the slow way to get results, and he needed something to speed this deal up.

Staring at the ceiling, he had wracked his brain for some foolproof way to clobber the Bannings once and for all. Just when he was about to chuck the whole mess and get some sleep, he remembered the old saw about divide and conquer. Look for the weakest link in the chain and twist till it broke. Once it snapped, Ed Banning would never get it spliced in time to save his own neck. With his grip on the town loosened, both the political machine and the gang itself would come apart at the seams. The more Stoudenmire thought about it the better he liked the idea. And unless he had lost the knack of sizing up men, Mayor Isaac Porter was the weak link.

Stoudenmire found the politician alone in his office, seated behind a desk staring listlessly at a stack of ledgers. His heavy tread brought Porter's head around, and the marshal sensed that this wasn't the same man who had berated him the morning of Ramón's death. Something about his eyes had changed. Nothing a man could put a name to, but it was there just the same. Like a gopher when it's cut off from its hole and no place to run. Suddenly his plan took on a new dimension, for the easiest man to buffalo was the one that had already scared himself.

"Morning, Mr. Mayor," he said, nodding at the ledgers. "How goes the fight?"

Porter darted a nervous glance at the gray-bound records. "Oh, these. Nothing really. The city fiscal year is upon us, and I was just going over the books."

Stoudenmire was well aware that such matters were generally left to accountants, but he let it pass. "Well that's a little out of my bailiwick. Never was much of a hand with figures. If you can spare a minute, I thought I'd fill you in on my trip south."

"No, no. That's quite all right, Marshal." His eyes widened, flashing an unnatural amount of white. "We can dispense with your report. The story's all over town. As a matter of fact, people aren't talking about much else."

"Yeah, something like that would just naturally get people to beatin' their gums." The lawman dropped into a chair and crossed his long legs. "Course, I'd better give you the lowdown anyway. Folks have a way of twistin' things out of shape, and you might've heard the wrong version."

The mayor sighed and slumped back in his chair with an acute look of resignation. "If you insist. But keep it to official matters. I've already heard the gory details."

"You mean about Kale?" Stoudenmire's expression was deceptively bland, but when Porter stiffened at his words, he knew he was on the right track. "Damned if that didn't beat anything I ever saw."

"Please, Marshal." The politician squirmed uneasily and a nervous tic surfaced beneath his left eye. "Just hold it to the facts, if you don't mind."

"Well, Mayor, I reckon the way a wanted man goes under is part of the facts. Come to think of it, not much else matters when it comes down to an official report. Wouldn't you say?"

Porter opened his mouth to reply, but the lawman plowed dead ahead, waving aside his sputtering objections. "You see, it was like this. I was teamed up with this breed, and we had trailed Kale to the foothills this side of the Sierra Madres. That night we separated with the idea of sneakin into his camp and taking him alive. Well wouldn't you know that damned Injun got there before me. I came wormin' through the brush, and there he sat. Holdin' Kale's head up like he was huntin' for fleas. The sonovabitch had whacked it off the way a man would split a fresh melon."

Stoudenmire flicked his hand across his throat in a slicing motion, and beads of sweat popped out on the mayor's forehead. For a moment the lawman thought Porter was going to swoon dead away, but he somehow got a grip on himself and straightened in his seat. "That will do, Marshal. I'm not a violent man, and I see no need to belabor how Tom Kale died."

"Why hell, Mayor. How he died is only half the story. What happened the next night was the real gutbuster." Stoudenmire hitched his chair around and leaned forward, eyeball to eyeball with the little man. "Them Mexicans got a fiesta going and the guest of honor was none other than old Tom Kale himself. The bastards stuck his head on a pole and spent the whole goddamn night dancin' around it like a bunch of wild Apaches. Course, I'll have to admit that it smelled a little rank by then, and those eyes bulging out of their sockets was enough to gag a dog off a gut wagon. But it was purely something to see. Just think of it! Jammed up on a pole and grinnin' like a jack-o'-lantern."

Porter's face turned green, and the lawman scooted back, certain the mayor was going to puke at any moment. The politician jerked a handkerchief and clapped it over his mouth, breathing heavily. Then he fell back in his chair and closed his eyes, taking short, fast gasps like a man trying to clear his head of a sickening stench. After a brief struggle to hold down his breakfast, his color returned, and he slowly opened his eyes.

Stoudenmire poured him a glass of water from a beaker on the desk, then let him have it right below the gizzard. "Porter, I told you that little story just to give you an idea of what's in store for anybody that stands in my way. I intend to scuttle the Bannings and all their cronies, even if it means fighting dirty in the clinches. And when I said *all* their cronies, I meant you especially, Mister Mayor. Course, I don't need to paint you a picture. You're smart enough to figure who's gonna be left holdin' the bag when the rats start scurrying for safety."

Isaac Porter blanched, and he suddenly felt sick in a different way. Stoudenmire's last statement jibed perfectly with his own estimate of what would happen when the Bannings were finally put to flight. Someone would be left behind as a sacrificial goat, and he had a pretty fair idea of who that *someone* would be. But that didn't shake him nearly as much as the knowledge that the coldblooded bastard seated across from him would be right there waiting. Ready, willing, and able to supply the noose that would stretch his plump neck.

The mayor wanted desperately to talk to someone; to unburden himself and erase the sense of doom that was with him constantly now. Yet there was one unknown in this whole ghastly mess. *Could he trust Stoudenmire?* Or should he go to Seth Hart? Maybe even the governor. It was a critical decision, and a man in his position couldn't afford even one mistake.

Glancing back at the lawman, he spoke with a bravado that seemed curiously out of character. "You're just trying to frighten me. But you'll find I don't fold so easily, Mr. Stoudenmire."

The marshal regarded him with mild disgust. "Porter, I'll make it easy for you. Swap sides now and testify against the Bannings, and you can walk away a free man. Otherwise you'll swing with the rest of 'em. The offer's good for forty-eight hours. No longer."

Stoudenmire rose and walked to the door. Then he turned as though an afterthought had suddenly occurred to him. "Something you oughta keep in mind while you're thinking it over. I can protect you from the Bannings. But the Banning's can't protect you from me."

The door opened and closed, leaving Isaac Porter alone with his fear.

Crossing the plaza, Stoudenmire wondered if he really could deliver on that last statement. He damn sure hadn't had much luck protecting people from the Bannings so far. But, what the hell! There was plenty of time to start worrying about a grubby politician if and when he decided to switch horses. The thing to do now was to take up the slack and see if a little judicious pressure wouldn't pop that weak link right under the Bannings' nose.

4.

THE BANNINGS were involved in working out a scheme of their own. Late that afternoon Ed and Sam came together in the backroom office to discuss how it should be handled. Stoudenmire had to be snuffed out, on that they were agreed. The sooner the better for everyone concerned, particularly themselves. The marshal's bulldog tenacity showed no signs of weakening, and by his own word he wouldn't slack off until they had been plowed under. Even if they were disposed to let things rock along for a while, the surly bastard seemed determined to force their hand.

Each day he lived, he became a greater threat, that was plain enough for anyone to see. And only a fool greenhorn let another man pick the time and place for a fight.

Whatever remnants of the code duello that remained after the war hadn't taken root in El Paso. Here the only recognized code was survival, and whoever struck first was generally thought to have something besides beeswax between his ears. The logic was really quite simple, profoundly earthy in its own way. Stoudenmire had poked his nose where it didn't belong, which was the kind of thing a man could overlook only so long. The German clearly didn't know when to let well enough alone, therefore he had to be killed. That was the only kind of language some people understood, especially hard-nosed lawdogs.

But Ed Banning was of the opinion that it had to be handled discreetly, in a manner that could never be traced back to them. Although elections were still more than a year away, they couldn't afford to take any chances. Voters had a long memory when it could be proved that a town's political boss was playing dirty pool, which meant that the Banning name had to be kept out of it at all costs. And right there was where Sam bowed his neck.

"Dammit, Ed, that's not fair." Sam was just dense enough to think it should be kept in the family. "I've got a personal score to settle with that shithead, and you got no right to let somebody else do the job."

The elder Banning shook his head wearily, as though involved in a senseless argument with a slow child. "Brother, I'm tellin' you, it's not worth the risk. You can get your jollies off just as well watchin' somebody else do it."

"Ah, horse apples!" The burly ruffian slunk down in his chair and petulantly slewed his eyes around the room. "That's like sayin' I'd get my load off watchin' some jasper fuck my best girl."

"Now there you go again," Ed snapped. "Making dumb comparisons that you can't back up. You know goddamned well those things have nothing to do with each other. This is business." He sighed heavily, glancing sideways at the younger man. ''Besides, you don't even have a best girl.''

''Now look who's harpin' the same old tune. One of these days I'm gonna get tired of you raggin' me about girls. You just wait and see. I know a few stories about you that ain't been told. Don't think I don't.''

Ed's eyes scrunched up at the corners, and he regarded his brother with a wary gaze. ''Is that a fact? Well suppose you just tell me what you know if it's so goddamn earth-shattering.''

Sam darted a secretive look at him. ''Oh, I know something. Don't you worry about that. Them girls over at Lizzie Pride's do a lot of talkin', and I got big ears.''

''No shit? Up beside a jackass I'd never have known. Now suppose you quit playin' ring-around-the-rosie and tell me what the hell you've heard.''

Sam's mouth twisted in a juvenile smirk, and he giggled nervously, not unlike a schoolboy telling his first dirty joke. ''They say you can't get it up. They're all the time laughin' and carrying on about it when they think nobody's around. That redhead swears up and down you couldn't stick your pecker in a pail of soft lard.''

Ed Banning's features went red as ox blood, and he half rose from his chair. ''That rotten little bitch! I'll cut her tits off and stuff 'em down her gullet. Then we'll see how much talkin' she does.'' The rage slowly drained out of his face, leaving it a mottled purple. After a moment he settled back, raking his brother with a furious scowl. ''And you better keep your mouth shut, too. If I ever get wind of you talkin' out of turn, I'll crack your balls good. Savvy?''

''Sure, Ed. Whatever you say.'' Sam clamped his legs shut, dimly wondering why a sharp pain had suddenly pulsed through his seeds. ''I was just funnin.' You know I didn't mean no harm.''

Ed drew a deep breath and released it slowly, forcing his mind back to the more immediate problem. ''All right, let's drop it and start thinkin' about Stoudenmire. You're not gonna do it, and that's final, so don't give me any lip.

The way I've got it figured, we need ourselves a stalking horse."

When Sam gave him a baffled look, the gang leader broke it down into two-bit words. "That's someone who has reason to want the German six feet under. Then everybody'll think he had a personal motive, and we won't be connected to it. He does the killin,' and our hands are clean. Sort of like havin' your cake and eatin' it too."

Sam digested his brother's scheme in an unhurried way, and a brightness slowly kindled in his eyes. "Yeah, that's real smart. Maybe we could even hire us a greaser to do it. Folks around here think greasers are dumb enough to do anything."

"No, we don't have time to go scoutin' up some Mex pig-sticker. We need somebody that's handy, and it's got to be a man with a first class grudge against Stoudenmire. I've been giving it a lot of thought, and I think I know just the man."

"Well hell, there's your answer, slicker'n rat shit. Who is he?"

"Bill Johnson."

"Bill Johnson?" Sam parroted the words with gaping disbelief. "That goddamn alky couldn't hold a gun steady enough to hit a bull in the ass across a fence."

"That's the whole point. We're gonna get him stiffer'n a board. Then we'll start talkin' about Stoudenmire. How he fired Johnson and booted his ass out the door. How he killed George Campbell, the only friend Johnson had in his whole miserable life. Before you know it, we'll have him foamin' at the mouth like a blind dog in a butcher shop. Then we'll open the back door and turn him loose. Everybody in town'll figure he had a shitpot full of reasons to kill the German."

"You know somethin', Ed? You're nothin' but a goddamn wizard." Sam nodded sagely for a moment, then blinked as though some part of the riddle remained unanswered. "Say, I just now thought of somethin'. You never did tell me if it was true."

Ed was still preoccupied with engineering the marshal's sudden demise. "If what was true?"

"What them girls said. That you couldn't get a hard-on no more."

Banning came up out of his chair. "Get your ass out of here! Go find Johnson and tell him I want to see him tonight. And you'd better listen to me close, little brother. Don't you ever again start runnin' your tongue about what those girls said. Not unless you want me to cut it out."

Sam backed slowly across the room, easing through the door without once meeting his brother's smoky glare. When he was gone, it passed through Ed's mind that he looked like a little boy who had just had his wrists slapped. The hell of it was that the dumb brute would always look like that. If he lived to be a hundred, he'd still be a half-grown kid masquerading as a man. And big brother would still be giving him a sugartit to suck instead of letting him fend for himself. Shit!

Later that night Sam returned with Bill Johnson in tow. But as it turned out, they didn't have much of a chore getting Johnson squiffed. The former deputy had installed himself as the reigning town drunk, and he was generally able to cadge enough drinks to stay half-crocked around the clock. When he came through the door, he was already walking on his heels, and within an hour Ed had floated his gizzard with a liberal dose of forty-rod.

Things went pretty much as Banning had predicted. Once they had Johnson cross-eyed, the gang leader started baiting him. *Hadn't Stoudenmire fired him, made a fool out of him in front of the whole town? Hadn't the marshal also killed his best friend, shot him down in cold blood? No real man would take something like that flat on his back. Anybody with any guts would make sure that the sonovabitch was laid out stone-cold dead. The sooner the better!*

Johnson responded to the goad more readily than Banning had expected. Staggering about the room in an alcoholic rage, he swore he would settle Stoudenmire's hash that very night. Before he could have any second thoughts, Banning thrust a shotgun into his hands and shoved him out the back door. Get him when he makes his night rounds, the gang leader whispered, down by the old church on Texas Street. Johnson nodded drunkenly and reeled off into the darkness, mumbling to himself. Banning watched for a moment to make sure he was headed in the right direction, then stepped back inside.

Sam was grinning like a short-fanged hyena. "Ed, it's just like I said. You're a fuckin' wizard."

Banning's eyes swung around, boring holes clean through him. "Listen close you big ox, 'cause I've only got time to say this once. Stick on Johnson's trail like a leech. If he gets it when the fireworks go off, then we've got no problem. But if he's still kickin' after he gets Stoudenmire, then you kill him on the spot. Got that? Blast him before he moves out of his tracks. Make it look like the German got him. The one thing we sure as shit don't need is another witness. Now vamoose. And mind what I told you."

Shooting clay pigeons was old hat to Sam, and he took off like the dinner bell had just caught him out in the north forty. When the door closed, Ed Banning settled into his chair, pouring himself a long, tall drink. It had been a grueling night, but for the first time in weeks he felt like a man holding all the cards.

Then he chuckled. After tonight he'd be the *only* man holding the cards.

5.

DOC CUMMINGS came through the jail door shortly after eight that evening. His face was furrowed with solemnity and concern, the way an undertaker looks at an expensive funeral. The storekeeper had purposely avoided Stoudenmire's house for this discussion since he didn't want to upset Kate needlessly. Tonight he meant to talk some sense into his brother-in-law's thick head, and the kind of language he had in mind wasn't exactly suited to a lady's ears.

The marshal was seated behind the desk paring his fingernails. When Cummings entered, he glanced up, then casually went back to work with the jackknife. "Evenin', Doc. How's tricks?"

Somehow Stoudenmire's unruffled composure grated on the little merchant. It put him in mind of a big cat calmly cleaning its paws as the hunters closed in for the kill. His eyes darted about the office, noting that the lawman was alone. "Where's Gillette, out makin' rounds?"

"No, I gave him the night off." Stoudenmire met the older man's stare, then grinned furtively. "He was overdue, and tonight seemed as good as any."

Cummings couldn't speak for a moment; couldn't bring himself to believe that anyone would be that calculating. Then it came to him that the man his sister had married was just cold-blooded enough to do it.

"Jesus H. Christ. You let him have the night off just to bait somebody into takin' a shot at you. Didn't you?" When Stoudenmire didn't answer, the storekeeper dropped into a chair, now thoroughly exasperated. "Dallas, I'll swear to God, sometimes I get to thinkin' you're on a steady diet of loco weed."

"Doc, you're a born worrier." The lawman chuckled and went right on scraping his thumbnail with the big knife. The abrasive sound sent a chill down Cumming's spine, like chalk screeching across a blackboard. Without looking up, Stoudenmire commented, "The town's peaceful as a church social and I just figured Gillette could use a good night's sleep. Quit your frettin'. Nothin' is gonna happen that I can't handle."

The marshal had a point, and Cummings about halfway believed him. El Paso seemed to have recovered from the shock of the recent killings, or perhaps folks were just learning to take such things in stride. They had damn sure had plenty of practice in the last month or so, enough to last any sane man a couple of lifetimes. But whichever way a fellow looked at it, there was no disputing that the fear of bloodshed had subsided noticeably. Word had gotten around about Stoudenmire's peace talks with Pedro Vazquez, and the townspeople were convinced that they at last had a lawman worth his salt. Still, there was more to it than a bunch of grubby Mexicans. A hell of a lot more where the marshal was concerned.

Cummings made a church with his hands, then flexed his fingers into a steeple. Although Stoudenmire's concentration centered wholly on his fingernails, the storekeeper knew damn well he was watching out of the corner of his eye. Since shouting would obviously accomplish nothing, Cummings decided instead to play it cool and devastate the stubborn German with sheer logic.

"Dallas, I've just come from a meeting with Seth Hart and the rest of the boys. Since you're so all-fired touchy, they asked me to pass along their thoughts and see if we couldn't come to some sort of understanding."

"You mean Hart asked you to pass along his thoughts, don't you? I recollect that he does the talkin' and the rest of your crowd does all the listenin'."

The merchant reddened slightly, but kept his tone lowkey. "Seth's smarter'n you give him credit for, Dallas. While everybody else is runnin' around poppin' off at the mouth, he sits back and figures which way the frog is gonna jump."

"You're readin' the cards wrong, Doc. I'm not sayin' he isn't smart. I just don't want him meddling in my game. He's got his own ax to grind, and I'm not real sure I want any part of it. Not just yet, at any rate."

"For the life of me, I can't figure you out. Seth Hart is probably the most honorable man in this town, bar none. The only thing he wants is to get El Paso back in the hands of the people. Can't you see that, or is it that you just don't trust anybody?"

"Sure, I trust lots of folks. Just not all at once." The lawman left off paring his nails and pointed the blade in Cummings' direction. "You're the one that's got a lot to learn about who to trust. Nobody does nothin' out of Christian charity. Seth Hart included. Saintliness went out of style when they started feedin' people to the lions."

"Is that a fact?" The storekeeper's words came out a little waspish in spite of himself. "Well suppose you just tell me what Seth's got up his sleeve."

"Can't say as I've given it much thought, what with

one thing and another. But just for openers, let's suppose I've gotten rid of Banning, and the political goodies are up for grabs. Who do you think is gonna step in and fill his shoes?"

"Why Seth Hart, naturally. Every respectable person in El Paso looks to him for leadership. But that's no reason to suspect him. Good Lord, somebody has to run things. A town just doesn't run itself, you know."

"Nope, I guess not. Leastways there's generally plenty of people willing to take on the job." Stoudenmire regarded his nails critically for a moment, then snapped the knife shut. "Maybe Hart's everything you make him out to be. I'm not sayin' yay or nay. We'll more'n likely find out soon enough, and until then I'll just keep on playing 'em close to the vest."

Cummings bounded out of his chair and paced across the room, flailing the air with his arms. "Damnation! That beats anything I ever heard of. Do you want to know why Seth Hart called that meeting tonight?" Whirling, he advanced on the lawman. "Because he's worried about you, Mr. Doubting Thomas."

"Me?" Stoudenmire echoed skeptically.

"That's right, you. He believes you're in danger, and he means to do something about it."

Cummings' terse statement neatly skirted what had actually been said in the meeting. For over an hour Seth Hart had lectured his political cronies, building as always toward a predetermined and entirely logical conclusion. The Bannings were boxed in, damned if they did and damned if they didn't. Marshal Stoudenmire had become too popular with the townspeople for the city council to fire him, yet he was daily drawing closer to fitting the Bannings for a noose. They had no choice but to kill him. That or run. And the Bannings weren't the type to just fold camp and sneak off into the night. Still, one man wasn't a match for an entire gang. He could flush them, but when it came down to a shooting war, he couldn't stand alone. The conclusion was obvious. Stoudenmire needed help.

"Dallas, we've discussed this matter thoroughly and the solution is as plain as a bump on a log." Cummings met the lawman's gaze squarely. "What El Paso needs is a vigilance committee."

"Not on your tintype!" Stoudenmire's hoarse growl buffeted the storekeeper back on his heels. "The first sonovabitch that takes the law into his own hands is gonna get his ass handed to him on a platter. And I don't draw the line at anybody, Doc. Not even you."

"Man, stop and think for a minute. You're bucking impossible odds. The Bannings have to be made aware that this town won't abide further killing. Otherwise, you'll wind up trying to kick the slats out of a pine box. What we need is a group of armed citizens willing to back your play. That's what'll turn the trick, and once the Bannings see the town's behind you, we can end this dirty business."

"No dice. When a town resorts to vigilantes, they've the same as admitted that the law won't work. I'm tellin' you right now, Doc, that won't happen while I'm wearin' this star."

"But, Jesus Christ, you haven't got the chance of a snowball in hades. Are you so pigheaded you can't see that? Or are you just set on gettin' yourself killed?"

Stoudenmire ignored the merchant's nasty tone. "Doc, I appreciate the gesture, but I'll have to finish this job my own way. I was hired with no strings attached, and that's how we're gonna play it out. Worryin' about a bunch of amateur gunslingers would just slow me down, and right now I need to keep movin'."

Cummings started to object, but the lawman stilled him with an upraised hand. "Now let me tell you something for your own good, Doc. What would happen if Hart formed the vigilantes and I still ended up in a basket? Think about that, real hard. You might be trading one political kingfish for another. Maybe I'm pigheaded, but I reckon I'll take my chances without Hart standin' behind me with a gun."

When the storekeeper seemed inclined to argue, Stoudenmire decided it was time to make the evening rounds. But Cummings wasn't about to be put off by that old dodge. Like a feisty dog worrying a bone, he tagged along, talking a blue streak. Crossing the plaza, he extolled the many virtues of Seth Hart, lambasting Stoudenmire for being overly suspicious of the very people who could save his hide. When the marshal merely grunted and kept on walking, Cummings forgot about logic and launched into a harangue about the folly of pride and rockbound stubbornness. Turning off the plaza onto Oregon Street, the lawman headed for the southside, trying his best not to listen as Cummings haughtily pronounced him a brute for punishment.

Short of jailing his own brother-in-law, there seemed no way to end it, so Stoudenmire just plowed on, nodding every now and then to let the little storekeeper know he wasn't talking to himself. The southside dives seemed no more rowdy than usual, and the pair made quick time as they strolled through the quarter. Apparently the saloons and dancehalls had been able to handle their own troubles, and for once it appeared that Stoudenmire would get through a tour without making a single arrest. Still, the night was young and anything could happen. As a matter of fact, it usually did. On the southside every night was the same, some more so than others, and long before closing time the jail was generally packed to the gunnels with a motley assortment of belligerent drunks and weepy rumdums.

Nearing the end of Texas Street, the lawman was only vaguely aware that Cummings was still rambling on about the need for a vigilance committee. Leaving the boardwalk, he took to the street and headed for the far corner, figuring to shuck Doc for the night once they again reached the plaza. Suddenly there was a deafening explosion only yards behind them, and a load of buckshot kicked up dust at their feet. Cummings howled and grabbed at his leg, crow-hopping forward a few steps before he toppled over.

Staggering drunk, Bill Johnson wobbled from behind a stone pillar of an old mission and raised his scattergun for a better shot. But the lawman made a hellishly poor target. With the first report, he had hit the ground, rolled sideways, then reversed himself in the middle of a roll. Even as Johnson pressed the trigger, he swung around on his belly with his pistol out and cocked. The Colt roared a fraction ahead of the shotgun's hollow boom, and Johnson stumbled backwards into the crumbling pillar.

The buckshot tore a sign loose over a store on the other side of the street, and even as it fell, Stoudenmire dusted the former deputy with three quick shots. Johnson hung against the pillar, jerking with the impact of each slug, then pitched face down in the street.

Stoudenmire came to his feet just in time to glimpse a man dart from the shadows and take off running down Stanton Street. Hurriedly, he snapped off two shots as the dim figure disappeared around a corner, knowing even as he fired that he had missed. There was no sense in giving chase with an empty gun, and he turned back to see what could be done for Cummings. But the storekeeper was already up and hobbling toward the fallen bushwhacker, gripped by a curiosity that for the moment overshadowed the pain in his leg. Both men reached the body at the same time, and Stoudenmire toed it over with the point of his boot. In the faint starlight, the dead man's glassy eyes shone like cloudy agates.

"Well I'll be double-dipped," Cummings croaked. "It's old Bill Johnson. Who'd have thought that miserable bastard would've had the guts for it."

Stoudenmire started kicking out empties and reloading. "They've all got the guts for it when they're shootin' at your back."

Holstering the Colt, he draped Cummings arm around his shoulders and took off at a slow walk. After a few steps he nodded down at the storekeeper's bloody leg. "That's the very reason I didn't want your vigilantes roaming the streets. Amateurs always end up gettin' shot."

CHAPTER EIGHT

1.

EARLY NEXT morning Stoudenmire sent word to Seth Hart calling for a meeting. Things were coming apart at the seams, and unless they did something fast, the whole damn town was going to look like a shooting gallery.

Johnson's assassination attempt had fooled no one, least of all the respectable element. The Bannings were behind the bushwhacking just like they were behind every other dirty thing in El Paso, and trying to gun down a peace officer was the last straw. The town had split right down the middle, the southside scum against the decent folks, and battle lines were already being drawn. Word about the proposed vigilance committee had somehow leaked out, and knots of men were even then gathering on the plaza, bolstering one another's courage with loud talk and cheap whiskey. The general feeling seemed to be that Stoudenmire needed a hand in ridding the town of its undesirables, and for the first time, the people of El Paso were openly declaring their opposition to Boss Banning.

Stoudenmire wasn't too keen on meeting with the Hart faction, but he saw no alternative. The townspeople had to be headed off before armed mobs took to the streets, and much as he hated to admit it, that was something he couldn't handle alone. Hart and his cronies had started this crazy business about vigilantes, and they were the only ones who could quell the hotheads gathering on the plaza. The important thing now was to get the leaders talking against mob action, and damned quickly. Otherwise, good men were going to die needlessly.

Although he would have been the last to admit it, the marshal could have used a little breather himself. Getting bushwhacked hadn't bothered him so much, but things were getting pretty fierce around the house. Kate had given him the roughest night yet, railing at him for getting Doc shot, then blistering him in the next breath for being so careless with his own life. Stoudenmire couldn't tell which had infuriated her more; she had skipped from one to the other for the better part of two hours. Finally he had stalked out of the house and returned to the office, leaving her to stew in her own juices. Women were damn strange creatures, temperamental as a mare in heat and about as predictable as a landslide.

Still, taking the shooting back to back with Kate's tantrum didn't gall him nearly as much as this meeting with Hart. The plain fact was that he would have to ask for their help, and it curried him the wrong way to be forced into that position. Seth Hart was a horsetrader from way back, and an exchange of some kind would have to be made before the lard-faced politician agreed to back off. But Stoudenmire didn't have a hell of a lot to bargain with. Except maybe to reveal the next step in his war on the Bannings. And that really grated on the bone! So far no one knew what he was going to do until he did it, and that was the biggest edge a lawman could ask for. Once somebody else was made privy to his plans, the cheese could get binding, real fast. Yet it was sort of like the fellow caught in a blizzard with only the shithouse in sight. He had damned little choice.

The morning passed uneventfully enough, but a hard core of troublemakers were still congregated on the plaza. Stoudenmire resisted the temptation to send them packing; they would only gather somewhere else, and as long as they remained on the square, he at least had them in sight. The time to start worrying was when he couldn't see them. With the way things were breaking, that'd be the time some spellbinder would get them all fired up and start a march on the southside. Crossing the plaza on his way to the meeting, it occurred to the lawman that El Paso was a town that seemed damned set on getting itself leveled to the ground. Oddly enough, some folks had the quaint notion that the only way to bring about change was to burn everything down and start all over. And unless Seth Hart got off his ass, the hammerheads in town might just get their way.

Upon arriving at Hart's home back of the mill, he found the clique assembled and waiting. Looking them over as Hart led him into the room, the lawman was struck by a certain sameness about their appearance. Then it came to him. They were seated in exactly the same chairs as on his first visit to this house. Each man probably had squatter's rights on his chair by now, and doubtless there was some hierarchy involved that made the whole thing seem vastly important to them. *Little men playing for big stakes*. That's what it all boiled down to, whichever way a man came at it.

Doc Cummings was the only one who greeted him by name. Horace Adair merely nodded, letting the lawman know that he hadn't forgotten their last encounter. John Simmons and Nate Hobart ran a dead heat to see who could cake the most ice around the word *marshal*, and curiously enough, they both won. So far as Stoudenmire was concerned, the whole damn room was swathed in frost, and he had the distinct feeling it was going to be all uphill in the next few minutes. Hart waved him to a chair, then took his own seat and sat back with his hands folded over his ample stomach. Watching him, Stoudenmire was reminded of an old bullfrog hunkered down on a lily pad flicking his tongue at passing flies. The trouble being that he seemed to be the only fly in sight.

Hart purposely let the silence build for a moment, then looked over at the lawman with a gloating smile, "Marshal, I'll have to admit you've got us curious. Doc relayed your feelings about a vigilance committee, and I suspect he toned them down for our benefit. Be that as it may, you called this meeting, and we'll listen to whatever you've got on your mind."

Stoudenmire didn't even bother looking at the other men. They reflected Hart's mood like images on still water, and he addressed himself directly to the miller. "Mr. Hart,

I'm gonna give you some cold facts. What you do with 'em is your own affair. But I'm warnin' you straight out, if you jump the wrong way, you'll wind up getting a lot of people killed."

"Like I said, Marshal, we'll listen." Hart's eyes roved around the table, and the other men nodded hastily. "I can't promise any more than that."

"Suit yourself. I'm just hired to keep the peace. Whichever way it goes, it won't be any skin off my nose." Horace Adair's jaw popped open, but Hart stilled him with a sharp glance. The lawman went on as if the Irishman didn't even exist. "Let's take first things first, just to clear the air. You're out to form a vigilance committee, and I mean to stop you. If I have to, I'll toss every man here into the hoosegow and forget where I hid the key."

"That's pretty strong talk for a hired hand." Adair broke in before Hart could silence him.

"Nothin' I can't back up, Mr. Adair. But unless I'm pushed, I'd prefer to handle it another way. Right now it's between the Bannings and me. That's the way I'd like to keep it. If you fellas organize the vigilantes, that means Banning will have to muster his own army on the southside. Since he controls the vice district, it wouldn't be any sweat to raise more guns than you could count. Once your vigilantes cross the line, it'll mean open warfare in the streets, and nobody knows where that'll end. Not even Mr. Hart, here."

Seth Hart moved his hand in a dismissive gesture. "We're not the amateurs you think, Marshal. These same thoughts have occurred to us. But we figure to raise enough men to counter anything Banning could scrounge up."

"What kind of men? Clerks and bank tellers." Stoudenmire's lips curled back from his teeth in a grin that was more like a grimace. "Maybe you men can run a business, but when it comes to killin', you haven't got sense enough to wad a birdgun load. Those hardcases on the southside would eat you alive and spit out the seeds. But that's not what troubles me."

"Well now, that's a damn curious thing for a lawman

to say,'' Hart rumbled. ''Just exactly what is it that troubles you, Mr. Stoudenmire?''

''Anybody that goes huntin' trouble deserves what he gets, no matter which side of town he's from. But if you turn the vigilantes loose, a lot of innocent people are gonna get killed in the bargain. I've seen mobs before, and once they get a taste for blood, there's no telling where it'll stop. You people have just missed a couple of showdowns with the Mexicans by the skin of your teeth. Seems to me it'd be damned foolish to start a war among yourselves that could be just as bad. Maybe worse.''

Horace Adair snorted derisively and slapped the table with his open palm. ''By God, Stoudenmire, for sheer gall you take the cake. You haven't got any evidence, your witnesses have all been murdered, and the Bannings are still running El Paso like they had a patent. But you have the audacity to come in here and ask us to hold back. Hell man, you haven't done the job you were hired to do. It's time somebody else took a crack at it.''

Stoudenmire's flinty gaze swung around and settled over the Irishman like a cold mist. ''Mister, I'm tryin' to overlook your bad manners, but it's gettin' to be a chore. Don't press your luck.''

''All right, boys,'' Hart said, ''let's not fly off the handle. Suppose everybody just calms down and tries using a little reason for a change.''

''Seth, I'm all for reason, but it seems to me that Horace has a point.'' Nate Hobart rarely said anything, and his unexpected comment brought the other men's heads around. ''Just think about it for a minute. The Bannings are so deeply entrenched in politics that we'll never get any evidence of corruption. All the witnesses that could link them to these killings are dead, so there's no way we can legally bring them to justice on that. Now the marshal tells us they're too well organized for vigilantes to be of any use. If that's the case, then just what is it he's suggesting?''

There was a moment of profound silence. The normally laconic hotel owner had deftly hit the nail right on the head. *Just what the hell did Stoudenmire have in mind?*

Doc Cummings had held back up to this point, not wanting to put his own brother-in-law on the spot. But he could see Adair priming himself, and he decided to jump in before the meeting disintegrated into a real donny-brook.

"Dallas, don't get your hackles up. John's question seems like a fair one to me. If you want us to keep sittin' on our thumbs, then you've got to give us a reason. Have you got an ace in the hole, or are you just giving the Bannings more rope in the hopes they'll hang themselves?"

The lawman looked around the table, fixing each man in turn with a probing stare. Finally he spoke, not to anyone in particular but to the five men as a whole. "I'm not in the habit of tellin' people my plans. The fewer that know, the less chance of a leak. You figure you've got a right to hear it, so I'll tell you. But if it gets out, I'll know where to come lookin'."

Stoudenmire's cold eyes again traveled around the table, and the men felt their innards shrivel under his gaze. The threat was only thinly veiled, and not one among them doubted that he would kill the first man who opened his mouth in the wrong place. Like he said, they wanted to hear, and with it they accepted the responsibility of keeping their traps shut.

"The Bannings are vulnerable in three spots." The marshal selected three poker chips from a rack in the center of the table and stood them on edge, side-by-side as he spoke. "Their rustling operation, their corrupt deals with city officials, and the protection racket they run in the vice district. Starting tomorrow, I'll be probing for the weak links in each of these operations. What I'm after is hard evidence that'll stand up in court. It's a gamble, I grant you, but keep in mind that it only takes one informer to topple the whole shootin' match." Stoudenmire flicked one of the chips with his finger, and it fell sideways, toppling the others in turn. "With a little luck I might just have a songbird in the bag within a couple of days. But even if that peters out, we'll still be giving Banning the cold nose every time he squats."

Seth Hart nodded solemnly, studying the top of the table for a moment. Then he looked up. "Marshal, we want shed of the Bannings, but by the same token we don't want you killed. Quite frankly, I'm not sure you can pull it off by yourself."

Stoudenmire's mouth quirked a little at the corners. "Well if it doesn't pan out, you can always storm the Coliseum. I might even go along with you."

Hart's belly rumbled, and his mouth parted in a wet chuckle. The decision had been made. Stoudenmire would have his chance, but the vigilantes would be held in reserve. Just in case.

2.

WHEN THE train pulled in next morning, a swarthy, dark-haired man stepped off onto the platform and stretched his arms, like a great black cat warming itself in the mellow sun. The only baggage he carried was strapped to his hips, twin Colts with darkened walnut grips and as deadly looking as the man himself. There was nothing fancy about his hardware, just tools of the trade, weathered, well oiled, and always close at hand. But two guns singled a man out, even in a border town, and it didn't take a swami to come up with his profession.

Still, guns and all, the thing that made people stare after this man were his eyes. Sort of dark and impassive, like thin ice on a winter pond. The kind of eyes a fellow didn't forget and, more often than not, went out of his way to avoid meeting directly. They weren't cruel eyes, or even pitiless, they were just black orbs that looked at nothing, yet saw everything, and registered absolutely no emotion whatsoever.

Somehow he put most folks in mind of a sleek carnivore stalking its supper, moving sort of soft and lithe like he was walking on padded feet. And if he came scratching at the door some dark night, a smart man would have blown out the lamp and thrown the bolt.

After working the kinks out of his back, the man ambled off toward the vice district. There was a certain arrogance to his walk, like maybe he had just foreclosed on the sidewalk, and even burly, ham-fisted teamsters gave him a wide berth. Though his gaze touched on everything and everyone along the street, there was no sign on his face of either like, dislike, or even passing curiosity. Just a stoic disinterest that looked through and past whatever happened to cross his path. Which wasn't a hell of a lot. Most people just naturally got out of his way and left well enough alone.

Ten minutes later he walked into the Coliseum Saloon and planted his foot on the brass rail. When the bartender meandered over, the man nodded just once, as though he was conserving his strength. "Where can I find Ed Banning?"

The stranger's slow, guttural words put the barkeep in mind of a mission-schooled Kiowa he had once known. But something about the man warned him that this was one pilgrim who wouldn't take kindly to questions. Jerking his thumb toward the rear of the room, the barkeep said, "That's his office back there. Best knock before you go in."

The man didn't even acknowledge that he had heard. Moving away from the bar, he crossed the room, rapped once on the door, and entered. The bartender shook his head in a mild quandary and went back to polishing glasses. Some minutes later the door opened again, and the stranger came out, trailed closely by Ed and Sam Banning. The men bellied up at the end of the bar, with the soft-spoken jasper between the two brothers. Ed Banning signaled for drinks, and the barkeep hustled forward with a bottle, growing more puzzled by the moment. The boss looked fidgety as a whore in church, and that was one for the books. Up till now he had always thought the skinny bastard didn't have any more nerves than a gorged snake.

"Jack, let's have some of the good stuff," Banning ordered. Looking about the saloon, he called out to a scattering of early morning patrons. "Boys, the drinks are on the house! Step up and name your pleasure."

The men sitting about the room exchanged startled glances, them made a rush for the bar. Ed Banning wasn't especially noted for his generosity, and everybody figured they had best get to drinking before he recovered his senses. The hubbub gradually died down after the men got their drinks, but Banning waited till everyone was swilling contentedly before he let them in on the reason for the celebration.

"Boys, in case you're wonderin' who this gent is, I'd like you to meet Choctaw Tyler." Banning placed his hand on the man's shoulder, then pulled it back like he had touched a hot stove. "From now on he's gonna be my right-hand man. Next to Sam here, of course."

There was a sudden stir of interest from the men crowding the bar. The name was known and feared, at least by anyone with sense enough to pour piss out of a boot. Choctaw Tyler, the scourge of Indian Territory, deadlier than smallpox and scarlet fever back to back.

Although facts were sketchy, he was reputed to have killed a dozen men in gunfights, maybe even twice that number. No one knew for sure. They only knew that, next to Doc Holliday and Wes Hardin, he was the most feared gun in the west. Perhaps the most deadly of all according to some folks, for it was a well known fact that gut-eaters placed no value whatever on human life, their own or anyone else's. And a man had only to look at him to know that Choctaw Tyler was a full blood, just a hop and a skip from carrying a scalping knife instead of a six-gun. Even the US marshals working out of Ft. Smith steered clear of him, and with good reason. Word out of the Nations had it that he was tougher'n boiled owl, and some even swore that wherever he spit, nothing ever again grew on that spot.

Now he was standing right before their eyes in the flesh, and he looked just about as mean as his reputation claimed. And the Bannings had imported him all the way from Indian Territory! By Christ, that would make folks sit up and talk, sure enough. But not a man at the bar needed to ask why Choctaw Tyler had been brought to El Paso. They knew. Just as sure as they knew their own names.

After a couple of drinks, the Bannings and their new hired gun returned to the office. The little charade at the bar had been nothing more than a means of letting everyone know that the Indian was in town. Word would spread through El Paso like a dose of clap in a whorehouse, and by noon folks wouldn't be talking about anything else. Maybe the uptown crowd wouldn't like it, but they'd wait around to see how it came out. Even Bible-thumpers had a certain morbid curiosity about such things.

Once they were seated in the office, Ed Banning briefly related the events leading to the present stalemate with Stoudenmire. Choctaw Tyler sat and listened, making no comment one way or the other about the killings, the political maneuverings, or the near misses. When the gang leader finally wound down, Tyler just looked at him, like he was watching a talking dog and waiting for the next trick.

"Right now we've got ourselves a Mexican standoff," Banning declared, slightly unsettled by the Indian's fishy stare. "But sooner or later, there'll be a showdown. Stoudenmire will either come lookin' for us, or else the vigilantes'll suck up their balls and start a free-for-all. Whichever way it falls, we want your gun backing our play."

"Money talks." Tyler's dark eyes hooded, revealing nothing. "Five hundred now. Another five when it's done. Sundays extra, and I buy my own shells."

Banning wasn't sure if the inscrutable sonovabitch was pulling his leg or not, but he let it pass. "Fair enough. We've got no gripes about payin' top dollar. This shitheel marshal has got the whole town walkin' on eggshells, and it'll be worth every penny of it to watch him eat dust."

Choctaw Tyler's mouth set in an ugly grin, like a skullhead covered with burnt rawhide. "Just pick a spot. I'll drop your hick lawdog like a load of bricks. They all go down when *Tai-me* rattles the bones."

Banning didn't have the least idea who *Tai-me* was, but he had a notion that the fullblood seated across from him would tackle a turpentined catamount if the price was right. While he started counting out five hundred in greenbacks, Sam got busy pouring another round of drinks. Maybe their celebration was jumping the gun a little, but what the hell! Choctaw Tyler had just signed on for the duration.

3.

SETH HART was as good as his word. Along with Doc Cummings and his other cronies, the miller had circulated around the plaza talking his own brand of horse sense. The time wasn't right, he cautioned the men standing on street corners and crowding the boardwalks. The Bannings knew every move they were making, and the only way to invade the southside without needless killing was to take them by surprise. Wait, he told them, stand ready. Vigilantes may yet be needed, and when the right moment came, he would put out the call. Until then, everyone was to go about their business just as usual and avoid trouble with the Banning crowd.

When a handful of hotheads tried to argue the point, Hart gave it to them straight. Lay off or get your ears pinned back, he growled. Any man who started trouble today would find hard times camping on his doorstep. The warning had its effect. Once the Bannings were gone, Seth Hart would be the most influential man in El Paso, and everyone knew it. Crossing him now would only make for lean pickings farther down the road. The miller would eventually wield the power in the basin, and the man who got on his wrong side might just find himself starved out of town.

But Hart was too good a politician to send them away disgruntled. He had given his word to the marshal that the townspeople would hold off until the law had had its chance. That meant that the vigilantes would probably be needed after all, since Stoudenmire was fast working himself into a corner. Keep it confidential, he told them, but sleep light and have your guns handy. The call could come at any time.

Seth Hart had few illusions about his fellow townsmen. They would keep it about as confidential as a medicine man hawking elixir water. By nightfall what he had said would be all over El Paso, in ten different versions. But it had gotten them off the streets, and as long as they had some burgeoning conspiracy to occupy their minds, they wouldn't be out hunting trouble.

Stoudenmire and Gillette watched Hart's performance from the door of the jail. While the fat man wasn't exactly their cup of tea, they grudgingly admitted that he was a slick operator. The crowd had been manipulated without even knowing it, which was the mark of a true bunco artist. Maybe Hart called himself a politician, but he was a kissing cousin to a con man, and the two peace officers found the knowledge a little unsettling. Still, the mob had been dispersed, and for the moment that was the only thing that counted.

The lawmen stepped back inside the jail and started tussling with their own problems. Stoudenmire had purposely held off discussing the next step in their campaign against the Bannings until they could get more information on the latest development. Namely, Choctaw Tyler.

Word of the redskin gunfighter had spread through town at a dizzying pace, and rumors were flying thick and fast. The Indian was here, that much they knew, and everyone suspected why he had been imported. After that it was pure speculation as to how the Bannings intended to use him.

Stoudenmire had his own ideas on the subject, but right now he was more concerned with other matters. Tilted back in his chair, he spoke absently, as though trying to flush his mind of distractions and focus only on the job ahead. "Jim, we've been losin' ground fast in this deal, and it appears to me we've got to play hurry up and catch up. Everybody in this town seems bent on givin' us the fast shuffle, including the ones that're supposed to be on our side."

"Ain't that the godawful truth," Gillette agreed sourly. "I never seen people so damn set on gettin' their brains blowed out. Seems like they're bound to get in a fight with somebody. Now that you put a damper on the greasers, they're half froze to start cuttin' on one another. Beatenest thing I ever run across."

"Well in a way it is, and in another way it's not." The marshal flipped his hat on the desk and locked his hands behind his head. "Most folks'll live and let live if they're left alone. Hell, wolves and cougars live right alongside one another, and they hardly ever tangle. People are the same way. They figure every man has a right to his own game, whether it's crooked or straight, so long as he don't step on their toes.''

Gillette ran a hand through his unruly shock of hair, and his forehead wrinkled in a bemused way. ''Pard, you just lost me on the turn. People ain't much different than the beasties, I grant you. But what the hell's that got to do with live and let live?''

''Why, I reckon I'm tryin' to say that, whether it's man or beast, they just naturally don't go huntin' trouble. Now you take wolves, for instance. Sometimes an old stud wolf'll get the hots for another outfit's territory. Before you know it, he'll start a battle royal and get his whole pack chewed to shreds just because he wants what the other fellow's got. Same thing happens with people. They let some sorry bastard get 'em all riled up, and before anybody takes the time to think it through, they're squared off lookin' for the other fellow's jugular.''

''You're sayin' it's the leaders that cause the trouble. If the people was left to their own hook they'd figure out some way to get by without all this fightin'.'' The deputy scratched his head and mulled it over, unmindful of the shower of dandruff that flaked down over his vest. ''Well, it's somethin' to think about. Don't know's I ever heard it put just that way.''

''No other way to put it,'' Stoudenmire commented. ''Just take a look around you. Ed Banning's got this town locked up tighter'n a drum, and Seth Hart figures he oughta be king of the hill. Between 'em they're liable to get half the people in El Paso laid out with their toes curled backwards. What folks oughta do is let those two fight it out man to man and then hang the winner. That'd solve most of the probems this town's got.''

''Well you sorta set Hart back on his haunches for the time bein'. Leastways he called off the vigilantes.''

''Not for long. He's only giving us enough time to make himself look good. If we don't come up with something fast, he's gonna have that mob back on the street yellin' for blood."

"You wanna know somethin,' Dallas? If I didn't know you better, I'd think you had rocks in your head. You got a hired *pistolero* sniffin' your trail, and you sit around worryin' about what's gonna happen to the little folks when the big dogs finally tangle. That's some kinda nervy, but I ain't sure it's too bright."

The lawman just chuckled, more amused than offended by Gillette's tone. This crotchety old fart was the only man on earth who could talk to him like that, and they both knew it. In some curious way, that made it all right. Perhaps everybody needed their own personal devil's advocate, someone who constantly looked on the dark side simply because they were too damned cantankerous to play it any other way. Oddly enough, it helped to keep things in perspective, and he always felt uneasy when Gillette wasn't around to nettle him with testy remarks.

"Jim, the way I see it, Choctaw Tyler's the least of our worries. The Bannings can't use him openly 'cause it would ruin 'em politically. Course, they could have him bushwhack me, but I sorta doubt that, too. I've got an idea they brought him in as a bodyguard more'n anything else. Like as not, the only time I'd trade lead with him is if I went lookin' for the Bannings."

"Jesus Pesus!" the deputy woofed. "You make it sound like a shootout with him wouldn't be no more'n a friendly game of mumblety-peg. You better check your paint pots again, *amigo*. I hear tell that gut-eater has already filled a couple of graveyards all by his lonesome."

Like most peace officers, Gillette and Stoudenmire kept themselves fairly well informed on the activities of the West's more publicized bad men. Even now they knew that Wyatt Earp and Doc Holliday were involved in a fracas out in Tombstone. Luke Short was still in Dodge, and Billy the Kid had recently gone under at old Ft. Sumner. Wes Hardin was serving twenty-five years at Huntsville, of course. And incredible as it seemed, Ben Thompson had been elected city marshal of Austin. There was just no explaining some people's taste in lawmen. Then there was

Choctaw Tyler. Never been indicted, much less in jail, and reportedly as sudden as a snake with either hand.

Stoudenmire slowly unfolded from his chair, then crossed to the stove and poured himself a cup of coffee. Turning, he gave Gillette a searching look. "Jim, think back to all the gunslingers we've run across in our time. Every one of 'em had a reputation about a mile long and a yard wide. But when it got down to cases, their rep assayed out to one part fact and nine parts bullshit. Seems to me they trade on the fact that people are scared of 'em, sorta bluff their way through just because folks have heard they're sudden death. When it comes to shootin' at somebody that's gonna shoot back, they head for the hills. *Muy pronto*. I'm bettin' Choctaw Tyler's not any different. Just more so."

"I can't argue it. Likely as not you're right." Gillette returned his look levelly. "But I still say it's a piss-poor bet. What we oughta do is come up on either side of that knothead and throw his ass in the can."

Before Stoudenmire could reply Doc Cummings popped through the door. The little merchant's bearing was square-shouldered and somewhat martial, like he had just led the Light Brigade through the Valley of Death. Halting before the marshal's desk, he stuck his thumb in his vest pocket and puffed out his chest.

"Well gents, we've disbanded the troops and sent 'em home. But all you have to do is say the word, and we'll have 'em formed and ready to march before you can bat an eye."

Gillette and Stoudenmire exchanged sardonic looks. After a moment, the marshal returned to his chair and glanced up at Cummings, who seemed frozen in his pose. "Relax, Doc. Have a seat. I was just getting ready to fill Jim in on what we discussed at the meeting. Maybe you could give us some advice."

Stoudenmire saw Gillette cover his mouth to hide a grin, but Cummings didn't tumble to the joke. The storekeeper dragged up a chair and plopped down, immensely gratified that his expertise in such matters had at last been recognized. "Fire away, Dallas. I won't interrupt unless I see something that's out of kilter."

"Thank you, Doc. I appreciate your help." The lawman cocked an eye in Gillette's direction and stifled a smile. "Now here's what I've got in mind. Jim, I want you to rent a packhorse, lay in some supplies, and go find yourself a spot where you can spy on the Banning ranch. What I'm hopin' is that they figure it's safe to start rustlin' again. If so, you trail 'em and spot the outfit they hit. Assuming it works, we'll call in the Rangers, get the Mexican rancher over here to identify the cattle, and sack the Bannings with a federal warrant."

"Sounds fair enough to me," Gillette observed. "But what if they've retired from the rustlin' business?"

"Good question," Doc interjected soberly. "That leaves us out in the cold."

"Not exactly," Stoudenmire noted. "While Jim's gone, I'm gonna visit every dive in town and put the pressure on 'em for evidence of kickbacks to the Bannings. Along with that, I'll also be nosin' around to see if we can turn up any political payoffs. Like that waterworks contract to Pud Brown's brother. We'll be hittin' 'em from three sides at once, and all we need is one good lick to bring them to their knees."

"Yeah, it might work," Gillette allowed. "But if it don't, they'll suck their ass up so tight we'll never get a hold on 'em."

"We'll cross that bridge when we come to it." The marshal paused watching the other two men intently for a moment. "If we come up between a rock and a hard place, I've still got an ace in the hole. I had a meeting with the mayor after I left Hart's this morning. The second meeting, as a matter of fact. He's scared shitless, and I've about got him sold on testifying against the Bannings. The only thing holding him back is that he wants another witness to back up his story. He's afraid we won't get an indictment otherwise." Again he hesitated, looking them both squarely in the eye. "I don't have to tell you to keep this under your hats. And, Doc, that includes Seth Hart. If this ever got out, Isaac Porter is cold meat. Savvy?"

Both men nodded solemnly, and Cummings came up on the edge of his seat. "Dallas, I just volunteered to help you. By God, if anybody knows what's happening in this town, it's me, and I'll betcha I can turn up a wagonload of evidence on corruption and bribes."

"Doc, I appreciate the offer, but I'll have to turn you down. The stakes are just too damn high. Banning and his crowd play for keeps, and they'd kill you dead as hell if they caught you diggin' for skeletons. This is a rough game, and there's no room in it for eager beavers."

Cumming's face purpled with indignation, and they argued briefly, but Stoudenmire was adamant. Under no circumstances was the storekeeper to get involved, and that was final. If he did, he'd find himself locked in a cell under protective custody. With that, Cummings kicked back his chair and marched out with his nose in the air. As he went through the door, they heard him muttering to himself. "By Christ, it's a sorry goddamn mess when your own brother-in-law treats you like a snot-nosed kid. Believe you me, Kate's going to hear about this."

Stoudenmire just grinned and went back for a refill on coffee. Some folks just didn't know when they were well off. Especially storekeepers trying to convince themselves that they didn't belong among the fainthearted.

4.

OVERNIGHT SOME disturbing rumors had drifted back to Ed Banning. Stoudenmire was making the rounds of various gaming dives and whorehouses on the southside. The message he carried was blunt and to the point. Cooperate in greasing the skids for the Bannings, or else. The latter part of his threat wasn't spelled out, but it was plain enough. Those who refused would be hauled down and trampled in the shitstorm that was sure to follow. Clearly the marshal had begun a war of nerves with the madams and gamblers in the vice district, and he damn sure wasn't pulling any punches about what he had in mind.

That in itself didn't disturb Banning. The trick was as

old as the hills, and every highroller and whore on the southside knew what would happen if they opened their mouths. What really bothered him was the fact that only two dive owners had reported the incident. That meant the sporting crowd was spooked, uncertain who would win in the end; otherwise they would have come running to him the moment they were contacted. Sam's bullying tactics had kept them in line in the past, true enough, but in a deal like this, nothing could be taken for granted. Even the threat of Choctaw Tyler couldn't be counted on now that Stoudenmire was out cracking knuckles. Some dunghead might get a case of the shakes and decide to hedge his bet. It only took one loose tongue to start the ball rolling, and it might just turn into a goddamn avalanche if something wasn't done fast.

Then, along about his third cup of coffee, Banning's morning turned even darker. One of the boys brought in word that Deputy Gillette had ridden out of town shortly after dawn leading a packhorse. The stablehand who had passed the information along didn't know Gillette's destination, but any numbskull could figure that out. Even Sam had tumbled fast enough. The old lawdog was headed for the ranch, only it was a cinch he wouldn't be paying a social visit. Once he got into the hills back of the spread, even a bloodhound couldn't track him down, and with a spyglass he could count the whiskers on everything that moved down below. The rustling operation would have to be shut down tight as a drum. Banning sent a rider pounding out of town with a terse message. Until he gave the word, nothing moved!

Ten minutes later Banning began wishing he had stayed in bed. One of his men from city hall came tapping at the back door and damn near wet down his leg while he was trying to spit out the story. These political hacks were all alike; they never made a move without mulling it over for at least a day, and even then you couldn't be sure they weren't playing both ends against the middle. Still, this one had finally decided his bread was best smeared with Banning butter, and the story he had to tell was the worst news yet.

Yesterday Stoudenmire had paid a call on the mayor, and they had holed up in the politico's office for the better part of a half-hour. Although the man didn't know what they had talked about, Isaac Porter appeared visibly shaken when the marshal left, and it seemed pretty certain they hadn't been discussing official business. Banning gave the man a good tongue lashing for not reporting sooner, then booted his ass out the back door.

Turning back to Sam and Choctaw Tyler, he had the look of a man who had just been served fried dog turds for breakfast. "Well you have to hand it to that goddamn German. When he cuts the wolves loose, he goes all the way. The bastard's kickin' over rocks in every direction."

"Yeah, but what's it mean?" Sam frowned, now thoroughly baffled by the morning's rash of problems. "Is Porter talkin', or did Stoudenmire just brace him the way he did everybody down here?"

"I don't know," Banning pondered aloud. "After all we've done for him, I'd hate to think the mayor would double-cross us. On the other hand, I'm damned if I'd put it past him." Then he blinked, glancing around at his brother. "But I'll tell you one thing. Porter could be real trouble. He knows enough to put us all away, and if he ever got on a witness stand, we're lookin' at a jail cell. Maybe even a neck stretchin'."

Sam's bemused look suddenly turned to anger. "Goddamnit, it's just like I been sayin' from the start. We gotta get rid of that fuckin' marshal once and for all."

"Don't worry, little brother. We're gonna dig his hole real soon. But we have to pick the time and the place, and it's gotta look right. Otherwise, the reformers'll start beatin' drums all over town."

Choctaw Tyler grunted and smiled like a cat with a mouthful of feathers. "Anytime you say suits me. Sooner I earn my money, the sooner I can hit the road."

Banning darted a glance at the Indian. "I'll tell you when. And you can bet your boots it won't be long in comin'." He seemed on the verge of saying something else, then fell silent, and after a moment looked over at Sam. "What we need is to buy a little time, and it occurs to me there's a trick we haven't tried. Send the swamper over to Stoudenmire's office. Tell him I've got something to say that he'll be real interested in hearin'. But only over here. Nowhere else."

Sam's mouth popped open, but he never got a chance to speak. Banning shot him a withering look, and the burly ruffian obediently made tracks for the door. Choctaw Tyler just smiled and pulled out the makings. Watching him, Banning decided that the gut-eater would be hard to take as a steady diet. All he did was look at you with that shiteatin' smile and stink up the place with his goddamn Bull Durham.

Sam returned shortly, and they all sat around looking at one another in deadened silence. Twenty minutes later Stoudenmire walked through the door, and it escaped no one's attention that Tige padded along at his side. The brute looked meaner than ever if such a thing were possible, and it was clear that he hadn't forgotten his trip to this room. It was equally clear that the lawman had come loaded for bear. If the gang leader wanted trouble, he figured that between Tige and himself they could dish out enough to go around.

Stoudenmire ignored the Indian as though he didn't exist, leveling down instead on Banning. "Whatever you've got to say, get it said. I haven't got all day."

Banning smiled, but only with great effort. "I don't think your time will be wasted, Marshal. But first I'd like to ask you a question. Just what do you hope to gain by badgering my people down here? They're not gonna spill their guts to you in a month of Sundays."

"Banning, you'd be surprised what folks'll spill when they see the writing on the wall." The lawman saw the other man's eyes narrow, and he drove the needle a little deeper. "Your outfit's got more leaks'n a rusty sieve. Damned interestin' the way people'll talk when they know the string's about played out."

Ed Banning's thin blade of a face suddenly lost its smile. "You oughta've been a poker player instead of a lawman. With a bluff like that you could've made a fortune."

Stoudenmire's chuckle had a mocking ring to it. "The only way to find out is to call the bet. Course, when you take another peek at your hole card, you're gonna discover I've got you by the short hairs."

"One hand don't make a game. Not the way I play." Banning dismissed the subject with a wave of his hand, plastering another shallow smile across his face. "Look, I didn't call you over here to trade insults. I've got a proposition to make, and I'll give it to you straight out. You're not gonna turn up anything I can't handle, but you are sort of a nuisance. Not that it bothers me all that much, you understand. Just takes my mind off more important matters. Suppose I was to open the safe and count out . . . say three thousand dollars. Hell, I might even go as high as five thousand. Don't you reckon that'd get your mind back on your own business?"

Stoudenmire felt his pulse quicken. The bastard was running scared! One more push and he might just crack. "Banning, I've got a better idea. Why don't you stuff that money up your ass and set a match to it. That's about the only way you'll get me off your back."

Sam started out of his chair, but the gang leader stayed him with a short, chopping motion of his hand. Then Banning leaned forward and nodded toward the Indian. "Marshal, I don't think you've met Choctaw Tyler. He's been hearin' about the big *pistolero* we've got for a lawman, so we brought him down to have a look-see for himself."

Stoudenmire gave the gunslinger a slow, appraising look. For a moment Choctaw Tyler just puffed on his cigarette, seemingly absorbed in the aimless drift of the smoke. Finally he turned and met the marshal's stare with an insolent smirk. His mouth was like a hard slit that had been traced across his face with a razor, and when he spoke, his words came out a soft, guttural hiss.

"Mister, you'd best listen to reason. Else you're gonna end up on the short end of the stick. Shit, he's offerin' you more money to stay alive than he's givin' me to kill you. Take it, 'fore I decide to do the job for free."

The lawman's pale eyes riveted into the full blood, and his voice was gritty as ground glass. "Tyler, I'm gonna give you some advice, maybe the best you ever got. Start makin' tracks out of here and don't look back. If you do, you're liable to lose an eye.''

Choctaw Tyler tensed, ready to come up out of his chair, but Banning stopped him cold. ''Choctaw, leave it be! He's just tryin' to get you riled up, and we can't afford a shootout in here.''

When Tyler eased off, the gang leader looked back at Stoudenmire. ''Marshal, I reckon we know how everybody stands, so let's just play the cards as they fall. Only don't ever say I didn't warn you that you're playin' with a cold deck.''

''That's real white of you, Banning. I'll remember it when I put a noose around your neck.''

Stoudenmire walked from the room with Tige bringing up the rear. Sam jumped out of his chair and spat a wad of phlegm at the door as it closed. Banning and Choctaw Tyler exchanged disgusted looks and watched silently as the spittle slowly wormed its way toward the floor. There wasn't much left to say, and besides, it had been one turd-knocker of a morning, start to finish.

5.

THAT EVENING Banning sent for Isaac Porter. Things were at a point that he couldn't afford another miscue, and one way or the other he had to find out if the mayor was going soft in the guts. Something was boogering the old scoundrel, that was for damn sure. Over the past few weeks he had steadily grown more jumpy, almost choleric in his drunken fits of gloom. That was another thing, his drinking. Since becoming mayor, he had religiously avoided the booze, finding solace instead at the gaming tables around town. But lately he had been soaking up whiskey like a sponge, and so far he hadn't shown any signs of slackening off. Having a rummy as a frontman was a risky proposition, particularly in a business where corruption and graft were the order of the day. The cause of Porter's dismal moods was easily traced. In a word, Stoudenmire.

Until the German came to town, Isaac Porter had been a glad-handing, back-slapping, bon vivant. The rotund, rosy-cheeked, little charmer that everyone liked to think typified the warmth and casual hospitality that made El Paso what it was. This jocular, ever sprightly disposition was the big factor in getting Porter elected, and it had made him a perfect show-horse for Banning's political machine. But with Stoudenmire's arrival, a gradual transformation had taken place, almost as though Porter had been sapped of his vitality and amiable wit. Banning didn't give a tinker's damn for the dissolution of the man himself, but when it endangered the organization, that was a different ball of wax altogether. And if Porter had any notions of talking out of school, he would become expendable faster than a bat fart in a windstorm.

When the mayor arrived, he looked like a man with a mild touch of St. Vitus's dance. His face was pale and drawn, and he couldn't seem to sit still, squirming nervously in the chair like his chubby rump was stuck to a hot griddle. Around the Bannings he was normally as docile as a circus elephant, accepting their sarcasm and biting remarks with quiet good humor. But tonight he had a real case of the shakes, and Choctaw Tyler's flat stare did little to settle his nerves. Obviously he had spent the afternoon in company with John Barleycorn, for he reeked of stale whiskey, and his eyes were a watery shade of red. Yet even the whiskey had had no apparent effect on his frayed spirits. He was a bundle of raw, suppurating nerves, and whatever rode astraddle his shoulders had raked him bloody with fear and uncertainty. A man had only to look to see it gnawing on him, and none saw it more clearly than Ed Banning.

The gang leader worked up what passed for a smile. "Well, Isaac, what's new over at city hall? We haven't seen you much lately. Thought maybe you'd forgotten old friends."

"No, no. Nothing like that, Ed." Porter's eyes flicked around the room, like timorous sparrows unable to find a perch. "Just closing the books on the fiscal year and preparing the new city budget. Have to keep burning the midnight oil, you know."

"Sure," Banning agreed congenially. "Running this town is a big job. And we're damned lucky to have a man like you to shoulder the load. Being mayor's not all rose water and kissin' babies, is it?"

Porter dredged up a spastic smile, trying to ape the gang leader's easy manner. "That's right, Ed. It's more of a burden than folks suspect. Carries a great responsibility, and sometimes it gets to weighing on a man."

"Now it's funny you mention that, Isaac." Banning motioned over at Sam and Choctaw Tyler, who looked like a couple of men watching a snake mesmerize a plump field mouse. "I was just telling the boys today that we've been workin' you too hard. By God, overseeing this operation is no soft touch. Man needs a little time off every now and then. Fact is, I was thinkin' of treating you to a vacation. St. Louis maybe, or Kansas City. That wouldn't be too hard to take, would it?"

The mayor's rubbery features brightened with surprise. "Why no, that wouldn't be hard to take at all. Tell you the truth, I have been off my feed a bit here lately."

Banning lit a cigar and casually drifted into a long monologue on the merits of various eastern cities, making it clear that he considered Chicago the best watering hole east of the Big Muddy. Isaac Porter listened and nodded like an eager schoolboy as the gang leader spoke. Slowly he began to relax, inwardly deriding himself for the groundless fears he had conjured up about this meeting. Banning just wanted to chat, deliver one of those rambling, disconnected lectures he was so fond of on occasion. Porter slouched back in his chair with renewed confidence. Hell, he wasn't in any danger! Banning had himself a captive audience, and he was going to make the most of it. And if Mother Porter's youngest son played his cards right, he might just get a ticket east. A one way ticket! Where didn't matter, just so he never had to return to this murderous hell-hole.

Porter was jarred out of his reverie as Banning neatly switched directions. "Say, Isaac, before I forget it. Stoudenmire has been down here bracing my people with threats. The knothead actually thinks somebody's gonna rat on me. Heard anything about it uptown?''

The mayor felt cold beads of sweat pop out on his forehead. Should he jeopardize this trip back east by telling the truth, or would it be better to play dumb? It was a knotty question, but he hesitated only a moment. ''No, not a thing. You mean to say he's actually making threats against the people down here?''

''Worse than that. He's telling 'em that the only way they'll save their own hides is to swap sides and testify against me. Matter of fact, a little bird told me he'd even paid you a call.''

Porter was taken completely off guard, and he suddenly had the look of a trapped animal. He was sweating profusely now, fighting desperately to keep his hands from shaking. ''You mean yesterday? Oh, yes, he dropped by for a few minutes. Completely slipped my mind till you mentioned it. Just wanted to tell me that he'd taken steps to put the quietus on this vigilante scare. Nothing really. Nothing at all.''

The mayor's voice had cracked only once during his short recital, but he had lied poorly, unconvincingly, and even now his face had the look of a constipated warthog. Banning betrayed nothing of what he was thinking, nodding absently as if the subject had been only of passing interest. The gang leader easily returned to events of a lighter nature, smiling and poking fun in his usual caustic manner. Porter once again relaxed, congratulating himself for having brought it off so smoothly. *By damn, when it came to tricky dodges, it took more than these louts to outfox an old con-man like Isaac Porter.*

Shortly the gang leader's banter wound down, and he allowed as how it was time to get back to business. If the mayor wouldn't mind, he had some things to talk over with Sam and Tyler. They'd get together again soon, real soon, and work out the details for his trip east. Porter's spunk and jaunty disposition were again restored, and he took his leave appearing vastly relieved. Easing through the door, he cocked his hat at a rakish angle and got busy planning a real rip-snorter to celebrate his own devilish cleverness.

When the door swung shut behind the old politico, Ed Banning put it to a vote. Not that his outfit was anything even mildly related to a democracy, but he just wanted a sounding board for his own opinion. Sam and Choctaw Tyler both agreed. *Porter had been lying.*

Banning tilted back in his chair and considered the matter at some length. The minutes ticked by, and the other two men began to wonder if he had gone to sleep. After a while his eyes opened, and he came back to the present, outlining in clipped, brutal words how it would be handled. They had no recourse but to kill Porter before he spilled his guts to the law. Tyler was to shadow him and wait until he headed home for the night. When he caught the mayor alone on some dark street, he was to finish him off. But it had to be done with a knife. Make it look like the old prick had been robbed and killed by some drunk greaser. That way the townspeople would have something to piss and moan about besides the Bannings.

Choctaw Tyler found the idea of using a knife vastly appealing. Somehow when a man felt it slip home, grating on bone, rending flesh, there was a greater sense of accomplishment; then, too, the smell of warm, fresh blood had always aroused him in some strange way, and that made it all the better. Happy to be functioning at last, he nodded to Banning and slipped out the back door.

Some three hours later Isaac Porter was weaving along a sidestreet when the Indian caught up with him. The mayor was carrying a heavy load, but when he saw the knife, his deadened senses surged back with alacrity. Still, it was a short and savagely unequal struggle. Porter managed only one bleating cry before Choctaw Tyler sunk the knife up to the hilt beneath his breastbone. The politician shuddered like a bolt of lightning had just fired up his rectum, then collapsed at the knees, and folded to the ground. Hunkering down beside the dead man, Tyler wiped his knife clean, then expertly went over the body for wallet, watch, and other valuables. Just as he finished, he heard the crunch of a footstep in loose soil.

Someone was standing directly behind him, and from the nearness of the sound, he wasn't more than ten feet away.

"Don't move!" the deadly click of a Colt hammer being earred back had a logic all its own. "Stand up slow and get your hands over your head. Then turn around."

The Indian obeyed, and when he came about, he found himself facing a Peacemaker in the hand of Dallas Stoudenmire. *Tai-me* was indeed a god of strange whims. Grinning, he jerked a thumb back at Porter's body. "Marshal, you're trickier than I thought. Looks like the fat man wasn't the only one being followed tonight."

Stoudenmire felt his guts constrict into a hard knot. The mayor hadn't been much, but he deserved better than this. "Tyler, I sure wish I had been on your tail. From the looks of things, I should've been. But just between you and me, I was makin' night rounds when I heard the ruckus. Course, it's not like I came up empty-handed, is it?"

Choctaw Tyler's guttural chuckle sounded softly in the narrow street. "Tell you what, Marshal. There's just you and me here. Why don't you poke that Colt back in the holster and give me an even break. If you don't, we never are gonna find out who's the fastest."

Stoudenmire just shook his head, his eyes cold and hard as hailstones. "No dice. I want you alive. The only choice you've got is between hangin' or doing some tall talkin' about who set this deal up. Course, if you're stupid you could go for your gun. But that'd just get you dead." The Colt moved slightly in a sideways motion. "Unbuckle your gunbelt and be real careful."

The Indian shrugged, a look of stoic resignation coming over his face. His left hand moved toward the belt buckle, but in the same instant his right hand snaked down and swept up with a six-gun. It was the old magician's trick with a deadly twist; distract the eye with one hand and work your magic with the other.

But as his pistol cleared leather, Stoudenmire Colt belched flame in a blinding roar. Three bright dots appeared on Choctaw Tyler's shirtpocket, and he stumbled backwards, tripping over the mayor's body. Dead even as he fell, he hit the ground with a dusty thud.

Stoudenmire walked forward and stood for a moment inspecting the Indian's spread-eagled form. Satisifed that the man was dead, he turned and headed toward the plaza, shucking empties and reloading as he walked.

Killing men was one thing, but he never could stand the stench when death released its grip on their bowels.

CHAPTER NINE

1.

JIM GILLETTE awakened only moments after the dusky glow of false dawn erased the darkened sky. The stars that hung suspended in the heavens each night, all cold silver and iced blue, had disappeared, and he shivered in the chill morning air. The resinous, piney odor from the embers of his fire had a sharp bite, and through the cobwebs of his drowsiness came images of a cherry blaze and a coffee pot perking delicious aromas. His camp was high on a mesa overlooking the Banning ranch in the valley below. These huge orange and golden buttes jutted skyward from the flatlands, forming sheer palisades that dominated the countryside in every direction. Above the escarpment there was an expanse as level as a billiard table, as though the gods had cleaved the top away in a moment of petulance and outrage. Over this barren, windswept rock-pile nothing grew save a profusion of piñon trees, gnarled and deformed by time and altitude into a stunted mockery of green things. Yet even atop these grotesque battlements, a man always had the taste of grit in his mouth, as though powdery granules of some tasteless filth were forever lodged between his teeth.

The deputy curled up into a tight ball, drawing his blanket closer against the damp cold. Something had roused him, and he tried to push back the fuzziness that clouded his brain, but for a moment his wits slogged along like a crippled mule. Then it hit him. What he heard was the pounding of hooves, and it was coming from the valley below. Not just horses either but cattle, lots of cattle. *Great smokin' Jesus! The gang must have ridden out during the night without him hearing them. But how the hell could that be?*

Whipping the blanket off, Gillette scrambled to his feet and ran toward the forward edge of the mesa. Taking cover behind a huge rock, he eased down on his belly and peered over the cliff. Suddenly he went slack-jawed with astonishment, rocked back on his haunches as though someone had dashed him in the face with a pan of cold water.

The Mexicans were raiding the Banning ranch! Goddammit, it just couldn't be possible.

Unable to believe what he had seen, he rubbed his eyes and took another look. This time there was no mistaking what he saw. Maybe it wasn't possible, but it was sure as hell a fact. The greasers were rustling Banning's cattle herd, and from up there, it looked like they were flat going to clean him out.

Gillette was staggered, his mind reeling with this quirky turn of events. Christ almighty, what Stoudenmire wouldn't give to be here right now! Although it was the last thing they would have imagined when he set out to scout the Banning ranch, it was damn sure a fine joke on those meatheads down below. The best joke he had ever heard, in fact. The rustlers getting rustled! Jesus, that was rich.

Evidently, Don Miguel Salazar figured it was time the *gringos* had a taste of their own medicine. Banning's night riders had sure as shit driven off enough of his stock, and the turnabout was long overdue, no two ways about it. Hell, the Mexicans could raid Banning every night for the next year, and they would probably still come out with a hole in their pockets. Not to mention the number of men they had had killed trying to protect their own herds. *¡Bueno!* Now maybe the pack of scutters working for Banning would hit leather and keep on riding until they found a place where folks weren't so all-fired persnickity about a bunch of cows.

Though it tickled his funnybone to see the Mexicans raiding Banning, the old lawdog would have much preferred it the other way around. That way he could have stuck to the plan and maybe come up with some hard evidence that would carry a little clout in a court of law. But at least something was happening, even if it wasn't what the marshal had set his sights on.

Gillette had been perched atop this windswept mesa for two nights now, and he was growing dismally bored with the whole deal. The gang had done nothing but loaf around all day and drink whiskey far into the night ever since he arrived. They had no apparent concern for the operation of the ranch itself, and quite obviously weren't planning a raid any time soon. Things were so peaceful, downright stultifying as a matter of fact, that he had intended returning to El Paso that very morning. It was a waste of time watching rustlers who for all intents and purposes had retired from the rustling business. Broiling under a hot ball of fire during the day and freezing his ass off at night wasn't exactly calculated to improve a man's frame of mind. Especially when those sapsuckers down in the valley had all the whiskey.

But all that had suddenly changed. Maybe the Mexicans had thrown a monkey wrench into his plans, but they had sure as hell livened things up. Even now they were driving the Banning herd right past him as they pushed south toward the river. In the faint glow from the sky, Gillette could see the *vaqueros* using their *reatas* as whips, hazing the longhorns into a ground-eating lope that shook the earth with a dull rumble. They had a ways to go, nearabout twenty miles before they hit the border, and it looked like the Mexicans figured to stampede the stolen cattle every foot of the way. Watching them, the deputy couldn't help but think that they were real greenhorns at this rustling game. They should have hit just after midnight; that way they would have been across the border long before first light. The way things were shaping up, they would be damned lucky to get that herd into Mexico much before dinner time.

Out of the corner of his eye, he suddenly picked up movement around the ranch house. Changing positions for a better view, he saw men running helter-skelter across the compound, shouting and waving their arms toward the fast disappearing herd. Then they turned and raced for the corral, grabbing any horse that came to hand in their haste to get mounted. Within moments they were saddled and pounding out the gate, clearly intent on carrying the fight to the Mexicans.

While the *vaqueros* could save themselves by making a run for it, Gillette saw it as a profound injustice that they should lose the cattle. That presented him with a thorny problem, one which he couldn't debate overly long, for the Banning gang was riding fresh horses, and they would close the gap in a matter of minutes.

Should he side with the Mexicans or remain strictly an observer?

His instinctive reaction was to stick with his own countrymen even though they were outlaws, nothing more than border scum when a man got down to cases. Simply by doing nothing he would be taking their side, and no matter how it was sliced, it wasn't any of his business to start with. The smart move was to just sit back and play like a spectator; let them fight it out amongst themselves and devil take the hindmost. But then nobody had ever accused him of being smart, or even bright for that matter. Besides, he felt a nagging sense of loyalty to something greater than those two-bit desperados, whether they were American or not. Like Stoudenmire always said, personal feelings shouldn't get between a man and what's right, especially if it's got to do with the law.

Just then a small band of *vaqueros* fell back to fight a rear-guard action, and his debate came to a skidding halt.

Grabbing his rifle, Gillette jacked a shell into the chamber and steadied himself against the boulder. Yet even with the decision made, he couldn't bring himself to ambush the no-account bastards. Waiting until they passed beneath his hideout, the deputy drew a bead on the lead horse and squeezed off a shot. When the rider pitched headlong to the ground, the rest of the gang reined up short and milled around him in swirling confusion. Methodically, Gillette aimed and fired, dropping their horses from beneath them like cattle in a slaughterhouse chute. With each report another animal fell, thrashing and squealing in blind terror, and before he could empty the rifle, the gang had scattered over the countryside, running for their very lives.

The Mexicans were no less astounded than the Texans themselves, but only a fool would stop to question divine intervention such as this. Waving their rifles in salute, they wheeled their mounts and thundered off after the herd. Whoever the *hombre* was up on that cliff, he was a great artist with a rifle, and he wouldn't be forgotten in their prayers tonight.

Gillette wasted no time gloating over his handiwork. Striding back to his camp, he quickly packed his gear and saddled up. Ten minutes later he was riding down the narrow trail on the backside of the buttes and damned glad to be on his way. This deal had been a washout from the start, and it was high time to get his skinny rump on back to El Paso.

Suddenly he wondered what Stoudenmire would have to say about this little fracas. Probably wouldn't be too amused, but he'd be damn hard put to fault it. Compromise wasn't the marshal's way of doing things. He'd doubtless have shot the men instead of the horses. Still, all things considered, Gillette felt like it had been a pretty good morning.

2.

STOUDENMIRE WAS discovering that there was more to catching fish than baiting the hook. The murder of Isaac Porter had silenced the sporting crowd as if a steel trap had clamped shut. Since he had caught Choctaw Tyler with knife in hand, there wasn't much doubt about who had ordered the killing. But knowing it and proving it was sort of like spreading horseshit on a soda cracker. Everybody admitted it looked good, but nobody wanted to take the first bite. Rightly enough, the marshal figured that the Bannings had somehow tumbled to his deal with Porter, yet the knowledge did little except add to his already sullen disposition.

Porter's death had soured his mood enough for one

night, but Kate had really finished the job off. After rousing the undertaker and getting the bodies attended to, he had gone home prepared for another bitter argument. But Kate had already heard the whole story from Doc, and she didn't care to discuss the matter further. As it turned out, she didn't care to discuss anything. She had decided that if yelling and screaming couldn't sway him, then maybe the silent treatment would get better results. Not only was she silent, she was downright aloof, even to the extent of turning her back on him when they crawled into bed. While it was a childish thing to do, and damned irritating coming on top of everything else, Stoudenmire found it to be a grimly humorous joke on her. His tallywhacker wouldn't have stood on end right then if a whole troop of vestal virgins had swarmed over him buck-assed naked.

Somehow killing took its toll on a man in a way that he had never fully understood. After the shooting was over and the other man lay dead, it was like the hot juices inside him had all been drained away. Often during the war he could have laid down and slept for a whole week after an especially busy day on the killing ground. It had always puzzled him, even disturbed him in a way, for it was as though killing sucked him dry of passion and left his twig as limber and lifeless as a doddering old man's. Over the years he had finally come to accept it for what it was. Killing just plain wore him out, and there wasn't anything to be done about it. But he often wondered if it had the same effect on other men. It wasn't rightly something a man would talk about, and he had never felt close enough to anyone to ask. Not even Jim Gillette.

Staring into the darkness last night, listening to Kate pretend she was asleep, it came to him that the joke was really on her. She thought she was punishing him by cutting him off, when all the time, he had about the same urges as a gelded hog. Still, wanting it or not, her peevish little contrivance had left him with a foul taste in his mouth.

The chilly atmosphere around the southside this morning hadn't done much to improve his mood either. The Bannings hadn't wasted any time circulating the word, and overnight it became known that the mayor had met the same fate that awaited any double-crosser. The warning didn't pass unheeded, and Stoudenmire had been rebuffed at every turn on an early morning jaunt through the vice district. Those who had considered talking yesterday now wouldn't even give him the correct time. Maybe he would end up putting them in jail, they conceded, that remained to be seen. But if they spoke out of turn, Ed Banning would put them in a box, and dead was a damnsight more permanent than a visit to the pokey.

Yet there was one aftereffect the Bannings hadn't counted on. Although Porter was generally regarded as a corrupt politician, the townspeople took a dim view of anyone murdering their mayor. Even if he was a crook. More than ever before, the people of El Paso closed ranks against the Bannings. There was even talk of forming a coalition ticket to defeat them in the forthcoming elections. Reflecting back over the vigilante scare, Stoudenmire was pleased to see that folks were thinking in terms of ballots rather than bullets. Once they were united against gang rule, they wouldn't have much trouble ridding city hall of its resident scoundrels.

But simply defeating the Bannings at the polls wasn't enough for the lawman. He wanted their hides nailed to the wall, and he had no intention of slackening the pressure. Gillette might return at any moment with evidence of rustling, and he had already made arrangements with the banks to inspect the records of various politicians. Still, he was going to need a witness, someone who knew all the details behind the Bannings' skulduggery. Gamblers, saloonkeepers, and madams had met his most recent overtures with stony silence, and obtaining proof of protection kickbacks now seemed highly unlikely. That left official corruption, and with nothing much to lose, Stoudenmire decided to brace the second most powerful cog in the Banning machine.

Judge Marcus Hamer was an imposing figure of a man. He was tall, stoutly built, with a mane of white, wavy hair, and he had the disconcerting habit of staring a man straight in the eye whenever he spoke. Moreover, he was a man of some refinement, cultured in his ways, highly educated, and obviously from a background of considerable breeding. Though it was common knowledge that his family had once ruled Atlanta society, not even his closest friends knew what quirk of fate had brought him west. Local gossip attributed it to a family scandal of some sort, but the only thing known for certain was that he had chosen El Paso for reasons of his own and, having done so, quickly aligned himself with the Bannings. He owed both his soul and his position as circuit judge to the machine, yet he gave every impression of being his own man. One who didn't flinch when the political waters got choppy.

Stoudenmire found him affable, somewhat amused by the Bannings' bumbling peccadillos, and quite willing to talk. But strictly off the record. After offering the lawman a chair, he lighted a thin cheroot much favored by southern gentlemen, then settled back with a patronizing smile.

"Well, Marshal, I presume you're here to offer me immunity from justice. Frankly, I'm just the least bit affronted that it took you so long to get around to me. I understand you have been all over town extending the same inducement to the more scurrilous element."

Stoudenmire missed some of the words, but not the tone. This man was an old campaigner, and he might just be the toughest nut to crack in the whole organization. "Judge, I won't waste your time beatin' around the bushes You know I'm after the Bannings, and I suspect you know I'll get 'em. What I'm offering you is a chance to come out on the winning side. It's as simple as that."

Hamer smiled wryly and exhaled a thick cloud of smoke through his nostrils. "My boy, an Englishmen by the name of Spencer once said that the ultimate result of shielding men from the effects of folly is to fill the world with fools. Now by no means am I inferring that you're a fool. But I do believe that you are perpetuating a folly. If it won't offend you, I would be happy to explain why."

"Fire away." Stoudenmire returned the smile, finding himself liking the old reprobate even if he was a thief. "I've got a thick skin."

"So I've heard." The judge flicked ashes from his cheroot and glanced around slyly. "But it will take more than that to bring Ed Banning to earth. Quite candidly, Marshal, you put me in mind of a man trying to shovel quicksand. The faster you shovel the deeper you sink, and the only way it ends is when you have sunk into obscurity. Now, as a case in point. You've been flitting about town trying to drum up a chink in Banning's armor. But there's not a man in El Paso who would dare to speak openly. Isaac Porter's death was a deplorable thing, but most effective, you'll have to admit. The denizens of our vice district have had their lips sealed forever. Whoever talked would be killed even though the Bannings went to jail, and that rather salient fact hasn't gone unnoted. Your folly, my friend, is that whoever deals with you ends up dead. I might also add that it is a folly that has now been exposed fully in a most impressive manner."

"What you're trying to tell me is that I've played out my string. That there's no way to get the Bannings."

"Precisely. By election time this whole affair will have blown over. I regret to say that most people live out their lives in thimbles. The dolts that populate El Paso are no different. They will gladly take the path of least resistance and be quite content to return to their humdrum existence."

Hamer chuckled to himself, as if amused by the profundity of his own statement. "Ofttimes, to win us to our harm, the instruments of darkness tell us truths. You and I, Marshal, must suffer under the knowledge that nothing ever changes. Politicians and lawmen come and go, but corruption never falters. It feeds on itself as well as the people, and in our benevolent form of government, it is the only constancy that remains."

Stoudenmire's eyes narrowed, regarding the older man speculatively. "What about you, Judge? Haven't you ever had an urge to make it work better? Could be El Paso is the place to start."

Hamer blinked and gave him a wry look. "My boy, it occurs to me that you are considerably smarter than Ed Banning gives you credit for. But don't waste your energies trying to lure an old curmudgeon like myself into your schemes. I no longer feel a young man's compulsion to wager against time and life. Like the apathetic masses, I am content to exist."

Later, after having left the judge's office, Stoudenmire crossed the plaza under a cloud of foreboding. Maybe the high-toned old bastard was right. Everywhere he turned he found nothing but blank walls. And damned if each one didn't seem to be constructed of solid granite.

3.

KATE HAD suddenly found her voice again. That evening when Stoudenmire came home for supper, she was primed and raring to go. The moment he walked in the door the lawman knew she was out for blood; even Tige crawled off in a corner and played possum. Her eyes crackled with a smoky brilliance that put him in mind of a treed wildcat, and he knew it was only a matter of time until her claws came unsheathed. Watching her bustle back and forth between the kitchen, clanging pots, slamming dishes down on the table, he thought again how complex and outright bewildering females became once they got married. Evidently a wedding band wrought some powerful change inside their skulls, and what it did to their tongues was an absolute marvel. Not the good kind, or even pleasant, just damned baffling and more than a man could handle on an empty stomach.

Maybe it had something to do with the moon. Hell, everybody knew what wild things went squirrely at certain times of the month, and the longer he was married the more certain he became that women weren't anywhere near as tame as folks made out. Leastways the one he slept with wasn't, and by Christ, now that he stopped to think about it, he had the scars to prove it.

After they were seated at the table, the silence lasted only as far as the mashed potatoes. Kate let him get a big glop piled up on his plate, but when he reached for the gravy, she came out swinging. "Dallas, there's something we have to discuss. Things have gone far enough, and I think it's about time we started being honest with each other."

"Goddamn, Kate, can't you pick some place besides the supper table to start these squabbles? Let me at least eat my meals in peace."

"Please don't blaspheme my house with your crude language." She got that prim look on her face, like she had just led a prayer meeting in scripture reading. "Just for your information, the only time I ever see you is when you get hungry. You're so busy being a rootin'-tootin' lawman that you've forgotten you're also a husband. You've even gotten to where you come home at night and flop down in bed like I was some kind of wooden Indian not worth talking to."

"Me!" Stoudenmire almost choked on a mouthful of corn bread. "Now, by God, that takes the cake. Last night you acted like somebody had hemstitched your mouth shut. You've sure got a lot of room to rake somebody over the coals for not talkin'."

"Well I had every right," Kate replied indignantly. "You can't come tromping in after killing another man and expect me to be a cuddly little furball."

"Why not, for Chrissakes?" the lawman grated out. "The sonovabitch was trying to kill me! What should I have done, took off runnin' and let him pump my ass full of lead?"

"Dallas, I'm going to leave the table if you can't talk civil."

Stoudenmire almost laughed in spite of himself. She was like a spoiled little girl trying to play the great lady. So proper and chock full of decorum. Except in bed. By Jesus, she wasn't any lady then. After a moment he became aware that she was waiting for him to say something. "Kate, I'm damned if I can figure out what's got you riled up. Are you worried about me getting killed? Or is it the fact that I have to use a gun on other men every now and then?"

"Oh, what a horrible thing to say." Her face squinched up tight, and she looked on the verge of tears. "Dallas Stoudenmire, you ought to be ashamed of yourself. Every time you walk out that door, I die a little inside thinking you won't come back." Yet that was only part of the truth, she thought to herself. For she found it increasingly difficult to sleep with a man who killed so callously, almost as if he considered it his calling, maybe even enjoyed it. Still those were fears she was barely able to admit to herself. Never to him. "Of course it's you I worry about. With half the people in this town wanting to kill you, I'm almost out of my mind with fear."

"C'mon now. You're paintin' it darker than it is." He smiled, letting a joshing tone creep into his voice. "Besides, the other half's on my side. So that sorta evens things out."

"Very funny. But it's not a joking matter. You've risked your life enough for this dirty town. After all, only so much can be expected of one man, and it's time these people took a hand in their own troubles."

"That's what they pay me for. If people were willing to weed their own garden, then there wouldn't be any need for men like me."

"But that's no reason for you to keep on doing it," Kate insisted angrily. "They've stood by and watched it happen for years, and whatever El Paso is, it's just what they deserve. It's their fight, Dallas, not yours. If you can't see that, then you're either bullheaded or blind as a bat."

"Maybe. But I'm a lawman, and you'd better get used to the idea, missy. That's what I was when we got married, and that's what I'm gonna stay. So you just might as well quit flouncin' around with your tailgate up in the air and learn to live with it."

Stoudenmire sighed wearily, noting the wounded look on her face. "Let's talk about something else. I've got a meeting, and I'd like to get through it without belchin' up this meal all night."

Later, walking toward Hart's mill, the marshal thought back to Kate's last stinging comment. *Bullheaded or blind as a bat.* Damned if he didn't know but what he agreed with her. The way things had worked out a man had to be one or the other just to keep on going.

After inspecting the bank records of various politicians

that afternoon, he had reached the conculsion that crooks must bury their money in tin cans. Despite his time and effort, the idea was simply another in a long row of wash-outs. Then Gillette had ridden in shortly afterwards with an astonishing report. The rustlers not only weren't stirring from the ranch, they were now being raided by the Mexicans! Even if the Banning gang was caught crossing the river with a whole goddamn herd, it probably wouldn't stand up in court after this. What judge was going to sign extradition papers against men who were merely retaliating against Mexican *bandidos?*

Jesus, it was enough to give a man the blue swivets. And the hell of it was, he couldn't think of a damn thing to do to get things straightened out. It was like old Judge Hamer had said. He had shoveled himself ass-deep in quicksand, and nobody seemed to have a rope handy. Maybe somebody was getting their shits and giggles out of this sorry mess, but it sure hadn't given him any laughs lately.

Stoudenmire found Seth Hart and his cohorts in their usual chairs. As he took his seat, it passed through his mind that he was getting to be a regular member of this little conclave. But it was a damned disquieting thought. Still, these men had brought him to El Paso, and he owed them an explanation, if nothing else.

Looking around the table at their silent faces, he found that the words came hard. "Gents, I'll make it short and sweet. What I've got to say speaks for itself."

The grave tone hardly seemed necessary, for the businessmen could tell from the look on the marshal's face that the news wasn't good. Briefly, he outlined the latest setbacks in their war on the Bannings. The rustling operation had been brought to a standstill. There wasn't a solitary soul in the vice district who would consider turning on the gang. The political hacks absolutely refused to cooperate in exposing corruption, even if granted immunity. Ed Banning had everyone in town scared shitless, and without hard evidence, the law was running dead last. Shrugging his shoulders with a futile gesture, Stoudenmire observed that it was a Mexican standoff. Short of forcing the Bannings into a gunfight, he didn't know where to turn.

When he finished, the businessmen merely stared at him in stony silence. What they were thinking was best left unsaid, and much as they hated to admit it, none of them had any worthwhile ideas anyhow. Seth Hart finally broke the uncomfortable lull. "Well, it's not like we haven't gained something out of all this. The people are fed up with the Bannings and their methods, and by election time we might just put a reform ticket across. One thing's for sure, Ed Banning will never again exert the influence he has in the past."

"Horseshit!" Everyone turned to look at Horace Adair, startled that he would dispute the old miller so openly. "Elections are more than a year off, Seth, and you're just kidding yourself if you think Banning won't have the town weighed and sacked by then. Goddammit, what we need are the vigilantes! I've said it all along, and I still contend it's the only way we'll ever rid ourselves of those bastards."

"Horace, you might have a point there." Hart studied the Irishman for a moment, then turned to Stoudenmire. "I seem to recall that the marshal said if his way didn't work, he'd be glad to lead the first charge on the southside."

The lawman's face was wooden, clearly the look of a man absorbed in reflections all his own. "Mr. Hart, I reckon that's one charge you'll have to lead yourself. I don't believe in mob law, and I won't have any part of it. If that's what you decide, then I'll resign and leave you to do what seems best. Otherwise I'll keep right on till I find some way to put Banning under."

"That's all very commendable, Marshal," Hart said. "But it appears to me you're fresh out of ideas. What's left to do that you haven't already done?"

Every man at the table regarded him with somber gravity, and a deep stillness settled over the room. The moments ticked by with excruciating slowness while the lawman considered. When he spoke, his words were as cryptic as his expression. "I don't know. Maybe nothing. Maybe more of the same. Whatever it is, it'll separate the men from the boys."

Seth Hart just nodded, then suggested they all think it over and meet again the next evening. There was a quick murmur of agreement, almost as though each of the men wanted to escape the tension that hung between them. Dispirited, they trooped from the mill and walked off into the darkening night. They had much to reflect on before the harsh light of day brought them face to face with themselves, and a man was best left to his own devices when he crawled away to lick his wounds.

4.

DOC CUMMINGS trailed along with Stoudenmire when they left the meeting. Not saying much, they crossed Santa Fe Street and headed uptown, each man lost in his own thoughts. The little storekeeper had remained silent during the brief exchange between Hart and the lawman. As far back as he could remember, it was the first time he had ever been at a loss for words. But how could a man speak up when he knew that every word out of his mouth would only add to a friend's already grinding misery? Stoudenmire had been brought to El Paso on his say-so, which sort of left him betwixt and between. Anything he said now would have the ring of sour grapes, and he wasn't about to badger the marshal like some old fishwife, particularly when recriminations would serve no useful purpose. Stoudenmire had failed and the less said the better. The whys and wherefores of that failure now seemed meaningless, something that required neither explanation nor discussion. They knew, and that was enough. Even Hart and the boys hadn't been too rough on the lawman, and Cummings was thankful for that. The man was being devoured whole by furies of his own, and he damn sure didn't need anyone to tell him that he'd fallen flat on his ass. He knew, and whatever he was saying to himself right at this moment was a damn sight worse than anything Seth Hart's crowd might be thinking.

Reflecting back over the past month or so, that first night flashed through Cumming's mind. The night Stoudenmire had come to El Paso to discuss cleaning up the town. He had seemed so sure of himself, cocky almost, and if ever a man looked the part of a town tamer it was Dallas Stoudenmire. *Town tamer*. That was the term John Simmons had used, and everyone readily agreed that such a man was exactly what they needed. Then, when Stoudenmire had walked into the room, they knew that this was the man for the job, sensed it somehow, like when a fellow gets a hunch at the faro table and goes whole hog. Whatever kind of inner steel that it took to belt other men in the head, intimidate them, shoot them if necessary, Stoudenmire had it. When he left that night to catch the train back east, they had laughed and carried on like kids. Slapping one another on the back, they had congratulated themselves on picking a real stem-winder, even drinking numerous ribald toasts to Ed Banning's early demise.

Now that night seemed long ago, as though each week had been a year in itself, and he felt like he had aged just about that much waiting for Banning to fall. Seth Hart always said that a man had to think big if he wanted to make his mark. What he forgot to add was that anyone who reached for the sun was just naturally bound to get blisters. *Blisters!* Hell, they had gotten enough to make them look like they had been scalded in boiling oil. Enough to make fools of them all.

Still, Stoudenmire's tenure as marshal hadn't been a complete loss. He had put the quietus on the Mexican trouble, and there was some solace in that. Not much, but you had to give the man credit. They had hired him to put the damper on the greasers as well as get rid of the Bannings, and he had done half the job anyway. But with the Mexicans peaceful again, everyone tended to ignore that and remember only that he hadn't axed Ed Banning's skinny neck. Christ, it was a grudging world. Full of fat old men who paid others to do their fighting and then bellyached like foundered mules when the hired gun didn't get himself killed just on cue.

Suddenly a very curious thought raced through Cumming's head. What if Dallas had been right all along? Maybe Seth Hart was another Ed Banning after all. Not so cold and deadly perhaps, but a man of ruthless ambition nonetheless, one who merely clothed it under the guise of civic benevolence. The more he thought about it, the better sense it made. Hart had never been overly concerned about the Mexicans, not even at the start. It was always the Bannings he harped on, and it stood to reason that he had engineered this whole deal just to rid himself of a troublesome obstacle. Namely, Ed Banning.

Even now the old devil was laying the groundwork to sack Stoudenmire as marshal. That benign little speech he made tonight was only so much crap. *Let's think it over and meet again tomorrow night*. Bullshit! He had seen Hart use that gambit a hundred times. Let the other man stew in his own juices for a day and then chop his head off with a few kindly, well chosen words. Stoudenmire wasn't going to get another shot at the Bannings. He was on his way out. Then, after things had returned to normal, Hart would recruit another fast gun and start the whole bloody business all over again.

Before Cummings could carry the thought further, he realized the lawman had said something. "Sorry, Dallas, I didn't hear you. My mind was a thousand miles off."

Stoudenmire jerked his head toward a sleezy cantina at the side of the street. "Just said I feel like a drink. Wanta join me?"

"Sure. I could stand a little fortifying myself, come to think of it." The storekeeper looked away, fearing his face would somehow betray the surprise he felt. Things must really be bad. Never had he known Stoudenmire to take a drink while on duty. The man was like a monk, spartan in his habits, limiting the pleasures other men took for granted to within the four walls of his own home.

Without another word Stoudenmire led the way into the cantina and took a seat at a table along the far wall. The men ranged around the room were mostly Mexican, and they studiously avoided any show of curiosity. *Gringos* seldom frequented this place, but if *el hombre* wanted to drink here, then who were they to object. Presently a barmaid materialized at their table, and the marshal ordered tequila.

When the girl returned with a bottle and two glasses, Stoudenmire calmly poured both brimful. Sprinkling salt over the web of flesh beside his thumb, he licked sparingly and tossed the drink off in one gulp. The tequila hit his gut like molten lead and bounced dangerously, but he held it down. Breathing deeply, he shuddered like a wet dog, then glanced over at the storekeeper.

"Doc, get that stupid look off your face. You've seen grown men drink before. What's so strange about that?"

Cummings still hadn't touched his glass. "Nothing, Dallas. Nothing at all. Except that you're going about it for the wrong reasons. Hell, tomorrow things won't look half so bad, and I'm layin' odds you'll figure a way out of this deal yet."

"Thanks for those kind words, brother-in-law." The lawman refilled his glass and stared at it listlessly. "But you and I both know that Big Daddy Hart is gonna give me the gate tomorrow night. So if I was you, I wouldn't be coverin' any bets."

The storekeeper started to say something, then tossed of his own drink and gasped when it hit bottom. After a moment he looked up. "Much as I hate to admit it, you've been right about a lot of things. Looks like old friend Seth is out to crown himself king, and near as I can figure, you're not arranging the coronation as fast as he'd like it."

Stoudenmire grinned wryly. "You figure pretty good, Doc. The old fart is gonna get rid of the Bannings even if he has to raise the vigilantes. That hogwash he was dishin' out tonight didn't mean a damn thing. Just as soon as he ties a can to my tail, there won't be anyone to stop him, and he'll put this whole goddamn town to the torch if that's what it takes."

"Yeah, but you're still US marshal. Don't forget that. You could stop him no matter what."

"Maybe. If I want to get myself killed facin' down a mob. I'm not real sure El Paso's worth it. The only other way is to send for the Rangers, and I doubt they could get here in time to head off what he's got in mind."

"Well hell, there's more'n one way to skin a cat." Cummings leaned over the table and tapped the lawman's arm. "Listen, there's plenty of good people in this town that won't hold still for that kind of crap. Why, I bet I could round up twenty, thirty men who'd stand with you when the time came."

Stoudenmire jiggled his glass, watching the tequila swirl around in tiny circles. "What good would it do gettin' them killed? It's like I told you before, Doc. When you've got two men who figure that there's room for only one kingfish, it's the folks in the middle who end up gettin' hurt. Maybe that's not how the Good Lord intended it, but that's damn sure how she works out."

Cummings nodded absently, staring into his empty glass. "Funny. When we were walkin' over here, I had it all figured out that Hart wanted to can you so he could hire another fast gun. Never occurred to me that the tricky bastard was just workin' up to an excuse for calling out the vigilantes." His voice faltered, as though the thought had touched a raw nerve. "Shitfire, let's have another drink. Maybe the sonsabitches'll kill each other off and we can start this town off right, the way it should've been."

Stoudenmire regarded the older man for a moment, then shook his head. "Guess I didn't want a drink as bad as I thought. Like the fella said, answers come sorta hard at the bottom of a bottle. Think I'll call it a night, Doc. Maybe tomorrow we'll wake up and find out we're both just a couple'a damn fools."

He tossed a coin on the table and headed for the door. They parted outside, and Cummings watched him walk off into the night, a deeply troubled man. Musing on it for a moment, the little merchant hoped that Kate didn't give him too hard a time tonight. Whatever else he was, Dallas Stoudenmire wasn't a quitter. But right now he was feeling mighty close to being one. He would need all the understanding Kate could give him, and then some.

Cummings wandered aimlessly for a while, then struck off toward the plaza and his store. After entering through the back door, he lit a lamp, broke open a fresh bottle, and sat down to do some serious thinking of his own. If Stoudenmire couldn't rid El Paso of the Bannings and hold Seth Hart in check, then what the hell was left? The question disturbed him, but the lack of an answer was downright chilling.

Puzzling over it, Cummings realized that the marshal was essentially a man of action, one who always chose the most direct solution to a problem. He wasn't a devious man, a schemer, the kind who could employ subterfuge or guile to put an opponent under. Moreover, he believed in the sanctity of the law, respected it fiercely. He wouldn't bat an eye at facing another man's gun, but it would never occur to him to acquire evidence in an illegal manner.

Like stealing the Bannings' records!

The thought came to him like a bolt from the blue, and with it the gut reaction that it was the solution to their dilemma. The Bannings must keep records. They couldn't run an organization without books of some sort. Whatever dirty work had gone on in this town and whoever had gotten paid off would be in those books. He knew it just as sure as he knew his own name, instinctively and without a doubt in the world. And the first place to look was the safe in Ed Banning's office.

The storekeeper had another drink and mulled it over. He wasn't a particularly brave man even by his own standards, but by Christ, he wasn't a coward either. It would be risky, and he'd have to be slicker than greased owlshit to pull it off. But he owed it to the town to try. And to Stoudenmire. Goddammit, that's what it all boiled down to! He owed it to Stoudenmire more than any of those mealy-mouthed bastards who sat around waiting for someone to save them from their own gutless palpitations.

By damn, he would drink to that. And to his first little sortie as a burglar. Down with Ed Banning and up Seth Hart's fat ass! Sonovabitch, that had a good ring to it, and if anybody could pull it off, it was that sneaky little shit by the name of Doc Cummings.

Late that night, after the southside dives had closed, Cummings gingerly stalked through the alley behind the Coliseum. He had downed the better part of a quart, just to steady his nerves, he told himself. Still, he wasn't feeling any pain, and his step was about as light as a bull elephant.

After looking up and down the alley, he forced the lock on the rear door of Banning's office and scuttled inside. There he found himself confronted by what seemed the biggest goddamned safe in Christendom. It was an ugly, black brute that towered over him like a barge, but he had to snicker in spite of himself. In the dark its round, shiny dial looked like Cyclop's beady eye watching his every movement, and somehow that struck him as damned humorous, hilarious almost. Shushing himself he went to work.

Although he was a fledgling thief, he knew how to use a crowbar, and he tackled the job with all the finesse of an ore-crusher. Gouging and prying, he went to work on the safe's doors.

But as he heaved and sweated over the cold steel, he failed to see the door knob slowly turning. In his fuzzy euphoria, the storekeeper had forgotten one salient detail. Sam Banning didn't live at the Parker House with his brother. He kept a room upstairs.

The door suddenly flew open, and Sam leaped into the office, covering him with a cocked six-gun. Cummings didn't cower or beg for mercy. He was looking the grim reaper straight in the eye, and it wasn't exactly the moment to go fainthearted. Whirling, he threw the crowbar with all his strength and jumped for the back door. But he never made it.

The Colt roared twice, and the game little merchant crashed to the floor dead.

Lighting a lamp, Sam turned the body over and stared in slack-jawed bewilderment. *Doc Cummings!* He lumbered back a step, head spinning in a witless stupor, and for a moment he went cold with sweat. Then he slammed the lamp down on the desk and raced out the back door. Whatever had happened here was over his head, and right now the only thing he wanted was to get his big brother.

By Jesus, that was the ticket. Let Ed figure it out!

5.

EARLY NEXT morning Jim Gillette knocked on Stoudenmire's door. The deputy was filled with a sense of dread; unable to shake the feeling that he had unwittingly become a messenger of death. Last night he had restrained himself with no little effort from awakening the marshal, knowing full well what would happen if he did so. Instead, he had downed a pot of coffee and waited for the first, golden streamers of sunrise, telling himself that Stoudenmire would be more reasonable with Cumming's body already laid out in the undertaking parlor.

From years of watching men kick out their lives on saloon floors and dusty cowtown streets, he knew that time often worked a curious change on the dead man's friends and family. Those who were notified immediately experienced a mixture of shock, sorrowful bereavement for their loved one, and blind rage for the man who had killed him. But if they found out about it later, often even as little as a few hours, their pain and mindless fury was mitigated in a quirky sort of way. Somehow the hurt faded almost as fast as it began, and instead of mourning the dead man, they felt sorry for themselves. It was as if they regretted the poor fellow's death not nearly so much as they resented him leaving them in the lurch on such short notice.

Gillette had always thought it was damned odd, but then most folks were sort of queer in the head anyway if a fellow stood off and watched the numbskull things they did. Like trying to crack Banning's safe with a crowbar. Jesus!

Still that was over and done with, and there was no way to bring the dead back. Right now he had to face the living, and whatever gods were watching, he sure as hell hoped they would lend a hand in putting the damper on Stoudenmire's temper.

When the lawman opened the door, he knew immediately that something was bad wrong. "C'mon in, Jim. You look like a man carrying a heavy load."

Gillette stepped inside and pulled his hat off, twisting

it nervously between his fingers. ''Dallas, I wish to Christ I wasn't the one that had to tell you, but there ain't no other way. Doc Cummings is dead.''

Stoudenmire just stared at him, showing nothing. ''Who got him?''

''Sam Banning.'' The deputy knew what was coming and he added hurriedly, ''But it ain't like it sounds.''

Stoudenmire's face went ashen, and every muscle in his body seemed taut as strung catgut. ''Tell me.''

''Doc broke into Banning's office and tried to crack the safe. Hadn't no more'n got started when Sam caught him.'' Gillette's voice faltered then, and he looked down at the floor. ''Doc heaved a crowbar and took off runnin'. Sam drilled him twice goin' away.''

''What about witnesses?''

''Nary a one. Just the two of 'em involved. The sign's all there to read though. Sam went over and rousted Banning out of bed, and then they come and got me. I went over it real careful, and it's just like I said.''

The marshal's color had returned, but his eyes were like death warmed over. ''When did it happen?''

''Somewheres after two this mornin'.'' Gillette hawked and cleared his throat. ''I had Doc taken over to Pritchard's funeral parlor.''

Stoudenmire nodded vaguely, suddenly aware that Kate would have to be told. Then he glanced back at Gillette, and his gaze hardened. ''What'd you do with Sam Banning?''

The deputy shifted his cud of tobacco and swallowed heavily. Now came the hairy part. ''Nothin.' There ain't no way we can touch him legally. Doc was caught in the act, and every man's got the right to defend his own property. Even if his name's Banning.''

Some moments passed as the lawman digested that. Then he grunted skeptically. ''That sounds like something Ed Banning would say.''

''Matter of fact, he did. Just used more words, that's all.'' Gillette took a hitch at his belt and met the younger man's look head-on. ''Dallas, I got an idea what you're thinkin', but it won't wash. Whatever Doc was lookin' for in that safe, he was out of line. There ain't nothin' we can do to the Bannings, and you'd best set your mind to it."

"What's that about Doc and the Bannings?" Kate's voice came from the kitchen doorway. Turning, they found her staring at them with mild alarm. Gillette was reminded of a young doe, all wide-eyed and nervously alert at some strange sound, and he suddenly wanted very much to be somewhere else.

Stoudenmire spoke without looking around. "Jim, you'd better get on back to the office. I'll be down a little later."

The deputy shot a glance at Kate, seeing her tense, then ducked out the door. Stoudenmire was left with the dirtiest job of all, but he was damn glad the lawman had let him off the hook. Relieved was more like it, as though somebody had just pulled him clear of a load of granite. Telling people their kinfolks had gone under was a messy business, and no matter how many times a man did it, he always walked away feeling soiled and kind of rotten at the core.

When he went through the gate, it came just about like he expected it would. First the stifled cry, then a scream of shock and disbelief, and finally the wretched, sobbing moan that was enough to tear a man's heart out by its roots. The wail of Indian women was worse, but not a hell of a lot. Whatever kind of female it was, animal or human, the sound stuck with a man for days, and even worse sometimes in the night when he couldn't chase it away. Lengthening his stride, the old lawdog struck out for the plaza, not the least bit shamed that it was Stoudenmire back there instead of him.

When Gillette reached the office, men slowly began drifting in to discuss this latest calamity. They cursed and grumbled, drank coffee, swilled whiskey out of pint bottles, and talked incessantly of raising the vigilantes. Seth Hart waddled in before long with his somber-faced cronies, and the crowd swarmed around him demanding some action be taken against the Bannings. The miller talked a hell of a lot without saying anything one way or the other, and the morning ground on with deadly slowness. Listening to them jabber on and on, it passed through Gillette's mind that, if a man was to put their brains in a jaybird, the sonovabitch would probably fly backwards.

Then, shortly before noon, Stoudenmire walked through the door. Tige was at his side, and for a moment the two of them regarded the crowded room with a hollow stare. The lawman's face was grim as weathered tombstone, and it was obvious that he had just come from a house where death now resided.

Seth Hart stepped forward and extended his hand. "Marshal, we all want you to know how sorry we are, and we'd be beholden if you would pass along our condolences to Mrs. Stoudenmire. Doc was a fine man, a friend to every decent person in this town, and he'll be missed around here."

The lawman's face remained blank, and he dropped the politician's hand after a perfunctory shake. "Thanks. My wife'll be glad to know he had so many friends."

Hart glanced around uncomfortably, wondering if the others had caught the marshal's sardonic tone. But he came right back, blustering with authority and purpose. "I might add that his friends mean to do something about this cowardly act, Marshal. The boys have been talking it over, and we think it's high time to call out the vigilantes. The Bannings absolutely can't be allowed to go any further. Naturally, we'd prefer it if you'd deputize everyone and make it legal and above board."

"Naturally." Stoudenmire's reply was clipped, with just the faintest trace of insolence. "Tell you what, Hart. It's gettin' along toward dinner time so why don't you get these boys fed and meet back here in a couple of hours. By then we oughta know what's what."

Seth Hart got a funny expression on his face, like he had heard it but he couldn't quite believe it. There was something more to this than met the eye, and he had the distinct feeling that the marshal had just snookered him into a corner. But he couldn't very well refuse, and it would look fishy if he demanded they march now. Stoudenmire's suggestion seemed very practical and everyone knew it. Hell, nobody wanted to fight on an empty stomach.

The men filed out with Hart in the lead, and within moments Stoudenmire and Gillette had the place to themselves. Gillette was more than a little thunderstruck himself by this sudden turn of events but he just waited for whatever was coming next. The lawman had something up his sleeve, and knowing him, it would probably be a real ball-buster.

After a moment the marshal sat down at his desk, took out pen and paper, and began writing. Finished, he unpinned his badge and tossed it on the desk. Then he handed Gillette the note. "Jim, that's my resignation. As of right now, you're marshal of El Paso."

Gillette studied the paper for a moment, then looked up. "I reckon you mean to call the Bannings out."

"That's about the size of it," Stoudenmire observed.

"And you just suckered Hart into gettin' the vigilantes out of your hair so you could do it all by your lonesome."

"You're a foxy old buzzard." Stoudenmire gave him a wry look. "Didn't figure I had you fooled."

Gillette dropped the note on the desk. "You didn't have Hart fooled neither. But that's nothin' one way or the other. What's important is that you're settin' out to do something that goes against everything you ever stood for. Call the Bannings out and you're gonna be spittin' in the teeth of the law you've sworn to uphold. Now you tell me how that differs from the vigilantes marchin' over there and lynching 'em?"

Stoudenmire's mouth set in a hard line. "Jim, I'm fresh out of answers. Maybe there's times when the law's just not enough. The Bannings toe-dance around it and make it bend to suit themselves. I couldn't stop 'em, and Doc got himself killed trying to help me. I reckon if I had put 'em under when I should've that wouldn't have happened."

He paused, staring at his scrawled resignation for a moment. "I failed as marshal, but I'm not gonna fail Doc. Sometimes a man has to fight just because he couldn't live with himself if he walked away. Right or wrong, that's how my stick floats."

Their eyes met and Stoudenmire flashed his old grin.

Then the moment passed, and he came up out of the chair, heading for the door. "Look after yourself, pardner."

Gillette moved to block his path. "Listen goddammit, there ain't no law that says you get to have all the fun. I'd sorta like a whack at them pricks myself, so just count me in."

"Thanks, Jim, but it's no go. This is personal. Besides, this town's got to have some law even if it's a crotchety old coot like you."

Smiling tightly, Stoudenmire brushed past him and walked out with Tige at his heels. Crossing the plaza, he felt a strange numbness settle over him. He had lived with danger all his life; sometimes it seemed as though he had no memory back beyond those first bloody days on the killing ground. But this was different. There was a cold, icy feeling in his spine, like death's ugly, fleshless hand was squeezing down on his backbone. Maybe it was a sign. Something warning him of what was to come. Then he chuckled. There weren't any signs. Just fast men and slow men. The quick and the dead.

Absently he noted the shops and people on the streets as he walked along. Curiously, it was as if he were seeing it all for the first time. Again he chuckled to himself. Or maybe for the last time. Then it came to him that first, last, or never, it really didn't make a damn. The only friends he had in this town was the one he had just left behind and the dog padding along at his side. Come to think of it, they were the only friends he had in the world. Whatever the reason, he just naturally couldn't take people except in small doses. But what the hell, a man in his game needed allies, not friends. After all, the friends you didn't have couldn't weasel out when the shooting started. That was the nice thing about Tige. The surly sonovabitch wouldn't back off from a bull alligator if he was hamstrung and blind in both eyes. Which was a hell of a lot more than you could say for most men. Even the best of them.

Without realizing it, he found himself standing in front of the Coliseum. The icy feeling was still with him, but he felt calm now, loose and easy inside where it counted. Then he knew that it was all right. Once the tightness drained away, everything else fell into place, and he didn't even have to think. Just react.

The moment he pushed through the bat-wing doors, he sensed that the Bannings had known he would come. Ed stood at the bar, while Sam casually studied a shot on the billiard table across from the door. They had him in a cross fire, no matter who drew first. But even so, he liked the odds. Somehow it made the game sweeter, more inviting, just the way he would have wanted it.

Glancing from one to the other, he decided to take Sam first. The overgrown crock of shit deserved it, and besides, Doc would have liked it that way. Watching Sam out of the corner of his eye, he laid it out for Banning.

"Banning, I've come to punch your ticket. Maybe you recollect I warned you once not to be around when your number was called."

Banning turned from the bar, brushing his coat back over the handle of his pistol. "Stoudenmire, you'd better turn around and walk out of here. Cummings got what was coming to him, and we've got the law on our side. Don't push it."

Stoudenmire's pale eyes went cold as chilled stone. "Shit, there's no law here. There's just you and me and your dumb-ass brother. Make your fight, mister. You're about to get killed."

Sam Banning's nerve suddenly broke, and he clawed at the pistol on his hip. Stoudenmire's arm moved in a blurred motion, and a Colt appeared in his fist. The gun bucked, and Sam was thrown across the billiard table, dusted front and back.

Crouching, Stoudenmire spun around, noting that Ed was no slouch with a gun. The gang leader had fired even as Sam died, but Tige was leaping for his throat, and the big dog took the ball straight through his spine. Banning thumbed off another shot as Tige dropped at his feet, and the slug caught Stoudenmire in the chest. Hurled backwards, he crashed into the wall and felt his knees start to buckle. Banning's mouth tightened in an evil grin, and he popped off a third shot. But he had rushed it, overanxious for the kill, and the window at Stoudenmire's side exploded in a shower of glass.

Steadying himself against the wall, Stoudenmire raised the Colt very deliberately, as if he had all the time in the world. When it jumped in his hand a small fountain of blood spurted out over Banning's shirtfront. Drunkenly, he staggered away from the bar and began to sag, groping blindly with his hands like a man trying to break a fall.

Extending his gun arm, Stoudenmire drew a fine bead and gut-shot Banning just as his rump hit the floor. The gang boss jerked upright, as if he were rowing a boat, his eyes bursting with pain and shock. Then the stench came as death loosed his bowels, and he settled to the floor. His leg jumped once, then stiffened, and he lay very still.

Stoudenmire's eyes glazed over, and he wiped his hand across his face. When his vision cleared, he looked down on the dead men for a moment, then shoved away from the wall. Willing himself to stand, to walk, to remain erect, he lurched across the room and pushed out through the doors. Gillette was there, and he rushed forward, eyes glistening wetly without shame.

Stoudenmire looked up through a bright haze of pain and grunted hoarsely. "Jim, you'd better call the undertaker. They killed Tige."

Then the Colt dropped from his hand, and he fell into Gillette's arms.

EPILOGUE

STOUDENMIRE STEPPED to the door, then paused to kiss Kate once more. Her arms encircled his neck, and she planted one square on his mouth, long and slow with a naughty little probing just for good measure. The kind of kiss nice girls weren't supposed to know about. The lawman squeezed her in a bearish grip, feeling the soft flesh yield and melt against him.

Christ! She was a shameless hussy about some things. Putting a kiss like that on him, right in the doorway where all the neighbors could get a real eyeful. But who the hell cared what other people thought? They didn't know about the wildcat that crawled into his bed every night, and by God, if she wanted a little kiss every now and then, he was damn sure going to oblige her.

Kate's soft lips curved in a teasing smile, and she stepped back, straightening his coat lapel. "There now. That ought to hold you till suppertime anyway. You just make sure you don't wear yourself out jayhawking around town."

"Lady, you oughta be arrested for carryin' dangerous weapons." He spun her about and swatted her on the bottom. "And don't be givin' people advice about getting their rest. It's not me that yells uncle in the clinches."

"Oh, what conceit!" Her mouth curled in a tiny pout. "Run along, Mr. Stoudenmire. Go on downtown and let everyone gawk at the big bad lawman. You'll get your comeuppance tonight."

Stoudenmire chuckled, then turned and hobbled off

down the walk. "Is that a promise or a threat?"

"Both. But I'll let you take it out in trade." Kate giggled wickedly and slammed the door shut when he looked back.

The lawman went through the gate chortling to himself. Damned if things didn't have a way of doing a bellyflop just when a man least expected it.

The last couple of months had brought a warm glow of discovery in the Stoudenmire household. Doc Cummings' death and the subsequent shootout with the Bannings had wrought a startling transformation in Kate. Somehow she had sifted it out for herself and come to the conclusion that certain men just weren't meant to be gelded. Once that dawned on her, and she came to grips with it, her entire attitude had changed. Now she made jokes about other women and their henpecked husbands, laughingly dubbing them *mansos*, the tame bulls, a term she had picked up from her Mexican housekeeper. Though Kate never said anything openly, she had become fiercely proud of her man, and quietly confident that he could handle anything that came down the pike. When she looked at other women nowadays, she felt something akin to pity, or perhaps merely compassion, for they would have to live out their lives never knowing what it was to take a real man to bed. And under the Stoudenmire roof, there was no longer the slightest doubt who ruled the roost.

Kate had become a woman, and she reveled in the sheer joy of using feminine wiles to get her way. Dallas Stoudenmire was just a big, lumbering teddy-bear now that she had figured him out, and Mrs. Stoudenmire had his number anytime she wanted to punch it.

The lawman himself had spent considerable time reflecting on this volatile and highly mercurial creature who now shared his life. But he still wasn't sure that he understood her, or for that matter that he ever would. Maybe the fact that he had broken with his own code to avenge Doc had triggered the change in her. Though she had never said one way or the other, he sensed that a bond of some sort had taken root between them the day he killed the Bannings. Love. Venegeance. An eye for an eye. Simple gratitude for not letting her brother go to his grave with the debt unsettled. Damned if he knew what made her tick, and somehow it didn't seem so important anymore that he try and decipher it. She had turned out to be the kind of woman he had always wanted, the loving, gutsy, spitfire who was "root hog or die" all the way. And that was enough.

Still, he had to laugh sometimes when he saw that sparkle come into her eye, and she started wheedling and conniving. Women just weren't happy unless they had some little plot going; scheming and finagling new ways to twist a man's ying-yang so he'd sit up and bark like a lap dog. But what the hell! Long as a man didn't lose his balls in the bargain, it was a pretty comfortable arrangement.

Strolling along the street, he greeted merchants and townspeople with an easy smile as they inquired after his health. The briskness of winter had settled over the basin, and it was good to be walking again, even though he felt slightly ridiculous using a cane. The crisp air made him forget the dull throb in his chest, and the sight of snow-capped mountains in the distance brought new strength to the rubbery joints in his knees. His recuperation had been slow and painful, and damned uncertain at times. But he was back on the job, part way anyhow. And that was what counted most.

After circling the plaza, he entered the office to find Gillette catnapping. The old lawdog roused himself with a lazy stretch and started grumbling right off. "Dallas, we gotta do something to stir up a little excitement around here. This goddamn town's so peaceful it's downright mortifying."

Stoudenmire hobbled around the desk and eased down in his chair. "Pardner, you name it and we'll do it. What'd you have in mind? A little mumblety-peg. Rackin' up some horseshoes. Maybe a fast game of marbles?"

"Aw, quit your joshin'." Gillette opened the door on the little pot-bellied stove and tossed in a load of wood. "You know what I'm talkin' about. Maybe we oughta pull up stakes and find us a town that ain't had a dose of law yet."

"Christ almighty," the lawman snorted. "We've just

got started in El Paso. As long as there's whorehouses and gambling dives, some bonehead is gonna try to get his meathooks on the whole box of goodies. The game's the same, Jimbo. Only the faces change."

"Like Seth Hart, maybe?" The deputy cocked one eye with a sly smirk.

"Maybe, Maybe not. Looks like the old devil might just run for mayor." Stoudenmire explored the thought for a moment before resuming. "Which means he'd have to play it strictly on the up and up, leastways if he wants the reformers' vote. But that doesn't change nothin'. If it's not him, someone else'll come along. There's always somebody that wants to sandbag the bets and skim off the cream."

"Damn me, if you ain't right. Matter of fact, it looks like that particular ailment is goin' around like measles." Gillette pulled a newspaper off his cot and tossed it on the desk. "Accordin' to that, the Earp boys just had 'emselves a turkey shoot over in Tombstone. Caught a bunch of the opposition in some corral and just flat plowed 'em under. You reckon Wyatt's tryin' to do the same thing over there that Banning done here?"

Stoudenmire studied the newspaper article, nodding to himself. Some moments passed before he looked up. "From what I saw of Earp in Dodge, I wouldn't put it past him. Course, you never can tell. Some towns need more law than others. Hell'sfire, there's even times when the law itself has to have its neck jerked back in joint."

"Well, much as I hate to say it, I don't look for no more trouble in this burg." The deputy wagged his head ruefully and squirted the stove with tobacco juice. "Folks've just naturally got the idea you're half-bear and half-alligator, and they don't want no part of it."

The marshal let that pass. Everybody in town had been goggling over him like he was some circus freak, and it was growing a bit wearisome. "I'll tell you something, Jim. It's the elections that are gonna tell the tale in El Paso. People have got a right to choose whatever kind of leaders they want, and they generally get just what they deserve. But whichever way it works out, lawmen can't take sides.

We're sorta like spectators at a cock fight. The best we can do is try to keep the lid on and make sure the good ones don't die for nothin'."

"Like Doc Cummings?" Gillette observed.

There was a momentary lull, and even the pot-bellied stove seemed to be thinking it over, holding its angry crackling to a simmering whisper.

Gilette quickly shifted the conversation around to routine matters of policing the town, and after a while Stoudenmire decided he would call it a day. Cane in hand, he hobbled out the door and headed back uptown. He still tired easily, and he had begun to look forward to his afternoon naps.

Moving slowly along the street, it occurred to him how much he missed Tige trotting along at his side. Maybe this afternoon he would take a stroll over to the big dog's grave. They had buried him back close to Commanche Peak where the wild things still ran free. Tige would have liked that, being out there among his own kind. *El lobo hambre*, the Mexican kids had called him that first day in town. Well, hell, he never was what a man would rightly call civilized. Never wanted to be either, just like his master.

Stoudenmire chuckled to himself. Damn, they'd made a pair, sure enough. Maybe they would cut trails again when it came his time to cross over. The thought brought a warm glow deep down in his belly, and just a touch of the old cockiness crept back into his stride.

Hefting the cane, he slung it into the middle of the road and struck off at a fast limp toward home.

PRAISE FOR SPUR AWARD-WINNING AUTHOR MATT BRAUN

"Matt Braun is one of the best!"

—Don Coldsmith, author of the Spanish Bit series

"Braun tackles the big men, the complex personalities of those brave few who were pivotal figures in the settling of an untamed frontier."

—Jory Sherman, author of *Grass Kingdom*

ACTING THE PART . . .

Lillian finally joined the fight. After a struggle to cock both hammers on the shotgun, she found it required all her strength to raise the heavy weapon. She brought it to shoulder level, trying to steady the long barrels, and accidentally tripped both triggers. The shotgun boomed, the double hammers dropping almost simultaneously, and a hail of buckshot sizzled into the charging Indians. The brutal kick of the recoil knocked Lillian off her feet.

A warrior flung out his arms and toppled dead from his pony. The others swerved aside as buckshot simmered through their ranks like angry hornets. Their charge was broken not ten feet from the overhang, and Fontaine and Chester continued to blast away with their Henry repeaters . . .

DON'T MISS THESE OTHER
CLASSIC WESTERN ADVENTURES FROM

MATT BRAUN

Dodge City
Dakota
A Distant Land
Windward West
Crossfire
Highbinders
The Warlords
The Spoilers
Hickok and Cody
The Overlords
Tombstone
Rio Grande
Brannocks
The Gamblers
Rio Hondo
Savage Land
Noble Outlaw
Cimarron Jordan
Lords of the Land
One Last Town
Texas Empire
Jury of Six

AVAILABLE FROM ST. MARTIN'S PAPERBACKS

THE WILD ONES

MATT BRAUN

St. Martin's Paperbacks

THE WILD ONES

ISBN: 978-1-250-01351-4
EAN: 1250013518

Printed in the United States of America

St. Martin's Paperbacks edition / June 2002

St. Martin's Paperbacks are published by St. Martin's Press, 175 Fifth Avenue, New York, NY 10010.

P1

IN MEMORY OF ALL THOSE LOST AT
THE WORLD TRADE CENTER
AND THE PENTAGON
SEPTEMBER 11, 2001

THE WILD ONES

Chapter 1

THE TRAIN was some miles west of Boonville. Lillian sat by the window, staring out at the verdant countryside. She thought Missouri looked little different from Indiana or Ohio, though perhaps not so flat. Her expression was pensive.

September lay across the land. Fields tall with corn, bordered by stands of trees, fleeted past the coach window under a waning sun. There was a monotonous sameness to the landscape, and the clickety-clack of steel wheels on rails made it all but hypnotic. She wondered if she would ever again see New York.

Chester, her brother, was seated beside her. Three years older, recently turned twenty-two, he was a solid six-footer, with chiseled features and a shock of wavy dark hair. His head bobbed to the sway of the coach and his eyes were closed in a light slumber. He seemed intent on sleeping his way through Missouri.

Alistair Fontaine, their father, was seated across from them. A slender man, his angular features and leonine head of gray hair gave him a distinguished appearance. He was forty-four, an impeccable dresser, his customary attire a three-piece suit with a gold watch chain draped over the expanse of his vest. He looked at Lillian.

"A penny for your thoughts, my dear." Lillian loved the sound of her father's voice. Even as a young child, she had been entranced by his sonorous baritone, cultured and uniquely rich in timbre. She smiled at him.

"Oh, just daydreaming, Papa," she said with a small shrug. "I miss New York so much. Don't you?"

"Never look back," Fontaine said cheerfully. "Westward the sun and westward our fortune. Our brightest days are yet ahead."

"Do you really think so?"

"Why, child, I have no doubt of it whatever. We are but stars following our destiny."

She sensed the lie beneath his words. He always put the best face on things, no matter how dismal. His wonderfully aristocratic bearing gave his pronouncements the ring of an oracle. But then, she reminded herself, he was an actor. He made reality of illusion.

"Yes, of course, you're right," she said. "Abilene just seems like the end of the earth. I feel as though we've been . . . banished."

"Nonsense," Fontaine gently admonished her. "We will take Abilene by storm, and our notices will have New York clamoring for our return. You mark my words!"

Chester was roused by his father's voice. He yawned, rubbing sleep from his eyes. "What's that about New York?"

"I was telling Lillian," Fontaine informed him. "Our trip West is but a way station on the road of life. We've not seen the last of Broadway."

"Dad, I hope to God you're right."

"Never doubt it for a moment, my boy. I have utter faith."

Lillian wasn't so sure. On the variety circuit, *The Fontaines*, as they were billed, was a headline act. Her earliest memories were of traveling the circuit of variety theaters throughout the Northeast and the Eastern Seaboard. Originated in England and imported across the Atlantic, variety theaters were the most popular form of entertainment in America.

A child of the theater, Lillian had been raised among performers. Her playmates were the offspring of chorus girls, song-and-dance men, comics, contortionists, and acrobats. At an early age, she and Chester became a part of the family troupe, acting in melodramas with their parents and sometimes accompanying their mother in song. The family ensemble presented entertainment for the masses, something for everyone.

Alistair Fontaine played to popular tastes by appearing in the sometimes-histrionic melodramas. At heart, he considered himself a tragedian, and his greatest joy was in emoting Shakespearean soliloquies in full costume. Yet it was his wife, Estell Fontaine, who was the true star of the show. Her extraordinary voice rendered audiences spellbound, and she might have had a career in opera. She chose instead her family. And the variety stage.

The magnitude of her stardom became apparent just three months ago, in the early summer of 1871. A bout of influenza quickly turned to pneumonia, and two days later she died in a New York hospital. Her loss devastated Alistair, who stayed drunk for a week, and left Lillian and Chester undone by grief. Estell was the bulwark of the family, wife, mother, and matriarch. They were lost without her, emotionally adrift. Yet, strangely, made somehow closer by her death.

Their personal tragedy was compounded in their professional lives. With Estell gone, the Fontaines soon discovered they were no longer a headline act. Her voice was the stardust of the show, and without her, they were suddenly unemployable anywhere on the variety circuit. Theater owners were sympathetic, but in the months following Estell's death there were no offers for an engagement, even on the undercard. Their booking agent suggested they try the budding variety circuit in the West.

Alistair Fontaine was at first opposed and not a little offended. But then, after three months without work and facing poverty, he reluctantly agreed. Their agent finally obtained a booking in Abilene, Kansas, the major railhead for shipping Texas cattle. Whatever was to be learned of their destination was to be found in the pages of the *Police Gazette.* Abilene was reported to be the wildest town in the Wild West.

Today, watching her father, Lillian wasn't at all convinced that he had reconciled himself with their situation. In off moments, she caught him staring dully into space and sensed his uncertainty about their trip West. Even more, she knew his posturing and his confident manner were meant to reassure herself and Chester. His oft-repeated assertion that they would return to New York and Broadway was fanciful, a dream at best.

She longed for the counsel of her mother.

"When's our next stop?" Chester abruptly asked. "I wouldn't mind a hot meal for a change."

There was no dining car on the train. A vendor periodically prowled the aisles, selling stale sandwiches and assorted sundries. Their last decent meal had been in St. Louis.

Fontaine chuckled amiably. "I fear you'll have a wait, my boy. We're scheduled to arrive in Kansas City about midnight."

"Wish it was New York instead."

"Be of stout heart, Chet. Think of us as thespians off on a grand adventure."

Lillian turned her gaze out the window. Abilene, for all her father's cheery bluster, hardly seemed to her a grand adventure. The middle of nowhere sounded a bit more like it.

She, too, wished for New York.

The train hurtled through the hamlet of Sweet Springs. Coupled to the rear of the engine and the tender were an express car and five passenger coaches. As the locomotive sped past the small depot, the engineer tooted his whistle. On the horizon, the sun dropped toward the rim of the earth.

A mile west of town, a tree had been felled across the tracks on the approach to a bridge. The engineer set the brakes, wheels grinding on the rails, and the train jarred to a screeching halt. The sudden jolt caught the passengers unawares, and there was a moment of pandemonium in the coaches. Luggage went flying from the overhead racks as women screamed and men cursed.

Then, suddenly, a collective hush fell over the coaches. From under the bridge where trees bordered a swift stream, a gang of riders burst out of the woods. Five men rode directly to the express car, pouring a volley of shots through the door. Another man, pistol drawn, jumped from his horse to the steps of the locomotive. The engineer and the fireman dutifully raised their hands.

Four remaining gang members, spurring their horses hard, charged up and down the track bed. Their pistols were cocked and pointed at the passengers, who stared openmouthed through the coach windows. No shots were fired, but the men's menacing attitude and tough appearance made the message all too clear. Anyone who resisted or attempted to flee the train would be killed.

"My God!" Alistair Fontaine said in an awed tone. "The train is being robbed."

Lillian shrank back into her seat. Her eyes were fastened on the riders waving their pistols. "Are we in danger, Papa?"

"Stay calm, my dear," Fontaine cautioned. "I daresay the rascals are more interested in the express car."

The threat posed by the armed horsemen made eminent good sense to the passengers. Like most railroads, the Kansas Pacific was not revered by the public. For years, eastern robber barons had plundered the West on land grants and freight rates. A holdup, according to common wisdom, was a matter between the railroad and the bandits. Only a fool would risk his life to thwart a robbery. There were no fools aboard today.

From the coaches, the passengers had a ringside seat. They watched as the five men outside the express car demonstrated a no-nonsense approach to train robbery. One of the riders produced a stick of dynamite and held the fuse only inches away from the tip of a lighted cigar. Another rider, whose commanding presence pegged him as the gang leader, gigged his horse onto the roadbed. His voice raised in a shout, he informed the express guards that their options were limited.

"Open the door or get blown to hell!"

The guards, much like the passengers, were unwilling to die for the Kansas Pacific. The door quickly slid open and they tossed their pistols onto the ground. Three of the robbers dismounted and scrambled inside the express car. The leader, positioned outside the car, directed the operation from aboard his horse. His tone had the ring of authority, brusque and demanding. His attitude was that of a man accustomed to being obeyed.

"Holy Hannah!" one of the passengers exclaimed. "That there's the James boys. There's Jesse himself!"

Jesse and Frank James were the most famous outlaws in America. Their legend began in 1866, when they rode into Liberty, Missouri, and robbed the Clay County Savings Association of $70,000. It was the first daylight bank robbery in American history and created a furor in the nation's press. It also served as a template by which the gang would operate over the years ahead, robbing trains and looting banks. Their raids were conducted with military precision.

A master of propaganda, Jesse James frequently wrote articulate letters to editors of influential midwestern newspapers. The letters were duly reprinted and accounted, in large measure, for the myth that "he robbed from the rich and gave to the poor." Comparisons were drawn between Jesse and Robin Hood, the legendary outlaw of Sherwood Forest. Not entirely in jest, newspaper editorials made reference to "Jesse and his merry band of robbers."

Tales were widely circulated with regard to Jesse's charitable nature toward the poor. The loot taken in the robberies, so he contended in his letters, was simply liberated from the coffers of greedy bankers and corrupt railroads. In time, with such tales multiplying, Jesse became known as a champion of the oppressed and the downtrodden. To backwoods Missourians and gullible Easterners alike he came to represent a larger-than-life figure. A Robin Hood reborn—who wore a six-gun and puckishly thumbed his nose at the law.

The holdup took less than five minutes. The robbers inside the express car emerged with a mail sack that appeared painfully empty of cash. There was a hurried conference with their leader, and his harsh curses indicated his displeasure. He dismounted, ordering one man to guard the train crew, and waved the others toward the passenger coaches. They split into pairs, two men to a coach, and clambered up the steps at the end of each car. The leader and another man burst through the door of the lead coach.

A murmur swept through the passengers. The two men were instantly recognizable, their faces plastered on wanted dodgers from Iowa to Texas. Jesse and Frank James stood at the front of the car, brandishing cocked pistols.

"Sorry to trouble you folks," Jesse said with cold levity. "That express safe was mighty poor pickin's. We'll have to ask you for a donation."

Frank lifted a derby off the head of a notions drummer. He started down the aisle, the upturned hat in one hand and a pistol in the other. His mouth creased in a sanguine smile as passengers obediently filled the hat with cash and gold coins. He paused where the Fontaines were seated.

Lillian blushed under his appreciative inspection. She was rather tall, with enormous china blue eyes and exquisite features. Vibrant even in the face of a robber, she wore her tawny hair upswept, with fluffs of curls spilling over her forehead. Her demure dimity cotton dress did nothing to hide her tiny waist and sumptuous figure. She quickly averted her eyes.

"Beauty's ensign"—Frank James nodded, still staring at her—"is crimson in thy lips and in thy cheeks."

Alistair Fontaine was an avid reader of periodicals. He recalled a curious item from the *Police Gazette,* noting the anomaly that robber and mankiller Frank James was a student of Shakespeare. He rose as though taking center stage.

"M'lord," he said in a mellifluous voice. "You see me here before you a poor man, as full of grief as age, wretched in both."

"King Lear," Frank said, grinning. "I take it you fancy the Bard."

"A mere actor," Fontaine replied modestly. "Known to some as a Shakespearean."

"Well, friend, never let it be said I'd rob a man that carries the word. Keep your money."

"Frank!" Jesse snapped. "Quite jawin' and tend to business. We ain't got all night."

Frank winked slyly at Fontaine. He went down the aisle and returned with the derby stuffed to overflowing. Jesse covered his retreat through the door and followed him out. Some moments later the gang mounted their horses and rode north from the railroad tracks. A smothered sun cloaked them in silty twilight.

The passengers watched them in stunned silence. Then, as though a floodgate was released, they began babbling to one another about being robbed by the James Boys. Chester shook his head in mild wonder.

"Some introduction to the Wild West," he muttered. "I hope Abilene's nothing like that."

Lillian turned to her father. "Oh, Papa, you were wonderful!"

"Yes," Fontaine agreed. "I surprised myself."

Twilight slowly faded to dusk. Fontaine stared off at the shelterbelt of woods where the riders had disappeared. Abruptly, his legs gone shaky with a delayed reaction, he sank down into his seat. Yet he thought he would remember Frank James with fondness.

It had been the finest performance of his life.

CHAPTER 2

ABILENE WAS situated along a dogleg of the Smoky Hill River. The town was a crude collection of buildings, surrounded by milling herds of longhorn cattle. The Kansas plains, flat as a billiard table, stretched endlessly to the points of the compass.

The Fontaines stepped off the train early the next afternoon. They stood for a moment on the depot platform, staring aghast at the squalid, ramshackle structures. Eastern newspapers, overly charitable in their accounts, labeled Abilene as the first of its kind. One of a kind. A cowtown.

"Good heavens," Fontaine said in a bemused tone. "I confess I expected something more . . . civilized."

Lillian wrinkled her nose. "What a horrid smell."

There was an enervating odor of cow dung in the air. The prairie encircling Abilene was a vast bawling sea of longhorns awaiting shipment to eastern slaughterhouses, and a barnyard scent assailed their nostrils. The pungency of it hung like a fetid mist over the town.

"Perhaps there's more than meets the eye," Fontaine said, ever the optimist. "Let's not jump to hasty conclusions."

Chester grunted. "I can't wait to see the theater."

A porter claimed their steamer trunks from the baggage car. He muscled the trunks onto a handcart and led the way around the depot. The Kansas Pacific railroad tracks bisected the town east to west, cleaving it in half. Texas Street, the main thoroughfare, ran north to south.

Lillian was appalled. Her first impression was that every storefront in Abilene was dedicated to separating the Texan cattlemen from their money. With the exception of two hotels, three mercantile emporiums, and one bank, the entire business community was devoted to either avarice or lust. The street was lined with saloons, gambling dives, and dancehalls.

The boardwalks were jammed with throngs of cowhands. Every saloon and dancehall shook with the strident chords of brass bands and rinky-dink pianos. Smiling brightly, hard-eyed girls in gaudy dresses enticed the trailhands through the doors, where a quarter bought a slug of whiskey or a trip around the dance floor. The music blared amidst a swirl of jangling spurs and painted women.

"Regular circus, ain't it?" the porter said, leading them past hitch racks lined with horses. "You folks from back East, are you?"

"New York," Fontaine advised him. "We have reservations at the Drover's Cottage."

"Well, you won't go wrong there. Best digs this side of Kansas City."

"Are the streets always so crowded?"

"Night or day, don't make no nevermind. There's mebbe a thousand Texans in town most of the trailin' season."

The porter went on to enlighten them about Abilene. Joseph McCoy, a land speculator and promoter, was the founder of America's first cowtown. Texans were beef-rich and money-poor, and he proposed to exchange Northern currency for longhorn cows. The fact that a railhead didn't exist deterred him not in the least. He proceeded with an enterprise that would alter the character of the West.

McCoy found his spot along the Smoky Hill River. There was water, and a boundless stretch of grassland, all situated near the Chisholm Trail. After a whirlwind courtship of the Kansas Pacific, he convinced the railroad to lay track across the western plains. In 1867, he bought 250 acres on the river, built a town and stockyards, and lured the Texas cattlemen north. Four years later, upward of 100,000 cows would be shipped from Abilene in a single season.

"Don't that beat all!" the porter concluded. "Dang-blasted pot o'gold, that's what it is."

"Yes indeed," Fontaine said dryly. "A veritable metropolis."

The Drover's Cottage was a two-story structure hammered together with ripsawed lumber. A favorite of Texas cowmen, the exterior was whitewashed and the interior was sparsely decorated. The Fontaines were shown to their rooms, and the porter lugged their steamer trunks to the second floor. They agreed to meet in the lobby in an hour.

Lillian closed the door with a sigh. Her room was appointed with a single bed, a washstand and a rickety dresser, and one straight-backed chair. There were wall pegs for hanging clothes and a grimy window with tattered curtains that overlooked Texas Street. The mirror over the washbasin was cracked, and there was a sense of a monk's cell about the whole affair. She thought she'd never seen anything so dreary.

After undressing, she poured water from a pitcher into the basin and took a birdbath. The water was tepid and thick with silt, but she felt refreshed after so many days on a train. Then, peering into the faded mirror above the washstand, she rearranged her hair, fluffing the curls over her forehead. From her trunk, she selected undergarments and a stylish muslin dress with a lace collar. She wanted to look her best when they went to the theater.

Her waist was so small that she never wore a corset. She slipped into a chemise with a fitted bodice and three petticoats that fell below the knees. Silk hose, ankle-high shoes of soft calfskin, and the muslin dress completed her outfit. On the spur of the moment, she took from the trunk her prize possession, a light paisley shawl purchased at Lord & Taylor in New York. The shawl, exorbitantly expensive, had been a present from her mother their last Christmas together. Lillian wore it only on special occasions.

Shortly after three o'clock the Fontaines entered the Comique Variety Theater. The theater was a pleasant surprise, with a small orchestra pit, a proscenium stage, and seating for 400 people. Lou Gordon, the owner, was a beefy man with a walrus mustache and the dour look of a mortician. He greeted the men with a perfunctory handshake and a curt nod. His eyes lingered on Lillian.

"High time you're here," he said brusquely. "You open tomorrow night."

Fontaine smiled. "Perfect timing, my dear chap."

"Hope for your sake your booking agent was right. His wire said you put on a good show."

"I have every confidence you will be pleased. We present a range of entertainment for everyone."

"Such as?"

"All the world's a stage." Fontaine gestured grandly. "And all the men and women merely players. They have their exits and their entrances. And one man in his time plays many parts."

Gordon frowned. "What's that?"

"Shakespeare," Fontaine said lightly. *"As You Like It."*

"Cowhands aren't much on culture. Your agent said you do first-rate melodrama."

"Why, yes, of course, that, too. We're quite versatile."

"Glad to hear it." Gordon paused, glanced at Lillian. "What's the girl do?"

"Lillian is a fine actress," Fontaine observed proudly. "And I might add, she has a very nice voice. She opens our show with a ballad."

"Cowhands like a pretty songbird. Just don't overdo the Shakespeare."

"Have no fear, old chap. We'll leave them thoroughly entertained."

"You know Eddie Foy?" Gordon asked. "Tonight's his closing night."

"We've not had the pleasure," Fontaine said. "Headliners rarely share the same bill."

"Come on by for the show. You'll get an idea what these Texans like."

"I wouldn't miss an opportunity to see Eddie Foy."

Fontaine led the way out of the theater. He set off at a brisk pace toward the hotel. "The nerve of the man!" he said indignantly. "Instructing me on Shakespeare."

Lillian hurried to stay up. "He was only telling you about the audience, Papa."

"We shall see, my dear. We shall indeed!"

* * *

The chorus line kicked and squealed. They pranced offstage, flashing their legs, to thunderous applause from the crowd. The house was packed with Texans, most of them already juiced on rotgut liquor. Their lusty shouts rose in pitch as the girls disappeared into the wings.

The orchestra segued into a sprightly tune. The horns were muted, the strings more pronounced, and the audience quieted in anticipation. Eddie Foy skipped onstage, tipping his derby to the crowd, and went into a shuffling soft-shoe routine. The sound of his light feet on the floor was like velvety sandpaper.

Foy was short and wiry, with ginger hair and an infectious smile. Halfway through the routine, he began singing a bawdy ballad that brought bursts of laughter from the trailhands. The title of the song was *Such a Delicate Duck.*

> *I took her out one night for a walk*
> *We indulged in all sports of pleasantry and talk*
> *We came to a potato patch; she wouldn't go across*
> *The potatoes had eyes and she didn't wear no drawers!*

Lillian blushed a bright crimson. She was seated between her father and brother, three rows back from the orchestra. The lyrics of the song were far more ribald than anything she'd ever heard in a variety theater. Secretly, she thought the tune was indecently amusing, and wondered if she had no shame. Her blush deepened.

Foy ended the soft-shoe number. The orchestra fell silent with a last note of the strings as he moved to center stage. Framed in the footlights, he walked back and forth with herky-jerky gestures, delivering a rapid comedic patter that was at once risque and hilarious. The Texans honked and hooted with rolling waves of laughter.

On the heels of a last riotous joke, the orchestra suddenly blared to life. Foy nimbly sprang into a high-stepping buck-and-wing dance routine that took him cavorting around the stage. His voice raised in a madcap shout, he belted out a naughty tune. The lyrics involved a girl and her one-legged lover.

Toward the end of the number, Foy's rubbery face stretched wide in a clownish grin. He whirled, clicking his heels in midair, and skipped offstage with a final tip of his derby. The audience whistled and cheered, on their feet, rocking the walls with shrill ovation. Foy, bouncing merrily onto the stage, took three curtain calls.

The crowd, still laughing, began filing out of the theater. Fontaine waited for the aisle to clear, then led Lillian and Chester backstage. They found Foy seated before a mirror in his dressing room, wiping off greasepaint. He rose, turning to greet them, as Fontaine performed the introductions. His mouth split in a broad smile.

"Welcome to Abilene," he said jauntily. "Lou Gordon told me you're opening tomorrow night."

"Indeed we are," Fontaine affirmed. "Though I have to say, you'll be a hard act to follow. You're quite the showman."

"Same goes both ways. The Fontaines have some classy reputation on the circuit back East."

"The question is, will East meet West? We certainly had an education on Texans tonight."

Foy laughed. "Hey, you'll do swell. Just remember they're a bunch of rowdies at heart."

"Not to mention uncouth," Fontaine amended. "I'm afraid we haven't your gift for humor, Eddie. Gordon warned us that culture wouldn't play well in Abilene."

"You think I'd try the material you heard tonight in New York? No sir, I wouldn't, not on your tintype! You have to tailor your material to suit your audience. Westerners just like it a little . . . raunchy."

"Perhaps it's herding all those cows. Hardly what would be termed a genteel endeavor."

"That's a good one!" Foy said with a moonlike grin. "Nothing genteel about cowboys. Nosiree."

"Well, in any event," Fontaine said, offering a warm handshake. "A distinct pleasure meeting you, Eddie. We enjoyed the show."

"All the luck in the world to you! Hope you knock'em in the aisles."

"We'll certainly do our very best."

Fontaine found the way to the stage door. They emerged into a narrow alley that opened onto Texas Street. Lillian fell in between the men and glanced furtively at her father. She could tell he was in a dark mood.

"How enlightening," he said sourly. "I hardly think we'll follow Mr. Foy's advice."

"What would it harm, Papa?" Lillian suggested. "Melodrama with a few laughs might play well."

"I will not pander to vulgarians! Let's hear no more of it."

On the street, they turned toward the hotel. A group of cowhands, ossified on whiskey, lurched into them on the boardwalk. The Texans stopped, blocking their way, and one of them pushed forward. He was a burly man, thick through the shoulders, with mean eyes. He leered drunkenly at Lillian.

"Lookee here," he said in a rough voice. "Where'd you come from, little miss puss? How about we have ourselves a drink?"

"How dare you!" Fontaine demanded. "I'll thank you to move aside."

"Old man, don't gimme none of yore sass. I'm talkin' to the little darlin' here."

Chester stepped between them "Do as you're told, and quickly. I won't ask again."

"Hear that, boys?" the cowhand said, glancing at the other Texans. "Way he talks, he's from Boston or somewheres. We done treed a gawddamn Yankee."

"Out of our way."

Chester shoved him and the cowhand launched a murderous haymaker. The blow caught Chester flush on the jaw and he dropped to his knees. The Texan cocked a fist to finish him off.

A man bulled through the knot of trailhands. He was tall, with hawklike features, a badge pinned to his coat. His pistol rose and fell, and he thunked the troublemaker over the head with the barrel. The Texan went down and out, sprawled on the boardwalk.

"You boys skedaddle," the lawman said, motioning with the pistol. "Take your friend along and sober him up."

The cowboys jumped to obey. None of them said a word, and they avoided the lawman's eyes, fear written across their faces. They grabbed the fallen Texan under the arms and dragged him off down the street. The lawman watched them a moment, then turned to the Fontaines. He knuckled the brim of his low-crowned hat.

"I'm Marshal Hickok," he said. "Them drunks won't bother you no more."

Lillian was fascinated. His auburn hair was long, spilling down over his shoulders. He wore a frock coat, with a scarlet sash around his waist, a brace of Colt pistols tucked cross-draw fashion into the sash. His sweeping mustache curled slightly at the ends.

Hickok helped Chester to his feet. Fontaine introduced himself, as well as Lillian and Chester. The marshal nodded politely.

"I reckon you're the actors," he said. "Heard you start at the Comique tomorrow."

"Yes indeed," Fontaine acknowledged. "I do hope you will attend, Marshal."

"Wouldn't miss it for all the tea in China."

"Allow me to express our most sincere thanks for your assistance tonight."

"Never yet met a Texan worth a tinker's damn. Pleasure was all mine."

Hickok again tipped his hat. He walked off upstreet, broad shoulders straining against the fabric of his coat. Fontaine chuckled softly to himself.

"Do you know who he is?"

"No," Lillian said. "Who?"

"Only the deadliest marshal in the West. I read about him in *Harper's Magazine*."

"Yes, but who is he, Papa?"

"My dear, they call him Wild Bill Hickok."

Chapter 3

A JUGGLER dressed in tights flung three bowie knives in a blinding circle. The steel of the heavy blades glittered in the footlights as he kept them spinning in midair. His face was a study in concentration.

The Comique was sold out. Tonight was opening night for *The Fontaines*, and every seat in the house was taken. The crowd, mostly Texas cowhands, watched the juggler with rapt interest. They thought he might slip and lose a finger.

The juggler suddenly flipped all three knives high in the air. He stood perfectly still as the knives rotated once, then twice, and plummeted downward. The points of the blades struck the floor, embedded deep in the wood, quivering not an inch from his shoes. The Texans broke out in rollicking applause for his death-defying stunt.

The orchestra blared as the juggler bowed, collecting his knives, and skipped off the stage. A chorus line of eight girls exploded out of the wings, squealing and kicking as the orchestra thumped louder. The girls were scantily clad, bosoms heaving, skirts flashing to reveal their legs. They bounded exuberantly around the stage in a high-stepping dance routine.

Lillian stood in the wings at stage right. She was dressed in a gown of teal silk, with a high collar and a hemline that swept the floor. Her heart fluttered and her throat felt dry, a nervous state she invariably experienced before a performance. Her father appeared from backstage, attired in the period costume of a Danish nobleman. His hands lightly touched her shoulders.

"You look beautiful," he said softly. "Your mother would have been proud of you."

"If only I had Mama's voice. I feel so . . . inadequate."

"Simply remember what your mother taught you. You'll do fine, my dear. I know you will."

Her mother had had an operatic voice, with the range of a soprano. Lillian's voice was lower, a husky alto, and her mother had taught her how to stay within her range, lend deeper emotion to the lyrics. Yet she never failed to draw the comparison with her mother, and in her mind she fell short. On her best nights, she was merely adequate.

The chorus line came romping offstage. The curtain swished closed, and Lou Gordon stepped before the footlights, briefly introducing his new headliner act. When the curtain opened, Lillian was positioned center stage, her hands folded at her waist. By contrast with the chorus girls, she looked innocent, somehow virginal. The orchestra came up softly as she opened with *Darling Nelly Gray.*

There's a low green valley
On the old Kentucky shore
There I've whiled happy hours away
Sitting and singing by the cottage door
Where lived my darling Nelly Gray

Something extraordinary happened. A hushed silence fell over the audience as her clear alto, pitched low and intimate, filled the hall. She acted out the song with poignant emotion, and her sultry voice somehow gave the lyrics a haunting quality. She sensed the cowhands were captivated, and she saw Wild Bill Hickok watching intently from the back of the theater. She played it for all it was worth.

Oh, my darling Nelly Gray
Up in heaven there they say
They'll take you from me no more
I'm coming as angels clear the way
Farewell now to the old Kentucky shore

There was hardly a dry eye in the house. The Texans were Southerners, many having served under the Confederate flag during the late war. They were caught up in a melancholy tale that was all the more sorrowful because of Lillian's striking good looks. She held them enthralled to the last note, and then the theater vibrated to rolling applause. She took a bow and bowed a final time before disappearing into the wings. The Texans chanted their approval.

"Lilly! Lilly! Lilly!"

The curtain closed as the clamor died down. Gordon again appeared before the footlights, announcing that the famed thespian Alistair Fontaine would now render a soliloquy from Shakespeare's masterpiece *Hamlet*. A moment later the curtain opened with Fontaine at center stage, bathed in the cider glow of a spotlight from the rear of the theater. He struck a classic profile, arresting in the costume of a Danish prince. His voice floated over the hall in a tragic baritone.

To be, or not to be: that is the question:
Whether 'tis nobler in the mind to suffer
The slings and arrows of outrageous fortune,
Or to take arms against a sea of troubles,
And by opposing end them? To die, to sleep . . .

The cowhands in the audience traded puzzled glances. They knew little of Shakespeare and even less of some strangely dressed character called Hamlet. Though they tried to follow the odd cadence of his words, the meaning eluded them. Fontaine doggedly plowed on, aware that they were restive and quickly losing interest. He ended the passage with a dramatic gesture, his features grimly stark in the spotlight. The Texans gave him a smattering of polite applause.

The finale of the show was a one-act melodrama titled *A Husband's Vengeance.* Chester played the husband and Lillian, attired in a cheap print dress, the attractive wife. Fontaine, following a quick change from Danish prince to top-hatted villain, played a lecherous landlord. In Scene 1, Chester and Lillian's love-struggling-against-poverty was established for the audience. In Scene 2, with the husband off at work, the lustful landlord demanded that the wife surrender her virtue for the overdue rent or be evicted. The crowd hissed and booed the villain for the cad he was.

Scene 3 brought the denouement. Chester returned from work to discover the landlord stalking his wife around the set, with the bed the most prominent item of furniture in the shabby apartment. The husband, properly infuriated, flattened Fontaine with a mighty punch and bodily tossed him out the door. The cowhands jumped to their feet, whooping and hollering, cheering the valorous conquest of good over evil. Then, to even greater cheers, the curtain closed with Chester and Lillian clinched in a loving embrace. The crowd went wild.

The show might have ended there. But the Texans almost immediately resumed their chant. They stood, shouting and stomping, the jingle of their spurs like musical chimes. Their voices were raised in a collective roar.

"We want Lilly! We want Lilly! We want Lilly!"

Lou Gordon hastily improvised an encore. After a hurried backstage conference with Lillian, he ran out to distribute sheet music to the orchestra. Some minutes later the curtain opened with Lillian center stage, still costumed in the cheap print dress. A hush settled over the audience as violins' from the orchestra came up on *Take Back the Heart.* Her dulcet voice throbbed with emotion.

Take back the heart that thou gavest
What is my anguish to thee?
Take back the freedom thou cravest
Leaving the fetters to me
Take back the vows thou hast spoken
Fling them aside and be free
Smile o'er each pitiful token
Leaving the sorrow for me

The ballad went on with the story of unrequited love. By the time she finished the last stanza, hardened Texans were sniffling noisily and swiping at tears. Their thoughts were on mothers and sisters, and girlfriends left behind, and there was no shame among grown men that night. Lillian bowed off the stage to tumultuous applause.

Gordon caught her as she stepped into the wings. "Little lady, from now on you're Lilly Fontaine! You hear what I'm saying—*Lilly Fontaine!*"

Lillian was in a daze. Her father was waiting as she turned backstage. He enfolded her into his arms, holding her close. His voice was a whisper.

"Thou art thy mother's glass, and she in thee calls back the lovely April of her prime."

"Oh, Papa!" She hugged him tightly. "You know that's my favorite of all the sonnets."

Fontaine grinned. "Your mother and the Bard would be proud of you."

She desperately hoped it was true.

Hickok was waiting at the stage door. The alleyway was deep in shadow, faintly lighted by a lamppost from the street. He knuckled the brim of his hat.

"Evenin'," he said pleasantly. "You folks put on a mighty good show. Liked it a lot."

"Why, thank you, Marshal," Fontaine said. "We're delighted you enjoyed yourself."

Hickok shrugged. "Figured I'd see you back to your hotel. Things get a little testy on the streets this late at night."

"How kind of you, Marshal. As it happens, Mayor McCoy invited Chester and myself for a drink. Perhaps you wouldn't mind escorting Lillian."

Joseph McCoy, the town founder, was also Abilene's mayor. His invitation, extended backstage following the show, did not include Lillian. Women of moral character never patronized saloons.

"Be an honor, ma'am," Hickok said, nodding to Lillian. "A lawman don't often get such pleasurable duty."

Lillian batted her eyelashes. "How very gallant, Marshal."

On the street, Fontaine and Chester turned north toward the Alamo Saloon. The Alamo catered to wealthy Texas cattlemen and local citizens of means. Lillian and Hickok walked south along the boardwalk.

"Tell me, Marshal," Lillian said, making conversation. "Have you been a peace officer very long?"

"A spell," Hickok allowed. "I was sheriff over at Hays City before I came here. How about you?"

"Pardon?"

"How long you been in variety work?"

"Oh, goodness, all of my life. I was born in the theater."

Hickok looked at her. "You was *born* in a theater?"

"A figure of speech," Lillian said gaily. "I started on the stage when I was five. The theater's all I've ever known."

"Well, now, don't that beat all."

A young man stopped in front of them. He was dressed in cowboy gear, a pistol holstered at his side. His eyes were cold slate blue, and Lillian placed him at about her own age. He gave Hickok a lopsided smile.

"How's tricks, Wild Bill?"

"Tolerable, Wes," Hickok said shortly. "You stayin' out of trouble?"

"Yeah, I'm on my good behavior. Wouldn't do to get on your bad side, would it now?"

"Never figured you any other way."

"Well, I'll see you around, Marshal. Don't take any wooden nickels."

The young man stepped around them, never once looking at Lillian. As they moved on, she darted a glance at Hickok. His expression was somber.

"How strange," she said. "I really don't think he likes you."

"Miss Lillian, the feeling's mutual."

"Who is he?"

"John Wesley Hardin," Hickok said. "Got himself a reputation as a gunman down in Texas. I warned him to mind his manners here in Abilene."

"Gunman?" Lillian said, shocked. "You mean he killed someone?"

"More'n one, so folks say."

"He doesn't look old enough."

"They raise'em quick in Texas."

Hickok bid her good night in the lobby of the Drover's Cottage. From her father she knew that Hickok himself was a notorious gunman. Apparently, a raft of dime novels had been written about his exploits on the frontier, dubbing him the "Prince of Pistoleers." She wondered how many men he had killed.

Upstairs, she undressed and changed into a nightgown. She got into bed, too exhilarated for sleep, remembering the applause. In her most fanciful dreams, she would never have imagined the reception she'd received tonight. The thought of men shedding tears at the sound of her voice made her shiver. She closed her eyes and fervently prayed it would last. An image of her mother formed. . . .

A gunshot brought her out of bed. She realized she'd fallen asleep, dreaming of her mother. There was no noise from the street, and she thought it must be late.

She went to the window, still confused by the gunshot, and looked out. Three rooms down from hers, she saw a man leap from the window and land heavily on the boardwalk. He jumped to his feet.

The spill of light from a lamppost momentarily froze his features. She recognized him as the young man she'd seen earlier, John Wesley Hardin. She saw now that he appeared disheveled, shirttail flapping, boots in one hand, his pistol in the other. He searched the street in both directions, spotting no one, and then sprinted off in his stocking feet. He disappeared around the corner.

Some minutes later she heard voices in the hall. She opened the door a crack and saw her father and Chester, barefoot, their nightshirts stuffed into their trousers. Other men, similarly awakened from sleep, were gathered before a door two rooms down from hers. They all turned as Hickok pounded up the stairs into the hall, his gun drawn. He brushed past them, entering the darkened room. A moment later lamplight glowed from the doorway.

"Good Lord!" her father exclaimed. "He's been shot."

Hickok stepped out of the room. His features were grim as he looked around at the men. "Anybody see what went on here?"

There were murmurs of bewilderment, men shaking their heads. Then, stuffing his pistol back in his sash, Hickok saw Lillian peering out of her door. He walked down the hall.

"Miss Lillian," he said. "Some poor devil's been shot and killed in his own bed. You hear anything unusual?"

"I saw him," Lillian said on an indrawn breath. "The gunshot awoke me and I went to my window. It was the young Texan you and I met on the street earlier. He leapt out the window of his room."

"You talkin' about Wes Hardin?"

"Yes, the one you said was a gunman."

"Where'd he go?"

"Why, he ran away," Lillian replied. "Around the corner, by the mercantile store."

"I'm most obliged for your help."

Hickok hurried to the stairwell. Fontaine and Chester, who were listening to the conversation, entered her room. She explained how she'd met Hardin and later recognized him as he fled the hotel. Fontaine slowly wagged his head.

"I'm sorry, my dear," he said, clearly shaken. "I've brought you to a place where murderers lodge just down the hall."

"Oh, Papa," she said quickly. "You mustn't blame yourself. It might have happened anywhere."

"I am reminded of the Bard by this dreadful affair. 'As flies to wanton boys, are we to the gods; they kill us for their sport.' "

Chester snorted. "Shakespeare should have seen Abilene!"

Several days later they learned the truth. John Wesley Hardin, after a drunken night on the town, was annoyed by the rumbling snores of a hotel guest in the next room. Hardin fired through the wall and killed the man where he lay fast asleep. Then, rather than face Hickok, he fled on foot to a cowcamp outside Abilene. From there, he made good his escape to Texas. He was eighteen years old.

Lillian, thinking back on it, was struck by how very little changed with time. Shakespeare, nearly three centuries before, had penned an axiom for all time.

Wanton boys, like the gods, still killed for sport.

CHAPTER 4

A BRILLIANT sun stood fixed at its zenith. The weather was moderate for late September, with cottony clouds drifting westward against an azure sky. The bawling of cows was constant from the stockyards near the railroad siding.

Hickok arrived at the hotel shortly before one o'clock. Lillian was waiting in the lobby, wearing a corded cotton dress with delicate stripes worked into the fabric. She carried a parasol and wore a chambray bonnet that accentuated her features. She gave him a fetching smile as he tipped his hat.

"I see you're punctual, as always."

"Never keep a lady waiting," Hickok said smoothly. "All ready to see the sights?"

"Oh, yes, I'm so looking forward to it."

Outside, on the boardwalk, she took his arm. They drew stares from passersby as they walked south along Texas Street. After a fortnight at the Comique, Lillian was the talk of the town. The *Abilene Courier* referred to her as a "chanteuse," and beguiled cowhands flocked to her performances. The theater was sold out every night.

The town was no less interested in her curious relationship with Hickok. He was a womanizer of some renown, having carried on liaisons with several ladies since arriving in Abilene. Even more, at thirty-four, he was fifteen years Lillian's senior, and the difference was the source of considerable gossip. Yet, for all anyone could tell, it was a benign relationship. Hickok appeared the perfect gentleman.

Lillian was attracted to him in the way a moth flirts with flame. She knew he was dangerous, having been informed by her father that he had killed at least a dozen men, not including Indians. He was a former army scout and deputy U.S. marshal and lionized by the press as the West's foremost "shootist." The term was peculiar to the frontier, reserved for those considered to be mankillers of some distinction. Other men crossed him at their own peril.

For all that, Lillian found him to be considerate and thoughtful, gentle in a roughhewn sort of way. Her father at first forbade her to see Hickok, and she deflected his protests with kittenish artifice. She was intrigued as well by Hickok's reputation as a womanizer, for she had never known a lothario, apart from Shakespeare's plays. One of the chorus girls at the Comique told her Hickok had lost his most recent lady friend to a Texas gambler named Phil Coe. Lillian thought, perhaps, the loss accounted for his courtly manner. He was, she sensed, a lonely man.

Every night, Hickok escorted her from the theater back to the Drover's Cottage. There, assured she was safe, he left her in the lobby and went about his duties as marshal. On three occasions, before the evening show at the Comique, he had invited her to dinner at the restaurant in the hotel. Today, leaving his deputy, Mike Williams, to police Abilene, he had invited her for an afternoon ride in the country. They had never been alone together or far from her father's sight, and she somehow relished the experience. She felt breathlessly close to the flame.

The owner of the livery stable was a paunchy man, bald as a bullet. He greeted Hickok with a nervous grin and led them to the rig, hired for the afternoon. Hickok assisted her into the buggy, which was drawn by a coal black mare with ginger in her step. He had a good hand with horses, lightly popping the reins, urging the mare along at a brisk clip. They drove east from town, on a wagon trace skirting the Smoky Hill and the Kansas Pacific tracks. Dappled sunlight filtered through tall cottonwoods bordering the river.

On the southeast corner of the town limits, they passed what was derisively known as the Devil's Addition. Abilene, with hordes of randy cowhands roaming the streets, attracted prostitutes in large numbers. The decent women of the community, offended by the revelry, demanded that the mayor close down the bordellos. Joseph McCoy, ever the pragmatist and fearful of inciting the Texans, banished the soiled doves instead to an isolated red-light district. The cowhands simply had to walk a little farther to slake their lust.

Lillian stared straight ahead as they drove past the brothels. She was no innocent, even though she had managed to retain her virginity despite the advances of handsome and persuasive admirers on the variety circuit. She knew men consorted with prostitutes and that the world's oldest profession could be traced to biblical times. Sometimes, wakeful in the dark of night, she tried to imagine what services the girls provided to their clientele. She often wished she could be a fly on the wall, just for a moment. She thought she might learn wicked and exotic secrets.

One secret she already knew. Her mother had taught her that the way to a man's heart was through his vanity. Men loved nothing quite so much as talking about themselves and their feats, imagined or otherwise. A woman who was a good listener and expressed interest captivated men by the sound of their own voices. Lillian had found what seemed an eternal axiom to be no less true with Wild Bill Hickok. She turned to him now.

"I've been wondering," she said with an engaging smile. "Why do people call you Wild Bill?"

"Well," Hickok said, clearly pleased by her interest. "One time durin' the war I had to fight off a passel of Rebs and swim a river to make my escape. The Federal boys watchin' from the other side was plumb amazed. They up and dubbed me Wild Bill."

"What a marvelous story!"

"Yeah, ceptin' my name's not Bill. It's James."

"James?" Lillian said, looking properly confused. "Why didn't they call you Wild *Jim?*"

"Never rightly knew," Hickok said. "The name stuck and I've been tagged with it ever since. Finally got wore out tryin' to set folks straight."

"I think James is a fine name."

"So'd my ma and pa."

Lillian urged him on. "So you were with the Union army?"

"Worked mostly as a scout behind enemy lines. The Rebs would've shot me for a spy if I'd ever got caught."

"How exciting!"

Hickok brought the buggy to a halt. They were stopped on a low bluff, overlooking the river and the prairie. The grasslands stretched endlessly in the distance, broken only by the churned earth of the Chisholm

Trail. A herd of longhorns, choused along by cowhands, plodded north toward Abilene.

"How beautiful!" she said. "I wish I were a painter."

"You're mighty pretty yourself." Hickok casually placed his arm on top of the seat behind her. "Somebody ought to paint you."

Lillian felt his fingers brush her shoulder. She thought she might allow him to kiss her, and then, just as quickly, she changed her mind. She knew he wouldn't be satisfied with a kiss.

"I'm simply fascinated by your work," she said, shifting slightly in the seat. "Do you enjoy being a peace officer?"

The question distracted Hickok. She seemed genuinely interested, and young as she was, she was probably impressionable. Talking about himself might lead to more than a kiss.

"Guess every man's got his callin'," he said with a tinge of bravado. "Turns out I'm good at enforcin' the law."

"Yes, but everyone out here carries a gun. Aren't you sometimes afraid . . . just a little?"

Hickok explained the code of the West. There were no rules that governed conduct in a shootout, except the rule of fairness: A man could not fire on an unarmed opponent or open fire without warning. Apart from that, every man looked for an edge, some slight advantage. The idea was to survive with honor intact.

"Not likely I'll ever be beat," he bragged. "Don't you see, I've already got the edge over other men. I'm Wild Bill."

Lillian at first thought he was joking. But then she realized he was serious, deadly serious. She wished her mother were there, for how they would have laughed. Wild Bill Hickok proved the point.

No man, given an attentive female, could resist tooting his own horn.

The spotlight bathed Lillian in an umber glow. She stood poised at center stage, the light caressing her features, the audience still. The house was again sold out, and every cowhand in the theater stared at her with a look of moony adoration. The orchestra glided into *The Rose of Killarney* as her voice filled the hall.

There's a spot in old Ireland still dear to my heart
Thousands of miles 'cross the sea tho I'm forced to part
I've a place now in the land of the free
Tho the home there I shall never forget
It brings a tear for thoughts I so regret
When I bid goodbye to the rose of Killarney

Her eyes roved over the audience. At the rear of the hall, she saw Hickok in his usual post by the door. Even in the midst of the song, she wondered if he regretted the loss of a kiss, having talked about himself all the way back to town. When she finished the last stanza, the crowd whooped and shouted, their hands pounding in applause. The spotlight followed her as she bowed her way offstage.

Fontaine came on next with a piece from *The Merchant of Venice.* The audience slumped into their seats, murmuring their displeasure, as though Shakespeare were an unwelcome guest at an otherwise festive occasion. Then, suddenly, the door at the rear of the hall burst open with a resounding whack. A cowboy, mounted on a sorrel gelding, ducked low through the door and rode down the center aisle. He caterwauled a loud, screeching Rebel yell.

Hickok was only a step behind. He levered himself over the horse's rump with one hand, grabbed a fistful of shirt with the other, and yanked the cowboy out of the saddle. The Texan hit the floor on his back, and as he scrambled to his feet, Hickok thumped him across the head with a pistol. The impact of metal on bone sounded with a mushy *splat*, and a welter of blood geysered out from the cowboy's scalp. He dropped into the arms of a man seated directly beside the aisle.

The horse reared at the railing of the orchestra pit. Terrified, the members of the orchestra dived in every direction, scattering horns and violins. By now thoroughly spooked, the gelding whirled around, wall eyed with fright, and started up the aisle. Hickok stepped aside, whacking him across the rump, and the horse bolted out of the theater. As he went through the door, the Texans in the audience erupted from their seats, angered that Hickok had spoiled the fun. All the more, they were outraged by his treatment of the cowboy.

"You sorry sonovabitch!" someone yelled. "You got yours comin' now!"

A knot of cowhands jammed into the aisle. Hickok backed to the orchestra pit, pulling his other Colt. He leveled the pistols on the crowd.

"Stop right there!" he ordered. "I'll drill the first man that comes any closer."

"You cain't get us all!" one of the cowhands in the front rank shouted. "C'mon, boys, let's rush the Yankee bastard."

A shotgun boomed from the rear of the theater. The Texans turned and saw Hickok's deputy, Mike Williams, standing in the doorway. Plaster rained down from a hole in the ceiling, and he swung the double-barrel scattergun in a wide arc, covering the crowd. Hickok rapped out a command.

"Everybody back in your seats!" he barked. "Any more nonsense and I'll march the whole bunch of you off to jail."

"Yore jail ain't that big, Hickok!"

"Who wants to try me and find out?"

No one seemed inclined to accept the offer. Order was restored within minutes, and the Texans, still muttering, slowly resumed their seats. Hickok walked up the aisle, both pistols trained on the audience, and stopped at the door. Mike Williams, who was a beefy man with a thatch of red hair, gave him a peg-toothed grin. They stood watching as the crowd settled down.

The Fontaines went directly into a melodrama titled *A Dastardly Deed.* When the play was over, Lillian came back onstage alone, for her nightly encore was by now part of the show. In an effort to further dampen the cowhands' temper, she sang their favorite song, *Dixie*. She sang it not as a stirring marching ballad but rather as a plaintive melody. Her voice was pitched low and sad, almost mournful.

I wish I was in the land of cotton
Old times there are not forgotten
Look away! Look away! Look away, Dixieland!

The Texans, unrepentant Confederates to a man, trooped out of the theater in weepy silence. They jammed into saloons along the street, drinking maudlin toasts to the Bonnie Blue Flag and blessing the gracious sentiment of Lilly Fontaine. Some of them, after a few snorts of popskull, wandered off to the Devil's Addition. There they found solace in the arms of whores.

Hickok escorted Lillian, as well as Fontaine and Chester, back to the hotel. He bid them a solemn good night, his features grave, and rejoined Mike Williams on the street. His manner was that of a man off to do battle, and the Fontaines fully expected to hear gunshots before the night was done. They went to their rooms wondering if the Texans would leave well enough alone.

Later, lying awake in the dark, Lillian was reminded of Abilene's former marshal. One of the chorus girls had related the gory end of Hickok's predecessor, Tom Smith. By all accounts a respected peace officer, Smith had gone to arrest a homesteader, Andrew McConnell, on a murder warrant. McConnell waylaid the marshal, grievously wounding him with a Winchester rifle. As Smith lay helpless, McConnell hefted an ax and chopped off his head. Abilene gave the slain lawman a stately funeral.

Lillian shuddered at the image. Still, the grisly death of Tom Smith helped her to better understand Hickok. Tonight's incident at the theater was part and parcel of what he'd tried to explain on their buggy ride that afternoon.

Wild Bill Hickok lived by a code ancient even in olden times: Do unto them before they do unto you.

CHAPTER 5

THE EVENING of October 5 was brisk and clear. A full moon washed the town in spectral light and stars dotted the sky like diamond dust. Texas Street was all but deserted.

A last contingent of cowhands wandered from saloon to saloon. Earlier that day the final herd of longhorns had been loaded at the stockyards and shipped east by train. The trailing season was officially over, for the onset of winter was only weeks away. Two months, perhaps less, would see the plains adrift with snow.

The mood was glum at the Comique. Abilene, the first of the western cowtowns, was sounding the death knell. The railroad had laid track a hundred miles south to Wichita, a burgeoning center of commerce located on the Arkansas River. By next spring, when the herds came north on the Chisholm Trail, Wichita would be the nearest railhead. Abilene would be a ghost town.

Lou Gordon planned to move his operation to Wichita. With the coming of spring, he would reopen the Comique on the banks of the Arkansas and welcome the Texans with yet another variety show. He had offered the Fontaines headliner billing, for Lillian was now a star attraction with a loyal following. But that left the problem of where they would spend the winter and how they would subsist in the months ahead. So far, he'd uncovered only one likely alternative.

Alistair Fontaine was deeply troubled. Though he usually managed a cheery facade, he was all but despondent over their bleak turn of fortune. Upon traveling West, he had anticipated a bravura engagement in Abilene and a triumphant return to New York. Yet his booking agent, despite solid notices in the *Abilene Courier,* had been unable to secure a spot for them on the Eastern variety circuit. A hit show in Kansas kindled little enthusiasm among impresarios on Broadway.

Fontaine saw it as a descent into obscurity. To climb so high and fall so far had about it the bitter taste of ignominy. He'd begun life as John Hagerty, an Irish ragamuffin from the Hell's Kitchen district of New York. Brash and ambitious, he fled poverty by working his way up in the theater, from stagehand to actor. Almost twenty-five years ago, he had adopted the stage name Alistair Fontaine, lending himself an air of culture and refinement. Then, seemingly graced, he had married Estell.

Yet now, after thirty years in the theater, he was reduced to a vagabond. The descent began with Estell's untimely death and the realization that he was, at best, a modest Shakespearian. In Abilene came the discovery that his daughter, though a lesser talent than her mother, nonetheless brought that indefinable magic to the stage. But he hadn't foreseen the vagaries of a celebrated return to New York or the growth of the railroad and the abrupt demise of Abilene. He wasn't prepared to winter in some primitive outpost called Dodge City.

The crowd for tonight's show was sparse. There were fewer than a hundred cowhands still in Abilene and perhaps half that number in the audience. The melodrama finished only moments ago, Fontaine and Chester stood in the wings, watching Lillian perform her encore. For their last night in Abilene, she had selected as her final number a poignant ballad titled *The Wayfarer*. She thought it would appeal to the Texans on their long journey home, south along the Chisholm Trail. Her voice gave the lyrics a sorrowful quality.

The sun is in the west,
The stars are on the sea,
Each kindly hand I've pres't,
And now, farewell to thee.
The cup of parting done,
'Tis the darkest I can sip.
I have pledg'd them ev'ry one
With my heart and with my lip.
But I came to thee the last,
That together we might throw
One look upon the past
In sadness ere I go

On the final note, the cowhands gave her a rousing ovation. They rose, calling out her name, waving goodbye with their broad-brimmed hats. She smiled wistfully, waving in return as the curtain closed, throwing them a kiss at the last moment. Her eyes were misty as she moved into the wings, where Fontaine and Chester waited. She swiped at a tear.

"Oh, just look at me," she said with a catch in her throat. "Crying over a bunch of cowboys."

"Well, it's closing night," Chester consoled her. "You're entitled to a few tears."

"I feel like crying myself," Fontaine grumped. "We've certainly nothing to celebrate."

"Papa!" Lillian scolded gently. "I'm surprised at you. What's wrong?"

"We are not traveling to New York, my dear. To paraphrase Robert Burns, the best laid schemes of mice and men often go awry."

"Yes, but Lou felt almost certain he could arrange a booking in Dodge City. It's not as though we're out of work."

"Dodge City!" Fontaine scoffed. "Gordon seemed quite chary with information about the place. Other than to say it is somewhere—*somewhere*—in western Kansas."

Chester grinned. "Dad, you were talking about a grand adventure when we came out here. This way, we get to see a little more of the West."

"And it's only for the winter," Lillian added. "Lou promised an engagement in Wichita in the spring."

Fontaine considered a moment. "I've no wish to see more of the West. But your point is well taken." He paused, nodding sagely. "Any engagement is better than no engagement a'tall."

Lou Gordon appeared from backstage. Over the course of their month in Abilene, he had become a friend, particularly where Lillian was concerned. He felt she was destined for big things on the variety stage. He extended a telegram to Fontaine.

"Got a wire from Frank Murphy just before the show. He's agreed to book you for the winter."

"Has he indeed?"

Fontaine scanned the telegram. His eyes narrowed. "Two hundred dollars a month! I refuse to work for a pauper's wages."

"Lodging and meals are included," Gordon pointed out. "Besides, Alistair, it's not like you've got a better offer."

"Papa, please," Lillian interceded. "Do we really have a choice?"

"I appear to be outnumbered," Fontaine said. "Very well, Lou, we will accept Mr. Murphy's parsimonious offer. How are we to accomplish this pilgrimage?"

Gordon quickly explained that railroad tracks had not yet been laid into western Kansas. He went on to say that he'd arranged for them to accompany a caravan of freight wagons bound for Dodge City. He felt sure they could make an excellent deal for a buggy and team at the livery stable. With the loss of the cattle trade, everything in Abilene was for sale at bargain prices.

"A buggy!" Fontaine parroted. "Good Lord, I'd given it no thought until now. We'll be sleeping on the *ground*."

"Afraid so," Gordon acknowledged. "You'll be cooking your own meals, too. The hardware store can supply you with camp gear."

"Is there no end to it?" Fontaine said in a wounded voice. "We are to travel like . . . Mongols."

Chester laughed. "No adventure as grand as an expedition. Nostradamus has nothing on you, Dad."

"I hardly predicted a sojourn into the wilderness."

"How marvelous!" Lillian clapped her hands with excitement. "We'll have such fun."

Fontaine arched an eyebrow. He thought perhaps her mother had missed something in her training. There was, after all, a certain limit to hardship.

Overland travel was hardly his idea of fun.

* * *

Hickok checked his pocket watch. He rose from behind his desk in the jailhouse and went out the door. He walked toward the theater.

All evening he'd been expecting trouble. As he passed the Lone Star Saloon, he glanced through the plate glass window. Phil Coe and several cowhands were standing at the bar, swilling whiskey. He wondered if Coe would at last find courage in a bottle.

Their mutual antagonism went back over the summer. Coe was a tinhorn gambler who preyed on guileless cowhands by duping them with friendship and liquor. Hickok, sometime in early July, put out the word that Coe was a cardsharp, the worst kind of cheat. He gulled fellow Texans in crooked games.

The charge brought no immediate confrontation. Hickok heard through the grapevine that Coe had threatened his life, but he suspected the gambler had no stomach for a fight. Coe retaliated instead by charming a saloon girl widely considered to be Hickok's woman and stealing away her affections. The animosity between the men deepened even more.

Word on the street was that the last of the Texans planned to depart town tomorrow. Coe, whose home was in Austin, would likely join them on the long trek down the Chisholm Trail. Without cowhands for him to fleece, there was nothing to hold Coe in Abilene any longer. So it made sense to Hickok that trouble, if it came at all, would come tonight. Coe, to all appearances, was fueling his courage with alcohol.

Hickok turned into the alley beside the Comique. He intended to see Lillian safely back to the hotel, just as he'd done every night since she arrived in Abilene. He planned to apply for the job of marshal in Wichita, and he thought that might have some bearing on their future. Lou Gordon was opening a variety theater there, and Hickok assumed the Fontaines would tag along. He would arrange to talk with her about it in the next day or so. Tonight, given the slightest pretext, he would attend to Phil Coe.

The stage door opened as he moved into the alleyway. Lillian stepped outside, accompanied by her father and brother. He greeted Fontaine and Chester as she waited for him by the door. Her features were animated.

"Aren't you the tardy one," she said with a teasing lilt. "You missed my last performance."

"Not by choice," Hickok begged off. "Had some business that needed tendin'."

"Wait till you hear our news!"

Lillian was eager to tell him about their plans. She fantasized that he would join them on the trip, perhaps become the marshal of Dodge City. She wasn't sure she loved him, for she still had no idea of what love was supposed to feel like. But she was attracted to him, and she knew the feeling was mutual, and she thought there was a good man beneath the rough exterior. A trip west together would make it even more of an adventure.

"What news is that?" Hickok asked.

"Well, we just found out tonight we're going—"

A gunshot sounded from the street. Then, in rapid succession, two more shots bracketed through the still night. Hickok was moving even as the echoes died away.

"Stay here!" he ordered. "Don't go out on the street."

"Where are you—"

"Just stay put!"

Hickok rushed off into the darkness. He moved to the far end of the alley, turning the corner of the building across from the Comique. Headed north, he walked quickly to the rear of the third building and entered the back door of the Alamo Saloon. He hurried through the saloon, startled customers frozen in place as he drew both pistols. He stepped through the front door onto the boardwalk.

Phil Coe stood in the middle of the street. A dead dog lay on the ground at his feet, the earth puddled with blood. He had a bottle in one hand and a gun in the other, bantering in a loud voice with four Texans who were gathered around. He idly waved the bottle at the dog.

"Boys, there lies one tough scutter. Never thought it'd take me three shots to kill a dog."

"Hell, it didn't," one of the cowhands cackled. "You done missed him twice."

"What's going on here, Coe?"

The men turned at the sound of Hickok's voice. He was framed in a shaft of light from the door, the pistols held loosely at his sides. Coe separated from the Texans, a tall man with handsome features, his mouth quirked in a tight smile. He gestured with the bottle.

"No harm done, Marshal," he said. "Just shot myself a dog, that's all."

"Drop your gun," Hickok told him. "You're under arrest."

"What the hell for?"

"Discharging firearms within the town limits."

"Bullshit!" Coe flared. "You're not arresting me for shootin' a goddamn dog."

"I won't tell you again—drop it."

Coe raised his pistol and fired. The slug plucked the sleeve of Hickok's coat and thunked into the saloon door. He extended his right arm at shoulder level and the Colt spat a sheet of flame. Coe staggered backward, firing another round that shattered the Alamo's window. Hickok shot him again.

A crimson starburst spread over the breast of Coe's jacket. His legs tangled in a nerveless dance, and he slumped to the ground, eyes fixed on the starry sky. Footsteps clattered on the boardwalk as a man bulled through a crowd of onlookers, gun in hand, and hurried forward. Hickok caught movement from the corner of his eye, the glint of metal in silvery moonlight. He whirled, reflexes strung tight, and fired.

The man faltered, clutching at his chest, and tumbled off the boardwalk into the street. One of the onlookers, a railroad worker, eased from the crowd and peered down at the body. His face went taut and he turned to Hickok with an accusing stare. "It's Mike Williams!" he shouted. "You've killed your own deputy."

A look of disbelief clouded Hickok's features. He walked to the body and knelt down, pistols dangling from his hands. His hard visage seemed to crack, and he bowed his head, shoulders slumped. The onlookers stared at him in stony silence.

The Fontaines watched from the alleyway. They had witnessed the gunfight, then the senseless death of a man rushing to help his friend. Fontaine was reminded of a Greek tragedy, played out on the dusty street of a cowtown, and Chester seemed struck dumb. Lillian had a hand pressed to her mouth in horror.

Fontaine took her arm. She glanced one last time at Hickok as her father led her away. Chester followed along, still mute, and they angled across the street to the Drover's Cottage. The desk clerk was standing in the door, drawn by the gunshots, on the verge of questioning them. He moved aside as they entered the lobby, reduced to silence by the expression on their faces. They mounted the stairs to their rooms.

Some while later, changed into her nightgown, Lillian crawled in bed. She felt numb with shock, her insides gone cold, and she pulled the covers to her chin. She had never seen a man killed, much less two in a matter of seconds, and the image of it kept flashing through her mind. The spectacle of it, random violence and death, was suddenly too much to bear. She closed her eyes to the terror.

A thought came to her in a moment of revelation. She could never love a man who so readily dealt in killing. The fantasy she had concocted was born of girlish dreams, silly notions about honor and knights of the plains. She saw now that it was all foolish whimsy.

Tomorrow, she would say goodbye to Wild Bill Hickok.

CHAPTER 6

THE CARAVAN stretched nearly a mile along the river. The broad, rushing waters of the Arkansas tumbled over a rocky streambed that curved southwestward across the plains. A fiery sun tilted lower toward the distant horizon.

Lillian was seated between her father and Chester. She wore a linsey-woolsey dress with a fitted mantle coat that fell below her knees. The men were attired in whipcord trousers, plaid mackinaws, and wide-brimmed slouch hats. They looked like reluctant city folk cast in the role of pioneers.

Their buckboard, purchased in Abilene, was a stout four-wheeled vehicle designed for overland travel. The rig was drawn by a team of horses, one sorrel and one dun, plodding along as though hitched to a plow. The storage bed behind the seat was loaded with camp gear, food crates, and their steamer trunks. The goods were lashed securely and covered with a tarpaulin.

"Ah, for the outdoor life," Fontaine said in a sardonic tone. "My backsides feel as though I have been flailed with cane rods."

Chester, who was driving the buckboard, chuckled aloud. "Dad, you have to look on the bright side. We're almost there."

"How would you know that?"

"One of the teamsters told me this morning."

"Well then, we have it from an unimpeachable source."

"Honestly!" Lillian said with a perky smile. "Why do you complain so, Papa? I've never seen anything so wonderful in my life." She suddenly stopped, pointing at the sky. "There, look!"

A hawk floated past on smothered wings. Beyond, distant on the rolling plains, a small herd of buffalo grazed placidly beneath wads of puffy clouds. The hawk caught an updraft, soaring higher into the sun. Lillian watched it fade away against a lucent sky.

"Oooo," she said softly, her eyes round with wonder. "I think it's all so . . . so magnificent."

"Do you really?" Chester said all too casually. "I'll wager you don't think so when you have to do your business. You sure look mortified, then."

"You're such a ninny, Chester. I sometimes wonder you're my brother."

Her indignation hardly covered her embarrassment. There were fifty-three wagons in the caravan and more than a hundred men, including teamsters, laborers, and scouts. The upshot, when she needed to relieve herself, was scant privacy and a desperate search for bushes along the river. She absolutely dreaded the urge to pee.

Yet, apart from the matter of privacy, she was content with their journey. Fifteen days ago, south of Abilene, they had joined the freight caravan on the Santa Fe Trail. The muleskinners were a rough lot, unaccustomed to having a woman in their company, and at first standoffish. But Josh Ingram, the wagon master, welcomed them into the caravan. He worked for a trading firm headquartered in Independence, Missouri.

The Santa Fe Trail, pioneered in 1821, was a major trading route with the far southwest. The trail began in Independence, crossing the Missouri line, and meandered a hundred-fifty miles across Kansas to the great northern bend of the Arkansas. The trail then followed the serpentine course of the river for another hundred-twenty miles to Fort Dodge and the nearby civilian outpost, Dodge City. From there, the trail wound southwest for some five hundred miles before terminating in Santa Fe, the capital of New Mexico Territory. Hundreds of wagons made the yearly trek over a vast wilderness where no railroads yet existed.

Lillian was fascinated by the grand scheme of the venture. One aspect in particular, the Conestoga wagons, attracted her immediate attention. Over the campfire their first night with the caravan, Josh Ingram explained that the wagons dated back to the early eighteenth century. Developed in the Conestoga River Valley of Pennsylvania, the wagons bore the distinctive touch of Dutch craftsmen. The design, still much the same after a hundred and fifty years, had moved westward with the expansion of the frontier.

The wagon bed, as Ingram later showed her, was almost four feet wide, bowed downward like the hull of a ship. Overall, the wagon was sixteen feet in length, with immense wheels bound by tire irons for navigating rough terrain. The wagon box was fitted with oval wooden bows covered by sturdy canvas, which resulted in the nickname prairie schooner. Drawn by a six-hitch of mules, the wagons regularly carried up to 4,000 pounds in freight. The trade goods ran the gamut from needles and thread to axes and shovels and household furniture.

Late every afternoon, on Ingram's signal, the wagons were drawn into a four-sided defensive square. So far west, there was the constant threat of Indian attack and the imperative to protect the crew as well as the livestock. There were army posts scattered about Kansas, and west of Fort Dodge, where warlike tribes roamed at will, cavalry patrols accompanied the caravan. But an experienced wagon master looked to the defense of his own outfit, and before sundown the livestock was grazed and watered. Then everyone, man and beast, settled down for the night within the improvised stockade.

The Fontaines made their own small campfire every evening. They could have eaten with the crew, for the caravan employed a full-time cook. But the food was only passable, and Lillian, anxious to experience life on the trial, had taught herself to cook over open coals. The company scouts, who killed a couple of buffalo every day to provision the men, always gave Lillian the choice cuts from the hump meat. Chester took care of the horses, and Fontaine, adverse to menial chores of any nature, humbled himself to collect firewood along the river. He then treated himself to a dram from his stock of Irish whiskey.

By sundown, Lillian had the cooking under way. She worked over a shallow pit, ringed with rocks and aglow with coals scooped from the fire. Her battery of cast-iron cookware turned out stews and steaks and sourdough biscuits and an occasional cobbler made from dried fruit. Fontaine, who had appointed himself armorer, displayed a surprising aptitude for the care and cleaning of weapons. In Abilene, the hardware store owner had convinced him that no sane man went unarmed on the plains, and he'd bought two Henry .44

lever-action repeaters. His evening ritual included wiping trail dust from the rifles.

"Fate has many twists," he said, posing with a rifle as he looked around at the camp enclosed by wagons. "I am reminded of a passage from *King Lear.*"

Lillian glanced up from a skillet of sizzling steaks. She knew he was performing and she was his audience. "Which passage is that, Papa?"

" 'When we are born we cry that we are come to this great stage of fools.' "

"You believe our journey is foolhardy?"

"We shall discover that by the by," Fontaine said, playing the oracle. "Some harbinger tells me that our lives will never again be the same."

"Evenin', folks."

Josh Ingram stepped into the circle of firelight. He was a large man with weathered features and a soup-strainer mustache. He nodded soberly to Fontaine.

"Figgered I'd best let you know. Our scouts cut Injun sign just before we camped. Wouldn't hurt to be on guard tonight."

Fontaine frowned. "Are we in danger of attack?"

"Never know," Ingram said. "Cheyenne and Kiowa get pretty thick out this way. They're partial to the trade goods we haul."

"Would they attack a caravan with so many men?"

"They have before and they doubtless will again. Don't mean to alarm you overly much. Just wanted you to know."

"We very much appreciate your concern."

Ingram touched his hat, a shy smile directed at Lillian. "Ma'am."

When he walked off, Fontaine stood for a moment with the rifle cradled over his arm. At length, he turned to Lillian and Chester. "I daresay we are in for a long night."

Chester took the other Henry repeater from the buckboard. He levered a shell into the chamber and lowered the hammer. "Wish we had practiced more with these rifles. I'd hate to miss when it counts."

"As the commander at Bunker Hill told his men, wait until you see the whites of their eyes. What worked on British Red Coats applies equally well to redskins."

Lillian thought it a witty pun. She knew her father's levity was meant to allay their fears. She was suddenly quite proud of him.

Alistair Fontaine was truly a man of many parts.

A noonday sun was lodged like a brass ball in the sky. The caravan followed a rutted track almost due west along the river. Scouts rode posted to the cardinal points of the compass.

The Fontaines' buckboard was near the front of the column. Josh Ingram, mounted on a blaze-faced roan, had stopped by not quite an hour ago with a piece of welcome news. He'd told them the caravan, by his reckoning, was less than twenty miles from Fort Dodge. He expected to sight the garrison by the next afternoon.

Lillian breathed a sigh of relief. The likelihood of confronting Indians seemed remote so close to a military post. Even more, from a personal standpoint, she would no longer have to suffer the indignity of squatting behind bushes to relieve herself. Her spirits brightened as she began thinking about the civilized comforts—

A scout galloped hell for leather over a low knoll to the north. He was waving his hat in the air and his bellow carried on the wind. *"Injuns! Injuns!"*

Ingram roared a command at the lead wagon. The teamster sawed hard on the reins and swung his mules off the trail. The wagons behind followed along, the drivers popping their whips, and the column maneuvered between the river and the rutted trace. The lead wagon spliced into the rear wagon minutes later, forming a defensive ring. Chester halted the Fontaines' buckboard in the center of the encircled caravan.

A war party boiled over the knoll even as the men jumped from their wagons. The massed Indians appeared to number a hundred or more, and they charged down the slope, whipping their ponies, at a dead run. The warriors rapidly deployed into a V-shaped formation and fanned out into two wings. They thundered toward the caravan whooping shrill battle cries.

The men behind the barricaded wagons opened fire. Before them, the buckskin-clad horde swirled back and forth, the wings simultaneously moving left and right, individual horsemen passing one another in opposite directions. The warriors were armed for the most part with bows and arrows, perhaps one in five carrying an ancient musket or a modern repeater. A cloud of arrows whizzed into the embattled defenders.

Ingram rushed about the wagons shouting orders. Fontaine instructed Lillian to remain crouched on the far side of the buckboard, where she would be protected from stray arrows. He left her armed with a Colt .32 pocket pistol he'd bought in Abilene, quickly showing her how to cock the hammer. She watched as he and Chester joined the men behind the barricade, shouldering their rifles. Here and there mules fell, kicking in the traces, pincushioned with feathered shafts. The din of gunfire quickly became general.

Ten minutes into the battle the warriors suddenly retreated out of rifle range. Several teamsters lay sprawled on the ground, dead or wounded, and beyond the wagons Lillian saw the bodies of dark-skinned braves. She thought the attack was over and prayed it was so, for neither her father nor Chester had suffered any wounds. Then, with hardly a respite, the Indians tore down off the knoll, again splitting into two formations. Lillian ducked behind the buckboard, peering over the seat, racked with shame and yet mesmerized at the same time. She was struck by something splendid and noble in the savage courage of the Indians.

A man stumbled away from one of the wagons, an arrow protruding from his chest. In the next instant, a lone brave separated from the horde and galloped directly toward the wagons. He vaulted his pony over a team of mules, steel-tipped lance in hand, and landed in the encirclement. All along the line men were firing at him, and Lillian, breath-taken, thought it was the most magnificent act of daring she'd ever seen. Suddenly he spotted her, and without a moment's hesitation he charged the buckboard, lance raised overhead. She froze, ready to crawl beneath the buckboard, and then, witless with fear, cocked the hammer on the small Colt. She closed her eyes and fired as he hurled the lance.

The warrior was flung forward off the back of his pony. He crashed onto the seat of the buckboard, a feather in his hair and a hole in his forehead, staring with dead eyes at Lillian. She backed away, oddly fixated on the war paint covering his face, her hands shaking uncontrollably. She couldn't credit that she had shot him—between the eyes—actually killed a man. The lance quivered in the ground at her side, and she knew she'd been extraordinarily lucky. A mote of guilt drifted through her mind even as she lowered the pistol. Yet she had never felt so exhilarated, so giddy. She was alive.

The Indians seemed emboldened by the one warrior's suicidal charge. Their ponies edged closer to the wagons, and the sky rained wave upon wave of arrows. Here and there a brave would break ranks and charge the defenders, whooping defiance, only to be shot down. But it appeared the Indians were working themselves into a fever pitch, probing for a weak spot in the defenses. There was little doubt that they would attempt to overrun the wagons and slaughter everyone in savage struggle. Then, so abruptly that it confounded defenders and attackers alike, the din of gunfire swelled to a drumming rattle. A bugle sounded over the roar of battle.

The Indians were enveloped from the rear by massed cavalry. Fully two troops of horseback soldiers delivered a withering volley as they closed on the warriors at a gallop. The lines collided in a fearsome clash, and the screams of dying men rose eerily above the clatter of gunfire. Lillian saw a cavalry officer with long golden ringlets, attired in a buckskin jacket, wielding a saber slick with blood. The warriors were caught between the soldiers and a wall of gunfire from the wagons, and scores of red men toppled dead from their ponies. Others broke through the line of blue coats and fled across the plains in disorganized retreat. A small group, surrounded at the center of the fight, was quickly taken prisoner.

One of the captured warriors was tall and powerfully built. His features were broad and coarse, as though adzed from dark wood, and his eyes glittered with menace. Lillian watched, almost transfixed, as the cavalry officer with the golden hair reined through the milling horses and stopped near the tall warrior. He saluted with his bloody saber.

"*Hao,* Santana," he said crisply. "We have you now."

The warrior stared at him with a stoic expression. After a moment, the officer wiped the blood from his saber with a kerchief and sheathed the blade in his saddle scabbard. He spun his horse, a magnificent bay stallion, and rode toward Josh Ingram and the men at the wagons. He reined to a halt, touched the brim of his hat with a casual salute. His grin was that of Caesar triumphant.

"Gentlemen," he said smartly. "The Seventh Cavalry at your service."

"The Seventh!" someone yelled. "You're Custer!"

"I am indeed."

Ingram stepped over a dead mule. "General, I'm the wagon master, Josh Ingram. We're damned glad to see you and your boys. How'd you happen on this here fracas?"

Custer idly waved at the tall warrior. "Mr. Ingram, you are looking at Santana, chief of the Kiowa. We've been trailing him and his war party for near on a week." He paused with an indulgent smile. "You are fortunate we were not far behind. We rode to the sound of gunfire."

"Mighty glad you did, General. We might've lost our scalps."

"Yes, where Santana's concerned, you're entirely correct. He keeps his scalping knife sharply honed."

Lillian had joined her father and Chester. She listened to the conversation while studying the dashing cavalry officer. Finally, unable to contain herself, she whispered to Fontaine, "Who is he, Papa?"

"The greatest Indian fighter of them all, my dear. George Armstrong Custer."

"Thank God he came along when he did."

Fontaine smiled. "Thank God and the Seventh Cavalry."

Chapter 7

THE FONTAINES were quartered in a billet normally reserved for visiting officers. There were two bedrooms and a sitting room, appointed in what Lillian assumed was military-issue furniture. She stood looking out the door at the garrison.

Fort Dodge was situated on a bluff overlooking the Arkansas. To her immediate front was the parade ground, and beyond that the post headquarters. Close by were the hospital and the quartermaster's depot and farther on the quarters for married officers. The enlisted men's barracks and the stables bordered a creek that emptied into the river. Everything looked spruce and well tended, orderly.

The caravan, accompanied by the cavalry, had arrived earlier that afternoon. The wagons were now encamped by the river, preparations under way to continue tomorrow on the Santa Fe Trail. Colonel Custer, courteous to a fault, had arranged for the Fontaines to stay the night in the officers' billet. Upon discovering they were actors, he had invited them to his quarters for dinner that evening. He seemed particularly taken with Fontaine's mastery of Shakespeare.

Fontaine, on the way to the fort, had spoken at length about the man many called the Boy General. He informed Lillian and Chester that their host was the most highly decorated soldier of the late Civil War. A graduate of West Point, his gift for tactics and warfare resulted in an extraordinary series of battlefield promotions. From 1862 to 1865, a mere three years, he leaped from first lieutenant to major general. He was twenty-five years old when the war ended.

Gen. Philip Sheridan personally posted Custer to the West following the Civil War. Though his peacetime rank was that of lieutenant colonel, he retained the brevet rank of major general. A splendid figure of a man, he was six feet tall, with a sweeping golden mustache, and wore his hair in curls that fell to his shoulders. He had participated in campaigns against the Plains Tribes throughout Kansas and Nebraska, culminating in a great victory in Indian Territory. There, on the Washita River, Custer and the Seventh Cavalry had routed the fabled Cheyenne.

Josh Ingram, listening to Fontaine's dissertation on Custer, had pointed out a parallel with Santana, the Kiowa war chief. His Indian name, *Se-Tain-te*, meant White Bear, bestowed on him after a vision quest. A blooded warrior at twenty, he began leading raids along the Santa Fe Trail and as far south as Mexico. He ranged across the frontier, burning and pillaging, leaving in his path a legion of scalped settlers and dead soldiers. What Custer was to the army Santana was to the Kiowa: a bold, fearless leader who dared anything, no matter the odds.

Lillian, reflecting on it as the sun went down over the parade ground, thought there was a stark difference. Santana, with his four followers who were captured in yesterday's battle, was in chains in the post stockade. George Armstrong Custer, victorious in every battle he'd ever fought, was yet again lauded for his courage in the field. She recalled him saying that he "rode to the sound of gunfire," and she mused that he was a man who thrived on war. She wouldn't be surprised if he one day replaced William Tecumseh Sherman as General of the Army. Custer, too, was a leader who never reckoned the odds.

Capt. Terrance Clark, Custer's adjutant, called for the Fontaines as twilight settled over the post. He was a strikingly handsome man, tall and muscular, resplendent in a tailored uniform. He shook hands with Fontaine and Chester and bowed politely to Lillian. Outside, he offered her his arm and led them across the parade ground in the quickening dusk. His manner somehow reminded her of Adonis, the young hero of Greek mythology. A warrior too handsome for words.

Custer's home was a military-style Victorian, with a pitched roof, square towers, and arched windows. The furniture in the parlor was French Victorian, with a rosewood piano against one wall flanked by a matching harp. The study was clearly a man's room, the walls decorated with mounted heads of antelope and deer and framed portraits of Custer and Gen. Philip Sheridan. The bookshelves were lined with classics, from Homer, to Shakespeare, to James Fenimore Cooper.

Elizabeth Custer was a small, attractive woman, with dark hair and delicate features. She insisted on being called Libbie and welcomed the Fontaines as though she'd never met a stranger in her life. She informed them that she was thrilled to have a troupe of professional actors in her home. Hardly catching her breath, she went on to say that she and the general were amateur thespians themselves. Lillian gathered that Libbie Custer, at least in public, referred to her husband only by rank.

"We have such fun," she rattled on. "Our last playlet was one written by the General himself. And he starred in it as well!"

"Libbie makes too much of it," Custer said with an air of modesty. "We stage amateur theatricals for the officers and their wives. Life on an army post requires that we provide our own entertainment."

"How very interesting," Fontaine observed. "And what was the subject of your production, General?"

Custer squared his shoulders. "I played the part of a Cheyenne war chief and one of the officers' wives played my . . . bride." He paused, suddenly aware of their curious stares. "We depicted a traditional Indian wedding ceremony. All quite authentic."

"I must say that sounds fascinating."

"Hardly in your league, Mr. Fontaine. Perhaps, after dinner, you would favor us with a reading from Shakespeare. We thirst for culture here on the frontier."

Fontaine preened. "I would be honored, General."

"By the by, I forgot to ask," Custer said. "Where will you be performing in Dodge City?"

"We are booked for the winter at Murphy's Exchange."

Fontaine caught the look that passed between Custer and his wife. Lillian saw it as well, and in the prolonged silence that followed she rushed to fill the void. Her expression was light and gay.

"We so wanted to see something of the frontier. And the timing is perfect, since we're between engagements until next spring. We open then at the Comique Theater in Wichita."

A manservant saved the moment. He appeared in the doorway of the dining room, dressed in a white jacket and blue uniform trousers, and announced dinner. Libbie, ever the gracious hostess, tactfully arranged the seating. Fontaine and Chester were placed on one side of the table, and Lillian was seated on the other, beside Captain Clark. Custer and Libbie occupied opposite ends of the table.

Dinner opened with terrapin soup, followed by a main course of prairie quail simmered in wine sauce. Throughout the meal, the Custers peppered their guests with questions about their life in the theater. Fontaine, though flattered, gradually steered the discussion to Custer's military campaigns against the warlike tribes. The conversation eventually touched on yesterday's engagement with the Kiowa.

"A sight to behold!" Fontaine announced, nodding to Libbie. "Your husband and the Seventh Cavalry at a full charge. I shan't soon forget the spectacle."

"*Au contraire*," Libbie said, displaying her grasp of French. "The General tells me your daughter was the heroine of the day." She cast an almost envious glance at Lillian. "Did you really shoot an Indian, my dear?"

Lillian blushed. "I'll never know how," she said with open wonder. "I closed my eyes when I fired the gun—and then . . . he practically fell in my lap."

Everyone laughed appreciatively at her candid amazement. Lillian was all too aware of Captain Clark's look of undisguised infatuation. He stared at her as if she were a ripe and creamy éclair and he wished he had a spoon. She noted as well that he wore no wedding ring.

After dinner, the men retired to the study for cigars and brandy. Lillian and Libbie conversed about New York and the latest fashions, discreetly avoiding any mention of the Fontaines' upcoming appearance at Murphy's Exchange. A short while later, the men joined them in the parlor. Captain Clark, rather too casually, took a seat beside Lillian on the sofa.

Fontaine required no great coaxing to perform. He positioned himself by the piano, his gaze fixed on infinity, and delivered a soliloquy from *King Richard II.* Custer and Libbie applauded exuberantly when he finished, congratulating him on the nuance of his interpretation. Then, with Libbie playing the piano, Lillian sang one of the day's most popular ballads. Her voice filled the parlor with *'Tis Sweet to Be Remembered.*

Terrance Clark watched her as though he'd seen a vision.

Dodge City was five miles west of Fort Dodge. A sprawling hodgepodge of buildings, it was inhabited principally by traders, teamsters, and buffalo hunters. Thousands of flint hides awaited shipment by wagon to the nearest railhead.

Late the next morning, when the Fontaines drove into town, they were dismayed by what they saw. Nothing had prepared them for a ramshackle outpost that looked as though it had been slapped together with spit and poster glue. Abilene, by comparsion, seemed like a megalopolis.

"To paraphrase the Bard," Fontaine said in a dazed voice. "I have ventured like wanton boys that swim on bladders. Far beyond my depth, my high-blown pride at length broke under me."

Chester nodded glumly. "Dad, no one could have said it better. We'll be lucky if we don't drown in this sinkhole."

The permanent population of the Dodge City looked to be something less than 500. At one end of Front Street, the main thoroughfare, were the Dodge House Hotel and Zimmerman's Hardware, flanked by a livery stable. Up the other way was a scattering of saloons, two trading companies, a mercantile store, and a whorehouse. The town's economy was fueled by buffalo hunters and troopers of the Seventh Cavalry. Whiskey and whores were a profitable enterprise on the edge of the frontier.

Fontaine directed Chester to the Dodge House. There were no porters, and they were forced to unload the buckboard themselves. Fortunately, it was a one-story building, and after registering with the desk clerk, they were able to slide their steamer trunks through the hall. Their rooms were little more than cubicles, furnished with a bed, a washstand, one chair, and a johnny pot. The clerk informed them the johnny pots would be emptied every morning.

Still shaking his head, Fontaine instructed Chester to take the buckboard to the livery stable. He expressed the view that it would not be prudent as yet to sell the horses and the buckboard. Their escape from Gomorrah, he noted dryly, might well depend on a ready source of transport. An hour or so later, after unpacking and changing from their trail clothes, they emerged from the hotel with their trepidation still intact. The men were attired in conservative three-piece suits and the Western headgear they had adopted while in Abilene. Lillian wore a demure day dress and a dark woolen shawl.

Murphy's Exchange was located across from one of the trading companies. Three buffalo hunters, lounging out front, gave them a squinted once-over as they moved through the door. The establishment was a combination saloon, dance hall, and gaming dive. Opposite a long mahogany bar were faro layouts and poker tables. A small stage at the rear overlooked a dance floor, with a piano player and a fiddler providing the music. Saloon girls in full war paint mingled with the crowd.

All conversation ceased as the soldiers and hide hunters treated Lillian to a slow inspection. She had the sinking sensation that they were undressing her with their eyes, layer by layer. Frank Murphy, the proprietor, walked forward from the end of the bar. He was a toadish man, short and stout, with jowls covered by muttonchop whiskers. His jaw cranked in a horsey smile, revealing a gold tooth, as he stopped in front of them. He regarded the finery of their clothes.

"From your duds," he said, flashing his gold tooth, "I'd say you're the Fontaines. Welcome to Dodge City."

"Thank you so much," Fontaine replied. "Our arrival was delayed by a slight skirmish with Kiowa brigands."

"Yeah, the word's all over town. Custer and his boys pulled your fat out of the fire, huh?"

"An apt if somewhat colloquial description."

"Well, you're here now and that's all that counts."

"Indeed we are."

Fontaine stared a moment at the miniature stage. His arm swept the room with a patrician gesture. "There is no sin but to be rich; there is no vice but beggary."

"Uh-huh," Murphy said, stroking his whiskers. "That wire I got about you folks, from Lou Gordon? He said you was partial to Shakespeare."

"Yes, I understand, Mr. Murphy. For the sake of your clientele, tread lightly with the verse."

"I guess it's sort of like bitin' into a green persimmon. A little bit goes a long ways."

"A green persimmon?" Fontaine said thoughtfully. "I've not heard the expression before. Is it a bitter fruit?"

"Right tasty when they're ripe," Murphy said. "A green one'll make your mouth pucker up worse'n wormwood."

"I have no doubt you dispense sound advice, Mr. Murphy. However, from the look of your customers, a dab of culture and a hot bath would do wonders. Charity demands that I acquaint them with the Bard."

"Don't say I didn't warn you."

"Consider your duty done."

Murphy turned his attention to Lillian. "You must be Lilly, the singer Gordon told me about. His wire said you're better'n good."

"How nice of him," Lillian said with a dimpled smile. "I'll certainly do my best, Mr. Murphy."

"Hope you've got some racy numbers in your songbook. The boys don't come here for church hymns."

"I sing all the popular ballads. The audiences in Abilene weren't disappointed."

"Hide hunters are a rougher lot than cowhands. Maybe just a little something off-color?"

"No, I'm afraid not."

"Too bad." Murphy examined her outfit. "Maybe you've got a dress that don't dust the floor. The boys like to see some ankle."

Lillian glanced at her father, clearly uncomfortable. Fontaine quickly intervened. "We are what we are, Mr. Murphy. Neither ribald nor risqué is included in our repertoire."

Murphy considered a moment. He thought he'd made a bad deal but saw no practical remedy. October was almost gone, and the chances of importing another act for the winter were somewhere between slim and none. He decided there was nothing for it.

"Guess we'll have to make do," he grouched. "I'm a man of my word, so I'll still pick up the tab for your lodging and your eats. Just try to gimme a good show."

"Have no fear," Fontaine said stiffly. "We never fail to entertain."

Outside, Fontaine led the way back toward the hotel. Lillian and Chester were silent, aware that his dour mood had turned even darker. He finally grunted a saturnine laugh. His expression was stolid.

"I believe our employer lacks confidence."

"Who cares?" Chester said. "We're a far cry from Broadway."

"You miss the point entirely, my boy."

"What point is that?"

"We are the Fontaines, and we thrive on challenge. Need I say more?"

Lillian thought that said it all.

CHAPTER 8

FONTAINE PROVED to a prophet. By the end of the week, Murphy's Exchange was the most popular spot in town. The other saloons were all but empty.

Every night, at show time, the house was packed. The audience, mainly buffalo hunters and soldiers, suffered through Shakespeare with only occasional jeers. The melodrama usually held their interest, though that was hardly the reason for their presence. They were there to see Lilly Fontaine.

Frank Murphy was the most amazed man in town. To his profound shock, he discovered that burly cavalrymen and rancid-smelling hide hunters all had a soft spot. A tender ballad, sung by a young innocent with the face of an angel, left them a-sea in memories of lost and long-ago yesterdays. Even the saloon girls wept.

The nature of the men made it all the more astounding. Buffalo hunters, who traveled where others feared to tread, lived from day to day. They wandered the plains, constantly under the threat of Indian attack, for they killed the beasts that were the very sustenance of nomadic tribes. The horse soldiers, even more inured to brutality, were in the business of killing Indians. Sentiment seemed lost in the scheme of things.

Yet none among them was so hardened that memory of gentler times failed. All of which made Frank Murphy the happiest saloonkeeper in Dodge City. Winters were harsh on the plains, with blizzards that sometimes left the land impassable, locked in snow and ice. The freezing cold drove men into town, often for weeks on end, seeking sanctuary from polar winds howling out of the north. The longer they stayed, the more they spent, and Murphy saw it as the winter of great fortune. He'd cornered the trade with Lilly Fontaine.

Lillian sometimes felt guilty. She was flattered by all the attention and adored the appreciative cheers of men who watched her perform. But she was saddened for her father, whose love of Shakespeare played to an unreceptive audience. He jokingly referred to them as "buffoons and jackanapes" and tried to slough off their indifference with nonchalant humor. Still, she knew he was disheartened, often embittered, while at the same time he gloried in her success. Her father's pride merely served to underscore her guilt.

On Monday morning, Fontaine's pride was put to the test. They were in his room, rehearsing the lines of a new melodrama he'd written, when someone knocked on the door. Fontaine moved across the room, opening the door, freshly inked script still in hand. A portly man in a checkered suit stood in the hallway.

"Mr. Fontaine," he said, "I'm Joe Porter. I own the Lucky Star Saloon and I'd like to talk to you."

"May I inquire the purpose of your call, Mr. Porter?"

"Let's just say it's a private matter. I'd sooner not discuss it standin' here in the hall. Could I come in a minute?"

"Of course."

Fontaine held the door. Porter entered, hat in hand, nodding mechanically to Chester. He smiled warmly at Lillian. "Miss Fontaine, a pleasure to see you."

"How may we assist you?" Fontaine asked. "I believe you said it was a private matter."

"Well, sir, just to be truthful, it's a business matter. I'd like to hire you folks over to the Lucky Star."

"As you must know, we are currently engaged."

"Yessir," Porter confirmed. "Everybody in a hundred miles knows about your daughter. And you and your boy, too, naturally."

Fontaine pursed his mouth. "I believe that rather nicely covers it, Mr. Porter."

"No, not just exactly it don't. What would you say if I was to offer you twice what Frank Murphy's payin' you?"

"I would have to say . . . no, thank you."

"Then name your price, if that ain't enough. I'd pay pretty near anything to have your girl singin' at the Lucky Star."

"Mr. Porter."

"Yeah?"

"We are not available," Fontaine said firmly. "We accepted a winter's engagement at Murphy's Exchange. We intend to honor our commitment."

"Look here," Porter insisted. "Your girl's runnin' the rest of us saloon owners out of business. We don't get no trade till your show's over every night. It just ain't fair."

"I most sincerely regret the inconvenience."

"Hell's bells, you gotta have a price! Name it!"

"Good day, Mr. Porter."

Fontaine opened the door. Porter gave him a look of bewildered disbelief, then marched out with a muttered curse. When the door closed, Fontaine turned back into the room. His gaze settled on Lillian.

"You appear to have the town bedazzled, my dear."

"I'm sorry, Papa," she said, genuinely contrite. "So very sorry."

"Never apologize for your talent. You deserve all the accolades one might imagine."

"What about the money?" Chester interjected. "Porter would have paid through the nose. We may never get another offer like that."

Fontaine smiled. "I daresay Mr. Murphy will be open to renegotiation. He most certainly will not be pleased, but then . . . business is business."

There were no secrets in a small town. Joe Porter made the mistake of grumbling about his unsatisfactory meeting with the Fontaines. The news spread on the moccasin telegraph, and Frank Murphy heard of it long before the noon hour. He took it as a personal affront.

"Tryin' to steal away my trade!" he huffed to one of the bartenders. "I always knew Joe Porter was a no-good sonovabitch."

Murphy's Exchange and the Lucky Star were located catty-corner from each other on Front Street. Porter, as was his custom, took his noon meal at the Silver Dollar Café, three doors down from his establishment. Shortly before one o'clock, he emerged from the café and turned upstreet. He had a toothpick wedged in the corner of his mouth.

Murphy stepped from the door of his saloon. He held a Colt Navy revolver at his side, and cognizant of the rules in such affairs, he prudently avoided being tagged a bushwhacker. He issued the proper warning to his opponent.

"Porter!" he shouted. *"Defend yourself!"*

Porter, taken by surprise, nonetheless reacted with dispatch. His stout legs pumping, he sprinted along the boardwalk as he drew a pistol from his waistband. Murphy fired, imploding a storefront window, and Porter winged a wild shot in return. He barreled through the door of the Lucky Star, diving for cover. Murphy wisely retreated within his own saloon.

The gunfight soon evolved into siege warfare. Murphy and Porter, after emptying their revolvers, switched to repeating rifles. They banged away at one another with more spirit than accuracy, bullets whizzing back and forth across the intersection. All along Front Street people took cover in saloons and dance halls, watching the duel as though it were some new and titillating spectator sport. By two o'clock, the windows in both Murphy's Exchange and the Lucky Star were reduced to shards of glass.

There was no law in Dodge City. The town was not incorporated and lacked either a city council or a town marshal. Law enforcement was the province of deputy U.S. marshals, who only occasionally wandered into western Kansas. An hour or so into the siege, someone decided a stray bullet would eventually claim the life of an innocent bystander. The military seemed the most likely solution, and a rider was dispatched to Fort Dodge. The onlookers settled down to await developments.

Capt. Terrance Clark, at the head of a cavalry troop, rode into town late that afternoon. He dismounted the company, stationing troopers armed with Springfield rifles around the intersection. The sight of fifty soldiers and the threat of military reprisal got the attention of Murphy and Porter. Clark arranged a cease-fire and then, ordering the saloonkeepers to lay down their arms, coaxed them into the street. There he negotiated a truce, which concluded with the two men reluctantly shaking hands. The onlookers applauded the end of what would later be called the Darlin' Lilly War.

Before departing town, Captain Clark seized the opportunity to call on Lillian at the hotel. She was already aware of the reason for the shooting and highly embarrassed rather than flattered. Yet her spirits were restored when he invited her to a military ball, two weeks hence at Fort Dodge. She was planning her wardrobe before he was out the door.

Terrance Clark, for his part, felt like clicking his heels. He'd taken the first step in his campaign to capture Lilly Fontaine.

I have done the state some service, and they
know 't;
No more of that. I pray you, in your letters,
When you shall these unlucky deeds relate,
Speak of me as I am; nothing extenuate,
Nor set down aught in malice: then, must you
speak
Of one that lov'd not wisely but too well.

The lines from *Othello* fell on deaf ears. Fontaine, in blackface and costumed as a Moorish nobleman, wrung agony from every word. The buffalo hunters and soldiers in the audience stared at him as if he were a field slave, strangely dressed and speaking in foreign tongues. He slogged on through the soliloquy.

There were times, alone on the stage, when Fontaine despaired that the majesty of the words had the least effect. He wondered now if the men watching him had any comprehension that he—Othello—had murdered Desdemona, a faithful wife falsely accused of betrayal. He despaired even more that he was acting out the tragedy for an audience of one. Himself.

The crude stage in Murphy's Exchange had no curtain. When he completed his oration, Fontaine paused with dramatic flair and then bowed his way offstage. The crowd, by now resigned to his nightly histrionics, gave him a smattering of applause. The fiddler and the piano player struck up a sprightly tune, allowing him time to run backstage and hurriedly scrub off the blackface. Saloon girls circulated with bee-stung smiles, pushing drinks.

The windows fronting the saloon, now empty holes, had been boarded over. The pitched battle that afternoon was all the talk, and Frank Murphy found himself something of a celebrity. He had, after all, defended what was rightfully his, and other men admired a man who would not tolerate insult. The crowd tonight was even larger than normal, standing-room-only and spilling out onto the boardwalk. Everyone wanted to see the sweet young temptress now known as Darlin' Lilly.

Lillian was repulsed by the whole affair. She thought it sordid and tawdry, and she felt soiled by the nickname bestowed on her just that afternoon. Earlier, when she performed her first number, she'd fixed her gaze on the front wall, ignoring the crowd. Where before she had given them the benefit of the doubt, she suddenly found the men brutish and coarse, rough vulgarians. She felt they stripped her naked with their loutish stares.

The melodrama that evening was titled *The Dying Kiss*. Fontaine, who recognized his limitations as a playwright, had plagiarized freely from Shakespeare's *Romeo and Juliet.* Lillian and Chester played the tragic young lovers, and Fontaine, casting himself as the villain of the piece, played the girl's father. The buffalo hunters and soldiers, caught up in what was a soppy tearjerker, roundly booed Fontaine off the stage. The final scene, when the lovers' suicide left them in eternal embrace, made tough men honk into their kerchiefs. Saloon girls wept so copiously they spoiled their war paint.

The audience gave the cast three curtain calls, albeit sans the curtain. Then, as though the brotherhood of men were of a single mind, they began chanting, *"Lilly! Lilly! Lilly!"* Lillian performed a quick change of costume, slipping into one of her two silk gowns, royal blue with white piping. The piano player and the fiddler, by now thoroughly rehearsed on her numbers, segued into Stephen Foster's immortal classic, *Beautiful Dreamer.* Her voice resonated poignantly through the saloon.

Beautiful dreamer, wake unto me
Starlight and dew drops are waiting for thee
Sounds of the rude world heard in the day
Lulled by the moonlight have all passed away

The crowd hung on her every word. The saloon was still as a church, the men and saloon girls a hushed tableau. Her face was turned as to the heavens and her eyes shone with emotion. On the last note there was an instant of impassioned silence, and then the audience erupted in raucous adulation and cheers. She bowed low, her features radiant.

A buffalo hunter lurched forward from the front of the crowd. His eyes were bloodshot with liquor and he drunkenly hoisted himself onto the stage. He spread his arms wide, reaching for her, and like a bull in rut bellowed, "Darlin' Lilly!" She backed away, unnerved and frightened, moving toward the wings. He lumbered after her.

She saw another man leap over the footlights. His features were wind-seamed, ruggedly forceful under a thatch of sandy hair and a bristling mustache. Though he wasn't a tall man, he was full-spanned through the shoulders, his wrists thick as a singletree. He grabbed the hide hunter by the collar, jerked him around, and lashed out with a splintering blow to the jaw. Clubbed off his feet, the hunter crashed to the floor.

The man stooped down, lifting the drunk by the collar and the seat of the pants. He walked to the footlights, carrying his load like a sack of potatoes, and hurled the buffalo hunter off the stage. Saloon girls squealed and men scattered as the inert form tumbled across the dance floor and skidded to a halt. The crowd roared with laughter as the man on the stage grinned and neatly dusted his hands. Their voices raised in a rowdy chant.

"Cimarron! Cimarron! Cimarron!"

Waving them off, the man turned and strode across the stage. Lillian noted he was dressed in the rough work clothes worn by the other buffalo hunters. But unlike them, his clothing was clean and freshly pressed and he smelled faintly of barber's lotion. His eyes crinkled with amusement as he stopped in front of her. He doffed his hat.

"Sorry for the trouble," he said, holding her gaze. "Some of these boys get liquored up and lose their heads." He paused, still grinning. "I'm Cimarron Jordan."

"How do you do," Lillian said warmly. "You saved me from a most unpleasant experience. Thank you so much."

"Why, anybody would've done the same for a pretty lady like yourself. No thanks necessary."

"Are you a buffalo hunter, Mr. Jordan?"

"That I am," Jordan said with amiable good humor. "Hope you haven't got nothin' against hunters."

"Oh, no, apart from the anarchy of Dodge City. I've never lived in a place where there isn't any law."

"Miss Lilly, you just whistle and I'll be your lawdog. Anytime a'tall."

Lillian sensed the magnetism of the man. He seemed to radiate strength and a quiet, but certain, force of character. She was amazed at herself that she found him attractive, although somewhat rough around the edges. She amazed herself even more by inviting him backstage to meet her father and brother. His unusual name intrigued her as well. Cimarron!

She thought she would ask him about that later.

Chapter 9

"I WON'T have it! Goddammit, it's Saturday night!"

"Lower your voice," Fontaine said curtly. "I will not permit you to curse at my daughter."

Murphy glowered at him. "Why'd she wait till tonight to tell me? I'd like to hear you answer that."

"For the very reason we see exhibited in your behavior. You are an intemperate man."

"You and your highfalutin words. What's that mean?"

"Quite simply, it means you are a hothead. You lack civility."

The Friday night show had concluded only moments ago. Lillian, with her father and Chester still in their melodrama costumes, had caught Murphy backstage. She explained as politely as possible that she had been invited to a military ball tomorrow night, Saturday night, at Fort Dodge. She asked for the night off.

"Tell me this," Murphy said gruffly. "When'd you get this invitation?"

"Two weeks ago," Lillian replied. "The day Captain Clark stopped you from killing Mr. Porter. He asked me while he was in town."

"And you waited till now to tell me?"

"Father has already explained that. I knew you wouldn't be . . . pleased."

"Pleased!" Murphy echoed. "You know good and well, Lilly—"

Lillian interrupted him. "I've told you over and over. I will not be called Lilly."

"All right then, Lillian, you know Saturday night's the biggest night of the week. And everybody in town turns out to hear you sing."

"I still have to have the night off."

Lillian was determined. After three weeks in Dodge City, she longed for the refinement and decorum that could be found only at Fort Dodge. Terrance Clark and sometimes Cimarron Jordan occasionally took her for afternoon buggy rides in the country. But she hadn't had a free night since she'd arrived in town. She meant to stand her ground.

"Let's be reasonable," Fontaine interceded. "We have performed every night—including Sunday, I might add—for three weeks running. Lillian deserves a night to herself."

Murphy laughed derisively. "You just don't get it, do you? Lillian's pipes are what draws the crowd. No songs, no crowd, no business!"

"On the contrary," Fontaine said indignantly. "Chester and I are perfectly capable of providing the entertainment for one night. We are, after all, actors."

Chester nodded eagerly. "I can even do a soft-shoe routine. I started practicing after we saw Eddie Foy in Abilene. I'm pretty good."

Fontaine and Lillian looked at him. Neither of them was aware that he had the slightest interest in dance routines. He had never once alluded to it, and so far as they knew, he had no talent as a hoofer. They could only conclude he'd been practicing secretly in his room at the hotel.

"There you have it," Fontaine jumped in with a confident air. "Chester will perform a soft-shoe number, with accompaniment from the piano. I will present a special rendering from Shakespeare. Perhaps something from *Macbeth.*"

"You're cracked, the both of you," Murphy growled. "You think anybody's gonna stick around to watch a couple of hams trod the boards? Lillian goes on and that's that!"

"No," Lillian said adamantly. "I insist on a night off."

"Well, insist all you want, little lady, but the answer's no. That's final."

"Then I quit."

Murphy looked as though his hearing had failed him. Fontaine and Chester, equally shocked, appeared speechless. The three men stared at her in startled apprehension.

"You leave us no choice," Lillian said, her eyes on Murphy. "We are forced to give you notice as of tonight. I feel quite sure Mr. Porter will welcome us to the Lucky Star."

"You'd do that to me!" Murphy exploded. "You'd take it across the street to that four-flusher—after I made you a star?"

"You made nothing," Lillian informed him. "We were The Fontaines long before we arrived in Dodge City."

Fontaine and Chester were struck dumb. The girl they'd known all their lives seemed to have stepped over the threshold into womanhood. She sounded eerily like her mother, quiet and strong and utterly certain of herself. They knew she wasn't bluffing.

Frank Murphy knew it as well. His toadish features mottled, and for a moment it appeared he would strangle before he recovered his voice. But he finally got his wits about him and recognized who was who in the scheme of things. He offered her a lame smile.

"Don't blame me if we have a riot on our hands. Hope you enjoy yourself."

"I'm sure I shall."

The officers' mess had been cleared of furniture for the occasion. Gaudy streamers festooned the ceiling, and several coats of wax, buffed since early morning by enlisted men, had brought the floor to a mirror polish. The regimental band, attired in gold-frogged uniforms, thumped sedately under the baton of a stern-eyed master sergeant.

Terrance Clark held Lillian at arm's length. He stiffly pushed her around the dance floor, neither light on his feet nor an accomplished dancer. Although perfectly tailored, splendid in a uniform bedecked with sash and medals, he was nonetheless overshadowed by his partner. As they moved about the floor, other men kept darting hidden glances at her. The women, more direct than their husbands, stared openly.

Lillian had dressed carefully for the ball. Her hair was arranged in an *en revanche* coiffure of ribbons and silk flowers, a French style she had copied from a ladies' periodical. Her svelte figure was stunningly displayed in the better of her two gowns, the teal silk with dark lace at the throat. Draped around her neck was her most prized possession, a string of black deep-sea pearls presented to her mother by her father on their tenth wedding anniversary. Lillian thought her mother would approve.

Tonight was her first formal ball. She'd never before kept company with a man, her mother wisely shielding her from the many Don Juans who populated variety theaters. Captain Clark, an officer and a gentleman, had assured her father she would be properly chaperoned during her stay at Fort Dodge. Arrangements had been made for her to spend the night with Colonel and Mrs. Custer, and Clark would drive her back to town Sunday morning. Still, chaperone or not, she wasn't worried about Terry Clark. His intentions were perhaps too honorable.

The band segued into a waltz. Custer claimed the dance while Libbie glided away on the arms of Clark. Lillian discovered that Custer was nimble of foot, clearly a veteran of ballroom engagements. He held her lightly, his golden ringlets bobbing as they floated off in time to the music. His mustache lifted in a foxy smile.

"I trust you are enjoying yourself."

"Oh, yes, very much."

"Excellent." Custer stared directly into her eyes. "Permit me to say you look ravishing tonight."

"Why, thank you," she said with a shy smile. "You're much too kind, General."

"A beautiful woman needs to be told so on occasion. Don't you agree?"

"You flatter me."

"Hardly more than you deserve."

By now, Lillian knew from gossips in town that Custer has an eye for the ladies. There were rumors he kept an Indian mistress tucked away somewhere, though he was circumspect around Fort Dodge. She'd also heard that his great victory over the Cheyenne was actually the massacre of a harmless band led by the peace chief Black Kettle. She chose not to believe the latter, for she remembered his valor the day he had rescued her from the Kiowa war party. But she accepted the story about his roving ways with women.

Long ago, her mother had warned her about smooth-talking men who could charm the birds out of the trees. She understood, though her mother had deftly employed a metaphor, that it was girls who were too often charmed out of their drawers. The world was full of glib, sweet-talking flatterers—George Armstrong Custer not being the first one she'd met—and she had long since taken her mother's lesson to heart. She would not be charmed out of her drawers.

Yet, on a moment's reflection, she realized that Custer was simply flirting. She was in no danger tonight, for Libbie rarely let her husband out of her sight. To put a point on it, Libbie reclaimed him as soon as the waltz ended. The foursome stood talking awhile, and then Custer, with Libbie on his arm, wandered off to mingle with the other guests. Clark suggested the refreshment table.

A grizzled sergeant served them punch from a crystal bowl. Their cups in hand, Clark led her across the room, where a row of chairs lined the dance floor. He chose a section with mostly empty chairs and courteously waited for her to be seated. She knew he wanted to be alone with her and sensed he had something on his mind. But Terry, as he insisted she call him, was not one of the smooth talkers and usually took the time to organize his thoughts. He finally got his tongue untied.

"Are you happy in Dodge City?" he asked. "I mean, do you enjoy theater work?"

Clark had only attended one show, and she'd intuited that he was disturbed by her working conditions. "I enjoy singing," she replied, pausing to take a sip of her punch. "I can't say I enjoy performing in a saloon."

"Army life is a good deal different." Clark seemed unaware of his awkward non sequitur. "Probably the main reason I chose a career as a soldier."

"Oh?" She wondered where he was trying to lead the conversation. "How is the army different?"

"Well, take this ball, for example. There's never a dull moment, and always something cultural to hold your interest. Do you see what I mean?"

"Like the ball?"

"Yes, and the theatricals we put on for ourselves. Not to mention our discussion groups on classical literature. And picnics in the summer and the evenings we get together for sing-alongs. You'd really enjoy that."

"I'm sure I would."

"The army's a fine life," he said with conviction. "Wonderful people, educated and intelligent, a stimulating culture. You couldn't ask for a better life."

All in a rush, Lillian realized he was trying to sell her on the army life. Or more to the point, the joys of the life of an army *wife.* He was, she saw in sudden comprehension, working himself around to a proposal. She thought it was a marvelous compliment, unbelievably flattering. He was so earnest, so handsome—and yet . . .

"Oh!" She sprang to her feet as the band swung into a lively tune. "Don't you just love a Virginia Reel!"

Before Clark knew what hit him, she had set their punch cups on an empty chair. She laughed, taking his hands, and pulled him onto the dance floor. There seemed no alternative but that she keep him dancing all night.

She wasn't yet ready to hear his proposal.

A warm sun flooded the streets of Dodge City. The weather was nonetheless brisk, for it was the middle of November and a chilly breeze drifted across the plains. Lillian wore her linsey-woolsey dress with a heavy shawl.

Jordan called for her at one o'clock. She'd arrived at the hotel with only enough time to change clothes. The drive back from Fort Dodge had required artifice and a good deal of chatter on her part. Terrance Clark had yet to complete the thought he'd started last night.

Fontaine had gently chided her about being a social butterfly. Out with the army last night, he slyly teased, and off with the buffalo hunter today. Still, he trusted her to do what was right and offered no real objection. He was secure in the knowledge that her mother had raised her to be a lady.

Today, with a buggy rented from the livery, Jordan drove west along the Arkansas. He and his crew of skinners returned to town every ten days or so with a load of hides. Lillian had learned that his nickname—Cimarron—derived from the fact that he was the only buffalo man willing to cross the Cimarron River and hunt in Indian Territory. His given name was Samuel.

She knew as well, from talking with the saloon girls, that he was widely admired by the other buffalo hunters. His daring had made him a legend of sorts, for he had returned time and again with his scalp intact from a land jealously guarded by hostile tribes. He was no less a legend for his ferocity in saloon brawls, though the girls vowed he'd never been known to start a fight. His temper, once unleashed, quickly ended any dispute.

Lillian found him different than his reputation. With her, he was quiet and gently spoken and always a gentleman. Today was their third ride into the country, and he'd never attempted to make advances, not even a kiss. He went armed with a pistol, and he carried his Sharps buffalo rifle whenever they traveled outside Dodge City. But she had never seen his violent side, and she sometimes wished he would try to kiss her. She found him a very attractive man.

Jordan stopped the buggy on a low rise some ten miles west of town. Off in the distance, a herd of buffalo numbering in the thousands slowly grazed southward against the umber plains. He explained that the herds migrated south for the winter, taking refuge in Palo Duro Canyon or on the vast uncharted wilderness known as the Staked Plains. At length, his explanation finished, he turned to her with a quizzical smile.

"How'd you enjoy the dance last night?"

"Very much," she said, taken aback. "How did you know where I went?"

"Well, I got to town expectin' to see you in the show. I asked your dad about it, thinkin' maybe you was sick. He told me you was sweet on that soldier-boy, Clark."

"Oh, that's just like Papa! He knows very well it's not true."

"Simmer down," Jordan said with an amused chuckle. "I was only funnin' you."

Lillian looked at him. "You don't care much for the army, do you? I've noticed you never speak to the soldiers in Murphy's. Why is that?"

"The cavalry tries to stop me from crossin' into Injun country. There's some treaty or another that says nobody's supposed to hunt down there."

"But you do it anyway?"

"I reckon somebody's got to keep the soldier-boys on their toes."

"You're shameless."

Her tone was light. Still, his casual manner made her wonder again at the violence of the frontier. The army fought the Indians, and the Indians pillaged settlements, and the buffalo hunters provoked the tribes even more with the slaughter of the herds. Hardly a night went by that hide hunters and soldiers weren't evolved in a brawl, just for the sheer deviltry of it. Everyone, white and red, fought everyone else.

First in Abilene, and now in Dodge City, it seemed to her that men fought without any great rhyme or reason. There was no real effort on anyone's part to live in peace, and the hostility inevitably led to more bloodshed. Of course, she had killed a Kiowa warrior—who thought he was justified in trying to kill her—so she had no right to be critical. But it all struck her as such a waste.

"Where'd you go?" Jordan asked. "You look like you're a million miles away."

"Oh, just daydreaming," Lillian fibbed. "Nothing important really."

"Thinking about that fancy ball last night?"

"No, actually, I was thinking about you. Am I the only one who calls you Samuel?"

"Most folks don't even know my real name."

"Then I want to know even more. How did you become a buffalo hunter?"

"That's a long story."

"We have all afternoon."

Jordan, like most men, was easily prompted to talk about himself. She listened, nodding with interest, seemingly all attention. Yet her mind was a world away, another time and another place. A time of gentler memory.

She longed again for the sight of New York.

CHAPTER 10

THE PLAINS were blanketed with snow. The air crackled with cold, and there were patches of ice along the banks of the Arkansas. Clouds the color of pewter hung low in the sky.

The Fontaines arrived shortly after eleven o'clock. They were bundled in heavy coats and lap robes, their breath like frosty puffs of smoke. An orderly rushed out to take charge of the buckboard and team as they stopped before the house. Libbie Custer met them at the door.

"Merry Christmas!" she cried gaily. "Come in out of the cold."

"Yes, Merry Christmas," Lillian replied, hugging her fondly. "Thank you so much for having us."

"Indeed," Fontaine added heartily. "You are the very spirit of the season for strangers far from home. We feel blessed by your charity."

"Don't be silly," Libbie fussed. "Now, get out of those coats and come into the parlor. Everyone's waiting."

Their coats were hung in the vestibule. Libbie led them into the parlor, where a cheery blaze snapped in the fireplace. Custer moved forward, his hand outstretched, followed by Clark. His manner was jovial.

"Here you are!" he said, shaking their hands. "To quote our friend Dickens, 'God bless us every one!' Welcome to our home."

Chester went to warm himself by the fire. Custer nodded to a manservant, who shortly returned with a tray of hot toddies in porcelain mugs. The mix of brandy, water, and sugar, heated with a red-hot poker, brought a flush to Lillian's face. Clark raised his mug in a toast.

"Merry Christmas," he said cordially. "You look lovely today."

"You're being gallant," she said with a smile. "I'm sure my nose is red as an apple. I thought I would freeze before we got here."

"I'm afraid it will be even colder when you drive back."

"Yes, but as you know, there's no rest for actors. The show must go on, even on Christmas night."

"We could change that easily enough. All you have to do is say the word."

Lillian avoided a reply. Over the past month Clark had proposed on several occasions, and each time she had gently turned him down. She was still attracted to him, just as she was to Jordan, who continued to court her whenever he was in town. But the thought of being stranded in Kansas, marriage or not, made her shudder. She looked for a way to change the subject.

"Oh, what a marvelous tree!" she said, turning to Libbie. "Why, it's absolutely gorgeous."

Libbie brightened. "I sent all the way to Chicago for some of the ornaments. I'm so happy you like it."

George Armstrong Custer was not a man to do things by half-measure. In mid-December, he'd had a fir tree imported from Missouri, freighted overland with a consignment of military stores. Libbie had decorated the tree with cranberries and popcorn strung together on thread and gaily-colored ribbon bows. Her most treasured ornaments, ordered from Chicago, were white satin angels with gossamer wings and shiny glass balls. The tree was crowned with a silver papier-mâché star.

The Custers were childless, but Christmas was nonetheless a time of celebration. Watching them, it occurred to Lillian that there was something childlike about the couple. They were forever inventing reasons for gala parties, amateur theatricals, or nature outings that often involved a dozen or more officers and their wives. Yet Christmas was clearly their favorite festivity of the year, eclipsing even the Fourth of July. The tree, imported all the way from Missouri, stood as testament to their Yuletide spirit.

The hot toddies were apparently a tradition in the Custer household. Apart from wine with dinner, women seldom drank hard liquor in the company of men. But Custer insisted, and before an hour was out Lillian felt as though her head would float away from her shoulders. Libbie coaxed her into singing a Christmas carol, and she managed to get through it without missing a note. She was giddy with delight.

Fontaine, who needed little prompting, was then asked to perform. To their surprise, he selected a poem written by Clement C. Moore, one that had gained enormous popularity in recent years. He positioned himself beside the tree and recited the poem with a Shakespearean flair for the dramatic. His silken baritone filled the parlor.

Twas the night before Christmas, when all
through the house
Not a creature was stirring—not even a mouse;

The stockings were hung by the chimney with care,
In hopes that St. Nicholas soon would be there . . .

"Bravo!" Custer yelled when Fontaine finished the last line. "Never have I heard it done better. Never!"

Libbie was reduced to tears. Lillian, still lightheaded from the hot toddies, was amazed. Apart from Shakespeare, she had no idea that her father had ever committed anything to memory. She glanced at Chester, who offered her an elaborate shrug. He seemed equally nonplussed.

The manservant, with impeccable timing, announced dinner. The table was decorated with greenery, bight red berries, and tall colored candles. A roasted goose, its legs tied with red and green bows, lay cooked to a crisp on a large serving platter. Custer, wielding a carving knife as though it were a cavalry saber, adeptly trimmed the bird. After loading their plates, he waited for the manservant to pour wine. He hoisted his glass.

"You honor Libbie and I with your presence on the day of Our Lord's birth. Merry Christmas!"

Everyone clinked glasses and echoed the sentiment. The serving bowls were passed and their plates were soon heaped with stuffing, winter squash, cranberry sauce, mashed potatoes, and a rich oyster gravy. Fontaine offered his compliments to the chef, though the army cook in the kitchen had never been seen on any of their visits to the house. The manservant kept their wineglasses full.

Lillian was acutely conscious of Clark seated on her right. He hadn't spoken since their earlier conversation in the parlor, when she'd blithely evaded his reference to marriage. His manner was sullen, and while the others ate with gusto, he merely picked at his food. No one else seemed to notice, but she saw Libbie glance at him several times during the meal. He drained his wineglass every time it was replenished.

Later, after dessert, the men retired to the study for cigars and brandy. Clark was bleary-eyed with wine on top of hot toddies and scarcely looked at Lillian as he walked from the room. Libbie led her into the parlor, where they seated themselves on a sofa before the fireplace. The gaiety of the party seemed diminished for Lillian, and she scolded herself for having hurt Clark with an unintentional rebuff. There was an awkward silence as she stared into the flames.

"I couldn't help but notice," Libbie finally said. "Did you and Terrance have words?"

Lillian smiled wanly. "I'm sure you knew he asked me to marry him."

"Yes, he mentioned it to the general."

"I've told him no any number of times. I think he realized today it's really final."

"What a shame," Libbie said sadly. "Terrance would make a fine husband."

"I know," Lillian said, a tear at the corner of her eye. "I just hate it, but I'm not ready for marriage. I haven't yet sorted out my own life."

"How do you mean?"

"Oh, it seems I'll never see New York again. And I so wanted a stage career."

"Aren't you scheduled to play Wichita next spring?"

"Wichita isn't New York," Lillian said fiercely. "I really loathe performing for cowboys and buffalo hunters, and drunken, brawling men. Everything in the West is so crude and . . . uncivilized."

"Yes, unfortunately, it is," Libbie agreed. "I often have those same feelings myself." She hesitated, considering. "Tell me, have you given any thought to Denver?"

"Denver?" Lillian looked at her. "Isn't that somewhere in Colorado? The mountains?"

"My dear, you have never seen anything like it. The Rockies are absolutely stunning, and Denver itself is really quite cosmopolitan. A very sophisticated city."

"Honestly?"

"Oh, goodness yes," Libbie said earnestly. "Theater, and opera, and shops with all the latest fashions. And scads of wealthy men. Just scads!"

Lillian's face lit up. "It sounds like the answer to a dream."

"Well, for someone who wants a career on the stage, it's perfect. I just know you would be a sensation there."

"Would you tell Father about it? Would you, please?"

"You mean, how grand and sophisticated it is? Perhaps a little hyperbole?"

"Yes! Yes!"

"Why, of course. What are friends for?"

The men trooped in from the study. Lillian caught Chester's eye and warned him to silence with a sharp look. Then, artful as a pickpocket, she got her father seated on the sofa. She gave the general's wife a conspiratorial wink.

Libbie Custer began her pitch on the wonders of Denver.

* * *

Murphy's Exchange was mobbed. The blizzard a few days past had driven every buffalo hunter on the plains into Dodge City. They decided to stay and celebrate Christmas.

Their idea of celebrating the Christ Child's birth was little short of heathen. The first stop was a saloon, where they got modestly tanked on rotgut whiskey. The second was a whorehouse, where the girls baptized them in ways unknown to practicing Christians. After a carnage of drinking, gambling, and whoring, they were ready at last for Christmas night. They came, en masse, to see Darlin' Lilly.

Lillian was beside herself with excitement. On the drive back from Fort Dodge, her father had spoken of little else but Denver. Libbie Custer's glowing account had left him intrigued by the thought of a cosmopolitan oasis in the heart of the mountains. The general, not to be outdone by his wife, had embellished the Mile High City with an aura of elegance second to none. His comments added authority to an already dazzling portrait.

The marvelous thing was that Alistair Fontaine adopted the idea as his own. New York was a tattered dream, and Wichita was yet another cowtown quagmire, hardly better than Dodge City. But Denver, he declared after the Custers' stirring narrative, was the affirmation of an actor's prayer. He hadn't committed to a journey into the Rockies, but Lillian told herself it was only a matter of time. A gentle nudge here and there and he would talk himself into it.

Tonight's show was almost ended. Lillian was waiting in the wings for the finale, her last song of the evening. Her father was farther backstage, involved in a discussion with Frank Murphy. Chester approached her, glancing over his shoulder to make sure the conversation was still in progress. He gave her a dour look.

"Dad's back there grilling Murphy about Denver. You sure put a bee in his bonnet."

"Me?" Lillian said innocently. "The Custers got him started on it, not me."

"Yeah, sure," Chester scoffed, "and the moon's made of green cheese."

"Listen to me, Chester. However much Papa talks, we're never going back to New York. Denver is our only hope for a decent life."

"I know."

"You do?"

"Of course I do," Chester said. "The chances are nil of our ever getting a booking back East. Either we go to Wichita or we take a crack at Denver."

"Well . . ." Lillian was relieved. "I hope you favor Denver."

"Don't worry, we'll talk Dad into it."

"No, he thinks it's his own idea. Let him talk himself into it."

Chester smiled. "I can almost hear Mom saying the same thing. You remind me more and more of her lately."

"Oh, Chet . . ."

The piano player opened with her introduction. She gave Chester a quick kiss on the cheek and moved out of the wings. The fiddler joined the piano, and the crowd of drunken buffalo hunters greeted her with rowdy applause. She walked to the footlights, hoping they would appreciate her selection. She thought it a fitting end to the Christmas season. On the musicians' cue, her voice seemed to fill the night.

Hark! the herald angels sing
Glory to the newborn King;
Peace on earth and mercy mild,
God and sinners reconciled!
Joyful all ye nations rise,
Join the triumph of the skies;
With th' angelic host proclaim
Christ is born in Bethlehem

The saloon went silent. She saw Cimarron Jordan at the bar, and he nodded with an approving smile. The hide hunters, heathen or not, stared at her as though suddenly touched by memories past. To a man, their thoughts slipped from whiskey and whores to long-gone times of Christmas trees and family. Many snuffled, their noses runny, and one blubbered without shame, his features slack with emotion. A carol sung in a saloon took them back to better days, gentler times.

The hush held until her voice faded on the last note. Then they recovered themselves, and a roar went up, whistles and cheers and drumming applause. She curtsied, warmed by their reaction, and made her way offstage. They brought her back for another ovation, and then another, and she thought there was, after all, some glimmer of hope for buffalo hunters. Yet it was a passing thought, and one quickly gone. Her mind was fixed on Denver.

Later, after she'd changed, Jordan took her to a café for a late supper. The food was greasy, thick slabs of buffalo fried in a skillet, and she hardly ate a bite. But she chattered on with growing excitement as she related her conspiracy with Libbie Custer. Her eyes sparkled whenever she mentioned Denver, and she could scarcely contain herself. She bubbled with the thrill of it all.

"What about your pa?" Jordan asked, when she paused for breath. "Think he'll go for the idea?"

"Oh, I know he will. I just know it! He's talked of nothing else."

"Well, I'm pleased for you. Mighty pleased."

Lillian saw his downcast expression. She knew he was taken with her and chided herself for not being more sensitive. She touched his hand.

"You could always come visit me in Denver."

"Suppose I could," Jordan said, studying on it. "Course, they'll turn you into a big-city girl with fancy notions. Likely you wouldn't have time for a rough old cob like me."

"That simply isn't true," she said, squeezing his hand. "I'll always have time for you, Samuel. Always."

Cimarron Jordan wanted to believe it. But he was a pragmatist, and he told himself there was a greater truth in what he'd heard tonight. Come spring, there was no doubt in his mind.

Dodge City would see the last of Darlin' Lilly.

Chapter 11

SPRING LAY across the land. The plains stretched onward to infinity, an emerald ocean of grass sprinkled with a riotous profusion of wildflowers. A late-afternoon sun heeled over toward the horizon.

Fontaine rode a bloodbay gelding. A Henry repeater was balanced behind the saddlehorn, and he wore a light doeskin jacket with fringe on the sleeves. Chester drove the buckboard, drawn by the mismatched sorrel and dun team, fat from a winter in the livery stable. Lillian was seated beside him, the brim of her bonnet lowered against the glare of the sun. They were three days west of Dodge City.

Lillian thought her father was in his glory. She glanced at him from beneath her bonnet, forced to smile at the striking figure he cut on the gelding. He rather fancied himself the intrepid plainsman and looked like he was playing a role that borrowed assorted traits from Daniel Boone and Kit Carson. She was amused that he played the part of stalwart scout with such élan.

Their immediate destination was Pueblo, Colorado. By her reckoning, she marked the date at April 18, and she hoped 1872 would prove more rewarding than the year just past. She had celebrated her twentieth birthday in February, and she felt immensely matured by her experiences in Abilene and Dodge City. So much so that she seldom fell into reverie about some grand and joyous return to New York. Her thoughts were on Denver.

By New Year's Day, Alistair Fontaine had sold himself on the idea. Over the next three months he'd devoted his time to planning their artistic assault on the Mile High City. The top nightspot in Denver was the Alcazar Variety Theater, and he had arranged for their New York booking agent to forward their notices and a glowing report on the show. The owner of the Alcazar had sent a lukewarm response, stating he was interested but offering no firm commitment. Fontaine, undeterred by details, went ahead with his plans. He was confident they would take Denver by storm.

George Armstrong Custer became their unofficial adviser. The Kansas Pacific railroad was laying track westward but had not completed the line into Colorado. The nearest railhead was Wichita, a week's journey to the east, and at least another week by train to Denver. The better route, Custer suggested, was to follow the Arkansas River overland, which would bring them to Pueblo within two weeks' time. From there, it was a short hop by train to Denver.

Cimarron Jordan considered the overland route to be foolhardy. He told Lillian, and then Fontaine, that Custer was playing daredevil with their lives. The country west of Dodge City, he explained, was a hunting ground for the Cheyenne, the Comanche, and other tribes. A strip of unsettled territory bordering their route, known as No Man's Land, was also haven to outlaws from throughout the West. He firmly believed they would be placing themselves in jeopardy.

Fontaine blithely ignored the warning. General Custer was a distinguished soldier and the greatest Indian fighter in the West. Jordan was a common buffalo hunter and, in the end, a man who lacked the wisdom of a military commander. To no small degree, Fontaine was influenced by Custer's derring-do and quixotic spirit. He saw the journey as another step in their westward adventure, and he cast himself in the role of trailblazer and scout. He declared they would take the overland route.

Their final week in Dodge City was spent in provisioning for the trip. Fontaine stocked all manner of victuals, including buffalo jerky, dried fruit, and four quarts of Irish whiskey. He purchased a ten-gauge shotgun, with powder and shot, announcing it was suitable for wild fowl or wild Indians. Then, in a picaresque moment, he bought a bloodbay gelding with fire in its eye and a quick, prancing gait. Custer, after seeing the horse, gave Fontaine a doeskin jacket taken in the spoils of war. He looked like a centaur with fringe on his sleeves.

Their departure brought out all of Dodge City in a rousing farewell. Custer was there, along with Libbie, who hugged Lillian with teary-eyed fondness and good wishes for the journey. Jordan and his crew of skinners accompanied them west for the first day and then turned south for the Cimarron River. Before they separated, Jordan again cautioned them to be wary at all times and to mount a guard over their livestock every night. Indians, he observed, might steal your horses and, rather than kill, leave you to a crueler fate. A man on foot would never survive the limitless plains.

Fontaine consulted his compass an hour or so before sundown. Encased in brass, indicating direction and azimuth without fail, the compass was largely a showpiece. The Arkansas River wound due west like a silver ribbon, and simply following its course would bring them to Pueblo. But Fontaine, immersed in his role as scout, wanted all the props to fit the part, and he'd bought a compass. After snapping the lid closed, he signaled Chester to a stand of cottonwoods along the riverbank. He announced they would stop for the night.

By now, they went about their assigned tasks with little conversation. Chester hobbled the horses and put them to graze on a grassy swale that bordered the river. Later, he would water them for the night and then place them on a picket line by the buckboard. Fontaine gathered deadwood from beneath the trees and kindled a fire with a mound of twigs. Lillian removed her cast-iron cookware and foodstuffs from the buckboard and began preparing supper. She planned to serve buffalo jerky, softened and fried, with beans and biscuits left over from breakfast.

Twilight settled over the land as she dished out the meal. The fire was like a beacon in the night, and they gathered around with tin plates and mugs of steaming coffee. She thought the scene was curiously atavistic, not unlike a primordial tribe, hunkered before a fire, sharing the end of another day. Three days on the trail had already toughened them, and though her father and Chester religiously shaved every morning, they appeared somehow leaner and harder. Every time she looked in her little vanity mirror, she got a fright. She was afraid the harsh plains sun would freckle her nose.

"Westerners do like their beans," Fontaine said, holding a bean to the firelight on the tines of his fork. "I've always found it amusing that they call them whistleberries."

"Oh, Papa," Lillian said, shocked. "That's disgusting."

"A natural function of the body, my dear. Beans produce wind."

"I really don't care to discuss it."

Lillian was still embarrassed by aspects of life on the trail. A call of nature required that she hunt down thick brush or hide behind a tree. Even then, she thought there was scarcely any privacy. She always felt exposed.

"Your modesty becomes you," Fontaine said understandingly. "In fact, it provides a lesson for us all. We mustn't allow ourselves to be coarsened by the demands of nomadic travel."

Chester laughed. "Buffalo jerky and beans are coarse all right. I'd give anything for a good steak."

"Capital idea!" Fontaine said. "The land fairly teams with wildlife. I'll set out on a hunt tomorrow."

Lillian was alarmed. Her father knew virtually nothing about hunting and even less about negotiating his way on the plains. She had visions of him becoming hopelessly lost on the sea of grass.

"Do you think that's wise, Papa?" she asked uneasily. "Shouldn't we stay together?"

"Have no fear," Fontaine said with a bold air. "I shan't stray too far from the river. Besides, I have my trusty compass."

Chester looked worried. "Lillian has a point. If we were separated somehow, we might never get back together. I can do without fresh meat."

"Nonsense," Fontaine said stubbornly. "You concern yourselves for no reason. The matter is settled."

Later, after the horses were picketed, they spread their bedrolls around the fire. Chester took the first shift of guarding the camp, stationed with his rifle near the buckboard. Fontaine would relieve him in two hours, and they would alternate shifts throughout the night. Neither of them would hear of Lillian standing guard. She was, after all, a girl.

Lillian was less offended than amused. They seemed to have forgotten that she'd killed a Kiowa warrior on the Santa Fe Trail last fall. But then, male vanity was as prevalent in the Fontaine family as any other. She was to be protected simply because she was a woman. Or in their minds, still a girl.

She snuggled into her bedroll. The sky was purest indigo, flecked with stars scattered about the heavens like shards of ice. She stared up at the Big Dipper, filled with wonder that they were here, roughing it on the plains, sleeping on the ground. Her father their scout and hunter.

She thought her mother would have been beyond laughter.

Fontaine rode out of camp at false dawn. He reined the bloodbay gelding north, toward a distant copse of trees bordering a tributary creek. He reasoned that deer would water there before sunrise.

Chester and Lillian, following his instructions, were to continue westward along the banks of the Arkansas. Fontaine was still touched by their concern for his welfare but nonetheless determined that plains travel was largely an exercise of the intellect. He planned to have his deer and rejoin them long before midday.

Hunting, he told himself, was a matter of intellect as well. He recalled reading somewhere—possibly Thoreau—that deer were by nature nocturnal creatures. So it made sense, after a night of foraging, they would water before bedding down for the day. He felt confident a fat buck awaited him even now at the creek.

The tree line was farther than he'd estimated. He reminded himself again that the vastness of the plains was deceptive; everything was more distant than it appeared to the eye. The sun burst free from the edge of the earth, a blinding globe of vermilion, just as he rode into the shade of the trees. He dismounted, tying the gelding to a stout limb. He moved into the shadows with the Henry repeater.

Fontaine was immensely pleased with himself. He'd taken equestrian lessons many years ago, and the rhythm of it had come back to him after a day or so in the saddle. He was armed with a rifle that shot true and perfectly capable of navigating across the vistas of open grassland. Everything considered, he felt the dime-novel exploits of Buffalo Bill and his ilk were greatly overrated, more myth than fact. Any man with a modicum of intelligence could become a plainsman, and the same was true of a hunter. All he needed was to spot—

A buck stepped out of the shadows across the creek, some fifty yards upstream. Streamers of sunlight filtered through the trees, glinting on antlers as the buck lowered his nose to the water. Fontaine thumbed the hammer on his rifle, slowly tucking the butt into his shoulder. His arms were shaking with excitement, and it took him a moment to steady the sights. He recalled a conversation with Cimarron Jordan, about the cleanest way to kill an animal. He aimed slightly behind the foreleg.

The gunshot reverberated like a kettledrum. The buck jerked back from the water, then whirled about and bounded off through the trees. Fontaine was too astounded to move, roundly cursing himself for having missed the shot. Before he could lever another cartridge into the chamber, the buck disappeared into a thicket far upstream. He lowered the rifle, still baffled by his poor marksmanship and struck by a vagrant, if somewhat unsavory, thought. There would be no fresh meat in the pot tonight.

The thud of hoofbeats sounded off to the east. Fontaine wondered if a herd of buffalo was headed his way, and in the next instant the notion was dispelled. Five Indians, drawn by the gunshot, topped the rise that sloped down to the creek and reined to a halt. Their eyes found him almost immediately, and for a moment he felt paralyzed, rooted to the ground. Then they gigged their ponies, whooping and screeching as they tore down the slope, and he scrambled to unhitch his horse. He flung himself into the saddle.

The Indians splashed across the creek. Fontaine had perhaps a hundred yards' head start, and he booted his horse hard in the ribs. The gelding responded, stretching out into a dead gallop, and he thanked the gods he'd bought a spirited mount. A quick glance over his shoulder brought reassurance that he was extending his lead, and he bent low in the saddle. Something fried the air past his ear, and a split second later he heard the report of a rifle from far behind. He thundered southwest toward the river.

Some twenty minutes into the chase Fontaine had widened the gap to a quarter-mile. He silently offered up a prayer that the gelding had stamina as well as speed, for if he faltered now all was lost. Then, as he rounded a bend in the river, he saw the buckboard not far ahead. Chester and Lillian turned in the seat as he pounded closer, and by the expression on their faces, he knew they'd seen the Indians. He frantically motioned them toward the riverbank.

"Get down!" he shouted. *"Take cover!"*

Chester sawed on the reins. He whipped the team off the grassy prairie and brought the buckboard to a skidding halt where a brush-choked overhang sheltered the streambed. He jumped to the ground, rifle in hand, as Lillian hopped out on the other side with the shotgun. Fontaine reined the gelding to a dust-smothered stop and vaulted from the saddle. His eyes were wild.

"Open fire!" he ordered. "Don't let them overrun us!"

The Indians galloped toward them at a full charge. The sight of a white woman and a buckboard full of supplies merely galvanized them to action. Fontaine and Chester commenced firing, working the levers on their rifles in a rolling staccato roar. The breakneck speed of the ponies made it difficult to center on a target, and none of their shots took effect. The warriors clearly intended to overrun their position.

Lillian finally joined the fight. After a struggle to cock both hammers on the shotgun, she found it required all her strength to raise the heavy weapon. She brought it to shoulder level, trying to steady the long barrels, and accidentally tripped both triggers. The shotgun boomed, the double hammers dropping almost simultaneously, and a hail of buckshot sizzled into the charging Indians. The brutal kick of the recoil knocked Lillian off her feet.

A warrior flung out his arms and toppled dead from his pony. The others swerved aside as buckshot simmered through their ranks like angry hornets. Their charge was broken not ten feet from the overhang, and Fontaine and Chester continued to blast away with their Henry repeaters. None of the slugs found a mark, but the Indians retreated to a stand of cottonwoods some thirty yards from the riverbank. They dismounted in the cover of the tree line.

"Help your sister," Fontaine said sharply. "I'll keep an eye on the red devils."

Lillian lay sprawled on the rocky shoreline. Her shoulder throbbed and her head ached, and there was a loud ringing in her ears. Chester lifted her off the ground and set her on her feet, supporting her until she recovered her balance. He grinned at her.

"You got one!"

"I did?"

"Look for yourself."

A gunshot from the trees sent a slug whizzing over their heads. They ducked beneath the overhang and quickly crouched beside their father. Fontaine gave them a doleful look.

"There are four left," he said. "They have only one rifle, but that is sufficient to keep us pinned down. I fear we're in for a siege."

"A siege?" Chester questioned. "You don't think they'll rush us again?"

"Not until nightfall," Fontaine remarked. "I daresay they are wary of Lillian's shotgun. You saved the day, my dear."

Lillian was still dazed. "Will they come after us tonight, Papa?"

"Yes, I believe they will. Chester, reload your sister's shotgun. We'll have need of our artillery."

Fontaine bent low behind the buckboard and tied his gelding to a wheel rim. He knew the Indians were as interested in their horses as in their scalps. A live horse was of equal value as a dead man.

He thought they were in for a long night.

Chapter 12

A BALL of orange flame rose over the eastern horizon. The heat of the sun slowly burned off a pallid mist that hung across the river. Somewhere in the distance a bird twittered, then fell silent.

The clearing between the riverbank and the cottonwoods was ghostly still. Fontaine was crouched at the right of the overhang, with Lillian in the middle and Chester at the opposite end. Lillian's shoulder was sore and bruised, and Chester had relieved her of the shotgun. She was now armed with a Henry repeater.

They were exhausted. Three times in the course of the night the Indians had attempted to infiltrate their position. Twice, using stealth and the cover of darkness, the warriors had crept in from the flanks. The last time had been an abortive assault from the river, floating downstream and trying to take them from behind. They had fought off every attack.

A starlit sky proved to be their salvation. The light was murky but nonetheless adequate to discern movement and form. Fontaine's instructions were to fire at the first sign of danger, and Lillian and Chester, their nerves on edge, were alert to the slightest sound. Accuracy was difficult in the dim light, and yet it did nothing to hamper volley after volley of rapid fire. The Indians beat a hasty retreat in the face of flying lead.

The horses reared and pitched with every skirmish. But Chester, exhibiting foresight long before darkness fell, had secured the team to thick, ancient roots jutting out from the overhang. The bloodbay gelding, tied to the near wheel of the buckboard, kicked and squealed with a ferocity that threatened to snap the reins. Still, with the coming of daylight, the horses dozed off standing up, as if calmed by the relative quiet. The only sound was a bird that twittered now and again.

Fontaine removed his hat. He cautiously edged his head around the side of the overhang and peered across the clearing. He saw no movement in the stand of cottonwoods and wondered if the Indians had pulled out under cover of darkness. His eyes narrowed as he realized that, sometime during the night they had recovered the body of the warrior killed by Lillian. A spurt of smoke blossomed from the tree line and a slug kicked dirt in his face. He jerked his head back.

"How depressing," he said with a mild attempt at humor. "Our friends are a determined lot."

Chester grunted. "Hope we killed some of them last night."

"I rather doubt it, my boy. Unless they still had us outnumbered, I suspect they would have given up the fight."

"So what do we do now?"

"Well, it is somewhat like a game of cat and mouse, isn't it? We have no option but to wait them out."

"Some option," Chester said dourly. "We could be here forever."

"Isn't there another way, Papa?" Lillian asked. "I dread the thought of another night like last night."

Fontaine smiled. "My dear, you are the only soldier among us. Chet and I have yet to kill our first savage."

"I can't say I'm proud of it. Besides, it was an accident with that stupid old shotgun anyway. It's a wonder I didn't break my shoulder."

"Or your *derriere*," Chester added with a sly grin. "You hit the ground so hard the earth shook."

Lillian was too tired to bandy words. Her face was smudged with dirt and the smoke of gunpowder, and stray locks of hair spilled down over her forehead. She was scared to death and felt as though she hadn't slept in a week. She wondered if they would live to see Denver.

Fontaine stuck his rifle around the edge of the overhang and fired. He turned back to them with a crafty smile. "A reminder for our friends," he said. "We musn't let them think we're not alert."

"I don't feel very alert," Lillian said. "I honestly believe I could close my eyes and go to sleep right now."

"Excellent idea, my dear. We need to be fresh for tonight's war of wits. You and Chet try to catch a nap. I'll keep watch for a while."

"You must be exhausted, too, Papa."

"On the contrary, I've never felt more—"

A herd of horses thundered around the bend in the river. At first glance, Fontaine estimated there were fifty or more, their manes streaming in the wind. Then, looking closer, he was never more heartened in his life. There were six men driving the horses. Six *white* men.

The four remaining Indians exploded out of the cottonwoods. They whipped their ponies, galloping north from the river, clearly no less startled by the sudden appearance of the herd. Several of the drovers pulled their pistols, jolted by the sight of Indians, and prepared to open fire. A man on a magnificent roan stallion raised his hand.

"Hold off!" he bellowed. "You'll spook the gawddamn herd!"

The men obediently holstered their pistols. They circled the herd and brought the horses to a milling standstill. One of them gestured off at the fleeing Indians.

"Them there's Comanche," he said in a puzzled voice. "Think they was fixin' to jump us, Rufe?"

"Tend to doubt it," the one named Rufe said. "Not the way they're hightailin' it outta here."

"Then what the blue-billy hell was they doin' here?"

Fontaine stepped around the overhang. Lillian and Chester followed him, all of them still armed. The six men stared at them as though a flock of doves had burst from a magician's hat. Fontaine nodded to the man named Rufe, the one who appeared to be the leader. He smiled amiably.

"Those heathens"—he motioned casually at the fast-departing Indians—"were here attempting to collect our scalps. You gentlemen arrived in the very nick of time."

"Who are you?"

"Alistair Fontaine. May I present my daughter, Lillian, and my son, Chester. And whom do I have the honor of addressing?"

"The name's Rufe Stroud."

"Well, sir," Fontaine said, the rifle nestled in the crook of his arm. "Never have I been more delighted to see anyone, Mr. Stroud. You are a welcome sight indeed."

Stroud squinted. "What brings you to this neck of the woods?"

"We are on our way to Denver."

"You picked a helluva way to get there. Them Comanche would've roasted you alive."

"All too true," Fontaine conceded. "You are, in every sense of the word, our deliverance."

"Mebbe so," Stroud said. "You folks on foot, are you?"

"Our buckboard is there on the riverbank."

One of the men rode to the overhang for a look. He turned in the saddle to Stroud. "Buckboard and three horses, Rufe. Got a bay gelding that's purty nice."

Stroud nodded. "I'm a mite curious," he said to Fontaine. "Why're you headed to Denver?"

"We are actors," Fontaine said in his best baritone. "We plan to play the Alcazar Theater."

"Your girl an actor, too?"

"Yes indeed, a fine actress. And a singer of exceptional merit, I might add."

"That a fact?"

Lillian felt uncomfortable under his stare. Fontaine smiled amicably. "From the size of your herd, I take it you are a horse rancher, Mr. Stroud."

"You take it wrong," Stroud said. "I'm a horse thief."

"I beg you pardon?"

"Drop them guns."

The men pulled their pistols as though on command. Fontaine looked at them, suddenly aware he was in the company of desperadoes. He dropped his rifle on the ground, nodding to Lillian and Chester, who quickly followed his lead. Then, ever so slowly, he fished the Colt .32 revolver from his jacket pocket and tossed it on the ground. He looked at Stroud.

"Those are all of our weapons. May I ask your intentions, Mr. Stroud?"

Stroud ignored him. "Shorty," he said to one of the men. "Get them into the buckboard and let's make tracks. Them Comanche might have friends hereabouts."

Shorty Martin was well named. He was hardly taller than a stump post, a thickset man with beady eyes. "Whyn't we kill'em now?" he said flatly. "They're just gonna slow us down."

Lillian's heart skipped a beat. She seemed unable to catch her breath as Stroud inspected them as if they were lame horses that might slow his progress. His eyes suddenly locked onto her and held her in a gaze that was at once assessment and raw lust. The look lasted a mere instant, though she felt stripped naked, and his eyes again went cold. He glanced at Martin.

"Do like you're told."

Martin knew an order when he heard one. Within minutes, the outfit proceeded west along the river. The Fontaines were in the buckboard, and the bloodbay gelding, now unsaddled, ran with the herd. Fontaine, nagged by a worrisome thought, wished he had kept the pistol.

He'd seen the way Stroud looked at Lillian.

The sun was high when they crossed the Arkansas. At a wide spot in the river, where the water ran shallow, they forded through a rocky streambed. Their direction was now almost due southwest.

Fontaine watched the operation with increasing vigilance. His mind was already exploring how they might escape, and he was committing the terrain and their direction to memory. Yet he discerned that the gang functioned like a military unit, relentlessly on guard and with an economy of commands. The men clearly knew what was expected of them.

The chain of command was clear as well. Stroud was the leader, and his orders were not open to question. The other men, though a rough lot, seemed wary of incurring his anger. Shorty Martin was apparently Stroud's lieutenant and nominally the second in command. But there was little doubt as to his place in the scheme of things. Every order originated with Stroud.

Lillian was frightened into stony silence. Her intuition told her that these men were far more dangerous than the Comanche warriors they'd fought off just last night. Their abductors were callous and openly cold-blooded, evidenced by the one who had so calmly suggested that killing them was the better alternative. Only by the whim of the gang leader were they still alive.

Their deliverance from the Indians seemed to her a harsher fate. She knew lust when she saw it, and she'd seen it all too plainly in Stroud's cool gaze. She thought they'd jumped from the frying pan into the fire, and all because of her. Some inner voice warned her that the lives of her father and Chester were hostage to how she behaved. She sensed it was only a matter of time until her virtue was tested.

Stroud called a halt at noon. A narrow creek lay across their path, and he ordered the horses watered. The men took turns watching the herd, some rolling themselves smokes while the horses crowded around the stream. Others dismounted, pulling their puds as if there weren't a woman within a hundred miles, and relieved themselves on the ground. Lillian kept her eyes averted.

Stroud rode over to the buckboard. Chester, whose face was white with fury, erupted in anger. "Don't your men have any decency? How can you let them. . . . do that! . . . in front of a woman?"

"Sonny, you'd best shut your mouth. I won't be barked at by pups."

"Listen here—"

"That's enough!" Fontaine broke in. "Do as he says, Chet. Say nothing more."

"Good advice," Stroud said. "Don't speak till you're spoke to. Savvy?"

"We understand," Fontaine assured him. "It won't happen again."

Stroud nodded. He hooked one leg around the saddlehorn and pulled the makings from his shirt pocket. After spilling tobacco from a sack into the paper, he licked the edges and rolled it tight. He popped a sulphurhead on his thumbnail and lit up in a haze of smoke. His gaze lingered on Lillian a moment as he exhaled. Then he looked back at Fontaine.

"I never met an actor," he said. "Go ahead, do something."

"Pardon me?"

"Let's see you act."

"Seated in a buckboard?"

"I ain't in the habit of repeatin' myself. Show me your stuff."

Fontaine realized it was a crude test of some sort. He knew he would have only one chance to make good and decided to give it his all. The other men, drawn by the spectacle, moved closer to the buckboard. His voice rose in a booming baritone.

The quality of mercy is not strained,
It droppeth as the gentle rain from heaven

Upon the place beneath: it is twice bless'd;
It blesseth him that gives and him that takes:
'Tis mightest in the mightiest; it becomes
The throned monarch better than his crown;
His scepter shows the force of temporal power,
The attribute to awe and majesty,
Wherein doth sit the dread and fear of kings

Stroud was silent a moment. He took a drag and exhaled a wad of smoke. Then he smiled. "I like that," he said. " 'The dread and fear of kings.' You just pick that out of thin air?"

Fontaine spread his hands. "I thought it appropriate to the occasion."

"The part about mercy wasn't bad, either. I can see you've got a sly way about you."

"A supplicant often petitions mercy. Under the circumstances, it seemed fitting."

Stroud turned to the men. "You boys ever hear Shakespeare before?"

The men traded sheepish glances, shook their heads. "Thought not," he said, flicking an ash off his cigarette. "Well, Mr. Fontaine, mebbe we won't have to kill you, after all. We're plumb shy on entertainment out our way."

Lillian thought he was evil incarnate. He was lithe and muscular, with square features and a bristly ginger mustache. His eyes were hooded and seemed to emanate menace. She found herself staring into them now.

"Your pa says you're—how'd he put it?—an exceptional singer."

"I try," she replied softly. "Some people think I have a nice voice."

"You be thinkin' up a good tune for when we camp tonight. I'll let you sing for the boys."

Stroud shifted his gaze to Chester. "What is it you do, sonny?"

Chester reddened. "I act in melodramas. And I do a soft-shoe routine."

"You'll be dancin' for your supper before we're done. Just don't gimme no more of your sass."

"We understand perfectly," Fontaine interjected. "You may depend on us for the spirit of cooperation."

Stroud snuffed his cigarette between thumb and forefinger. He gestured to his men. "Awright, we been jawbonin' long enough. Let's get them horses on the trail."

The men jumped to obey. Stroud swung his leg over the saddlehorn and jammed his boot in the stirrup. Fontaine cleared his throat.

"May I ask you something, Mr. Stroud?"

"Try me and see."

"Where, exactly, are you taking us?"

Stroud smiled. "Folks call it No Man's Land."

Chapter 13

THREE DAYS later they crossed into No Man's Land. Their line of march was due southwest, through desolate country parched by wind and sun. On the fourth day, they sighted Wild Horse Lake.

Rufe Stroud seemed to unwind a little when they neared the outlaw camp. He rode beside the buckboard, suddenly talkative, almost genial, chatting with Fontaine. Lillian got the impression that it was all for her benefit, meant to impress her with the man and the place. He was in a bragging mood.

The remote strip of wilderness, Stroud told them, was all but uninhabited. Centuries ago Spanish explorers had called it *Cimarron*, which loosely translated meant "wild and unruly." Through a hodgepodge of confused and poorly written treaties, it now belonged to none of the Western states or territories. So it was aptly dubbed No Man's Land.

Despite the name, there was nothing confusing about its borders. Texas and Kansas were separated by its depth of some thirty-five miles, while its breadth extended nearly two hundred miles westward from Indian Territory to New Mexico Territory. Along its northwestern fringe, the isolated strip of grasslands formed a juncture with Colorado as well. To a large degree, the raw expanse of wilderness had been forgotten by God and government alike. There was no law, Stroud idly warned them, but his law.

Wild Horse Lake was his headquarters. Known to few white men, the spot was situated on the divide between the Beaver and Cimarron Rivers. A prominent landmark, it was the haunt of renegades and desperadoes from across the West. Those who came there were predators, wanted men on the dodge, and the law of the gun prevailed. A man survived on cunning and nerve and by minding his own business. Too much curiosity, Stroud explained, could get a man killed.

The lake itself was centered in a large basin. Somewhat like a deep bowl, it served as a reservoir for thunderstorms that whipped across the plains. Above the basin, sweeping away on all sides, was a limitless prairie where the grasses grew thick and tall. Wild things, the mustangs that gave the lake its name, no longer came there to feed and water. The basin was now the domain of men.

Outlaws found refuge there. A sanctuary where those who rode the owlhoot could retreat with no fear of pursuit. Not even U.S. marshals dared venture into the isolated stronghold, for lawmen were considered a form of prey anywhere in No Man's Land. Discretion being the better part of valor, peace officers stayed away, and a man on the run could find no safer place. There was absolute immunity from the law at Wild Horse Lake.

Several cabins dotted the perimeter of the lake. A trail from the east dropped off the plains and followed an incline into the basin. Lillian counted seven cabins and upward of ten men lounging about in the late-afternoon sunshine. Three men on hoseback were watering a herd of longhorns, and she noticed that the cattle wore fresh brands, the hair and hide still singed. She knew nothing of such matters, but it appeared to her that the old brands had somehow been altered. The men watched her with interest as the buckboard rolled past.

Stroud's headquarters was on the west side of the lake. There were three cabins, one larger than the others, and off on the south side a corral constructed of stout poles. The men hazed the horses into the corral, and a woman came running to slam and bolt the gate. Lillian saw two other women standing outside the larger cabin, and for a moment her spirits soared. But then, looking closer, she was reminded of the prostitutes she'd seen in Dodge City. She would find no friends at Wild Horse Lake.

One of the women walked forward. She was plump and curvaceous, with a mound of dark hair and bold amber eyes. Her gaze touched on Lillian with an instant's appraisal and then moved to Stroud. Her mouth ovaled in a saucy smile.

"Hello there, lover," she said. "Glad to see you back."

"Glad to be back."

Stroud stepped down from the saddle. The woman put her arms around his neck and kissed him full on the mouth. After a moment, she disengaged and nodded to the buckboard. "What've you got here?"

"They're actors," Stroud said, his arm around her waist. "The old man's pure hell on Shakespeare. The boy dances a little and the girl's a singer. Got a real nice voice."

"You plan to keep them here?"

"Don't see why not. We could stand some entertainment. Liven up the place."

She poked him in the ribs. "Thought I was lively enough for you."

"Course you are," Stroud said quickly. "Wait'll you hear the girl sing, though. She's damn good."

"Just make sure singing's all she does."

"C'mon now, Sally, don't get started on me. I'm in no mood for it."

She laughed a bawdy laugh. "I guess I know how to change your mood."

The order of things soon became apparent. Stroud and his woman, Sally Keogh, shared one of the smaller cabins. The other small cabin was occupied by Shorty Martin and a frowsy woman with broad hips and red hair. The largest of the cabins was a combination mess hall and bunkhouse for the remaining four men. The third woman appeared to be their communal harlot.

Martin quickly got a rude surprise. Stroud motioned him over to the buckboard. "The actors," he said, jerking a thumb at the Fontaines, "are takin' over your place. You and Mae move your stuff into the big cabin."

"For chrissake!" Martin howled. "You got no call to do that, Rufe."

"Don't gimme no argument. Get'em settled and quit your bellyachin'."

"There ain't no extra bunk in the big cabin!"

"Work out your own sleepin' arrangements. Just get it done."

"Yeah, awright," Martin grumped. "Still ain't fair."

Stroud turned to the buckboard. "Listen to me real good," he said, staring hard at Fontaine. "You mixin' with my men—'specially the girl—that's liable to cause trouble. So I'm givin' you a cabin to yourselves."

Fontaine nodded. "We appreciate the courtesy, Mr. Stroud."

"You're gonna see we don't have no padlock to put on your door. Before long, you might get it in your head to steal some horses and make a run for it."

"I assure you—"

"Lemme finish," Stroud said coldly. "You run, I'll let Shorty have his way with you. Get my drift?"

"Yes, I do."

"Then don't do nothin' stupid."

By sundown, the Fontaines were settled in the small cabin. Not long afterward, Fontaine and Chester were ordered to carry armloads of firewood into the big cabin. Lillian was assigned to the kitchen, which consisted of a woodburning cookstove and a crude table for preparing food. The other women, who were frying antelope steaks and a huge skillet of potatoes, gave her the silent treatment. But as the men trooped in, taking seats on long benches at a dining table, Sally Keogh sidled up to her. The woman's features were contorted.

"Stay away from Rufe," she hissed. "You mess with him and I'll slit your gullet."

"Why not tell him that?" Lillian said, suddenly angry. "All I want is to be left alone."

"Just remember you were warned."

Stroud broke out the whiskey. He waved Fontaine and Chester to the table and poured them drinks in enamel mugs. His amiable mood left them puzzled until they realized he wanted to celebrate a successful horse raid. He once again began bragging about his operation.

The whiskey and other essentials, he informed them, were imported to Wild Horse Lake from a distant trading post. There were three gangs who made the basin their headquarters, and his was the largest of the bunch. Some rustled cattle, others robbed banks and stagecoaches, but none dealt in stolen horses. Stroud reserved that right to himself, and the other gangs went along, aware that he would fight to protect his interests. No one cared to tangle with him or his outfit.

Fontaine mentioned he'd been told that the Comanche and Cheyenne tribes were active in this part of the country. He alluded specifically to Stroud and his men saving them from certain death at the hands of the Comanche raiding party. He asked how Stroud and the other gangs managed to operate so openly in a land where warlike tribes traveled at will. Stroud laughed loudly.

"We buy 'em off," he said. "Injuns would trade their souls for repeatin' rifles. Bastards think we hung the moon."

Lillian listened as she worked at the stove. She knew all his bragging was like the sounding of their death knell. He would never have brought them here or expounded at such length on his operation if there was any chance they would be released. Or any chance they might escape.

He was telling them that they would never leave Wild Horse Lake.

Stroud threw a party that night. He invited all the members of the other gangs headquartered at Wild Horse Lake. By eight o'clock, some twenty people were jammed into the big cabin.

The announced purpose of the shindig was celebration of still another profitable horse raid. Yet it was apparent to all who attended that Stroud was eager to show off his captives, the Fontaines. Or as he insisted on referring to them in a loud, boastful manner: The Actors.

Jugs of whiskey were liberally dispensed to the revelers. Stroud and the other gang leaders were seated at the head of the long dining table, the position of honor. Their followers were left to stand for the most part, though some took seats on the bunks. The party steadily became more boisterous as they swilled popskull liquor.

One of Stroud's men whanged away on a Jew's harp. With the metal instrument clamped between his teeth, he plucked musical tones that were surprisingly melodious. A member of another gang was no less proficient on a harmonica, and the sounds produced on the mouth organ complemented those from the Jew's harp. They soon had the cabin rollicking with sprightly tunes.

Fontaine felt like he was attending some mad festivity hosted by an ancient feudal lord. The only difference in his mind was that the men were armed with pistols rather than broadswords and crossbows. Somewhat sequestered, he stood watching with Lillian and Chester by the woodstove as liquor flowed and the party got rowdier. He sensed they were about to become the court jesters of Wild Horse Lake.

Not quite an hour into the revelry Stroud rose to his feet. His face was flushed with whiskey and his mouth stretched wide in a drunken grin. He pounded on the table with a thorny fist until the Jew's harp and the harmonica trailed off in a final note. The crowd fell silent.

"I got a treat for you boys," he said with a broad gesture directed at the Fontaines. "These here folks are professional actors, come all the way from Dodge City.

Song and dance and, believe it or not, Shakespeare!"

Monte Dunn, the leader of a band of robbers, guffawed loudly. He was lean, the welt of an old scar across his eyebrow, with muddy eyes and buttered hair. He gave Stroud a scornful look.

"Shakespeare?" he said caustically. "Who the hell wants to hear Shakespeare? Ain't no swells in this bunch."

Stroud glowered at him. "Don't gimme none of your bullshit, Monte. This here's my show and I'll run it any damn way I see fit. Got it?"

"Don't get your bowels in an uproar. I was just sayin' it ain't my cup of tea."

"Like it or lump it, you're gonna hear it."

Stroud nodded to Fontaine, motioning him forward. Fontaine walked to a cleared area at the end of the table and bowed with a grandiose air. "For your edification," he said, glancing about the room, "I shall present the most famous passage from *Julius Caesar*."

The outlaws stared back at him with blank expressions. The thought crossed his mind that he might as well be a minister preaching to a congregation of deaf imbeciles. Yet he knew that his audience was Stroud alone, a man with the power of life and death. His eloquent baritone lifted with emotion.

Friends, Romans, countrymen, lend me your ears;
I come to bury Caesar, not to praise him.
The evil that men do lives after them,
The good is oft interred with their bones;
So let it be with Caesar . . .

Fontaine labored on to the end of the soliloquy. When he finished, the crowd swapped baffled glances, as though he'd spoken in Mandarin Chinese. But Stroud laughed and pounded the table with hearty exuberance. "You hear that!" he whooped. "That there's art!"

No one appeared to share the sentiment. Chester was the next to perform, accompanied by the Jew's harp and the harmonica. He went into a soft-shoe routine, which was made all the more effective by the sandpaper scrape of his soles against dirt on the floor. He shuffled in place, executed a few lazy whirls, and ended with legs extended and arms spread wide. The outlaws whistled and hooted their approval.

Lillian was to close with a song. She asked the men on the Jew's harp and harmonica if they knew the ballad *Molly Bawn*. When they shook their heads, she suggested they follow her lead and try to catch the melody as she went along. She moved to the end of the table, hands folded at her waist, and avoided the leering stares of a crowd now gone quiet. Her husky alto flooded the room.

Oh, Molly Bawn, why leave me pining,
All lonely, waiting here for you?
The stars above are brightly shining,
Because they've nothing else to do.
The flowers so gay were keeping,
To try a rival blush with you;
But Mother Nature set them sleeping,
Their rosy faces washed with dew.
Oh, Molly Bawn! Oh, Molly Bawn!

The ballad ended on a heartrending note. There was a moment's silence; then the outlaws rocked the cabin with applause and cheers. Stroud looked proud enough to bust his buttons, grinning and nodding until the commotion died down. He climbed to his feet.

"Listen here, Lilly," he said expansively. "Let's give these boys a real show. What say?"

"I don't understand," Lillian said.

"That old rag you're wearin' don't do you justice. Go change into one of them pretty silk gowns. The ones I saw in your trunk."

"Now?"

"Yeah, right now," Stroud said. "Get dolled up and come give us another song."

Lillian looked at Fontaine, who shrugged helplessly. She turned away from the table, unwilling to anger Stroud, and moved toward the door, As she went out, the Jew's harp twanged and the harmonica chimed in on *The Tenderfoot*. The men poured a fresh round of drinks, clapping in time to the music.

"Good-lookin' gal," Monte Dunn said, glancing at Stroud. "How'd you like to sell that little buttercup, Rufe? I'd pay you a handsome price."

"What d'you think I am?" Stroud said indignantly. "I don't sell humans like some gawddamn slave trader."

"Well, I don't know why not. You stole her just like you stole them horses out in the corral. You're gonna sell them horses for a profit. Why not her?"

"She ain't for sale."

Dunn laughed. "Hell, anything's for sale. Name a price."

"Monte, you stink up a place worse'n a polecat. Think I'll get myself some fresh air."

Stroud walked to the door. Sally started after him and he waved her off. She'd overheard his conversation with Dunn, and she didn't believe a word of it. She thought he was after more than fresh air.

Outside, Stroud hurried off in the direction of the Fontaines' cabin. A coal-oil lamp lighted the window, and he paused, darting a look over his shoulder, before he opened the door. Lillian was clothed only in her chemise, about to slip into her blue silk gown. She backed away, holding the gown to cover her breasts. He closed the door behind him.

"Well, looky here," he said, advancing on her. "I knew you was hidin' something special under that dress."

"Get out!" Lillian backed up against the wall. "Get out or I'll scream."

"Naw, you ain't gonna scream. That'd bring your pa runnin' and I'd have to kill him."

"Please don't do this, I beg you. I'm not that kind of woman."

"You're my kind of woman," Stroud said, reaching for her. "You and me are gonna have some good times."

Lillian swatted his hand away. "Leave me alone! Don't touch me!"

"I'm gonna do more'n touch you."

The door burst open. Before Stroud could turn, Sally whapped him over the head with a gnarled stick of firewood. The blow drove him to his knees, and he saved himself from falling by planting a hand against the floor. She shook the log in his face.

"You son-of-a-bitch!" she screeched. "You try any strange pussy and I'll cut your balls off. You hear me?"

Stroud wobbled to his feet. "You ought'nt have hit me like that, Sal. I was just talkin' to her, that's all."

"You're a lying no-good two-timin' bastard!"

She shoved him out the door and slammed it behind her. Lillian sat down on the bunk, the gown still clutched to her breasts. Her heart was in her throat, and she had to gulp to get her breath. Yet a small vixenish smile dimpled the corner of her mouth.

She thought Sally really would cut off his balls.

CHAPTER 14

LATE THE next morning, the first of the stolen horses was led to the branding fire. Outside the corral, thick stakes were driven into the ground several feet apart, and laid out near the fire were lengths of heavy-gauge wire and a lip twist. A wooden bucket, with a rag dauber fastened to a stick, was positioned off to the side.

The horse was thrown and the men swarmed over him. Within seconds, his legs, front and rear, were lashed to the stakes. One man held the gelding's head down, while two others kept his hindquarters from thrashing. The fourth man stepped into the fray with the twist. He attached the rope loop to the horse's lower lip, then began twisting it like a tourniquet. The pain, intensifying with every turn, quickly distracted the horse from all else.

Stroud stood watching with Fontaine and Chester. His eyes were bloodshot from last night's party, and his head pounded with a dull hangover. But he was proud of his operation, and he'd invited them to observe the crew in action. He wanted them to see how a stolen horse was transformed into a salable horse.

"Watch close now," he said. "Shorty's a regular brand doctor."

"Pardon me?" Fontaine said, curious despite himself. "A brand doctor?"

"Yeah, somebody that makes a new brand out of the old brand. He's a gawddamn wizard."

Shorty Martin walked to the fire. He studied the brand on the gelding's flank—Bar C—then selected a piece of wire. His hands worked the metal the way a sculptor fashions clay; with a twist here and a curl there, he shaped one end of the wire into a graceful but oddly patterned design. A quick measurement against the old brand apparently satisfied him.

"You gotta pay attention," Stroud urged. "Shorty works fast once't he gets started."

Martin pulled the length of wire, now cherry red, out of the fire. With a critical eye, he positioned the wire and laid it over the old brand. The smell of burnt hair and scorched flesh filled the air, and an instant later he stepped back, inspecting his handiwork. As if by magic, the original C had been transformed into a Δ.

"Ever see the like!" Stroud crowed. "Touch here and a touch there, and we got a Triangle O."

"Amazing," Fontaine said, truly impressed. "Mr. Martin is something of an artist."

Chester's brow furrowed. "I don't mean to question his work, Mr. Stroud. But isn't the burning and the redness something of a tip-off?"

Stroud chuckled. "Keep your eyes peeled, sonny. You're fixin' to see why Shorty's a sure-enough doctor."

Martin hefted the bucket. He stirred the contents, which appeared thick as axle grease and had the faint odor of liniment. Then he turned to the horse, and with a quick stroke of the dauber he spread a dark, pasty layer across the new brand. The entire operation had taken less than five minutes.

"I'm still at a loss," Chester said. "What does that do?"

"Shorty's secret recipe," Stroud announced. "Heals the brand natural as all get-out in a couple of days. Jesus Christ himself couldn't tell it'd ever been worked over."

The gelding was released and choused back into the corral. One of the men roped another horse and led it toward the fire. Fontaine wagged his head.

"I must say, you have it down to a science. Very impressive indeed."

"Tricks of the trade," Stroud said. "Stealin' horses takes a sight of know-how."

"I'm curious," Fontaine said in a musing tone. "How do you sell the rebranded horses?"

"You'll recollect I told you curiosity could get you killed around here."

"I withdraw the question."

"No, come to think of it, what's the difference? You gents are gonna be with us till hell freezes over. It ain't like you'll ever be tellin' anybody."

"I take your point," Fontaine said. "We are, in a manner of speaking, residents of Wild Horse Lake."

"Like I said, you won't be tellin' tales out of school."

Stroud was in an expansive mood. He went on to liken his operation to a thimblerigger's shell game. Several livestock dealers, spread throughout surrounding states and territories, represented the pea under the pod. Every week or so the gang would conduct a raid into Kansas, Colorado, New Mexico, or Texas. The stolen horses were then trailed back to No Man's Land, where the brands were altered with Shorty's magic wire.

The stolen stock, Stroud elaborated, was never sold on home ground. Horses from Kansas were trailed to Colorado and those from Texas to New Mexico. To muddy the waters further, the order of the raids was rotated among the states and territories. Local ranchers were never able to establish any pattern to the random nature of the raids. Yet it was all very methodical, nearly impossible to defend against.

The shell game was played out on many fronts. After being trailed to different locations, never on home ground, the horses were sold by livestock dealers over a widespread area. Usually, there was a mix of altered brands, and to all appearances, the stock had been bought here and there by an itinerant horse trader. In the end, horses stolen in random order were the shells of the game, sold across the breadth of four states. The livestock dealers, the pea under the pod, were known only to Stroud and his gang. Not one had ever been caught selling stolen stock.

"Nothin's foolproof," Stroud concluded, "but this here's mighty damn close. Them horses are scattered to hell and gone, and nobody the wiser."

Fontaine could hardly argue the point. There was a logistical genius to the operation, which virtually eliminated any chance of being detected. Yet Stroud had revealed the inner workings of the scheme with what amounted to a veiled threat. The Fontaines would never leave Wild Horse Lake. Not alive.

Lillian was watching them from the kitchen window. She and the other women were preparing the noon meal, and she wondered why her father and Stroud were involved in such lengthy discussion. As she turned from the window, she saw that Sally had taken a break, seated at the table with a mug of coffee. She decided now was the time.

"May I speak with you?" she asked, moving to the table. "We haven't talked about last night and perhaps we should."

Sally looked at her. "What's on your mind?"

"Well . . ." Lillian seated herself. "I wanted to apologize for what happened. I was as surprised as you were."

"Wasn't any surprise to me. Rufe never could keep his pecker in his pants."

"Do you think he'll try again?"

"Damn sure better not," Sally said evenly. "If he does, I won't stop with his balls. I'll lop his tallywhacker off."

The term was new to Lillian. She considered a moment and suddenly blushed with understanding. Her mother had always referred to that part of a man's anatomy as his "dingus." She mentally committed *tallywhacker* to her vocabulary.

"You sound unsure," she said. "Does he really believe you would—you know . . . do that?"

"Oh, he believes it," Sally said with a wicked smile. "Trouble is, he'd risk it if he caught you off alone somewhere. He knows you'd never talk."

"Why on earth wouldn't I?"

"Did you tell your pa about last night?"

"No . . . I didn't."

"Because you knew he'd get riled and start trouble and Rufe would kill him. That about cover it?"

"Yes."

"Well, dearie, Rufe figures it the same way."

Lillian was silent a moment. She glanced quickly at the kitchen area, to make sure they wouldn't be overheard by the other women. Then, lowering her voice, she took a chance. "Will you help us escape?"

"You're off your rocker!" Sally said, flummoxed by the very thought. "Why would I do a fool thing like that?"

"You know why we were brought here. It has nothing to do with my father or my brother, or with the fact that we're entertainers. It has only to do with me."

"So?"

"So where will it end?" Lillian coaxed her. "Will you kill him when he finally manages to . . . to rape me? Will you kill me just to remove the temptation?"

"You're some piece of work. Either I help you escape, or somebody—you, Rufe, maybe even me—winds up dead. That the general idea?"

"Yes, exactly."

"Wish to hell you'd stayed in Dodge City."

"So you'll help us get away?"

Sally sighed wearily. "I'll think about it . . . no promises."

The cabin was cramped. There was a single bunk, wedged into a corner, and wall pegs for hanging clothes. Last night Fontaine had insisted that Lillian take the bunk while he and Chester made do with pallets on the floor. Yet it was their only haven from Stroud and the gang. The one place they could talk in privacy.

By early afternoon all the horses had been doctored with new brands. Stroud, finally tired by a morning of braggadocio on the stratagems of a horse thief, had dismissed Fontaine and Chester. Lillian helped the women clean up in the kitchen following the noon meal and afterward was left to her own devices as well. The family gathered in the relative security of the cabin.

Fontaine related the details of Stroud's windy discourse on the triumphs of the gang. His tone was one of grudging admiration, and he admitted that the outlaw chieftain had a natural gift for organization. He readily admitted as well that Stroud's garrulous revelations of how the operation worked had come at a high price. They were, for all practical purposes, consigned to spend the rest of their lives at Wild Horse Lake. Stroud would never release them.

"You should have heard him," Chester added, looking at Lillian. "He as much as said he was confiding in us because we would never be able to tell anyone. He would kill us before he'd let that happen."

"Not in those exact words," Fontaine amended. "He has a clever way of issuing a threat without stating it openly. But you are nonetheless correct, Chet. Our lives are at peril."

"I had the feeling that we were being sworn in as members of the gang."

"With the proviso, of course, that anyone who betrays the trust signs his own death warrant. I feel sure Mr. Martin would gladly carry out the sentence."

"Huh!" Chester grunted dismally. "Shorty Martin would kill us just to get this cabin back."

Fontaine nodded. "I daresay you're right."

Lillian listened with growing concern. She desperately wanted to tell them of her conversation with Sally Keogh. But she wondered how to do it without revealing last night's failed assault by Stroud. She decided to shade the truth.

"We may have an ally," she said. "I spoke with Sally this morning. She might help us."

"Oh?" Fontaine inquired. "Help us in what way?"

"To escape."

Fontaine stared at her, and Chester's mouth dropped open. A moment elapsed before Fontaine recovered his composure. "Why in God's name would you ever raise the subject with her? She is Stroud's woman."

"That was exactly the reason," Lillian said with more confidence than she felt. "Sally thinks Stroud is attracted to me and she's worried. She told me so herself."

"One moment." Fontaine stopped her with an upraised palm. "Are you saying she is concerned Stroud would turn her out for you? She would lose his . . . affections?"

"Yes, Papa, that's what I'm saying."

"And she broached the matter with you?"

"Not about the escape," Lillian said evasively. "She expressed her concern that she might lose Stroud. I suggested the way around that was to help us escape. She promised to think about it."

"Extraordinary," Fontaine muttered. "Wouldn't that rather place her in jeopardy with Stroud?"

"Not unless she's caught."

"What if *we're* caught?" Chester interjected. "We already know what Stroud would do to us. He'd kill us!"

Fontaine thought that was only partially true. He suspected Stroud would kill Chester and himself without a moment's hesitation. Lillian, on the other hand, would be spared only to become Stroud's concubine. But all of that might happen anyway, for he'd seen Stroud's covetous attitude toward his daughter. He told himself that escape was their only option.

"Let me understand," he said. "Do you have reason to believe Sally will help us? Did she say anything to that effect?"

"Nothing definite," Lillian admitted. "But I really do believe she will, Papa. She loves Stroud very much."

"Talk about a revolting thought," Chester said. "She certainly has poor taste in men."

Fontaine crossed to the door. He stood staring out at the bleak landscape, trying to puzzle through all of the ramifications. A movement caught his eye and he saw a rider approaching from the northwest. The man rode into the compound, dismounted, and left his horse hitched at the corral. He walked toward the big cabin.

Lost in his own thoughts, Fontaine dismissed the man from mind. Some while later, as the sun dropped steadily westward, he suggested they leave for the main cabin. The women would be preparing supper, he noted, and their appearance would be expected at the dinner table. He cautioned Lillian and Chester to act as normal as possible, particularly around Sally Keogh. The slightest misstep might alert Stroud.

On the way across the compound, they saw Sally stagger around the corner of the cabin. Her lip was split, blood leaking out of her mouth, and her left eye was almost swollen shut. She lurched, all but losing her balance, and managed to recover herself. Lillian rushed forward.

"Sally, my God, what happened?"

"Watch yourself, kiddo," Sally mumbled. "I tried, but it got nasty. Rufe's on a tear."

"He hit you?"

"Slugged me a couple of times. Knocked me flat on my ass."

"That's terrible!" Lillian said angrily. "Why would he hit you?"

"Ed Farley's here," Sally said. "He's always had a thing for me and I thought I could trust him. Turns out I was wrong."

"Wait, you aren't making sense. Who's Ed Farley?"

"Ed's a livestock dealer. He buys all the horses Rufe trails to Colorado."

"And you told him about us?"

Sally, dabbing at her split lip, briefly explained. She'd gotten Farley aside and told him what great entertainers the Fontaines were. She suggested that he buy them from Stroud and make them sign a contract appointing him their manager. She convinced him there was money to be made on the variety circuit.

"Wasn't a bad idea," she concluded. "I figured you could escape lots easier in Colorado than here. Trouble is, Rufe popped his cork and Ed lost his nerve. He told Rufe it was my idea."

Lillian gently touched her arm. "I'm so sorry I got you into this."

"Worry about yourself," Sally warned her. "Rufe's never gonna let you go. He's like a madman."

"Yes, but what about you? Will you be all right?"

"Honey, that's anybody's guess. Rufe knows I'll kill him if he touches you or any other woman. Maybe he'll be cooled down by the time he comes to bed."

Sally tottered off toward her cabin. Fontaine appeared unsettled by what he'd heard. He finally squared his shoulders. "We'll have to have our wits about us tonight. Under the circumstances, we cannot afforded to provoke Stroud."

There was a moment of turgid silence when they entered the cabin. The women busied themselves in the kitchen, their eyes fixed on their tasks. Stroud was seated at the table with Ed Farley and the other gang members. His features were set in a sphinxlike mask.

"Well, here's the actors," he said curtly. "Look'em over real good, Ed. Make me an offer."

Farley was a heavyset man with a full beard. He shook his head. "Rufe, I think I'll stick to horses."

Stroud studied Lillian as if trying to read her mind. His gaze abruptly shifted to Fontaine. "Don't matter which one of you put Sally up to that nonsense. It was a dumb move."

"Yes, it was," Fontaine agreed. "Very foolish indeed."

"I warned you twice about tryin' to escape. There's not gonna be a third time. You follow me?"

"Implicitly, Mr. Stroud."

"You and your fancy words," Stroud said with a tight smile. "Tell you what, actor; let's see you act. Show Ed some of your Shakespeare."

"I would be honored to do so."

Fontaine felt like an organ grinder's monkey. Yet he knew there was no choice but to perform on command. He struck a dramatic pose.

"O, what a rogue and peasant slave am I . . ."

Chapter 15

THE LAKE was molten with sunlight. Stroud stood in the door of the main cabin with a mug of coffee. His gaze was fixed on the corral.

Four men, one of them Ed Farley, were saddling their horses. Farley finished tightening the cinch on his chestnut gelding and spoke to the men. One of them racked back the bolt on the gate while the others swung into the saddle. He led his horse toward the cabin.

"We're ready," he said. "Didn't forget to pay you, did I?"

"That'll be the day," Stroud said with a crooked grin. "You're off to an early start."

"Well, Rufe, I'm not a man of leisure. I've got a ways to go before those horses turn a profit."

"Don't give me no sob stories. You make out like a Mexican bandit."

Farley shrugged. "Guess I've got no complaints."

"Course you ain't." Stroud drained his coffee mug. "Make sure them boys head on back here when the job's done. I don't want'em lollygaggin' around whorehouses and such."

The men choused the stolen horses out of the corral. The herd now included Fontaine's bloodbay gelding and the team that had once pulled the buckboard. One of the men turned the lead horse, while the others circled from behind, and they drove the herd west from the cabins. Farley stepped into the saddle.

"Always good doing business with you, Rufe. See you in about a month."

"I'll be here."

Stroud moved back into the cabin. As the door closed, Farley and the three gang members pushed the herd up the western slope of the basin. Fontaine, watching from the door of his cabin, waited until the horses disappeared over the rim onto the plains. He shook his head with a frown.

"A pity," he said, almost to himself. "They've taken my horse and the buckboard team. We are, quite literally, afoot."

Chester laughed sourly. "Dad, that's how Stroud intended it all along. He knows we're not about to walk out of here."

"Quite so," Fontaine concurred. "Somehow, though, it makes me feel all the more a prisoner. I rather liked that horse."

Lillian was seated on the bunk. "We musn't despair, Papa. There has to be a way."

"Yes, of course, my dear. Spirits bright, for we are nothing without hope. I'm sure we will find a way."

Fontaine tried to sound optimistic. Still, given the circumstances, his spirits had never been lower. Last night, Stroud had made them perform until even the men grew bored. The lengthy show was punishment for their abortive escape attempt and a message as well. Their next attempt to flee would be their last.

For all that, Fontaine saw no alternative. Stroud, before too long, would try to force himself on Lillian. When that happened, Fontaine would resist, as would Chester, and they would both be killed. Even worse, Lillian would be doomed to a life of depravity and unremitting torment. Fontaine thought it preferable, if death was inevitable, to die trying to escape.

Lillian scooted off the bunk. "I think I'll go talk to Sally. Maybe she'll have another idea."

"Be very careful," Fontaine admonished. "We have no way of knowing what transpired overnight. She may report anything you say to Stroud."

"Oh, I doubt that very much, Papa. Not after the way he abused her."

"Exactly the point I'm trying to make. After last night, she may well fear for her own life."

"Don't worry, I'll be careful. I promise."

Lillian stepped out the door. Sally had failed to appear at breakfast that morning, and she was concerned about her. She was no less concerned about a means of escape, for she knew the stalemate with Stroud would not last much longer. Time was running out.

Sally was huddled in the bunk of her cabin. When Lillian entered, a bright shaft of sunlight filled the dim interior. Sally winced, her left eye swollen shut, bruised in a rosette of black and purple, and her lip caked with dried blood. She looked worse than last night.

"Close the door," she said. "I'm a sight not fit to see."

Lillian sat on the edge of the bunk. "I was worried when you didn't come to breakfast. Is there anything I can do to help?"

"No, thanks just the same. Time's the only thing that'll heal what I've got."

"Sometimes I wish I were a man. I'd give him a lesson he wouldn't forget."

"Honey, a half-dozen men sat there last night and watched him beat me. None of them said a damn word."

"Yes, but they're afraid of him."

"And you aren't?"

"Actually, I'm terrified," Lillian admitted. "I didn't sleep a wink worrying he might come for me."

Sally sniffed. "Rufe won't be comin' for you till he kills me. Not that he wouldn't, you understand."

"What happened?"

"I waited for him last night. Minute he got in bed, I put a knife to his throat. Told him if he ever hit me again I'd slit his gullet."

"You didn't!"

"Yeah, I did, too," Sally said hotly. "Told him it was him and me, or nothin'. I won't be thrown over for another woman . . . meanin' you, of course."

"Good heavens," Lillian breathed. "What did he say?"

"Oh, he tried to play lovey-dovey. Longer I held that knife to his throat, the more promises I got. But that don't mean a lot for either you or me."

"Why not?"

Sally went solemn. "Rufe's a born liar, that's why not. He might kill me to get at you." Her voice dropped. "Or he might turn you over to the men . . . just to spite me."

"The men?"

"Toss you to that pack of wolves in the big cabin. Way he thinks, that'd still give him the last laugh."

Lillian paled. She had been too worried about Stroud to conjure an even worse fate. The thought had never occurred to her that she might be forced to submit to the horror of several men, night after night. As she considered it now, she felt queasy and the bitter taste of bile flooded her throat. She silently swore she would kill herself first.

"Do you . . ." She faltered, groping for words. "There has to be some way we can escape from here. Do you know of anything that might have a chance?"

Sally looked defeated. "Wish I did. Trouble is, if I try anything else, Rufe *will* kill me. And it'd all be for nothing. He'd still get you."

"Oh, God, Sally, I feel so helpless."

"Honey, I've felt that way most of my life."

A distant gunshot brought their heads around. Then, in the space of a heartbeat, a rattling volley of gunfire echoed through the basin. Lillian rushed to the window, with Sally only a step behind. Across the way, they saw three columns of horsemen fanning out around Wild Horse Lake. One column was galloping directly toward Stroud's compound.

The attack caught everyone by surprise. Monte Dunn and his men, as well as the gang of cattle rustlers, were lounging in the sunshine outside their cabins. The men tried to put up a fight, but they were overwhelmed by sheer numbers. There appeared to be ten or more horsemen in each column, their pistols popping as they came on at a gallop. The outlaws were cut down in a withering maelstrom of lead.

Stroud ran out of the big cabin as the attack started from the southern rim of the basin. Shorty Martin and the other men followed him outside, guns drawn, their women watching from the door. They opened fire on the column headed toward the cabin, and then, too late, realized they were outnumbered. As they turned back to the cabin, Martin took a slug between the shoulders and pitched to the ground. The other men, riddled, dropped on the doorstep.

A swarm of bullets sizzled all around Stroud. His hat went flying and a slug clipped his bootheel, but somehow, miraculously, he was otherwise unscathed. Some visceral instinct told him he would be killed if he tried to make it into the cabin, and he abruptly gave up the fight. He flung his pistol into the dirt and stopped, still as a statue, his hands high overhead. He waited for a shot in the back, then the gunfire suddenly ceased. The riders reined to a halt before the cabin.

"My God," Lillian whispered. "Who are they?"

Sally swallowed hard. "I think you've just been saved."

"What do you mean?"

"I mean they're wearin' badges."

Capt. Ben Tuttle held court in front of the cabin. He was a large man, with the jaw of a bulldog and eyes the color of dead coals. The star of a Texas Ranger was pinned to his shirt.

Tuttle had been a Ranger for almost twenty years. He'd fought Comanche marauders who raided south of the Brazos and Mexican *banditos* who struck north of the Rio Grande. In his time, he had seen some strange things and yet nothing as strange as what he'd found at Wild Horse Lake. He thought it beggared belief.

The dining table had been brought outside and positioned before the cabin. Tuttle was seated behind the table, having adopted the role of judge and jury in today's hearings. The Rangers, throughout the organization's history, were notorious for dispensing summary justice in the field. Wild Horse Lake was no exception.

There were thirty Rangers in Tuttle's company. In the course of the raid, they had killed nine outlaws without suffering a casualty. They were now guarding the survivors, who were ranked before Tuttle's impromptu courtroom. Stroud waited with Sally and the other women off to one side. Monte Dunn, whose gang had been wiped out, was held with the two cattle rustlers. His left arm dripped blood from a bullet wound.

The Fontaines stood before the bench. Alistair Fontaine had just finished telling their saga of escaping wild Indians only to be taken captive by a band of outlaws. Lillian and Chester had said nothing, merely nodding affirmation as their father related one hair-raising exploit after another. Capt. Ben Tuttle, who knew a whopper when he heard one, considered them with a skeptical eye. He thought it was all a load of hogwash.

"Let me get this straight," he said. "You're being held here prisoner and forced to entertain this bunch, or they'd kill you. That about the gist of it?"

"Indeed so," Fontaine acknowledged. "You and your men were our very salvation. You have delivered us from certain death."

Tuttle scowled. "You never stole a horse, or rustled a cow, or robbed nobody. Have I got it right?"

"Never!" Fontaine intoned. "We are actors."

"And you're from New York City?"

"By way of Abilene and Dodge City."

"And George Armstrong Custer advised you to take the overland route to Denver."

"None other," Fontaine said. "General Custer and his wife Libbie are our very good friends."

Tuttle rolled his eyes. "That's the damnedest story I ever heard."

"Captain, I assure you every word of it is true."

"Your word don't count for much in this neck of the woods. I'll need some proof."

Fontaine assumed a classic profile. " 'O, I have passed a miserable night. So full of ugly sights, of ghastly dreams. That, as I am a Christian faithful man, I would not spend another such a night.' You may recognize a passage from *King Richard the Third.*"

"That ain't exactly proof," Tuttle said cynically. "Any dimdot might memorize himself some Shakespeare."

"Lillian, step forward," Fontaine prompted. "Sing something for the captain, my dear."

"Without music, Papa?"

"A cappella will do quite nicely."

Lillian composed herself. She knew all Texans were former Confederates, and she sang *The Bonnie Blue Flag*. Her clear alto voice finished on a stirring note.

Hurrah, hurrah, for Southern rights, hurrah!
Hurrah for the Bonnie Blue Flag that bears the single star!

"You sing right good," Tuttle complimented her. "Course, that don't mean you're a stage actress. I've heard near as good in a church choir."

"Like hell!" Sally interrupted loudly. "Not unless you're deaf as a post. She's the real article."

Tuttle squinted. "Who might you be?"

"Sally Keogh."

"You a singer, too, are you?"

"I'm his woman," she said, pointing at Stroud. "That's Rufe Stroud, all-round horse thief and woman beater. He abducted these folks, just like they told you."

Stroud blanched with rage. "You gawddamn lyin' bitch! Shut your mouth!"

Tuttle nodded to one of his Rangers. "Teach that rowdy some manners."

The Ranger whacked Stroud upside the jaw with a rifle butt. Stroud went down as though poleaxed, spitting blood and teeth. Tuttle looked pleased with the result.

"Mind your tongue," he said. "I won't have nobody takin' the Lord's name in vain in my courtroom."

"This ain't Texas!" Stroud said, levering himself to his knees. "This here's No Man's Land. You ain't got no . . . no . . ."

"Jurisdiction?"

"Yeah, you ain't got no jurisdiction here. You can't do nothin' to us."

"Don't bet on it," Tuttle said. "Time or two, I've taken jurisdiction across the border into Old Mexico. I reckon No Man's Land ain't no different."

"That's a crock!" Stroud sputtered, his front teeth missing. "You're breakin' the law yourself!"

"Have me arrested." Tuttle turned back to Fontaine. "Appears you folks was tellin' the truth, and this court won't hold you. You're free to go."

"Thank you, Captain."

Fontaine motioned Lillian and Chester away from the table. Tuttle riveted the outlaws with a look. "Rufe Stroud," he said, "we been huntin' you a long time now. Like your woman says, you're a top-notch horse thief."

"Go to hell," Stroud spat through bloody gums. "You ain't got nothin' on me."

"Monte Dunn." Tuttle fixed his gaze on Dunn. "Your name's pretty well known in Texas, too. Heard your description so often I would've knowed you in a crowd."

"You got the wrong man," Dunn blustered. "I never been in Texas in my life."

"There's many a stagecoach driver that would dispute that. You've robbed your last one."

"I'm tellin' you, I'm not your man!"

Tuttle straightened in his chair. "This here court sentences you gents to be hung by the neck till you're dead." He looked at the two cattle rustlers. "You boys are found guilty by the company you keep."

"You sorry sonovabitch!" Stroud roared. "You can't hang us without a trial!"

"Objection overruled." Tuttle got to his feet. "Let's get on with this business. Time's awastin'."

A lone oak tree stood between the cabin and the lake. Within minutes, the four men were bound, mounted on horses, and positioned beneath a stout limb. The Rangers tossed ropes over the limb and snugged them firmly to the trunk of the tree. The nooses were cinched around the necks of the doomed men.

Lillian turned away, unable to watch. Tuttle walked forward, staring up at the men. "You boys got any last words?"

"I do," Stroud said, glowering down at Sally. "Hope you're satisfied, you dumb slut. You got me hung."

"No, Rufe," she said in a teary voice. "You got yourself hung."

Tuttle motioned with his hand. The Rangers cracked the horses across the rumps, and the outlaws were jerked into the air. When the nooses snapped tight, their eyes seemed to burst from the sockets, growing huge and distended. They thrashed and kicked, their legs dancing, as though trying to gain a foothold. A full minute passed before their bodies went limp.

"We're done here," Tuttle called to his Rangers. "Get ready to move out!"

Fontaine was aghast. "Aren't you going to bury them?"

"We rode ten days to catch this bunch. I reckon we'll leave'em as warnin' to anybody that thinks they're safe in No Man's Land."

"I daresay that would be warning enough."

Tuttle studied him a moment. "You still set on headin' for Denver?"

"Yes, we are," Fontaine said. "Why do you ask?"

"Stroud's woman and them other two floozies. We don't take prisoners, specially women. You might want to cart 'em along to Denver."

"Good God!"

"Life's hell sometimes, ain't it?"

Lillian took Sally in her arms. She watched the Rangers mount, forming in a column, and ride out over the southern rim of the basin. In the silence, the creak of rope caught her attention, and she turned, staring at the bodies swaying beneath the tree. The brutal suddenness of it still left her in shock.

She prayed as she'd never prayed before for the bright lights of Denver.

Chapter 16

The Arkansas River brought them at last to Pueblo. They had been on the trail twelve days, and the tale of the journey was told in their appearance. They looked worn and weary, somewhat bedraggled.

Fontaine was mounted astride Rufe Stroud's roan stallion. Beside him, Chester rode the frisky gelding formerly owned by Shorty Martin. They thought it only fitting that they had appropriated the horses of their now-deceased captors. The irony of it had a certain appeal.

The buckboard was drawn by two saddle horses, drafted into service as a team. Lillian drove the buckboard, with Sally seated beside her and the other two women in the rear. Fontaine promised himself that he would never again undertake overland travel with four women. He felt somewhat like the headmaster of a seminary on wheels.

Pueblo was situated in the southern foothills of the Rockies. The surrounding countryside was arid, despite the proximity of the Arkansas River to the town. Eastward lay a vista of broken plains, and to the west towering summits were still capped with snow. The mountains marched northward like an unbroken column of sentinels.

By 1872, Pueblo was the railway center of Southern Colorado. The road into town crossed the Denver & Rio Grande tracks, which extended some ninety miles northward to Denver. Directly past the tracks, Pueblo's main thoroughfare was clogged with wagons and buggies and the boardwalks were crowded with shoppers. The street was jammed with stores, and a block away the new courthouse was under construction. The arrival of the railroad had transformed a once-isolated outpost into a bustling mecca of commerce.

Lillian was all eyes. She hadn't seen anything so civilized since they departed New York almost nine months ago. Abilene, then Dodge City and No Man's Land seemed to her a journey through a wasteland most memorable for its bloodshed and violence. Several times she'd had nightmares about the brutal hangings, bodies dangling with crooked necks beneath a tree limb. She was determined never again to stray far from a city.

Sally asked her to stop as they neared the edge of the business district. She reined the team to a halt by the boardwalk, wondering why Sally wanted to stop short of the uptown area. Over the past twelve days they had become friends, confiding in each other and sharing secrets. She called out to her father and Chester, who rode back to the buckboard. Sally faced them with a sober expression.

"We'll leave you here," she said, nodding to the other women. "We're obliged for everything you've done."

"Why?" Lillian asked, openly surprised. "We've only just arrived."

"You don't want to be seen with the likes of us. Wouldn't do much for your reputation."

"Who cares about reputation? You're as new to Pueblo as we are. How will you manage?"

"Don't worry about us," Sally said with a rueful smile. "We'll do lots better here than we did at Wild Horse Lake."

"I won't hear of it!" Lillian said adamantly. "At least wait until we get settled."

"No, trust me, it's best this way. We'll likely see you before you leave for Denver."

Sally gave her an affectionate hug. Lillian's eyes puddled with tears as the women crawled out of the buckboard. They were poorly dressed, and their belongings, brought from Wild Horse Lake, were hardly any better. She knew they would become prostitutes or, if they were lucky, kept women. She knew as well that Sally was fibbing about getting together. She would never see them again.

The women walked away, Sally waving back over her shoulder. Fontaine waited a moment for Lillian to collect herself, then reined his horse around. Uptown, he quickly surveyed the street and led them toward the Manitou House Hotel. An imposing brick structure, three stories high, the hotel had two bellmen. They wrestled the steamer trunks off the buckboard and carried them inside. Fontaine turned to Chester.

"Lillian and I will register," he said. "Find the nearest livery stable and sell the lot. Horses, buckboard, everything."

"All right," Chester said. "What price should I ask?"

"Take whatever you're offered. I'm happy to say we have completed our last overland expedition. We will travel by train from now on."

"Dad, that sounds good to me. Hope I never see a horse again."

"I devoutly second the motion."

Fontaine engaged a suite on the third floor. After their travails, he informed Lillian, they were due some modicum of comfort. The suite contained a sitting room and two bedrooms, with windows overlooking the street. Lillian would take one bedroom, and Fontaine would share the other one with Chester. He ordered the bellmen to bring corrugated metal tubs for each bedroom and loads of hot water.

Lillian thought it grand enough for royalty. By the time she unpacked her trunk, the tub and hot water arrived. She spent the next hour luxuriating in steamy bliss, unable to remember when she'd been so content. Her very soul seemed encrusted with grime from No Man's Land and the overland trek, and she gave herself over to the cleansing of a good scrub and washing her hair. She stepped from the tub reborn.

Some while later she wandered into the sitting room. She was barefoot, wearing a fluffy robe, her hair wrapped in a towel. Fontaine, already bathed, shaved, and dressed, was attired in a suit he'd had pressed while he was in the tub. He was standing by the windows, staring out over the town, and turned when she entered the room. Before he could speak, Chester came through the door.

"I was becoming concerned," Fontaine said. "What took you so long, Chet?"

Chester grinned, pulling a leather pouch from his coat pocket. He dumped a mound of gold coins on a table by the sofa. "I finally talked them out of three hundred dollars."

"Three hundred!" Lillian yelped excitedly. "We're rich!"

"Bravo, my boy," Fontaine congratulated him. "You obviously have a gift for finance."

"I don't know about that." Chester shrugged modestly. "But I have to say, I enjoyed the dickering. It's fun to get the better of the deal."

"Yes, of course," Fontaine said. "Now, hurry along and have your bath. Lillian will be ready before you are."

"Where are we going?"

"Why, we're off to see the town. I'm looking forward to a decent meal."

Early that evening they emerged from an Italian restaurant recommended by the hotel. Fontaine was impressed by the service and, even more so, the food; they were stuffed on fresh garden salad, beef cannelloni, and a rich assortment of pastries. On the street, Fontaine suggested they have a look at some of Pueblo's variety theaters. He was interested to see what played well in the Rockies.

The sporting district was south of the business center. There, as in most western towns, the stage shows were mingled among saloons and gambling establishments. The largest, and by far the most crowded, was the Tivoli Variety Theater. A barnlike structure, the Tivoli boasted the longest bar in Pueblo, assorted games of chance, and a wide stage at the rear of the room. Fontaine arranged for a table near the orchestra.

A waiter seated them as a magician produced a rabbit from a top hat. Then, playing to the audience, he brought forth a pair of doves from a silk scarf. By the time Fontaine and Chester were served drinks, the headline act, billed as the Ethiopian Minstrels, pranced onstage. The troupe of twelve men, all in blackface, proceeded to rattle their tambourines while they sang and ribbed one another with colorful badinage. Fontaine was fascinated.

"I know this act," he said. "They played many of the theaters we did on the circuit back East."

"By golly, you're right," Chester remarked. "I remember we followed them into Syracuse one time. I forget the name of the theater."

"The Rialto."

Fontaine fell silent. He watched the minstrels clown and trade barbs, but his thoughts seemed elsewhere. His features were a study in concentration, and when the curtain came down, he scarcely bothered to applaud. He looked around at Lillian and Chester with a buoyant expression.

"I've just had a marvelous idea," he said. "Do you recall the roundabout message we got from the owner of the Alcazar Theater in Denver? That we would have to audition before he would consider booking us?"

"Yes, I do," Lillian replied. "You thought it was awfully stuffy of him."

"Well, a better plan occurs to me now. We will make our name here and then storm the gates of Denver."

"You mean . . . here . . . in Pueblo?"

"Exactly!"

"Oh, Papa, I so wanted to go on to Denver. Libbie Custer said it is absolutely cosmopolitan."

"Think a moment, my dear," Fontaine said earnestly. "We haven't yet made our name on the Western circuit. A short time here and we enter Denver with headliner billing."

"Listen to him," Chester encouraged her. "Pueblo may not be cosmopolitan, but it's the right place to start.

We need good notices going into Denver."

"No question of it!" Fontaine said vigorously. "We will make them *beg* for The Fontaines!"

Lillian knew she'd been outvoted. However disappointing, her father was wise in the ways of the theater. Pueblo really was the place to start.

Denver would have to wait.

Late the following morning they returned to the Tivoli. Bartenders were busy stocking the shelves, and one of them pointed toward the rear. The office was off to one side of the stage.

Nate Varnum, the owner, was a sparrow of a man. He was short and slight, with thinning hair and a reedy voice. At their knock, he invited them into the office and offered them seats. Fontaine went straight to the point.

"Mr. Varnum, I'm quite confident you are familiar with The Fontaines. We have been a headline act back East for many years."

"No, can't say as I am," Varnum commented. "How'd you wind up in Pueblo?"

"We decided to come West," Fontaine said evasively. "Naturally, we've heard a good deal about you and your theater. All of it quite complimentary, I might add."

"Hottest spot in town, that's for sure."

"And the very reason we are here. I see by the billboard that the Ethiopian Minstrels are closing tonight."

Varnum grimaced. "You know Foster and Davis, the comedy act?"

"Indeed we do," Fontaine said. "They were on the undercard when we played the Orpheum in New York."

"Well, they were supposed to open tomorrow night. But I got a wire from Burt Tully, he owns the Alcazar in Denver. Davis dropped dead last night in the middle of the act. Heart attack."

"I am most distressed to hear that, Mr. Varnum. Phil Davis was a consummate performer."

"Well, anyway, your timing's good," Varnum said. "I need an act and you pop up out of nowhere. What is it you folks do, exactly?"

Fontaine explained the nature of their show. Varnum listened, his birdlike features revealing very little. He gave them a pensive look when Fontaine finished.

"I'll have to see it," he said. "We're not open for business till noon. You got any objection to doing it now?"

"Not at all, my dear fellow. We would be delighted, absolutely delighted."

Varnum led them out to the theater. He was a middling piano player and offered to accompany Lillian. She sang *Wondrous Love* as her opening number, and then Fontaine delivered a soliloquy from *Hamlet*. Working as an ensemble, they next performed the melodrama *A Husband's Vengeance*. Lillian closed the show with an evocative rendition of *Molly Bawn*.

On the last note, Varnum smiled at her, nodding his approval. He swung around on the piano stool, facing Fontaine and Chester, who were seated at one of the tables. His expression was neutral.

"Lillian's a natural," he said. "Great voice, good looks, lots of emotion. Anybody ever think of calling her Lilly?"

"Yes, they have," Lillian said, descending a short flight of stairs beside the stage. "I was billed that way at our last two engagements."

"Good, that's what we'll use." Varnum rose from the piano stool. "Now, let's talk about your material. You can hold an audience only so long with love ballads. Don't you know any snappy tunes?"

"I usually sing selections similar to what you heard."

"Little lady, you have to be versatile to get to the top. So let me put it another way. Do you want to be a star?"

"Mr. Varnum, if you please," Fontaine interrupted. "My daughter will not lower herself to the vulgarian."

"Hush, Papa," Lillian said sharply. "Let him talk."

Fontaine was stunned into silence by her tone. Varnum glanced from one to the other, then turned to Lillian. He spread his hands in a conciliatory gesture.

"I don't mean dirty stuff," he said. "I'm talking about songs with some spirit, a little oomph. You want to leave the audience feeling good. End it on an upnote."

"Could you give me an illustration?"

"How about *Buffalo Gals*? Or maybe *Sweet Betsy from Pike*? Do you know songs like that?"

"Yes, I know them."

"Well?"

Lillian considered it, slowly nodded. "I could open the show with a ballad and close with something more lively. Would that work?"

"You bet it would!"

"Then it's settled."

"Not just exactly." Varnum's gaze swung around to Fontaine. "Lilly's fine and the melodrama ought to play well. But I can't use the Shakespeare."

Fontaine stiffened. "May I ask why not?"

"Shakespeare's too highbrow for our crowd. They want to be entertained."

"For your information, Shakespeare has been entertaining audiences for almost three hundred years. I rather think it will play well in your . . . establishment."

"Don't try to teach me my business, Fontaine. I said it's out and that's final. No Shakespeare."

"Then we've wasted your time," Lillian said forcefully. "Our act is as you've seen it, Mr. Varnum. All or nothing."

"There's no place for you in Pueblo but the Tivoli. I doubt the other joints would even take the melodrama."

"Yes, but that leaves you without a headliner tomorrow night . . . doesn't it?"

"You'd do that to save ten minutes of Shakespeare?"

"I believe I just have."

Varnum clenched his teeth. "You're tougher than you look, Lilly. I'll give you fifty a week for the whole act."

"A hundred," Lillian countered. "Not a penny less."

"You know, it's a good thing you sing as well as you do. Otherwise the whole bunch of you would be out on the street. All right, a hundred it is."

"Thank you very much, Mr. Varnum."

Arrangements were made for Lillian to rehearse with the orchestra the next morning. Then, after a cursory round of handshakes, Fontaine stalked out of the theater. Lillian and Chester followed along, and they turned back toward the hotel. Fontaine let go a bitter laugh.

"Shakespeare has no currency with our new employer. As he said, it is a good thing you sing so well, my dear."

"Oh, Papa," Lillian said, taking his arm. "You'll be just wonderful, wait and see. You always are."

"To quote the Bard," Fontaine replied. " 'When he had occasion to be seen, he was but as the cuckoo in

June. Heard, not regarded.' I am about to become the cuckoo of Pueblo."

Fontaine began drinking that afternoon. The more he drank, the more his perception of things became clear. He realized that, but for Lillian's voice, they would not open at the Tivoli tomorrow night. Even more, he toyed with the idea that the West was no place for a thespian and thought perhaps it was true. He felt as though he'd lost control of some essential part of his life and wondered where and how. By early evening, he was too drunk to stand.

Chester put him to bed shortly before seven o'clock. Lillian was waiting when he returned, seated on the sofa. Her features were taut with worry, and she looked on the verge of tears. She waited until he sat down.

"I feel like I'm responsible. Why didn't I let Father deal with Varnum? He must resent me terribly."

"No, you're wrong," Chester said. "It's something else entirely."

"What?"

"You're the only thing keeping this act together. Varnum was right when he said we'd be out on the street except for you. Dad finally saw it for himself today."

"Oh, that simply isn't true! I don't believe it for a minute."

"Yeah, it was true in Abilene and Dodge City, and it's true here. Like it or not, you'd better get used to the idea. You're the star of the show."

A tear rolled down Lillian's cheek. Her father was so proud and dignified, so defined by his years in the theater. A Shakespearean who had devoted his life to his art. She swore herself to an oath.

She wouldn't let him become the cuckoo of Pueblo.

Chapter 17

A TEAM of acrobats gyrated around the stage. The Tivoli was packed for the opening night of the new headliners. Handbills had been plastered around town and an advertisement had appeared in the *Pueblo Sentinel.* The boldest line left no question as to the star of the show:

LILLY FONTAINE & THE FONTAINES

Lillian waited in the wings. She watched the acrobats as she prepared to go on with her opening number. Her hair was stylishly arranged in a chignon, and overnight she'd sponged and pressed her gowns. She looked radiant, her checks flushed with excitement.

Yet, appearances aside, she was worried. The Tivoli was the largest theater they'd played since leaving New York, and hopefully, their entrée to bigger things in Denver. Her father had read the ad in the newspaper and passed it along with no comment whatever about his second billing. She was deeply troubled by his silence.

The audience rewarded the acrobats with modest applause. The curtains swished closed as they bounded into the wings, and Lillian moved to center stage. As the curtains opened, she stood bathed in the glow of the footlights, and the orchestra segued into *We Parted By*

The River Side. Her voice sent a hush through the crowd.

The lyrics told the story of lovers biding fond adieu until they could be reunited. Lillian sang the ballad with ardent emotion, her eyes lingering here and there on members of the audience. Down front, seated at separate tables, she noticed two men dressed in frock coats and expensive silk cravats. Their attire set them apart from the other men in the crowd.

On the last note of the ballad, the audience exploded with applause. She bowed her way offstage, aware that the two well-dressed men were on their feet, trying to outclap one another. Her father was waiting in the wings, dressed in costume for *Macbeth,* and she gave him an encouraging kiss on the cheek. She smelled liquor on his breath.

Fontaine walked to center stage. He had been nipping at whiskey all day, and it had taken the edge off his hangover from last night. The liquor had dulled his dismal mood as well, for he was still unsettled by the ad in the morning newspaper. But he was determined that his sudden demotion to a supporting role would not affect his performance. His voice boomed out over the theater.

Tomorrow, and tomorrow, and tomorrow,
Creeps in this petty pace from day to day,
To the last syllable of recorded time;
And all our yesterdays have lighted fools
The way to dusty death. Out, out, brief candle!
Life's but a walking shadow, a poor player
That struts and frets his hour upon the stage,
And then is heard no more; it is a tale

Told by an idiot, full of sound and fury,
Signifying nothing. . . .

Lillian was overcome with emotion. Her eyes teared as she watched from the wings, never prouder of him than at this moment. She prayed there would be no catcalls or jeers from the crowd, and her eyes quickly scanned the theater. The two men she'd noted before, seated close to the stage, were following the performance with respectful interest. She got the impression that the audience, though restless, was looking to the men to set the example.

After a moment, she hurried backstage. She'd been given a tiny dressing room, and she began changing into her costume for the melodrama. She hung her teal gown on a hanger and slipped into the clinging cotton frock she would wear as a love-stricken young maiden. As she was brushed her hair to shoulder length, one of the chorus girls stopped in the doorway. Her name was Lulu Banes.

"Sweetie, I hafta tell you," she said with a bee-stung smile. "You got a real nice set of pipes."

"Why, thank you, Lulu."

Lillian had met her at rehearsal earlier in the day. Some of the chorus girls kept their distance, waiting to see if Lillian thought herself a prima donna. But Lulu was bubbly and outgoing, and they'd immediately hit it off. Lillian looked at her now in the mirror.

"Do you really think the audience enjoyed it?"

"Are you kiddin'?" Lulu said brightly. "You had those jokers eating out of your hand. They love you!"

"Oh, I hope so." Lillian paused with her hairbrush. "Did you see those nicely dressed gentlemen down near the front? The ones who look like bankers?"

"Spotted them, did you? That's Jake Tallant and Hank Warner, the biggest ranchers in these parts. And, sweetie, they're both rich as Midas!"

"I thought the crowd was watching them with unusual interest. Now I know why."

"No, that's not it," Lulu said archly. "Everybody was waiting to see which one pulled a gun. The crowd probably had bets down."

"Are you serious?" Lillian asked. "Do they dislike each other that much?"

"Hate would be more like it. Those two have been fighting a range war for almost a year. They're sworn enemies."

"Well, I must say I'm surprised. They look so refined."

"Not so refined they wouldn't shoot one another. They're on their good behavior tonight."

The stage manager called Lillian. She joined her father and Chester onstage for the melodrama *The Dying Kiss*. During the performance, she kept sneaking peeks at the two ranchers and found it difficult to concentrate on her lines. They were both handsome in their own way, one dark and the other fair, their mustaches neatly trimmed. She thought it a shame they were enemies.

The crowd applauded politely at the end of the melodrama. A juggler kept them entertained while Lillian rushed backstage and changed into her royal blue gown. She had rehearsed a new number most of the afternoon, and when the curtain opened her demeanor was totally changed. Hands on her hips, she gave the audience a saucy look as the orchestra launched into a sprightly melody. She belted out the tune.

Oh, don't you remember sweet Besty from Pike
Crossed the great mountains with her lover Ike
With two yoke of oxen, a large yellow dog
A tall Shanghai rooster and one spotted hog!

The lyrics about Betsy and Ike became suggestive, though never openly risqué. Lillian danced about the stage, with a wink here and a sassy grin there. She was enjoying herself immensely, and the audience, caught up in her performance, began clapping in time to the music. She ended with a pirouette, revealing a dainty ankle, her arms spread wide. The crowd went wild.

Lillian took four curtain calls. Finally, with the audience still cheering, she waved and skipped into the wings. Fontaine and Chester, along with Nate Varnum and the rest of the cast, were waiting backstage and broke out in applause. Her features were flushed with the thrill of it all—the freedom of letting go with a snappy, foot-stomping number—and she threw herself into her father's arms. His eyes were misty with pride.

"You were magnificent," he said softly. "How I wish your mother could have seen you tonight."

"Do you think she would have liked it, Papa?"

"My dear, she would have adored it."

A waiter appeared from the stairs by the stage. He nodded to Lillian. "Ma'am," he said formally. "Mr. Jacob Tallant sends his compliments. He requests you have champagne with him at his table."

A second waiter appeared. "Miss Lillian," he said, beaming. "Mr. Henry Warner extends his most sincere congratulations. He's asked you to join him and celebrate with champagne."

"Good God!" Varnum howled. "You can't pick one over the other, Lilly. We'll have a riot on our hands!"

Lillian shrugged. "Perhaps I should accept both invitations. The three of us could share a bottle of champagne."

"Never work," Varnum told her. "Jake Tallant and Hank Warner at the same table would be like lighting the fuse on a powder keg. They'd kill one another."

Fontaine stepped forward. "May I make a suggestion, my dear?"

"Yes, of course, Papa."

"There is no reason for you to become involved in other people's problems. Politely refuse both invitations."

"That'll work," Varnum quickly added. "Gets them off the premises without a fight. Smart thinking, Fontaine."

"You should read the Bard," Fontaine said with a mocking smile. "His plays are a treatise on the art of masterful scheming."

Lillian turned to the waiters. "Please inform Mr. Tallant and Mr. Warner that I decline their invitations—with sincere regrets."

Varnum heaved a sigh of relief. "Thank God."

"No, old chap," Fontaine reminded him. "Thank Shakespeare."

The *Pueblo Sentinel* gave the show rave notices. Fontaine and Chester were mentioned in passing, but Lillian was the centerpiece of the review. The editor rhapsodized at length on her voice, her stage presence, and her ethereal beauty. As though anointing a saint, he dubbed her the Colorado Nightingale.

Fontaine read the paper over breakfast. He'd arranged with the hotel to have room service in the suite every morning. The waiter brought the paper along with a serving cart loaded with eggs, ham, fluffy buttermilk biscuits, and coffee. The article was on the bottom fold of the front page.

Lillian wandered into the sitting room, still dressed in her robe and nightgown. Her face was freshly scrubbed, and her hair, cascading about her shoulders, was lustrous and tawny. Fontaine never ceased to marvel that she had the gift of awakening so exquisitely attractive that it took a man's breath. She was her mother's daughter.

Chester, who had finished reading the article, was slathering butter on a biscuit. He looked up as Lillian poured herself a cup of coffee. "Here she is," he said with a broad grin. "The Colorado Nightingale."

"Chet, really, it's too early for jokes."

"No joke," he said, spearing a hunk of ham with his fork. "Have a look at the paper."

Lillian sat down on the sofa. She placed her cup on the table and scanned the newspaper article. Then she read it again, more slowly. Her expression was pensive.

"Well, it's very nice," she said, folding the paper. "But I wasn't *that* good."

"Indeed you were," Fontaine corrected her. "I believe adding a number with quicker tempo inspirited your performance. You've found your true mêtier, my dear."

"Oh, Papa!" Her face was suddenly suffused with joy. "I'm so happy you think so. I felt so . . . so alive."

Fontaine nodded. "There is no question you held the audience enthralled. They would have listened to you sing all night."

"Why not!" Chester said, grinning around a mouthful of biscuit. "She's the Colorado Nightingale."

"I rather like it," Fontaine observed. "There's a certain ring to it, and it's catchy. Not to mention the metaphoric symmetry—the nightingale."

Lillian laughed. "I only wish it were true. I'd love to sound like a nightingale."

"Never underestimate yourself," Fontaine said, wagging his finger. "You have a lovely voice, and a range few singers ever attain. I see no limit to your career."

Lillian felt a stab of pain. She knew he was speaking as her father, and the pride was evident in his voice. Yet the newspaper article had scarcely mentioned his name or Chester's, and she sensed her father's hurt, the wound to his dignity. She sensed as well that she could offer no comfort, nothing to soothe his hurt. Anything she said would only make it worse.

"Aren't you going to eat?" Chester asked, buttering another biscuit. "A singer needs to keep up her strength. We're sure to pack the house tonight."

"Oh, nothing for me," Lillian said. "I'm having lunch with Lulu Banes. She's such a nice girl."

"Yes, I thought so, too," Fontaine remarked. "She struck me as a cut above the other girls. I'm delighted you've found a friend."

"She's really quite—"

A knock sounded at the door. Fontaine rose, crossed the room, and opened it to find a bellman in the hallway. The bellman gave him a sheepish smile.

"Sorry to bother you, Mr. Fontaine. We've got sort of a problem."

"Yes?"

"Well, sir, there's two cowhands downstairs. One sent here by Jake Tallant and the other from Hank Warner."

"How does that concern me?"

"Not you, your daughter," the bellman said nervously. "They've both got horses for Miss Fontaine."

Fontaine frowned. "Horses?"

"Yessir, outside on the street. Appears like Mr. Tallant and Mr. Warner both sent your daughter a present. Couple of real nice horses."

"One from each, is that it?"

"Yessir, and those cowhands are down there fit to fight. I mean to say, both of them showing up with horses at the same time. They're hot under the collar."

"Wait here a moment, young man."

Fontaine turned back into the suite. He looked at Lillian with a wry smile. "I believe you are being courted, my dear. Did you hear what was said?"

Lillian walked to the window. Fontaine and Chester followed, and they stared down at the street. Outside the hotel were two cowhands, studiously trying to ignore each other. One held the reins of a glossy sorrel gelding and the other those of a chocolate-spotted pinto mare.

"Horses!" Lillian said uncertainly. "What kind of gift is that?"

"Hardly the question," Fontaine advised. "More to the point, do you wish to accept gifts from men you've never met—albeit admirers?"

"No, I don't," Lillian said, after a moment's thought. "I think it would be inappropriate."

"Quite so."

Fontaine returned to the door. "If you will be so kind," he said to the bellman. "Inform the gentlemen downstairs that Miss Fontaine declines the gifts. They may so advise Mr. Tallant and Mr. Warner."

"Yessir, Mr. Fontaine," the bellman replied. "I'll tell'em just what you said."

"Thank you so much."

Lillian was flattered but nonetheless embarrassed. Chester attempted to josh with her about her new beaux, and she went to her bedroom. She stayed there the rest of the morning, emerging shortly before noon in a fitted cotton dress and carrying a parasol. She smiled at her father.

"I'm going to meet Lulu for lunch, Papa."

"Enjoy yourself, my dear."

"Take care, little sister," Chester called out. "Don't talk to men with strange horses."

"I wonder that I talk to you, Chester Fontaine!"

Lillian slammed the door. She was still steaming when she joined Lulu at a restaurant some ten minutes later. After a waiter took their orders, she told Lulu about the horses and how upset she was by the entire affair. Lulu was of a different opinion.

"Sugar, you ought to count your blessings. I wish I had those two scamps after me."

"Oh, honestly!" Lillian said. "Whoever heard of offering a lady *horses?* Everyone in town will be talking!"

"Who cares?" Lulu scoffed. "If they're wearing a skirt, they're just jealous. They'd give their eyeteeth to catch Jake Tallant or Hank Warner."

"Money isn't everything."

"A good-looking man with money is *definitely* everything. Take my word for it, sweetheart."

Lillian was silent a moment. "Tell me about them, will you? Why are they such enemies?"

Lulu quickly warmed to the subject. Jake Tallant was a widower, with two children, who owned an enormous ranch on the south side of the Arkansas River. Hank Warner, a bachelor, owned an equally large cattle spread on the north side of the river. For years, they had disputed water rights where the river curled through their separate spreads. Then, just within the last year, it had developed into a range war.

"I don't know all the details," Lulu concluded. "Something to do with one of those old Spanish land grants. You'd think either one had enough land for one man."

"How did the range war start?"

"Warner sued Tallant in court, and don't ask me what for. All that legal stuff makes me dizzy."

"How rich are they?"

"Sugar, they've both got more money than God!"

Lillian vaguely wondered why she'd even asked the question. She was still somewhat offended by the incident with the horses. Lulu finally uttered a sly laugh. "One thing's for sure."

"Oh?"

"Those two aren't through with you yet. The game has just started."

"What game?"

"Why, the game to see who wins your favor. You're the prize."

Lillian sniffed. “I have no intention of being anyone’s prize.”

“We’ll see.”

“What do you mean by that?”

Lulu smiled. “Get ready for the whirlwind, sugar. It’s headed your way.”

Chapter 18

THE FONTAINES' second night at the Tivoli was standing-room-only. The crowd spilled out of the theater into the barroom and onto the street. Everyone wanted to see the Colorado Nightingale.

Jake Tallant and Hank Warner were again seated at tables in the front row. Neither of them appeared in the least daunted by the unceremonious refusal of their gifts. Their eyes were glued to Lillian every moment she was onstage.

Bouquets of wildflowers from both men were delivered backstage following the show. There were cards with the flowers, the script tactfully phrased, requesting the honor of calling on Lillian. She was flattered by their perseverance but again declined the invitations. Still, she considered flowers a more appropriate gift than horses. She put them in a vase in her dressing room.

The next morning she awoke expecting some new enticement to appear at the hotel. She was oddly disappointed when nothing was delivered to the suite and no messages were left at the desk. There was something titillating about being courted by suitors who were not only handsome but also enormously wealthy. She wondered if she had offended them by her seeming lack of interest. She wondered even more why she cared.

Early that afternoon there was a knock at the door. Chester admitted a man who wore the dog collar of a minister and, in fact, introduced himself as the Reverend Buford Blackburn. He was portly, with a thatch of hair the color of a pumpkin and the ever-ready smile of a preacher. His manner indicated that he was the very soul of discretion.

Fontaine was seated in an easy chair, reading the paper. Lillian came out of her bedroom, curious as to who might be calling. Chester ushered the minister into the sitting room and performed the introductions. There was an awkward moment while everyone got themselves arranged, Fontaine and Blackburn in overstuffed chairs and Lillian and Chester on the sofa. Fontaine opened the conversation.

"Well now, Reverend, a man of God is always welcome in our humble abode. To what do we owe the pleasure?"

"I am here on a mission," Blackburn ventured in an orotund voice. "One might say at the behest of Jacob Tallant and Henry Warner."

"Indeed?" Fontaine arched an eyebrow. "I take it this has to do with my daughter."

"Mr. Fontaine, I am the pastor of the First Methodist Church. Jake Tallant and Hank Warner are among my most loyal and devoted parishioners. They have asked me to act as their emissary."

"In what regard?"

"A truce keeper," Blackburn said with a small shrug. "Jake and Hank are fine, honorable men, true servants of Christ. Unfortunately, they are also the bitterest of enemies."

"So we are told," Fontaine allowed. "And what, precisely, is your mission with respect to Lillian?"

"These gentlemen hold your daughter in the highest esteem. They wish to call on her, and I am here to plead their case."

"A jolly plot indeed, Reverend. Shakespeare might have written it himself."

Blackburn smiled. "These are men of honorable intentions. In the most formal sense of the word, they wish to court your daughter."

"I see," Fontaine said. "Perhaps your remarks should be addressed to Lillian. She is, after all, the purpose of your mission."

"Yes, of course." Blackburn turned to her with a benign expression. "Miss Fontaine, let me assure you most earnestly that Mr. Tallant and Mr. Warner are sincere in their admiration of you. They wish only to be given the opportunity to call on you in person."

Lillian felt like hugging herself. She was all the more flattered that the men had sent a minister as their emissary. Their persistence as well spoke to the matter of sincerity and a guileless, rather unaffected admiration. Yet she was still wary.

"May I be frank, Reverend?" She waited until he nodded. "I understand Mr. Tallant and Mr. Warner are involved in what's known as a 'range war.' I have no interest in associating with violent men."

"Your fears are unjustified, Miss Fontaine. The range war you speak of is being fought in a court of law. Nothing of a violent nature has occurred."

"Everyone I've spoken with believes they might shoot one another on a moment's notice. You said yourself they are the bitterest enemies."

"And so they are," Blackburn conceded. "But these men are good Christians, and despite their differences, neither of them has resorted to violence. I have utmost confidence they will settle the matter in a peaceful fashion."

Lillian considered a moment. "Very well," she said at length. "You may tell them I will be most happy to have them call on me. You might also tell them of my aversion to violent men."

"I shall faithfully follow your wishes, Miss Fontaine."

"How will I decide which one to see first?"

"Oh, yes, that is a problem," Blackburn confessed. "Neither of them would want to feel slighted."

"That's simple enough," Chester broke in with an amused laugh. "Draw straws for the lucky man."

"Bully!" Blackburn exclaimed in quick agreement. "Certainly no one could object to a random draw."

Fontaine thought the Bard would have written it as a farce. Lillian went along, even though she felt somewhat the object of a lottery. Rev. Buford Blackburn, intent on his mission, would have agreed to anything short of blasphemy. A cleaning maid provided the broom straws.

Jake Tallant, his luck running strong, won the draw.

Lillian bought a new dress for the occasion. She was a perfect size 4, and the clerk at Mendel's Mercantile was delighted with her patronage. By now, she was something of a celebrity, and virtually every man in Pueblo knew her on sight. Her visit to the store caused a minor sensation.

The fabric of the dress was sateen, snugly fitted to complement her figure. Her black pearls against the dove gray material made the outfit all the more spectacular. Her hair was upswept and she wore a hat adorned with feathers the color of her dress. She looked stunning.

Tallant called for her at six o'clock. The plan was to have an early get-acquainted dinner and deliver her to the theater in time for the eight o'clock curtain. Fontaine and Chester greeted the rancher with cordiality and made small talk until Lillian swept into the sitting room. Her entrance, Fontaine wryly noted, was staged for maximum effect.

The restaurant Tallant chose was the finest in Pueblo. With impeccable service and an atmosphere of decorum, it was where men of influence and wealth took their wives for a night out. The tables were covered with linen, appointed with crystal and silver and the finest china. The owner greeted Tallant effusively, bowing to Lillian, and personally escorted them to their table. A waiter materialized with menus.

Lillian was charmed by all the attention. Tallant was a man of impressive bearing with a leonine head of dark hair, somewhere in his early thirties. His features were angular, set off by a sweeping mustache, and he wore a tailored charcoal suit with a patterned cravat. His manner was soft-spoken, though commanding, and he was gentlemanly in an old-world sort of way. She thought he was even more handsome up close.

Over dinner, he tried to draw her out about her life in the theater. She entertained him with a brief but amusing account of her adventures in the West. Ever so deftly, she then turned the conversation to his life and interests. He quietly explained that he was a widower and that his wife, a woman of Mexican heritage, had died of influenza just over a year ago. He had two children, a son and a daughter, ages nine and ten.

"How wonderful you had children," Lillian said, trying for a cheerful tone. "You have something of your wife in them. I'm sure they're adorable."

"Yeah, they're a pair," Tallant said proudly. "I'd like you to meet them sometime. Maybe you could come to Sunday dinner."

"I think that would be very nice."

"Don't let Hank Warner sour you on the idea. He won't have anything good to say about me."

"Oh?" Lillian was momentarily flustered by his directness. "You apparently know I'm having dinner with Mr. Warner tomorrow night."

"Reverend Blackburn told me," Tallant said with a faint smile. "He's keeping us both informed."

"Yes, I can understand that he would. He's very concerned about the difficulty between you and Mr. Warner."

"Well, that's a long story. Not a pretty one, either."

Lillian sensed he was dying to tell his version. She thought he'd raised Hank Warner's name for that very reason. Tonight was his night to impress on her the justness of his cause and the strength of his character. With only a little coaxing, she got him talking. She found it a fascinating story.

All land north of the Rio Grande had been ceded to the United States following the 1846 war with Mexico. By the Treaty of Guadalupe Hidalgo, the U.S. government agreed to respect the holdings of Mexican landowners. Yet the title to all property in the ceded zone had evolved from ancient land grants; the issue of who owned what was clouded by a convoluted maze of documents. To compound the problem, many of the grants overlapped one another.

Nowhere was the issue more confused than in Southern Colorado. Some Mexican landowners claimed that their holdings spilled over the New Mexico line into the southern reaches of the Rockies. At various times, land grants had been awarded by the king of Spain, the Republic of Mexico, and provincial governors who haphazardly drew a line on a map. Ownership was often nine points physical possession and one point law. For generations, the force to back the claim overrode legal technicalities.

"Maria, my wife, was the last of her line," Tallant explained. "The land had been in her family for over a hundred years, and when we were married, it became our land. No one disputed that until Warner filed his lawsuit."

"Good heavens," Lillian sympathized. "Are you saying his lawsuit is frivolous?"

"Well, he contends that the Treaty of Guadalupe Hidalgo didn't cover land grants in Colorado. Nobody ever questioned it before, so why now? He's just greedy, that's all."

"Does he have any chance of winning?"

"Not according to my lawyers," Tallant said. "They think he's plumb loco."

"And if they're wrong?" Lillian asked "What would you do then?"

"I won't be thrown off the land my wife's ancestors worked to build. Not by some scoundrel like Hank Warner."

"Yes, that would be terrible."

Lillian felt sorry for him. From what she'd just heard, there was every reason for bad blood between the two men. She halfway hoped Warner wouldn't appear at the theater for tonight's performance. But that was wishful thinking.

She knew he would be seated front and center.

Lillian was prepared to dislike Henry Warner. All she'd heard last night led her to believe he was an out-and-out rogue. But to her surprise, he was a very engaging rogue.

Warner was lithe and muscular, with sandy hair and a neatly groomed mustache. He was so personable that he charmed her father and Chester in a matter of moments. His magnetism all but took her breath.

They went to the restaurant where she'd dined last night. The owner was equally effusive in his greeting of Warner and made a production of escorting them to their table. The waiter was the same as last night, and he gave Lillian a conspiratorial smile. She hardly knew what to think.

Warner took charge. He ordered braised squab with wild rice for both of them. Then he selected a delicate white wine with a marvelous bouquet. When they clinked glasses, Lillian only sipped, but the taste was like some heady nectar. His vivid blue eyes pinned her like a butterfly to a board.

"Before anything else," he said in a deep voice, "I want to say you are the most beautiful woman I've ever seen. I intend to marry you."

Lillian was aghast. "Mr. Warner, you're frightening me."

"Call me Hank," he said jovially. "And no, Lillian—you prefer that to Lilly, don't you?—no, Lillian, I'm not frightening you. Am I?"

"How did you know I prefer Lillian?"

"Nate Varnum told me everything about you. I think he's in love with you himself."

"I somehow doubt that," Lillian said. "Do you always sweep the ladies off their feet?"

Warner chuckled, a low rumble. "As they say, the race goes to the swiftest. Jake Tallant probably convinced you I'm an immoral bounder." He paused, looking deep into her eyes. "Get to know me and you'll know better. I never toy with a lady's affections—especially yours."

Lillian tried to deflect his onslaught. "What Mr. Tallant and I discussed was your lawsuit. He is very disturbed you're attempting to take his ranch."

The remark seemed to amuse Warner. He wagged his head with a satiric smile. "Did Jake tell you about his wife?"

"Yes, as a matter of fact, he did. He said the land had been in her family for generations."

"Did he tell you that I was in love with her, too?"

"No." Lillian was visibly startled. "You were in love with another man's wife?"

"A long time ago." Warner hesitated, sipping his wine. "Jake and me were both courting Maria back in '61. Her folks were still alive then. Best people you'd ever hope to meet."

"And she married Mr. Tallant . . . Jake."

"Well, don't you see, I wasn't the lighthearted rascal that I am now. Jake beat me out."

Lillian suddenly realized it was all an act. Beneath the glib manner, there was nothing lighthearted about Henry Warner. She felt an outrush of sympathy.

"And having lost Maria, you never married?"

"Never saw her match," Warner said with a debonair grin. "Leastways, not till the night I saw you. I'm liable to propose any moment now."

The waiter appeared with a serving tray. He set their plates before them, succulent squab on beds of brown rice. Their conversation momentarily dwindled off as they took cutlery in hand and began dissecting the plump birds. Lillian savored her first bite.

"It's wonderful!" she marveled. "I've never had squab before."

"Stick with me and I'll show you a whole new world. How'd you like to go to Paris on our honeymoon?"

"I do believe you're an incorrigible flirt."

"A gentleman never lies," Warner said with a contagious smile. "You're the girl for me and no two ways about. I'm plumb smitten."

Lillian was silent for a moment. "May I ask you a personal question?"

"Darlin', for you, I'm an open book."

"Why did you wait until Maria died to sue Jake Tallant?"

Warner stopped eating. "You're a regular little firecracker. Don't miss much, do you?"

"I don't mean to pry," Lillian said with guileful innocence. "I was just curious."

"Well, what with you and me practically at the altar, I've got no secrets. I waited because I'd never have done anything to hurt Maria."

"What does that have to do with Jake's ranch?"

"Couple of things," Warner said, more serious now. "For openers, the river corkscrews all through our boundary lines. We've been fightin' over water rights for years."

Lillian looked at him. "But that isn't the main issue . . . is it?"

"No, it's not. There's an old Spanish land grant handed down through Maria. Did Jake tell you about it?"

"Yes, last night."

"Thing is, it'll never stand up in court. Jake knows it and I know it. He's just burned I opened his can of worms."

"Do you really want his ranch that badly?"

Warner grinned. "I don't want his ranch at all. I've got enough land of my own."

"I—" Lillian was shocked. "Why have you sued him, then?"

"Take a guess."

"Maria?"

"None other," Warner acknowledged. "Jake stole her away from me. Laughed about it for ten years to anybody that'd listen. I figure to have the last laugh."

Lillian thought she had never heard of anything so vindictive. But then, on second thought, she knew she'd heard a deeper truth. Henry Warner was a victim of the most powerful emotion imaginable. He had lived with a broken heart until the day Maria Tallant died. She felt his sorrow beneath the veneer of devil-may-care nonchalance.

"Do you still love her . . . even now?"

"No, ma'am," Warner said with a bold smile. "You are the light of my life. I hear the wedding bells ringing!"

Lillian wondered if he saw in her the ghost of a dead woman. She hoped not.

CHAPTER 19

LILLIAN'S DRESSING room was scarcely more than a cubicle. She was stripped to her chemise, seated before a tiny mirror lighted by small coal-oil lamps. She began applying kohl to her eyelids.

Following dinner, Hank Warner had dropped her off at the stage-door entrance. Her first number was usually around eight-thirty, after the juggler, the fire-eater, and a comic who told risqué jokes. That gave her an hour or so to finish her makeup.

Decent women never wore makeup in public. Lillian wished social conventions were different; she thought pinching one's cheeks to give them color was prudish and outmoded. She liked the way kohl enhanced her eyes and how nicely rouge accentuated her features. Still, she had to limit herself to nightly appearances on-stage. Only prostitutes wore makeup on the street.

There was a light rap at the door. She slipped into a smock she'd bought to cover herself backstage. She was proud of her figure but cautious around stagehands and male performers of any variety. Her mother had taught her that a girl's physical assets, if kept a mystery, were all the more a temptation. She tightened the belt on the smock. "Come in!" she called out. "I'm decent."

Lulu Banes stepped into the dressing room. She was in full war paint, wearing a skimpy peekaboo gown that left little to the imagination. The chorus line always opened the show, and the girls were usually costumed before anyone else. She paused inside the door.

"I couldn't wait till later," she said with a bee-stung smile. "How'd it go with Handsome Hank?"

"Oh, very nice," Lillian said, seating herself before the mirror. "He was a perfect gentleman."

"Honey, they all are till they get their way. C'mon, skip straight to the hot stuff."

By now, Lulu was her confidante. Last night, Lillian had related the details of her dinner with Jake Tallant. She'd never before had a close woman friend, and she was pleased to have someone to talk to. She knew Lulu thrived on gossip.

"You have to remember," she said, "everything is in confidence. You can't repeat a word to anyone."

"Cross my heart." Lulu drew a sign over her breast. "My lips are sealed."

"Well . . ." Lillian patted rouge on her cheekbones. "I know it will be hard to believe. . . ."

"Uh-oh, here it comes. What'd he say?"

"Hank was really quite open. He told me he doesn't want Jake's ranch. That isn't why he sued."

"Nooo," Lulu said slowly, with a look of undisguised amusement. "And you bought that?"

Lillian nodded. "I most certainly did."

"Sounds like malarkey to me."

"Not when you know the reason. Hank was in love with Maria Tallant, Jake's wife. He waited until she died to bring legal action."

"Omigod!" Lulu's eyes went round. "He was having an affair with Tallant's wife?"

"No, no," Lillian said dismissively. "They were rivals for her affections long before she married Jake. Hank has loved her all this time."

"You lost me there, kiddo. What's that got to do with the lawsuit?"

"Hank wants Jake to suffer the way he's suffered. How tragic that they both loved the same woman . . . and lost her."

"Uh-huh." Lulu raised a skeptical eyebrow. "Sounds to me like Hank is after revenge. Don't you think?"

"Yes, perhaps a little," Lillian admitted. "But only because he'd loved her all these years. I mean, think about it, he never married!"

"Sweetie, I hate to say it, but you're a soft touch. That's the most cockamamy story I ever heard."

"I think it's rather romantic."

Lulu *humphed.* "Are you going to see him again?"

"Saturday," Lillian said. "He invited me to see his ranch. I accepted."

"And you're having Sunday dinner at Jake Tallant's ranch? You're an awfully busy little bee."

"Yes, but they're both such nice men. How could I refuse?"

"Far be it from me to give you advice. . . ."

"Oh, don't be silly, go ahead."

"Whatever sad tale they tell you . . . ?"

"Yes?"

"Forget a grain of salt, honey. Take it with a spoon."

Later that evening, Lillian went on for her opening number. Tallant and Warner, as usual, were seated at tables down front. They applauded mightily even as she stood bathed in the footlights, each trying to outdo the other. She blushed, avoiding their eyes, as the maestro lifted his baton and led the orchestra into *Aura Lee*. Her voice floated dreamily across the theater.

Aura Lee, Aura Lee
Maid of golden hair
Sunshine came along with thee
And took my heart for fair

Lillian thought the song was suitable to the moment. Never before had she had two such handsome and pleasantly wealthy men vying for her attention. She told herself that Lulu was simply too protective, perhaps too cynical. There was no need for a grain of salt.

No need for salt at all.

Hank Warner called for her the next morning. He was attired in range clothes, whipcord trousers stuffed in his boots and a dark placket shirt. His hat was tall-crowned, roweled spurs on his boots and a Colt pistol strapped on his hip. He looked every inch the cattleman.

Lillian wore a muslin day dress, a gay little bonnet atop her mound of curls. She carried her parasol and snapped it open as he assisted her into a buckboard drawn by a matched team of sorrel mares. The sun was in their faces as they drove east from town.

"I'm so excited," she said happily. "I've never seen an honest-to-goodness ranch."

Warner smiled secretly. "Well, you're in for a treat today. I arranged a surprise."

"Oh, I love surprises! What is it?"

"Wouldn't be a surprise if I told you, would it? You'll just have to wait and see."

"Will it be worth the wait?"

"I've got a notion you'll approve."

Near the edge of town, they had to wait until a train pulled out of the railroad station. As they crossed the tracks, she gave him a quick sideways inspection. He caught the look.

"What?" he said. "Something wrong?"

"Nothing really." Lillian titled her parasol against the glare of the sun. "It's just that I've never seen you wear a gun before."

"You've never seen it because I was wearing a suit. I carry it tucked in my waistband. You shy of guns?"

"No, not in the right hands."

"Well, I have to say, I'm right handy."

"I think you are making fun of me."

"You're too pretty to make fun of. I'm plumb struck blind."

"In that event"—Lillian playfully batted her eyelashes—"I insist you tell me your surprise."

Warner laughed, "Now that would spoil the fun. Wait till we get there."

The ranch was located some five miles east of Pueblo. Warner explained that he owned nearly a hundred thousand acres of grazeland, all of it north of the Arkansas River. The range was well watered, sheltered from plains blizzards by the walls of a canyon, and covered with lush grama grass that fattened steers. He ran about ten thousand head of cattle.

Lillian was stunned into silence. She couldn't imagine anyone owning so much land, and as the road wound along the canyon, she was mesmerized by vast herds of cattle grazing beneath a forenoon sun. The headquarters compound, situated leeward of the canyon walls, consisted of a main house, a large bunkhouse, and a corral. The buildings were stout log structures.

"Not the grandest in the world," Warner said, halting the buckboard in front of the main house. "But it's warm in the winter and cool in the summer. Built to last, too."

"Yes, I can see." Lillian thought it looked like a fort with windows. "It's really very nice."

She realized he was trying to impress her. The land, the cattle, the house, an empire built on an ocean of grass. There were at least thirty men gathered outside the bunkhouse, and Warner explained that they were some of the cowhands on his payroll. A whole steer, cleaved down the middle, was being roasted over a bed of coals. The day, he told her, had been planned to honor her visit to the ranch. Later they would celebrate with a traditional Western feast.

The festivities started with an exhibition by Warner's top broncbuster. A buckskin renegade was blindfolded with a gunnysack while Alvin Johnson, the broncbuster, got himself mounted. When the sack was removed, the horse exploded at both ends, like a stick of dynamite bursting within itself. All four feet left the ground as the buckskin swapped ends in midair and sunfished across the corral in a series of bounding catlike leaps. The battle went on for what seemed an eternity, with the men whooping and shouting as the horse whirled and kicked with squeals of outrage. Johnson rode the bronc to a standstill.

"Bravo! Bravo!" Lillian cried, clapping loudly when it was over. "I've never seen anything so exciting in my life. It was just wonderful!"

Warner seemed pleased. "No doubt about it, Alvin's the best. Glad you liked it."

"Your surprise really was worth waiting for."

"There's more to come, lots more. All for you."

The men took turns aboard pitching broncs. None of them were as good as Alvin Johnson, and most got thrown off. But there was a spirit of camaraderie about it, and everyone hooted and cheered when a rider got dumped. After the broncbusting, there was a demonstration of fancy work with a lariat. Longhorns were hazed onto open ground near the corral, and horsemen would cast loops at a dead run, snaring the steers' horns and hind legs, and neatly drop them in midstride. Lillian applauded the men's feats like a young girl at her first circus.

Late that afternoon the feast was served. Cooks sliced choice cuts off the roasted steer and loaded plates with beef, beans, and sourdough biscuits fresh from a Dutch oven. The men scattered about the compound, wolfing down their food, while Lillian and Warner were served at a table in the shade of a leafy oak tree. Afterward, Warner gave her a tour of the house, which, much as she expected, was a masculine domain. The parlor was dominated by a huge stone fireplace with a bearskin rug and lots of leather furniture.

Warner drove her back into town as sunset fired the sky beyond distant mountains. Lillian was exhilarated, still bubbling with excitement, and yet oddly reflective. She had the feeling she'd spent the day auditioning for a role. Mistress of the manor or perhaps queen of the cowboys.

She wasn't sure it was the part for her.

The Fontaines were invited to Jacob Tallant's for dinner the following day. The noon meal on Sunday, commonly called dinner by country folk, was considered the occasion of the week. Fontaine rented a buggy and team at the livery stable.

The ranch headquarters was located some three miles east of Pueblo. On the drive out, Lillian thought Jake Tallant was playing the diplomat by inviting her father and Chester. His intent, clearly, was to win over the entire Fontaine family. His designs on her would only be furthered by her father's blessing.

The *casa grande* reflected its Mexican heritage. The main house was one-story, constructed of native adobe, with broad wings extending off the central living quarters. Beneath a tile roof, hewn beams protruded from walls four feet thick. The window casements gleamed of tallowed oak, and the double doors were wider than a man's outspanned arms. The effect was one of old-world gentility.

The house, which overlooked the river to the north, commanded the ranch compound. The buildings formed a quadrangle, grouped with a symmetry that was at once functional and pleasing to the eye. Corrals and stables, flanked by storage sheds, angled off to the south. A commissary and an open-sided blacksmith forge were situated on a plot central to a compound that covered several acres. It looked like a small but prosperous village.

Fontaine brought the team to a halt in front of the house. Tallant hurried outside and assisted Lillian from the buggy. "Welcome to my home," he said cordially. "I trust you had a good drive from town."

"Yes, we did," Lillian replied. "The views are simply marvelous along the river."

"Quite an operation," Fontaine said, gesturing about the compound. "How large is your ranch?"

"Just over a hundred thousand acres. We run in the neighborhood of ten thousand head."

"How do you keep up with that many cows?"

"Mr. Fontaine, I often wonder myself. Please, won't you come inside?"

The interior of the house was even more impressive than the outside. The floors were tiled, and off the foyer was an immense parlor with furniture crafted of rich hardwood. Waiting in the parlor were Tallant's children, dressed in their Sunday best. The girl was nine, with the olive complexion of her mother and hair the color of a raven's wing. The boy, who was ten, favored his father, with dark, curly hair. Their eyes fixed immediately on Lillian.

"This is Jennifer," Tallant introduced them, "and this is Robert. And I warn you, they're dying of curiosity."

Lillian smiled warmly. "I'm so happy to meet you, Jennifer and Robert. Thank you for having us to your home."

"Father says you're a singer," Jennifer said, overcome with curiosity. "Will you sing something for us?"

"Why, yes, of course I will. Do you have a favorite song?"

"Father likes *Aura Lee*," Robert said with boyish enthusiasm. "He told us how you sang it the other night. He likes it a lot."

"Mind your manners," Tallant broke in. "Perhaps Miss Fontaine will favor us with a song after dinner. Although I'm afraid we don't have a piano."

"Miguel plays the guitar," Robert reminded him. "Want me to run down to the bunkhouse?"

"Not just yet, Son. I think it'll wait till we've eaten."

Dinner was served in a spacious dining room. There were two servants, a man and a woman, and they brought from the kitchen platters of spicy Mexican dishes. Fontaine, as well as Lillian and Chester, found the food delicious, if somewhat zesty to the palate. Jennifer and Robert peppered them with questions throughout the meal, eager to learn everything about their life in the theater. Fontaine, playing to a wide-eyed audience, gave them a running discourse on the wonders of Shakespeare.

After dinner, Miguel was summoned from the bunkhouse. Lillian hummed the melody for him, and he quickly found the chords on his guitar. Everyone got themselves seated in the parlor, and with Miguel strumming softly, she sang *Aura Lee*. The children were fascinated, watching her intently, and applauded wildly on the last note. When they clamored for more, Fontaine stepped into the breech, delivering a stirring passage from *Hamlet*. As her father's baritone filled the room, Lillian joined Tallant, who was standing behind the sofa. He gave her an apologetic shrug.

"I hope you don't mind," he said. "They get carried away sometimes."

"I think they're wonderful," Lillian said graciously. "You should encourage them in the arts. They enjoy it so much."

"Well, I don't have to encourage them about you. I've never seen them take to anyone so fast."

"Jennifer is so beautiful, and Robert is the very image of you. You must be very proud."

"Never more so than today, Lillian."

The afternoon sped past. Tallant gave them a tour of the compound, explaining the many facets of how a ranch operates. The children clung to Lillian, and she sensed they were starved for a woman's affection. Before anyone quite knew it, the sun heeled over to the west, and it was time to leave. Fontaine told them that actors, unlike the Lord, were allowed no rest on the Sabbath. The show, he noted jovially, must go on.

Tallant and the children saw them off. Jennifer and Robert hugged Lillian, begging her to return, and ran alongside until the buggy picked up speed. On the way into town, Lillian was silent, playing the afternoon back in her mind. Fontaine finally broke into her reverie, looking at her with an amused expression. He shook his head.

"I believe the Bard said it all," he observed wryly. " 'She's beautiful and therefore to be wooed. She is a woman, therefore to be won.' You have captured their hearts, my dear."

Lillian ignored the jest. She stared off into the fading sun and suddenly felt the race was too swift for her liking. All the more so after a visit to the Tallant ranch.

She thought she was too young to be a mother. Perhaps too young to be a wife.

Chapter 20

Lillian wrestled with her uncertainty all through Sunday night. Neither Tallant nor Warner attended the evening performance, and she was relieved by their absence. She needed time to sort out her feelings.

Her ambivalence was unsettling. She genuinely liked both men, though they were as different as night and day. One lived like an old-world Spanish *grandee* and the other like a devil-may-care plains buccaneer. She'd never known two men so dissimilar.

All of which was part of a larger problem. She had never been courted, and she'd never known any man intimately. Her experiences with men were of a flirtatious nature, a stolen kiss that never led to anything more. Her mother had imparted wisdom about men, but Lillian had no actual experience. She felt oddly like a vestal virgin in ancient Rome. Chaste, even wise, but nonetheless ignorant.

She wasn't sure she wanted to lose that ignorance to either of them. Jake Tallant was a gentleman of the old school, kind and considerate, almost chivalrous in manner. Yet his children, however delightful, posed the worrisome question of overnight motherhood. Hank Warner was perhaps more debonair, a puckish bon vivant with a devilish sense of humor. Still, for all his protests, he lived with the memory of a dead woman. A wife would never displace the ghost of Maria Tallant.

Lillian's ambivalence was underscored by an even more personal dilemma. Over the course of her Western odyssey, she had found some essential part of herself in the theater. She loved the audiences and the thrill of it all, the wave of adulation that came to her over the footlights. She thought she loved it more than she might ever love a man, and she wasn't willing to trade one for the other. Her stage career was, at least for now, her life.

By Monday morning, she had arrived at a partial solution. She wrote discreet notes to both Tallant and Warner, explaining that she felt overwhelmed by their attentions. The notes were identical except for the salutations, tactfully phrased word-for-word appeals for patience. She emphasized that she needed time, needed to be alone with her thoughts, for it had all happened too fast, too quickly. She asked that they not contact her until she was able to reconcile her own feelings.

The notes were secretly delivered to each of the men by Chester. He caught them separately, as they were entering the Tivoli Monday evening, and slipped them the notes in the course of a handshake. That night, and for the three days following, the men honored her wishes. They attended her performances every evening, seated at their usual tables, following her about the stage with the eyes of infatuated schoolboys. True to her request, neither of them attempted to contact her.

Friday morning she awoke with a vague sense of disquiet. Her father and Chester went out to attend to personal errands, and she was left alone with her thoughts. She couldn't identify the source of her unease, apart from the fact that she somehow felt lonely. She inwardly admitted that she missed the company of the men, Tallant for his courtly manner and Warner for his waggish humor. She wondered if a woman, after all, needed a man in her life.

Fontaine returned shortly before noon. He found her moping about, still dressed in her housecoat, staring listlessly out the window. She didn't move as he crossed the sitting room and stopped at her side. Her expression was pensive, vaguely sad. He tried for a light note.

"What's this?" he said. "I planned to take you out for lunch. Why aren't you dressed?"

"I just haven't gotten around to it."

"Come now, my dear, that is hardly an answer. What's wrong?"

"Oh, Papa." Her voice wavered. "I'm so confused."

Fontaine studied her with concern. "Need I ask the source of your confusion? Something to do with men, is it?"

"I was standing here thinking I miss them. And then I thought how perfectly ingenuous. How naive."

"No one would ever accuse you of naïveté. You are much more the sophisticate than you realize."

"Am I?" Lillian said with a tinge of melancholy. "One minute I want them out of my life, and the next I wish they were knocking on the door. How sophisticated is that, Papa?"

"You punish yourself unnecessarily," Fontaine said. "Quite often logic dictates one thing while the heart dictates another. Are you in love with either of these men?"

"No, of course not."

"And the stage is still your beacon?"

"Yes, more than anything."

"Then logic prevails, my dear. There are simpler ways to resolve matters of the heart."

Lillian turned from the window. "I'm not sure I understand, Papa. What is it you're suggesting?"

"Nothing unseemly," Fontaine assured her. "You are lonely for male companionship and nothing could be more natural. Amuse yourself without becoming involved."

"Wouldn't that be unfair to them?"

"I'm sure your mother educated you about the whys and wherefores of men. A woman need not worry about trifling with their affections."

"Yes, but how would—"

Chester burst through the door. His face was flushed and he looked as though he'd just run a marathon. He hurried across the room, gesturing wildly.

"Your gentleman friends just shot it out! Not five minutes ago in front of the bank."

Lillian appeared to stagger. "Hank and Jake?"

"None other," Chester said. "I saw it myself."

"Are they . . . dead?"

"Warner got it in the arm and Tallant lost a piece of his ear. They're both lousy shots."

Fontaine put an arm around Lillian's shoulders. He looked at Chester. "How did it happen?"

"Warner started it," Chester said. "Tallant was coming out of the bank and Warner stopped him on the street. They exchanged insults, and next thing you know, they pulled their guns. Wounded one another with the first shot."

"Unfortunate," Fontaine remarked. "I assume it had to do with Warner's lawsuit?"

"No, Dad, it was literally an *affaire de coeur.* They were fighting over Lillian."

"Me!" Lillian was nonplussed. "Why would they fight over me?"

Chester suppressed a grin. "Warner used some dirty language. Accused Tallant of stealing your affections."

"That's ridiculous!"

"You haven't heard the rest of it. Tallant cursed Warner out and accused him of the same thing. That's when they went for their guns."

"How dare they!" Lillian fumed. "I never gave either of them reason to believe I favored one over the other. I asked both of them to leave me alone!"

"Not to hear them tell it," Chester informed her. "They each think the other one stole your heart away. Talk about jealousy."

"I feel like a common streetwalker. Men fighting over me, for mercy's sake! It's disgusting."

A knock sounded at the door. Chester opened it and admitted Lulu Banes. She rushed across the room to Lillian.

"Have you heard?"

"Chester just finished telling me. I can't believe it."

"Believe it," Lulu said archly. "Lucky the fools didn't kill one another."

"I wrote each of them notes," Lillian said with a dazed expression. "And they weren't love notes, either. I told them to stay away."

"Honey, you think they compare dance cards?"

"What do you mean?"

"I mean your notes had the opposite effect. They both thought you ditched one for the other."

"Well, that's absurd," Lillian protested. "Neither of them has any claim on me. I made that very clear."

Lulu chuckled. "Not clear enough, sugar. They just got through fighting a duel for you. How's it feel to be fought over?"

"Absolutely revolting! I wish I'd never met either of them."

"And I'd give anything in the world to be in your place. How I wish, I wish, I wish."

Lillian sniffed. "You're welcome to them."

"Not in this lifetime," Lulu said woefully. "They've only got eyes for you, kiddo."

"Then I'll have to persuade them otherwise, won't I?"

"What are you talking about?"

"Lulu, I mean to put an end to it—permanently!"

* * *

For God's sake, let us sit upon the ground
And tell sad stories of the death of kings:
How some have been depos'd, some slain in
war,
Some haunted by the ghosts they have deposed,
Some poison'd by their wives, some sleeping
kill'd;
All murder'd: for within the hollow crown
That rounds the mortal temples of a king
Keeps Death his court . . .

Fontaine plowed on with the soliloquy from *King Richard II.* The patrons of the Tivoli were by now resigned to his nightly orations from Shakespeare. For the most part, they ignored him, milling about and carrying on conversations interspersed with laughter. He might have been playing to an empty house.

Two members of the audience were nonetheless attentive. Jake Tallant was seated at his usual table, his right ear heavily bandaged with gauze. Across the aisle, Hank Warner sat with his left arm cradled in a dark sling that matched the color of his suit. Fontaine was surprised to find them in the crowd, for their wounds were still fresh from the morning gunfight. He suspected their attendance had little to do with Shakepeare.

The magician kept the audience entertained between acts. The curtain then opened on the melodrama of the evening, *The Dying Kiss*. Lillian was all too aware of Tallant and Warner, for their tables were just beyond the orchestra, near the stage. She noted that they studiously ignored each other, but she thought their presence was scandalous. The eyes of every man in the room were on her, and she knew what they were thinking. She was the temptress who provoked men to gunfights.

After the melodrama, she hurried backstage to change for her final number. She was still seething as she slipped into her teal gown and tried to repair her makeup. When she went on, her face was scarlet and she had little doubt that everyone in the theater looked upon her as a scarlet woman. She was, in all likelihood, branded the lover of the two men seated down front. The orchestra led her into a lively tune.

I came from Alabama
With a banjo on my knee
I'm going to Louisiana
My true love for to see

It rained all night the day I left
The weather it was dry
The sun so hot I froze to death
Susanna, don't you cry
Oh! Susanna, oh don't you cry for me
I've come from Alabama with a banjo on my knee

The crowd gave her a rousing ovation. Tallant, undeterred by his mangled ear, applauded mightily. Warner, limited to one good arm, pounded the table with the flat of his hand. She took three curtain calls, then bowed offstage into the wings. Nate Varnum was standing nearby, and she asked him to invite Tallant and Warner backstage. Her look was such that he restrained himself from questioning her judgment. He hurried off.

Fontaine and Chester were finished removing their greasepaint. They exchanged glances, having overheard her conversation with Varnum, and joined her near her dressing room. Fontaine appeared troubled.

"Do you think this is wise?" he asked. "Bringing them together so soon after their altercation?"

"Their welfare doesn't concern me," Lillian said. "I intend to put an end to it here—tonight."

"I hope you know what you're doing, my dear."

"Yes, I know very well, Papa."

Varnum came through the door at the side of the stage. Warner was directly behind him, followed by Tallant. Everything came to a standstill as the cast—chorus girls, acrobats, jugglers, and the magician—paused to watch. Varnum led the ranchers backstage and stopped outside Lillian's dressing room. The men seemed disconcerted by her summons, nodding to her with weak smiles. Her eyes flashed with anger.

"Look at you!" she said in a stinging voice. "You should be ashamed of yourselves."

Tallant and Warner ducked their heads like naughty urchins. Lillian felt a momentary pang of sympathy, for they were proud men being humbled in public. But she was determined to see it end. She lashed out at them.

"Do you have any idea how you've humiliated me? Fighting like common thugs in the street. And all in my name!"

"Lillian, listen," Warner said, thoroughly abashed. "I wouldn't offend you for anything in the world. I just wasn't thinking straight."

Tallant nodded his head rapidly. "That goes double for me. I'm as much to blame as Hank."

"Yes, you are," Lillian said shortly. "Now, I want you both to shake hands. Let it end here."

Warner and Tallant swapped a quick glance. After a moment, Tallant stuck out his hand and Warner clasped it in a firm grip. Lillian allowed herself a tight smile.

"I hope you can behave like gentlemen from now on. You might even become friends."

"I tend to doubt it," Warner said.

Tallant grunted. "Yeah, not too likely."

"Well, you won't have me as an excuse." Lillian looked from one to the other. "I am leaving Pueblo and I never want to see you again. Either of you."

"Hold on!" Warner barked, and Tallant added a hasty, "Let's talk about this!"

Fontaine stepped forward. "Gentlemen, I believe my daughter—"

"Please, Papa," Lillian cut him off. "I have to do this myself."

"Of course, my dear."

"Goodbye, Hank. Goodbye, Jake." Lillian permitted herself a softer smile. "Please don't say anything to make it more difficult. Just leave now. Please."

Tallant and Warner seemed on the verge of arguing it further. But then, under her cool stare, they mumbled their goodbyes and turned away. No one said anything as they crossed backstage and went out the door. Fontaine looked at Lillian.

"Leaving Pueblo?" he said. "Wasn't that what you told them? I recall no discussion to that effect."

"Yes, Papa, we are leaving."

"You might have consulted me first."

"I'm sorry," Lillian said evenly. "I've had my fill of ruffians, Papa. It's time to go on to Denver."

Fontaine nodded judiciously. "Certainly our notices merit moving onward and upward. You may have a point."

"Just a damn minute!" Varnum jumped in. "You can't run off and leave me high and dry."

"Indeed?" Fontaine said, suddenly testy. "For a man who dislikes Shakespeare, you take umbrage rather too quickly. Do we have a contract with you, Mr. Varnum?"

"I gave you your start!" Varnum objected loudly. "And besides, it's not professional."

"Hmmn." Fontaine feigned deep consideration. "Never let it be said that the Fontaines are less than professional. What say, my dear, shall we give him another week?"

Lillian sighed. "One week, Papa, but no more. I'm anxious to see Denver."

"I concur," Fontaine said, gesturing idly in Varnum's direction. "There you have it, my good man. One week and we bid you *adieu*."

"Godalmighty," Varnum groaned. "I'll never find a headliner act in a week."

"Nor will you find one to replace The Fontaines, my dear fellow. We are, in a word, singular."

Lillian turned toward her dressing room. Lulu was waiting by the door and gave her Kewpie-doll smile. "Sugar, you sure know how to end a romance. I never saw two chumps dusted off so fast."

"I hope I wasn't too harsh on them. Although I must say they deserved it."

"Well, who knows, maybe I'll snag one of them while he's sobbin' in his beer. But whether I do or don't, I'm gonna miss you, kiddo."

"Oh, Lulu, I'll miss you, too."

"Yeah, but I can always say I knew you when. You're on your way to the big time now."

"Do you think so, honestly?"

"Sugar, I'd lay odds on it."

Theatrical people were superstitious and rarely counted their good fortune until it came true. Yet Lillian, who was caught up in the moment, cast her superstitions aside. She already knew it was true.

She saw her name in lights.

CHAPTER 21

THE ENGINEER set the brakes with a racketing squeal. A moment later the train rocked to a halt before the Denver stationhouse. Towering skyward, the Rockies rose majestically under a noonday sun, the snowcapped spires touching the clouds. Lillian thought it was a scene of unimaginable grandeur.

Passengers began deboarding the train. Fontaine signaled one of the porters who waited outside the stationhouse. When the baggage car was unloaded, the porter muscled their steamer trunks onto a cart and led them across the platform. In front of the depot, Fontaine engaged a carriage and told the cabbie to take them to the Brown Palace Hotel. From all he'd heard, the hotel was an institution, the finest in Denver. He planned to establish residence in proper style.

On the way uptown Lillian noted that the streets were cobbled and many of the buildings were constructed of brick masonry. She recalled Libbie Custer telling her that a town founded on a gold strike had become a center of finance and commerce. Over the years, the mining camp reproduced itself a hundredfold, until finally a modern metropolis rose along the banks of Cherry Creek and the South Platte River. Denver was transformed into a cosmopolitan beehive, with opera and a stock exchange and a population approaching 20,000. The city was unrivaled on the Western plains.

The Brown Palace was all they'd been led to expect. Thick carpets covered the marble floor of the lobby, and a central seating area was furnished with leather chairs and sofas. The whole of the lobby ceiling glittered with an ornate mural, and a wide, sweeping staircase ascended to the upper floors. The place had the look and smell of wealth, home away from home for the upper class. At the reception desk, Fontaine noted a calendar with the date May 25, and he marked it as an auspicious day. Their journey had at last brought them to Denver.

"Good afternoon," he said, nodding to the clerk. "You have a suite reserved for Alistair Fontaine."

"Yes, sir," the clerk replied. "How long will you be staying with us, Mr. Fontaine?"

"Indefinitely."

"Welcome to the Brown Palace."

"Thank you so much."

Fontaine signed the register with a flourish. Upstairs, led by a bellman, they were shown into a lavish suite. A lush Persian carpet covered the sitting room floor, and grouped before a marble fireplace were several chairs and a chesterfield divan. There were connecting doors to the bedrooms, both of which were appointed in Victorian style and equipped with a private lavatory. A series of handsomely draped windows overlooked the city.

Lillian whirled around the sitting room. "I can hardly believe we're here. It's like a dream come true."

"Indeed, my dear," Fontaine said. "Far more civilized than anything we've seen in our travels, hmmm?"

"And running water," Chester added, returning from the bedroom. "I think I'm going to like Denver."

"I'm going to *love* it!" Lillian said gaily. "Papa, when will we see the theater? Could we go this afternoon?"

"Tonight, I believe," Fontaine said. "We'll take in the show and get a feel for the crowd. No need to rush."

"I'm just so anxious, that's all. I wish we were opening tonight."

"What is one night more or less? We will have a long run in Denver, my dear. You may depend on it."

Fontaine exuded confidence. By telegraph, he'd spent the last week negotiating with Burt Tully, owner of the Alcazar Variety Theater. Their notices from Pueblo, just as he'd predicted, had made Tully eager to offer them headliner billing. Though Tully's principal interest was in Lillian, Fontaine had nonetheless struck a lucrative deal for the entire act. Their salary was $300 a week, with a four-week guarantee.

Early that evening, they took a stroll through the sporting district. For reasons lost to time, the district was known locally as the Tenderloin. There, within a few square blocks of Blake Street, gaming dives and variety theaters provided a circus of nightlife. Saloons and gambling, mixed with top-drawer entertainment, presented an enticing lure. Sporting men were attracted from all across the West.

One block over was Denver's infamous red-light district. Known simply as the Row, Holladay Street was a lusty fleshpot, with a veritable crush of dollar cribs. Yet while hook shops dominated the row, there was no scarcity of high-class bordellos. The parlor houses offered exotic tarts, usually younger and prettier, all at steeper prices. Something over a thousand soiled doves plied their trade on Holladay Street.

Hop Alley satisfied the more bizarre tastes. A narrow passageway off Holladay, it was Denver's version of Lotus Land. Chinese fan-tan parlors vied with the faint sweet odor of opium dens, and those addicted to the Orient's heady delights beat a steady path to this back-street world of pipe dreams. To a select clientele, dainty China dolls were available day or night. Vice in every form was available at a price.

Fontaine cut short their tour of Holladay Street. He realized within a block that they had strayed from the more respectable section of the sporting district. Lillian kept her gaze averted, though she felt shamelessly intrigued by the sight of so much sin for sale. Chester, on the other hand, oogled the girls and mentally marked a few bordellos that looked worthy of a visit. They quickly found themselves back on Blake Street.

The Alcazar Variety Theater was the liveliest spot in town. A two-story structure with leaded-glass windows, if offered diverse forms of entertainment for the sporting crowd. On the first floor was the bar and, through an arched doorway at the rear, the theater. The stage was centered on the room, with seating for 400, and a gallery of private booths circled the mezzanine. The upper floor of the club was devoted exclusively to gambling.

Their entrance was not altogether unnoticed. Lillian, though she was dressed in a simple gown, drew admiring stares from men at the bar. Fontaine purchased tickets to the theater and slipped the doorman a gold eagle, which resulted in a table near the orchestra. The audience was composed primarily of men, and waiters scurried back and forth serving drinks. As they were seated,

Fontaine saw a man emerge from a door leading backstage. He nodded at Lillian.

"Unless I'm mistaken," he said, "there goes our employer, Mr. Tully."

Lillian followed his look. The man was stoutly built, with salt-and-pepper hair and a handlebar mustache, attired in a dark suit and a colorful brocade vest. He stopped here and there, greeting customers seated at tables, and slowly made his way to the rear of the theater. She glanced back at her father.

"Shouldn't we introduce ourselves, Papa?"

"No need, my dear," Fontaine said idly. "We aren't expected until tomorrow. Time enough, then."

"Yes, I suppose," Lillian said. "He certainly has a nice theater."

"Let us hope he's a good showman as well."

The orchestra thumped into a spirited dance number. As the curtain opened, a line of chorus girls went high-stepping across the stage. The lead dancer raised her skirts, revealing a shapely leg, and joined them in a prancing cakewalk. The dance routine was followed by a comic, a sword swallower and his pretty assistant, a contortionist who tied himself in knots, and a team of nimble acrobats dressed in tights. The audience applauded appreciatively after every act.

The headliner was billed as The Flying Nymph. A trapeze bar flew out of the stage loft with a woman hanging by her knees. She was identified on the program as Darlene LaRue, and she wore abbreviated tights covered by flowing veils. She performed daring flips and at one point hung by her heels, all the while divesting herself of a veil at a time. The orchestra built to a cresendo as she swung by one hand, tossing the last veil into the audience, her buxom figure revealed in the footlights. The curtain swished closed to applause and cheers.

"Good Lord!" Fontaine muttered. "I thought I'd seen everything. That is positively bizarre."

Chester laughed. "Dad, it's the show business. You have to admit she's different."

"So are dancing elephants," Fontaine said. "That doesn't mean it is art." He turned to Lillian. "Don't you agree, my dear?"

Lillian thought Denver was no different than Pueblo. Or for that matter, Abilene and Dodge City. Men were men, and they wanted to be entertained rather than enlightened. Opera would never play on a variety stage.

"Yes, Papa, I agree," she said. "No dancing elephants."

Fontaine gave her a strange look. "Pardon me?"

"I won't sing from a trapeze, either."

"I should think not!"

She decided to humor him. His art was his life and not a subject for jest. Alistair Fontaine was who he was.

She hoped Shakespeare would play in Denver.

Springtime was the best of times in the Rockies. The air was invigorating, and on the mountains green-leafed aspens fluttered on gentle breezes. The slopes sparkled below the timberline with a kaleidoscope of wildflowers.

A horse-drawn streetcar trundled past as the Fontaines emerged from the hotel. The sun was directly overhead, fixed like a copper ball in a cloudless sky. Fontaine, who was in a chipper mood, filled his lungs with air. He exhaled with gusto.

"I do believe I'm going to like it here. There's something bracing about the mountain air."

"Not to mention the streetcars," Chester said. "Give me a city anytime, all the time."

"I endorse the sentiment, my boy."

Lillian shared their spirited manner. The sidewalks were crowded with smartly dressed men and women attired in the latest fashions. Everywhere she looked there were shops and stores, and the city seemed to pulse with an energy that was all but palpable. She thought she'd already fallen in love with Denver.

Fontaine set off briskly down the street. They were on their way to meet with Burt Tully, the owner of the Alcazar. Fontaine and Chester looked dapper in their three-piece suits, freshly pressed for the occasion. Lillian wore her dove gray taffeta gown, her hair upswept, a parasol over her shoulder. She had never felt so alive, or more eager to get on with anything. She was excited by their prospects.

"I'm looking forward to this," Fontaine said, waiting for a streetcar to pass. "From what we saw last night, Tully's establishment needs a touch of class. That is to say, The Fontaines."

Lillian took his arm. "Papa, will you do something for me?"

"Why, of course, my dear. What is it?"

"Try not to lecture Mr. Tully."

"Lecture?" Fontaine said in a bemused tone. "Why on earth would I lecture him?"

"You know," Lillian gently reminded. "What we were talking about last night? Dancing elephants and trapeze ladies."

"I see no reason to raise topics of an unpleasant nature. After all, we have Mr. Tully exactly where we want him."

"We do?"

"Yes indeed," Fontaine said confidently. "Three hundred a week speaks to the fact that we have the upper hand. His first offer, as you will recall, was rather niggardly."

"Papa, we mustn't let him think we're overbearing. Won't you be tactful . . . for me?"

"I shall be the very soul of discretion. You may depend on it."

Lillian exchanged a look with Chester. He tipped his head in an imperceptible nod. "Listen to her, Dad," he urged. "Denver's our big break and we don't want to spoil it. We might end up in Pueblo again."

Fontaine laughed it off. "Never fear, my boy, we have seen the last of Pueblo. Leave everything to me."

Some ten minutes later they entered the Alcazar. A bartender told them that Tully's office was on the second floor, at the rear of the gaming room. Upstairs, they found a plushly appointed room with faro layouts, twenty-one, chuck-a-luck, roulette, and several poker tables. Though it was scarcely past the noon hour, there were men gathered around the various gaming devices. The girls serving drinks wore peekaboo gowns that displayed their cleavage to maximum effect.

The office looked more suited to a railroad mogul. A lush carpet covered the floor, the furniture was oxblood leather, and the walls were paneled in dark hardwood. Burt Tully was seated at a massive walnut desk; a large painting of sunset over the Rockies hung behind his chair. He rose after they knocked and came through the door. His mouth lifted in a pleasant smile.

"Let me guess," he said, extending his hand. "You're the Fontaines."

Fontaine accepted his handshake. "A distinct pleasure to meet you at last, Mr. Tully. May I introduce my daughter, Lillian, and my son, Chester."

"An honor, Miss Fontaine," Tully said, gently taking her hand. "I've heard a good deal about the Colorado Nightingale. Welcome to the Alcazar."

Lillian smiled winningly. "Thank you so much, Mr. Tully. We're delighted to be here."

"Please, won't you folks have a seat?"

There were two wingback chairs before the desk. Fontaine took one and Chester stepped back, motioning Lillian to the other. He seated himself on a leather sofa against the wall, casually crossing his legs. Tully dropped into his chair behind the desk.

"Allow me to congratulate you," Fontaine said. "You have a very impressive operation here."

"I don't mean to brag—" Tully spread his hands with a modest grin. "The Alcazar is the top spot in the Tenderloin. We pack them in seven nights a week."

"And well you should, my dear fellow. You offer the finest in entertainment."

"All the more reason you're here. Darlene LaRue closes tonight and you open tomorrow night."

"Indeed!" Fontaine said jovially. "I'm sure we will fill the house."

"No doubt you will." Tully paused, his gaze shifting to Lillian. "I have ads starting in all the papers tomorrow. Everyone in town will want to see the Colorado Nightingale."

Lillian detected an unspoken message. There was no mention of The Fontaines but instead a rather subtle reference to the Colorado Nightingale. She returned his look.

"Are you familiar with the way we present our act?"

"Yes, of course he is," Fontaine interrupted. "I covered all that in our telegrams. Didn't I, dear fellow?"

"Let's talk about that," Tully said seriously. "You realize your daughter is the attraction? The real headliner?"

"I—" Fontaine seemed taken aback. "I would be the first to admit that Lillian draws the crowds. Was there some other point?"

Tully steepled his hands. "I have no objection to the melodrama. We haven't held one in a while and it ought to play pretty well." He hesitated, his features solemn. "I'd like you to consider dropping the Shakespeare."

"Nate Varnum said the same thing in Pueblo. Shakespeare played well enough there."

"No, Mr. Fontaine, it didn't. I exchanged telegrams with Nate, and he told me—you'll pardon my saying so—the crowd sat on their hands. The same thing will happen here."

Fontaine reddened. "You signed The Fontaines to an engagement, and The Fontaines are here. I expect you to honor the terms of our agreement."

"Think about it," Tully suggested. "Your daughter has a great career ahead of her. She's doing two songs a show, and she should be doing three or four. Without the Shakespeare, she could."

"Mr. Tully."

Their heads snapped around at the tone in Lillian's voice. She shifted forward in her chair. "Father speaks for The Fontaines. You have to accept us as we are . . . or not at all."

There was a moment of intense silence. Tully finally shook his head. "You're doing yourself a disservice, Miss Fontaine. Your father knows it and I know it. And you know it, too, don't you?"

"As I said, we are The Fontaines. Shakespeare is part of our act."

"Just as you wish," Tully said in a resigned voice. "I'll go along only because I want the Colorado Nightingale at the Alcazar. For you, personally, I think it's a big mistake."

Lillian smiled. "You won't think so tomorrow night. We'll fill the house."

"Yes, I'm sure *you* will, Miss Fontaine."

Tully arranged a rehersal schedule for her the next morning. After a perfunctory round of handshakes, they left his office. Outside, walking along Blake Street, it was apparent that Fontaine's chipper mood had vanished. He appeared somehow diminished, head bowed and shoulders hunched. Lillian knew he was crushed.

"Papa—"

"Later, my dear."

"Are you all right?"

"I think I need a drink."

Chapter 22

Lillian strolled along Larimer Street. The central thoroughfare of Denver, it was lined with shops and stores, banks and newspaper offices, and all manner of business establishments. She turned into Mlle. Tourneau's Dress Shop.

The shop was airy and pleasantly appointed, with a large plate glass window fronting Larimer Street. Dresses were displayed on mannequins, and from the rear, behind a partition, she heard the whir of sewing machines. A small woman with pince-nez glasses walked forward as the bell over the door jingled. She nodded amiably.

"Good afternoon," she said with a trace of an accent. "May I help you?"

"Are you Mademoiselle Tourneau?" Lillian asked.

"*Oui.*"

Lillian thought the accent was slightly off and wondered if the woman was really French. She smiled politely. "The manager at the Brown Palace told me you are the finest dressmaker in Denver."

"M'sieur Clark is very kind," Mlle. Tourneau said. "And whom do I have the privilege of addressing?"

"My name is Lillian Fontaine."

"*Enchanté*, Mademoiselle Fontaine. How may I serve you?"

"I'm in desperate need of some gowns. I hoped you might design them for me."

"But of course, with pleasure. What type of gowns do you require?"

"Stage gowns," Lillian replied. "I'm an actress and a singer. I open tomorrow night at the Alcazar Variety Theater."

Mlle. Tourneau laughed coyly. "There is much talk about you, I believe. You are the one called the Colorado Nightingale. *Non?*"

"Well, yes, that is how they have me billed."

"How very exciting! I will be honored to design your gowns."

Mlle. Tourneau began spreading bolts of cloth on a large table. As she prattled on about the quality of the fabrics, Lillian ran her fingers over the material, pausing to study various colors and textures. Finally, hardly able to choose from the delicate fabrics, she made three selections. The bolts were set aside.

Scarcely drawing a breath, Mlle. Tourneau pulled out a large pad of paper and a stick of charcoal shaved to a point. She began sketching gowns, rapidly filling in details as the charcoal flew across the paper. One was to be done in embroidered yellow tulle, another in Lyon silk with white lace trim, and the third in pleated ivory satin with guipure lace. She completed the last sketch with a flourish.

"Voilà!" she announced dramatically. *"C'est magnifique!"*

Lillian studied the sketches. She had given considerable thought to remarks made by both theater owners and stage performers over the last several months. The more discreet had alluded to the aura of innocence she projected onstage and how irresistible that was to men. The more plainspoken advised naughty but nice, a peek here and a peek there to heighten the sense of mystery. She decided now that some of both would enhance the overall effect.

"Here," she said, a fingernail on the sketch. "Perhaps we could lower it slightly . . . to here."

"Ahhh!" Mlle. Tourneau peered over her pince-nez. "You wish to accentuate the décolletage. *Tres bien*!"

"And here." Lillian pointed to the bottom of the gown. "Perhaps we could raise this just a . . . touch."

"*Mais oui!* You wish a tiny display of the ankle. How very daring."

"Nothing vulgar, you understand."

"Non, non! Never!"

Mlle. Tourneau led her to the fitting room. Lillian disrobed to her chemise and the dressmaker began taking measurements. She ran the tape around hips, waist, and bust, and her eyes went round. She clucked appreciatively.

"Extraordinaire!" she said merrily. "You will look absolutely lovely in these gowns. I predict you will break hearts. Many hearts."

"Well . . ." Lillian studied herself in the full-length mirror and giggled. "I'll certainly try."

"*Fait accompli, mon cher*. Men will fall at your feet."

"I have to ask you a favor, mademoiselle."

"Anything in my power."

"The ivory gown . . ." Lillian waited until she nodded. "I'll need it by tomorrow evening. I just have to have it for my opening show."

"Sacre bleu!" Mlle. Tourneau exclaimed. "Tomorrow?"

"Won't you please?"

Lillian looked at her with a beseeching gaze. Mlle. Tourneau's stern expression slowly gave way to a resigned smile. Her eyes blinked behind her pince-nez.

"How could I refuse you? I will work my girls throughout the night. You must be here first thing in the morning for a fitting. But you will have your gown. *Certainment!*"

"Oh, thank you! Thank you!"

The measurements completed, Mlle. Tourneau suggested an accessory to complement the outfit. She carried a line of low-cut slippers with a medium heel, which she could cover in the same fabric as the gown. She laughed a wicked little laugh.

"Show the shoe, show the ankle. Eh?"

"I think it's perfect!"

A short while later Lillian left the shop. She returned to the hotel, tingling with excitement at the thought of her new gown. When she entered the suite, her father was slumped in an easy chair, a bottle of whiskey at hand on a side table. His jaw was slack and his eyes appeared glazed. He lifted his glass in a mock toast.

"Welcome back to our cheery abode, my dear. How went the shopping?"

Chester was seated on the divan. As she crossed the room, he looked at her with an expression of rueful concern, wagging his head from side to side. She stopped by the fireplace. "I ordered a lovely gown," she said, forcing herself to smile. "I'll have it for the opening tomorrow night."

"Marvelous!" Fontaine pronounced in a slurred voice. "Never disappoint your public."

Lillian saw that he was already drunk. He laughed as though amused by some private joke and poured himself another drink. The bottle wobbled when he set it back on the table, and he watched it with an indifferent stare. He took a slug of whiskey.

"Papa," Lillian said tentatively. "Don't you think you've had enough to drink?"

Fontaine waved her off with an idle gesture. "Have no fear," he said. "John Barleycorn and I are old friends. He treats me gently."

"I worry anyway. Too much liquor isn't good for you."

"I am indestructible, my dear. A rock upon which a sea of troubles doth scatter to the winds."

Lillian knew he was trying to escape into a bottle. His optimism about their prospects in Denver and his pride in negotiating such a lucrative engagement at the Alcazar—all that had been dashed by their meeting with Burt Tully. Her father had heard all over again that no one was interested in Shakespeare. Or Alistair Fontaine.

She felt guilty about her own good fortune. The accolades accorded the Colorado Nightingale, first in Pueblo and now in Denver, had pushed her father out of the limelight and ever deeper into the shadows. She suddenly felt guilty about her new gowns, for while she was happy, her father was drunk and disconsolate. She simply didn't know how to erase his pain.

"Papa, listen to me," she temporized. "You're only hurting yourself, and I hate to see you like this. Won't you please stop . . . for me?"

Fontaine grunted. " 'Men's evil manners live in brass; their virtues we write in water.' I believe the Bard penned the line for me. Yes, indeed, quite apropos."

Lillian was reduced to silence. She looked at Chester, and he again shook his head in dull defeat. Fontaine downed the glass of whiskey, muttering something unintelligible, and slumped deeper in the chair. His eyes went blank, then slowly closed, and his chin sank lower on his chest. The glass dropped from his hand onto the carpet.

Lillian took a seat on the divan. She stared at her father a moment, listening to his light snore. "I feel so terrible," she said, tears welling up in her eyes. "Surely there's something we can do."

"Like what?" Chester said. "You know yourself, he lives and breathes Shakespeare. Tully might as well have hit him over the head with a hammer."

"Yes, you're right, he was just devastated. He thought Denver would be so much more cultured. His hopes were so high."

"Maybe he'll sleep it off and come to his senses. He's always bounced back before."

"I'm not sure sleep will solve anything."

"You tell me then, what will?"

"Perhaps Tully was wrong about the audiences. Perhaps they will appreciate Shakespeare."

"Anything's possible," Chester said with no great confidence. "I guess we'll find out tomorrow night."

"Oh, Chet, I feel so helpless."

"Let's cross our fingers and hope for the best."

Lillian thought they would need more than luck.

Denver turned out for opening night. The theater was full by seven o'clock, and men were wedged tight in the barroom. The crowd spilled out onto the sidewalk, and a police squad was brought in to maintain order. The backlit marquee blazed outside the Alcazar.

LILLY FONTAINE
THE COLORADO NIGHTINGALE

Lillian complained to Burt Tully. The marquee made no reference to her father or Chester, and she was upset by the oversight. Her father had sloughed it off, but she knew he was offended and hurt. Tully told her it was no oversight and then repeated what he'd said the day before. The crowd was there to see her, not The Fontaines. She was the headliner.

Before her opening number, she stopped by the dressing room her father shared with Chester. Fontaine was attired in the costume of a Danish nobleman, and his breath reeked of alcohol. His eyes were bloodshot, and though he tried to hide a tremor in his hand, he seemed in rare form. He nodded affably and inspected her outfit, the teal gown with the black pearls. He arched an eyebrow.

"What's this?" he said. "Not wearing your new gown?"

Lillian smiled. "I'm saving it for the closing number."

"Excellent thinking, my dear. Contrary to common wisdom, the last impression is the one most remembered."

"Are you all right, Papa?"

"I am in fine fettle," Fontaine said grandly. "I shall acquit myself admirably indeed."

Lillian kissed him on the cheek. "You will always be my Hamlet."

"And you the sweet voice in the darkness of my night."

"I have to go."

"Leave them enraptured, my dear. Hearts in their throats!"

A juggler came offstage as she moved into the wings. She walked to center stage, composing herself, hands clasped at her waist. The orchestra glided smoothly into *Nobody's Darling* as the curtain opened to reveal her awash in a rose-hued spotlight. Her voice brought an expectant hush over the audience.

They say I am nobody's darling
Nobody cares for me
While others are radiant and joyful
I'm lonely as lonely can be
I'm lonely indeed without you
But I know what I know in my heart
Dreaming at morning and evening
Of meeting, oh never to part

On the last note there was a moment of almost reverent silence. Then the crowd stood, everyone in the theater on their feet, their applause vibrating off the walls. She curtsied, her eyes radiant, and slowly bowed her way offstage. The uproar went on unabated, and the audience brought her back for four curtain calls. Her face was flushed with joy when at last the commotion subsided.

Fontaine was waiting in the wings. His eyes were misty and he hugged her in a fierce outpouring of pride. She again smelled liquor on his breath, and then he marched, shoulders squared, to the center of the stage. The curtain swished open, and he raised one hand in a dramatic gesture, caught in the glow of a cider spotlight.

He hesitated an instant, staring out over the audience, and launched into a soliloquy from *Hamlet*. His rich baritone resonated across the theater.

Neither a borrower, nor a lender be;
For loan oft loses both itself and friend,
And borrowing dulls the edge of husbandry,
This above all: to thine own self be true,
And it must follow, as the night the day,
Thou canst not then be false to any man . . .

The crowd watched him with a look of dumb bemusement. There was a sense of some misguided gathering come upon a man speaking in a tongue foreign to the ear. When he delivered the last line, they stared at him as though waiting for a summation that would make it all comprehensible. Then, just as Burt Tully had predicted, they sat on their hands. Their applause was scattered, quickly gone.

Fontaine took no curtain calls. The acrobats bounded onstage as he walked, head bowed, to his dressing room to change costumes. A few minutes later he joined Lillian and Chester in the presentation of the melodrama *A Husband's Vengeance*. All through the performance Lillian's concentration was on her father rather than on the play. She knew, even if the audience never would, why he had selected that particular passage from *Hamlet*. He wanted to deliver the one line that personified Alistair Fontaine.

To thine own self be true.

The crowd responded favorably to the melodrama. Following the performance, Fontaine's spirits seemed somewhat restored. He changed into his street clothes, leaving Chester backstage, and moved quickly to the door leading to the theater. Lillian came out of her dressing room just as he went through the door. She was wearing her new gown, resplendent in ivory, her hair loose to her shoulders. She saw Chester standing outside his dressing room, his face screwed up in a puzzled frown. She hurried forward.

"Chet?" she said anxiously. "Where did Papa go?"

"To the bar." Chester appeared troubled. "He said he'd watch your performance from there. He just rushed off."

"I'm worried about his drinking. Will you find him and stay with him?"

"The way he acted, I'm not sure he wants company. He didn't invite me along."

"Yes, but he shouldn't be left alone. Not tonight."

"You're right. I'll go find him."

Chester walked away. The stage manager motioned frantically to Lillian as the chorus line pranced offstage. She moved through the wings, taking her position at center stage, and struck a coquettish pose. The curtain opened as the orchestra swung into *Buffalo Gals* and the spotlight made her a vision in ivory. Her cleavage and the sight of a dainty ankle brought shouts from the audience. She performed a cheeky dance routine as she zestfully banged out the lyrics.

Buffalo gals, won't you come out tonight
Come out tonight, come out tonight

Buffalo gals, won't you come out tonight
And we'll dance by the light of the moon

Lillian twirled around the stage, her ivory slippers lightly skipping in time to the music. Her voice was animated and strong, every mirthful stanza of the song followed by the rollicking chorus. She spun about in a playful pirouette on the last line and ended with her arms flung wide and her hip cocked at a saucy angle. The uproar from the crowd rocked the theater with applause and cheers and shrill whistles of exuberance. A standing ovation drummed on through five curtain calls.

The cast surrounded her backstage. She was jubilant with the wild reception from the audience, and congratulations from the other performers made it all the more heady. Burt Tully pulled her into a smothering bear hug and told her she would play the Alcazar forever. As he let her go, she saw her father and Chester, followed by another man, come through the door from the theater. She threw herself into her father's arms.

"Oh, Papa!" she cried. "Wasn't it just wonderful!"

Fontaine was glassy-eyed with liquor. He kissed her with drunken affection. "You bedazzled them, my dear. You were magical."

"I could have sung forever and ever! And Papa, five curtain calls!"

"Yes, indeed, you brought the house down."

"Oooo, I'm so excited!"

"I'd like you to meet someone." Fontaine motioned the other man forward. "Permit me to introduce Otis Gaylord. I've invited him to join us for supper."

Gaylord was a man of imposing stature. He was tall, lithely built, with sandy hair and pale blue eyes. He took her hand in his and lifted it to his lips. He caressed it with a kiss.

"I am your most ardent admirer, Miss Fontaine. Your performance left me thoroughly bewitched."

Lillian smiled graciously. He wasn't the handsomest man she'd ever seen. But he was devilishly good-looking, strongly virile, with a cleft chin and rugged features. She thought she might drown in his pale blue eyes.

"Otis favors Irish whiskey," Fontaine said with a tipsy chortle. "I can think of no finer attribute in a friend. And lest I betray a secret, my dear—he is smitten with you."

Gaylord laughed. "I would be a liar if I said otherwise."

Lillian sensed they would celebrate more than her triumph tonight.

Chapter 23

Lillian was the toast of Denver. Her first week at the Alcazar Variety Theater was a sellout every night. The Colorado Nightingale was front-page news.

Articles appeared in the *Denver Tribune* and the *Rocky Mountain News*. The stories gushed with accolades and adjectives, unanimous agreement that she was a sensation, a singer with the voice of an angel. She was the talk of the town.

The response was overwhelming. Loads of flowers were delivered to her dressing room every night, with notes expressing adulation and all but begging her attention. Every man in Denver was seemingly a rabid admirer and intent on becoming a suitor. She was an object of adoration, the stuff of men's dreams.

Otis Gaylord was the envy of her many admirers. He managed to monopolize her time and squired her around town at every opportunity. Today, she joined him for lunch in the restaurant at the Brown Palace, and the maître d' greeted them with the fanfare reserved for the hotel's resident celebrity. Heads turned as they were led to their table.

Lillian was taken with Gaylord's urbane manner. He was courteous, thoughtful, and attentive to her every wish. His wit amused her, and if he was not the handsomest man she'd ever known, he was nonetheless the most attractive. So much so that she declined dozens of invitations every night, for she was drawn to him by an emotional affinity she'd never before felt. And apart from all that, he was enormously wealthy.

Gaylord was a mining investor. As he explained it, he owned blocks of stock in several gold mines in Central City, which was located some thirty miles west of Denver. The mining camp was called the richest square mile on earth, and upward of a hundred thousand dollars a week was gouged from the mountainous terrain. A shrewd financier might easily quadruple his investment in a year or less.

For Lillian, Otis Gaylord seemed the answer to a girl's prayers. Nor was she alone in that sense, for fortune had smiled on Chester as well. Earlier in the week he'd met Ethel Weaver, who kept the books at her father's store, Weaver's Mercantile. The girl was cute as a button, and to hear Chester tell it, she was one in a million. He spent every spare moment in her company, and he acted like a man who had fallen hard. He talked of nothing else.

Lillian's one concern was her father. His spirit seemed broken by the theater crowd's yawning indifference to Shakespeare and to him as an actor. His drinking had grown worse over the past week, starting in the morning and ending only when he fell into bed at night. His mind was fogged with alcohol, and on two occasions he'd forgotten his lines in the course of the melodrama. His escape into a bottle, just as Lillian had feared, was sapping him mentally and physically. He seemed a shell of his former self.

Gaylord tried to write it off as a momentary lapse. He enjoyed Fontaine's sardonic wit, and even more, he respected his integrity as an actor. Gaylord counseled Lillian to patience, and today, when she seemed particularly distressed, he assured her that her father, given time, would come to grips with the problem. No more had he offered his assurances than James Clark, the manager of the Brown Palace, interrupted their luncheon. He rushed into the dining room.

"Pardon the intrusion," he said earnestly. "Miss Fontaine, your father has been injured. Your brother asked that you come immediately to the suite."

Lillian pushed back her chair. "What kind of injury?"

"I'm afraid I haven't any details. I saw your brother and several men carry your father in from the street. He asked me to find you."

Lillian hurried from the restaurant. Gaylord escorted her upstairs, and three men came out of the suite as they arrived. They found Chester nervously pacing around the sitting room. He turned as they entered.

"Thank God you're here," he said. "Dad got run over by a lumber wagon. I was on the way to lunch with Ethel and I saw it. He just stepped off the curb into the path of the horses."

"How bad is he?" Lillian demanded. "Have you sent for a doctor?"

"There was a doctor there. On the street, on his way to lunch, I mean. He and some other men helped me carry Dad back here."

"The doctor's here, now?"

"Dr. Macquire." Chester motioned to the closed bedroom door. "Dad was unconscious when we brought him in. He didn't look good."

Lillian sagged and Gaylord put his arm around her shoulders. "Steady now," he said. "No need to think the worst."

"Oh, Otis, I feel so terrible. Drinking the way he does, he shouldn't have been on the street. I should have known better."

Chester grimaced. "We would have to keep him under lock and key. Or hide the whiskey."

The bedroom door opened. Dr. Thomas Macquire moved into the sitting room, his features solemn. He nodded to Lillian and Chester. "Your father has the constitution of an ox. Of course, in a way, being drunk was a lucky thing. Drunks can absorb more damage than a sober man."

Lillian stepped forward. "Are you saying he'll be all right?"

"There are no broken bones, and so far as I can tell, there's no internal injuries. I'll have to keep an eye on him for a few days."

"Has he regained consciousness?"

"Miss Fontaine, not only is he awake, he asked for a drink."

Lillian walked to the bedroom. Her father's features were ashen, a discolored bruise on his jaw and a large knot on his forehead. His eyes were rheumy and his breathing raspy. He looked at her with a forlorn expression.

" 'If I must die,' " he said in a slurred voice, " 'I will encounter darkness as a bride, and hug it in mine arms.' Send for a priest, my dear."

"You aren't going to die, Papa. Not as long as you can quote Shakespeare."

" 'The stroke of death is as a lover's pinch'! I could quote the Bard from my grave."

"Dr. Macquire says you'll live."

"What do doctors know?" Fontaine said dismissively. "I need a drink and a priest. Would you oblige me, my dear?"

"Try to get some rest," Lillian said, turning away. "We'll talk later, Papa."

She closed the door on her way out.

Lillian carried on the show by herself. She was forced to cancel the melodrama, as well as the Shakespearean act, for the immediate future. Neither could be performed without her father.

Burt Tully was almost deliriously happy. The crowds jamming the Alcazar shared the sentiment to a man. Lillian was now singing five songs a night, and the theater was sold out a week in advance. A cottage industry sprang up with street hustlers hawking tickets for triple the box office price.

Chester, much to Lillian's surprise, took it all in stride. He told her he was available to resume stage work whenever their father recovered. But he promptly obtained a job as a clerk in Weaver's Mercantile and seemed content to spend his days in close proximity to Ethel Weaver. His nights were spent in her company as well.

Dr. Macquire, at Fontaine's insistence, got the clergy involved. The Reverend Titus Hunnicut, pastor of the First Baptist Church, became a regular at Fontaine's bedside. The actor and the minister sequestered themselves, talking for hours at a time. A male nurse was hired to tend to Fontaine's physical needs, and Reverend Hunnicut tended to his spiritual needs. Fontaine, to Lillian's utter shock, stopped drinking.

Three days after the accident, Fontaine was on the mend. Dr. Macquire pronounced his recovery remarkable, for he'd been trampled by the horses and the lumber wagon had passed over his right leg. He was alert and sober, his cheeks glowing with health, and positively reveling in all the attention. Even more remarkable, he'd taken a vow of abstinence, swearing off demon rum forever. He basked in the glory of the Lord.

Lillian returned from rehearsing a new number late that afternoon. Reverend Hunnicut was on his way out and stopped to chat with her for a moment. A slight man, with oily hair and an unctuous manner, he seemed forever on the pulpit. He nodded as though angels were whispering in his ear.

"Praise the Lord," he said in a sepulchral voice. "Your father has been delivered from the damnation of hell's fires. He is truly blessed."

"How wonderful," Lillian demurred. "Thank you for all your concern, Reverend."

"I am but a humble servant of Christ, Miss Fontaine. God's will be done!"

"Yes, of course."

Lillian showed him to the door. The male nurse, who was seated on the divan reading a newspaper, started to his feet. She waved him down with a smile and proceeded on into the bedroom. Her father was propped up against a bank of pillows.

"Hello, Papa," she said, bussing him on the cheek. "How are you feeling?"

"Quite well." Fontaine studied her with an eager look. "I have something to tell you, my dear. Reverend Hunnicut convinced me it was time."

"Oh?"

"The day the wagon ran over me—actually it was that evening—God spoke to me in the moment of my death."

"You weren't dying, Papa. And since when have you become so devout?"

" 'Ye of little faith,' " Fontaine chided her. " 'They that wait upon the Lord shall renew their strength; they shall mount up with wings as eagles.' " He paused, holding her gaze. "I have been spared death for a greater mission in life."

"A greater mission?"

"Yes indeed, my dear. I shall carry the word of our Lord to the infidels in the mining camps. Their immortal souls are but a step away from perdition."

Lillian was never more stunned in her life. "Are you serious, Papa?"

"I most certainly am."

"What about the stage?"

"All the world's a stage." Fontaine's eyes burned with a fervent light. "I shall be an actor for our Lord Jesus Christ."

"Really?" Lillian said dubiously. "You intend to give up Shakespeare to become a preacher?"

" 'To every thing there is a season, and a time to every purpose under the heaven.' That comes from Ecclesiastes, not Shakespeare."

"Yes, but how can you forsake the stage?"

"On the contrary, the stage has forsaken me. I go now to spread the word of Him who so oft inspired the Bard."

"Are you certain about this, Papa?"

"I have been called," Fontaine said with conviction. "The Gospel will light my way."

Lillian returned to the sitting room in a daze. The male nurse rose from the divan and went past her into the bedroom. As she sat down, the door opened and Chester entered the suite. She gave him a look of baffled consternation.

"Papa has decided to become a preacher."

"I know," Chester said, crossing to the divan. "He's been working himself up to telling you. I found out last night."

"And you didn't say anything?" Lillian was astounded. "Do you think he's lost his mind? I have to talk to the doctor."

"Think about it a minute and you'll understand. What he lost was his faith in himself as a Shakespearean. He's adopted a new role in life—a man of God."

"Oh, Chet, how can you say that? He's an actor, not a preacher."

"As the Bard said," Chester quoted, " 'one man in his time plays many parts.' I'm taking on a new part myself."

"You?" Lillian said. "What are you talking about?"

"I've decided to quit the stage."

"I don't believe it!"

Chester sat down beside her. "You know yourself I was never much of an actor. I stayed with it because it was sort of the family tradition. I think it's time to move on."

Lillian's head was reeling. "Move on to what?"

"I really believe I was cut out to be a merchant. I can't tell you how much I enjoy working in the store. Ethel's father says I have a head for business."

"For business or for Ethel?"

"Well, her, too," Chester said with a goofy smile. "But the point is, what with the act breaking up, I have no future on the stage. Time to make a new career for myself."

"I'm speechless." Lillian felt dizzy and somehow saddened. "Papa a preacher and you a merchant. Where will it end?"

"As for Dad and myself, who's to say? You're the only sure bet in the family."

"I'd so much rather have you and Papa onstage with me."

"You don't need us where you're going, little sister. You never did."

Lillian snuggled close in his arms, her head on his shoulder. A tear ran down her cheek and she wondered how they'd come so far to have it end this way. So abruptly, so unforeseen. So final.

The end of The Fontaines.

* * *

My wild Irish Rose
The sweetest flower that grows
You may search everywhere
But none can compare
With my wild Irish Rose

Lillian's voice was particularly poignant that night. She was thinking not of the lyrics but of her father and Chester. Her eyes shone with tears, and the emotion she felt inside gave the song a haunting quality. She got hold of herself for the last refrain.

My wild Irish Rose
The dearest flower that grows

And someday for my sake
She may let me take
The bloom from my wild Irish Rose

A momentary lull held the audience in thrall as the last note faded away. Then the house rocked with applause, men swiping at their noses, their eyes moist with memories evoked by her performance. The noise quickened, went on unabated, the crowd on their feet, bellowing their approval. She left them wanting more with a fifth curtain call.

Some while later Otis Gaylord met her at the stagedoor entrance. She was dressed in a gossamer satin gown, a fashionable Eton jacket thrown over her shoulders, her hair pulled back in a lustrous chignon. A carriage took them to Delmonico's, one of the finer restaurants in Denver. The owner personally escorted them to their table.

"That was some performance," Gaylord said when they were seated. "You had the boys crying in their beer."

"I feel like crying myself."

"What's wrong?"

Lillian told him about her afternoon. Gaylord was no less amazed to hear that her father was to become a preacher. The news of her brother was no great surprise, for he'd always felt Chester was the least talented of the family. She ended on a rueful note.

"Nothing will ever be the same again. We've been an act since I was a little girl."

"Yeah, it's a shame," Gaylord agreed. "Of course, maybe it's the best thing for Alistair, and Chester, too. You have to look on the bright side."

"What bright side?" Lillian said. "We'll be separated now."

"Only on the stage. Sounds to me like Alistair and Chester will be doing something that makes them lots happier. Think of it that way."

The waiter appeared with menus. Lillian thought about Gaylord's advice, and after they ordered, she looked at him. Her eyes crinkled with a smile.

"I was being selfish," she said. "If they're happy, why should I be sad? Isn't that what you meant?"

Gaylord chuckled. "I think I put it a little more tactfully. But yeah, that's the general idea."

"Well, you were right, and I feel like a ninny I didn't see it for myself. No more tears."

"Maybe this will cheer you up even more."

Gaylord took a small box from his pocket. He set it before her on the table, his expression unreadable, and eased back in his chair. She opened it and saw a gold heart-shaped locket bordered with tiny diamonds, strung on a delicate chain. Her mouth ovaled with surprise.

"Oh, it's beautiful!" she said merrily. "No one ever gave me anything so nice!"

"We'll have to correct that," Gaylord said. "Lots of pretty presents for a pretty lady. I like it when you laugh."

Lillian batted her eyelashes. "Are you trying to ply me with favors, Mr. Gaylord?"

"I'll ply you any way I can, Miss Fontaine. I intend to be the object of your affections."

"Do you?"

"No question about it."

"Well . . ." She gave him a sultry look. "We'll see."

Gaylord ordered champagne. Lillian strung the locket around her neck, aware that he was watching her. She wondered if tonight was the beginning of what would lead to a proposal. She certainly wasn't going to surrender herself without a wedding band on her finger. But then, on second thought, she wasn't at all sure that love and marriage were the same thing. She felt awfully old to still be a virgin. Too old.

The waiter poured champagne, then moved away. Gaylord lifted his glass, staring at her over the rim. "To us," he said in a seductive voice. "And the future."

Lillian laughed vivaciously. "Yes, to the future."

CHAPTER 24

SOME DAYS mark a passage in time. Lillian was never to forget June 12, 1872, the day her world turned topsy-turvy. She felt alone for the first time in her life.

Alistair Fontaine stood at the curb in front of the Brown Palace Hotel. He was dressed in a black frock coat, with dark trousers and a white shirt, the crown of his hat rounded in a dome. His horse, a swaybacked gelding donated by the church, was black as well. Fontaine looked every inch the part of an itinerant preacher.

Lillian and Chester waited while he checked his saddlebags. Over the past week he had recovered fully from his encounter with the lumber wagon. By now, after daily sessions with Reverend Hunnicut, he virtually had the Bible memorized, and the paperwork, properly endorsed, had been submitted to have him ordained. He was a man of God.

Watching him, Lillian thought he'd never looked so fit. He held himself tall and straight, and there was fire in his eyes, the zealotry of a man reborn in faith. The saddlebags held all his worldly possessions, and he pulled the strap tight with a firm hand. He turned to face them with an expression that was beatific, at peace with himself.

"Come now," he said, looking from one to the other. "Will you send me off with dreary faces?"

"Oh, Papa!" Lillian sniffled, on the verge of tears. "We'll miss you so."

"The Spirit of the Lord God is upon me. I go forth to give light to them that sit in darkness. I am blessed among men, my dear."

"Dad, I'd like to hear your first sermon," Chester said, grinning. "You'll probably convert those miners in droves."

Fontaine chortled. "I will try to save my first wedding ceremony for you and Ethel."

Chester was himself like a man with a new lease on life. After a whirlwind courtship, he'd announced that morning his betrothal to Ethel Weaver. Her father, who knew a natural-born tradesman when he saw one, welcomed Chester into the family. They were to be married in October.

"God bless you both and keep you safe until I return."

Fontaine hugged Lillian and shook hands with Chester. He stepped into the saddle, tipping his hat with a jaunty air, and rode off along Larimer Street. They stood watching until he rounded the corner and turned west toward the distant mountains. Lillian dabbed at her eyes with a hankie.

"How things change," she said. "I expected him to leave us with a quote from Shakespeare. Something properly dashing, or adventurous."

"Actually . . ." Chester paused, nodding to himself. "I was thinking of Cervantes. A line he wrote in *Don Quixote* strikes me as perfect: 'Many are the ways by which God leads His children home.' "

"For a storekeeper, you're still very much the actor. Are you sure you've given up on the stage?"

"Never more sure of anything. And speaking of the store, I have to get back. I'll see you later."

Chester hurried off down the street. Lillian turned into the hotel, feeling lonely and blue. Upstairs, she wandered through the empty suite, reminded of her father everywhere she looked. She wished she had a rehearsal, or a dress fitting, anything to take her mind off the overwhelming loneliness. She thought she might go to the theater early tonight.

A short while later there was a knock at the door. Lillian was staring out the window, brooding, and she welcomed the distraction. She moved across the sitting room, opening the door, and found two men standing in the hall. One was short and stocky, the other one tall and lean, both attired in conservative suits. She nodded pleasantly.

"May I help you?"

"Miss Fontaine?"

"Yes."

"I'm David Cook," the short one said, "and this is my associate, Jeff Carr. I wonder if we might speak with you a moment."

"May I ask what it regards?"

"A personal matter involving Otis Gaylord."

Lillian invited them inside. Once they were seated, Cook explained that he was head of the Rocky Mountain Detective Association, located in Denver, and currently retained by Wells Fargo. Jeff Carr, he went on, was the county sheriff from Cheyenne, Wyoming. They wanted to ask her a few questions about Otis Gaylord.

"I don't understand," she said. "Why are you interested in Mr. Gaylord?"

Lillian would later discover that David Cook and Jeff Carr were renowned manhunters. Cook, the chief operative of the Rocky Mountain Detective Association, had tracked fugitives all across the West. Carr, who had killed several men in gunfights, was reputed to be the only lawman who had ridden into Hole-in-the-Wall, the outlaw sanctuary, and ridden out alive. Cook looked at her now.

"We have reason to believe that Gaylord's real name is Earl Miller. He's wanted for robbery and murder."

"You're mistaken," Lillian said tersely. "Mr. Gaylord is a mining investor. He's quite wealthy."

"Guess he oughta be," Jeff Carr said. "He robbed a Wells Fargo stagecoach outside of Cheyenne. Got forty-three thousand in gold bullion and killed the express guard."

"And those investments?" Cook added. "We checked out the story he uses, about owning mines in Central City. Nobody there ever heard of him."

Lillian sniffed. "That isn't proof. There could be any number of explanations."

"How's this for proof?" Cook said. "Gaylord sold almost forty thousand in gold bullion to Ed Chase for seventy cents on the dollar. Our informant saw the transaction."

Everyone in Denver knew the name Ed Chase. He was the underworld czar who controlled the rackets and ruled the Tenderloin with a gang of thugs. One of his sidelines was operating as a fence for stolen goods.

"I don't believe you," Lillian said tartly. "If you have evidence, why haven't you arrested Mr. Gaylord? Why come to me?"

Cook informed her that the gold bars, once in the hands of Ed Chase, were untraceable. As for Earl Miller, the robber and murderer, he always wore a bandanna mask and had yet to be positively identified. The break in the case came when they were informed of the underworld sale of the gold.

"We know of your relationship with Gaylord," Cook went on discreetly. "We hoped to solicit your assistance in identifying him."

"Really?" Lillian countered. "Why would I help you?"

"The man's a killer," Carr said bluntly. "Because of him that express guard left a widow and three kids. How's that for a reason?"

"And you might be doing Gaylord a service," Cook argued. "If he's not Earl Miller, you could clear his name. Prove we've got the wrong suspect."

Lillian was less certain of herself than a moment ago. Yet she couldn't believe that Otis Gaylord was a robber, not to mention a murderer. Still, the lawmen were determined, and unless he was cleared, they might very well destroy his reputation. She decided to cooperate.

"What do you want me to do?"

Cook told her what they had in mind.

Gaylord maintained rooms at the Windsor Hotel. Lillian sent a note by messenger, asking that their usual late supper be changed to an early dinner. She suggested their favorite restaurant, Delmonico's.

All afternoon she fretted over what seemed to her a conspiracy. For more than two weeks now, Gaylord had been her lone suitor and her constant companion. She wasn't in love with him, but she thought that might come with time. He was immensely attractive, and she'd even had wicked dreams about him. Wild, delicious dreams.

By five o'clock, she had all but convinced herself that she was betraying him. However much she rationalized it, the plot hatched with Cook and Carr left a bitter taste in her mouth. She went over it again as she was dressing for dinner and forced herself to justify it as a means to an end. Tonight, she would clear Gaylord's name!

Gaylord called for her at six. As they walked to the restaurant, she excused the early dinner by saying she was lonely. She told him about her father's departure that morning and Chester's announcement of his impending marriage. She was happy for them, for one had found salvation in God and the other with the girl of his dreams. But she'd never felt so alone, and a little lost. She missed her father terribly.

Over dinner, Gaylord sympathized with her sense of loss. She felt all the more guilty because he was so considerate and understanding, hardly the traits of a robber and murderer. Finally, when she declined dessert and Gaylord ordered chokecherry pie she knew she was unable to avoid it any longer. She waited until he was served, then leaned forward on her elbows. She lowered her voice.

"Today, two men called on me at the hotel . . . a detective and a sheriff."

"Oh?" Gaylord said curiously. "What was the purpose of their call?"

Lillian composed herself. "The detective works for Wells Fargo and the sheriff is from Wyoming. They're searching for a robber."

"That's the strangest thing I ever heard of. Why would they ask you about a robber?"

"I'm afraid they were asking about you. They said your name is really Earl Miller."

Gaylord's fork paused in midair. She saw something flicker in his eyes, and then he recovered himself. He forked the bite of pie into his mouth and looked at her with an open expression. He chewed away, seemingly puzzled.

"Well, I've been called many things, but never a robber. It must be a case of mistaken identity."

Lillian held his gaze. "They have a witness."

"A witness to what?"

"Someone who saw you sell the gold from the robbery to Ed Chase. And they know you haven't any mining properties in Central City."

"Lillian—"

"You are Earl Miller, aren't you?"

Gaylord placed his fork on his plate. "I'm sorry, more sorry than you'll ever know. I'd hoped to start fresh here in Denver."

"Omigod," Lillian whispered. "I wasn't sure until just now. I prayed it wasn't so."

"And I forgot what a good actress you are. They sent you here to get a confession, didn't they?"

"I thought I could clear your name. How silly of me."

"Where are they now?"

"Sitting right over there."

David Cook and Jeff Carr were seated at a table across the room. Gaylord looked at them and they returned his look with flat stares. He glanced back at Lillian.

"Time to go," he said with an ironic smile. "Wish I could stick around and see how we made out. I think it would've worked."

"Wait, please!" Lillian pleaded. "You musn't try to run."

"Didn't they tell you I killed a man?"

"Yes—"

"I won't be hung."

"Otis, please—"

"So long, Lillian."

Gaylord swung out of his chair. He walked quickly toward the front of the restaurant, snaring his hat off a wall rack. As he neared the door, Cook and Carr got to their feet. Carr pushed a waiter aside.

"Earl Miller!" he commanded. "Halt right there!"

Miller, alias Otis Gaylord, stopped at the door. His hand snaked inside his jacket and came out with a Colt Navy revolver. He whirled, bringing the Colt to bear, and found himself a beat behind. Jeff Carr, pistol extended at shoulder level, fired.

The slug struck Miller dead-center in the chest. His shirt colored as though a small rosebud had been painted on the cloth by an invisible brush. A look of mild surprise came over his face, and he staggered back, dropping the Colt, slamming into the door. His knees buckled and he slumped to the floor.

Lillian stared at him as though she'd been shot herself. Her mouth opened in a soundless scream and for a moment she couldn't get her breath. She buried her head in her hands.

Her low, choking sob was the only sound in Delmonico's.

The theater was mobbed. Within the hour, the news of the shooting had spread throughout the Tenderloin, and the star of the Alcazar became even more sensational.

Everyone wanted a glimpse of the woman assumed to be the dead man's paramour. The Colorado Nightingale.

Lillian somehow got through her first four numbers. She felt wretched about Gaylord's death and oddly guilty for having exposed him as an outlaw. But she kept reminding herself of what her father—and her mother—had always taught as the cardinal tenet of the theater. No matter what, the show must go on.

The oldest bromide in the business was her lodestone. A trouper, barring earthquake or flood, went out on the stage and performed. She sang the ballads with heartfelt emotion for Gaylord (she still couldn't think of him as Earl Miller, robber and murderer). And she belted out the snappy tunes with an insouciance that belied her sorrow.

A comic came offstage as she waited in the wings. Her final number for the evening was *Lily of the West*, which played well off her own billing. She walked to center stage, steeling herself to hold it all together and close out the night on a high note. She put on a happy face as the curtain opened and the orchestra swung into the tune. Her voice was bubbly and spirited.

When first I came to Denver
Some pleasure here to find
A damsel fresh from Durango
Was laughter to my mind
Her rosy cheeks, her ruby lips
Set things aflutter in my chest
Her name so sweet and dear was Dora
The Lily of the West . . .

The audience began clapping in time to the music. Her ivory gown shone in the spotlight as she whirled and skipped about the stage, revealing her ankles in a sprightly dance routine. She finished the song with a winsome smile and playfully threw kisses to the crowd, bowing low when she curtsied for a mischievous display of cleavage. The applause swelled into a standing ovation that brought her on for five—then six—curtain calls.

Backstage, she nodded politely to congratulations from the other performers. Burt Tully had earlier offered his condolences about Gaylord, and she hoped she'd seen the last of him for the night. She wanted nothing more than to hurry back to the hotel and climb into bed and hide. She thought she might burst into tears at any moment.

Before she could undo her gown, there was a light rap on the door. She sighed, thinking it was Tully, or Chester come to express his sympathy, and sulked across the room. When she opened the door, a man in his early thirties, dressed in an impeccably tailored suit, stood outside. His mouth flashed in an engaging smile.

"Miss Fontaine," he said in a modulated voice. "I'm Victor Stanton, from San Francisco. May I speak with you a moment?"

Lillian held her ground. "What is it you want, Mr. Stanton? How did you get backstage?"

"I talked my way past Burt Tully. As to my purpose, I own the Bella Union Theater. Perhaps you've heard of it."

Everyone in show business had heard of the Bella Union. Even in New York, which was considered the center of the universe for theater, the Bella Union was fabled for its opulent productions. Victor Stanton, the impresario, was considered a showman second to none. Lillian suddenly placed the man with the name.

"Yes, of course," she said pleasantly. "Won't you please come in?"

There was a small, sagging sofa against the wall. Lillian got him seated and took her chair by the dressing table. "How nice of you to drop by," she said, trying to gather her wits. "What brings you to Denver?"

"I come here once or twice a year," Stanton said amiably. "I'm always scouting for new acts, and I must say, tonight was my lucky night. You were absolutely brilliant, Miss Fontaine."

"Why, thank you!" Lillian gushed. "I'm very flattered you would say so."

"Let me ask, are you familiar with San Francisco?"

"Well, no, not really."

"We like to think of it as the Paris of North America. Even more cosmopolitan than New York."

Stanton went on like a civic booster, extolling the virtues of the City by the Bay. As he talked, Lillian noticed his dapper attire, his polished manner and his chiseled features, and the fact that he wore no wedding ring. A fleeting thought crossed her mind about the rotten luck she'd had with men on her odyssey through the West. She wondered if her fortunes might change.

"There you have it," Stanton said. "A city worthy of your remarkable talent."

Lillian realized she was focused on the man rather than his words. "Pardon me?"

"Miss Fontaine, I'm offering you star billing at the Bella Union. How much is Tully paying you?"

"Why . . . three hundred a week."

"I'll make it five hundred," Stanton said without hesitation. "With a one-year contract and my personal guarantee of fame beyond your wildest expectations. What do you say?"

"I . . ." Lillian thought she might faint. "I have almost two weeks left on my engagement here."

"Then you'll open at the Bella Union on Independence Day. We'll introduce you to San Francisco with fireworks on July Fourth! I couldn't think of anything more fitting."

Lillian felt a sudden rush of memory. Abilene and the Comique and Wild Bill Hickok. Dodge City and George Armstrong Custer and Cimarron Jordan. Pueblo and Denver and her long run as the Colorado Nightingale. And now, her name in lights in the City by the Bay.

"You'll love it there," Stanton said, staring directly into her eyes. "I can't wait to show you all the sights, Telegraph Hill and the Golden Gate. I predict you'll never leave."

"I've always heard it's very nice."

"Do you prefer to be called Lilly or Lillian?"

"All my friends call me Lillian."

"And mine call me Victor. I think this is the start of something big, Lillian. Do you feel it, too?"

Lillian all but melted under the warmth of his gaze. The Bella Union, her name in lights, and maybe, with just a little luck, Victor Stanton. Yes, she told herself with the wonder of it all . . .

San Francisco, here I come.

Epilogue

Victor Stanton made good on his promise. Lillian was billed simply as *The Nightingale*, and she quickly became the star of the Bella Union. By early summer of 1873, she was the sweetheart of stage and song.

Lillian loved San Francisco. The city was wondrously nestled in a natural amphitheater, with steep hills surrounding the center of the community. The bay was the finest landlocked harbor on the continent, and westward along the peninsula, through the Golden Gate, sailed tall-masted clippers and oceangoing steamers from around the world. The trade had transformed the City by the Bay into one of the richest ports on earth.

A profusion of cultures, it was also the premier city of the West. Along the waterfront was the infamous Barbary Coast, a wild carnival of dance halls and brothels where sailors were shanghaied onto ships bound for the Orient. Chinatown, an exotic city within a city, was like being transported backward in time to Old Cathay, where ancient customs still prevailed. The Uptown Tenderloin, a district reserved for society swells, was filled with theaters and cabarets and plush casinos. To Lillian, it was all a storybook come to life.

The Bella Union, located in the heart of the Uptown Tenderloin, was on O'Farrel Street. There was a casino for affluent high rollers upstairs and on the ground floor an ornate barroom fronting the building. Beyond the bar was a spacious theater, with a sunken orchestra pit and the largest proscenium stage west of Chicago. The floor was jammed with linen-covered tables for 500, and a horseshoe balcony was partitioned into private boxes for wealthy patrons. Crowds flocked there every night of the week to see The Nightingale.

Lillian's dressing room was decorated in pale blue. The furnishings were expensive and tasteful, a Louis XIV sofa and chairs and a lush Persian carpet. Victor Stanton, as was his custom, lounged on the sofa while she changed behind a silk screen that was all but translucent. For her last number of the night, she slipped into a bead-embroidered gown of lavender crepe de chine. When she stepped from behind the screen, Stanton stared at her as though spellbound. The gown clung like silken skin to her sumptuous figure.

"Do you like it?" she said, posing for him. "I ordered it especially for you."

Stanton seemed short of breath. "You have never looked lovelier," he said, his eyes glued to her. "I deeply regret I must share you with the audience."

"How gallant!" She laughed a minxish little laugh. "Perhaps I'll wear it only for you."

"No, no," Stanton said, ever the showman. "You owe it to your public, my dear. You are, after all, The Nightingale."

"Then you won't mind sharing me with the audience?"

"I smother my desires to the good of the show."

"Sweet Victor, you really are a naughty man. I somehow doubt your resolve will hold after the show."

Lillian was a very chic and sophisticated twenty-one. She was not a maiden any longer, but neither was she a fallen woman. Any number of times, Victor had asked her to become his bride and share his mansion in the posh Nob Hill district. She was content instead to be his lover, what the society grand dames, given to tittering euphemism, called his inamorata. She enjoyed her freedom.

On Telegraph Hill, her little house was done in the French style, with a magnificent view of the bay. No less than her own home, she loved the independence of $9,000 in the bank and a growing portfolio of railroad stocks. She had renegotiated her contract with Victor three times and now received 5 percent of the box office receipts at the Bella Union. She often thought there was a bit of the extortionist in every successful chanteuse.

Letters from Colorado merely added to her sense of well-being. Chester was happily married, his wife in a family way, and almost certainly destined to become the merchant prince of Denver. Alistair Fontaine, now an ordained minister, reveled in his role as an itinerant preacher in the mining camps. To hear him tell it in his letters, he had Satan on the run and waged war on sinners with the battle cry of "Onward Christian Soldiers." She suspected God had never had a warrior quite like her father. A Shakespearean was, in the end, more than a match for Satan.

"I've arranged supper at the Palace," Stanton said as she checked herself in the mirror. "I thought it only appropriate for our celebration."

"Oh?" Lillian adjusted the bodice of her gown. "What are we celebrating?"

"Why, it's June 28, the anniversary of your arrival from Denver. Surely you haven't forgotten?"

"How could I forget a year together? And because

of you, dear, sweet Victor . . . the happiest year of my life."

"Well, selfish fellow that I am, I planned it that way. I told you the night we met you would never leave San Francisco."

"Yes, it's true." Lillian turned, kissed him soundly on the mouth. "I will never leave."

"Does that mean you'll accept my proposal?"

"One day, someday, maybe a Sunday. We'll see."

"You're a little vixen to keep me waiting."

"I know!"

Stanton, as he did every night, walked her to the wings for her last performance. Onstage, a squealing troupe of dancers was romping through the 'Frisco version of the French *cancan.* Their frilly drawers and black mesh stockings were laughingly exposed as they went into the finale and flung themselves rump first to the floor in *la split.* Then, screaming and tossing their skirts, they leaped to their feet and raced offstage as the curtain closed. The crowd rewarded them with thunderous applause.

Lillian moved to center stage. The orchestra segued into *A Cozy Corner*, and when the curtain opened, she stood framed in a creamy spotlight. Her clear alto voice filled the theater, and she glided around the stage, pausing here and there with a dazzling smile and a saucy wink. She played to every man in the room.

A cup of coffee, a sandwich and you
A cozy corner, a table for two
A chance to whisper and cuddle and coo
With lots of loving and hugging from you
I don't need music, laughter or wine

Whenever your eyes look into mine
A cup of coffee, a sandwich and you
A cozy corner, a table for two

San Franciscans were fond of saying there was only one nightingale in all the world. Her name was Lilly Fontaine.

CPSIA information can be obtained at www.ICGtesting.com
Printed in the USA
LVOW050050191212

312338LV00001B/31/P